T0378996

THE MUDFLATS MURDER CLUB

BRIAN THIEM

Copyright © 2025 by Brian Thiem.

All rights reserved.

No part of this book may be reproduced in any form or by any electronic or mechanical means, including information storage and retrieval systems, without written permission from the author, except for the use of brief quotations in a book review.

Severn River Publishing
www.SevernRiverBooks.com

This is a work of fiction. Names, characters, businesses, places, events and incidents are either the products of the author's imagination or used in a fictitious manner. Any resemblance to actual persons, living or dead, or actual events is purely coincidental.

ISBN: 978-1-64875-628-3 (Paperback)

ALSO BY BRIAN THIEM

Mudflats Murder Club Mysteries

The Mudflats Murder Club

A Killer in the Cordgrass

A Death in the Deluge

To find out more about Brian Thiem and his books, visit

severnriverbooks.com

For the law enforcement professionals around the country who put their lives on the line on a daily basis to protect and serve their communities.

TIDAL MUDFLATS

Mudflats are found in tidal areas along the South Carolina coast, commonly in estuaries and along tidal rivers. They are formed by the rise and fall of the tide, which submerges and exposes the mudflats twice daily. They are a vital part of the Lowcountry ecology and form a habitat for shorebirds, crabs, shellfish, and fish.

SPARTINA (SPARTINA ALTERNIFLORA)

Smooth Cordgrass, commonly found in coastal salt marshes along the Atlantic coast of South Carolina. The growth of Spartina stabilizes the soil, prevents erosion, and protects the fragile shoreline from storm surges. It also provides food, habitat, and protection for many creatures that make the tidal rivers and marsh home, including various fish, crabs, shrimp, and numerous different bird species. The Spartina grass, along with the twice-daily tidal flow and salt water, is an essential component of the Lowcountry tidal marsh ecology. Spartina is critical to the very life of Lowcountry salt marshes.

From placards on the River Lodge dock at Sea Island Plantation, Spartina Island, South Carolina.

1

MONDAY

He finally stopped fighting and gave up.

Sean Tanner maneuvered his kayak so the bow faced the wind and the incoming tide, both coming off the mouth of the river that opened into the Atlantic Ocean. He then slowly reeled in the fish. When it was alongside his kayak, he reached under it with his net and raised it out of the water. A redfish, about fifteen inches long, good eating for those who fish for food. He carefully removed the fishhook and lowered the fish back into the brackish water. After a few seconds, the fish's mouth and gills opened and closed, and Sean released the fish and watched it swim off into the safety of the Spartina grass at the edge of the river.

With his wife gone and his law enforcement career behind him, Sean wondered if there was more to life than this. Something more than fishing and golfing, when all he had to show for it was the fish he released back into the salt marsh and a lousy golf game.

Sean's kayak rocked slightly as his pal, George Laughlin, paddled his fully outfitted fishing kayak alongside Sean's bare bones model. George was sixty-two, eight years older than Sean, and fully embraced his retired life on Spartina Island. He had an average build with a noticeable paunch that George said he could eliminate if he didn't love food so much. He had dark brown hair that Sean was sure was colored to hide the gray. He filled his days fishing, golfing, woodworking, and playing pickleball and bocce. He and his wife spent their evenings going to dinners, parties, and shows with other couples. He looked forward to every day, while Sean viewed each day as something to fill to avoid boredom. "You had enough, Sean?"

Even with the breeze coming off the ocean, Sean was baking inside the confined kayak in the midday August sun. "More than enough." The truth was he'd had enough hours ago, but if he weren't out here, he would've been sitting in his house alone.

"Lead the way," George said.

Sean dipped his paddle into the water, turning the kayak upriver, and set off with strong, rhythmic strokes. With the wind at his back and the tide with him, he streaked down the tidal river with the salt marsh grasses closing in on him the farther he paddled. Sea Island Plantation, the gated community in which they lived, soon appeared on his left. Two egrets flew past him just a few feet above the water, flared their wings and seemed to stop in the air as if they had jammed on their brakes. They dropped into the shallow water next to a sandy stretch of shore on the north side of the river and began poking their beaks into the water in search of lunch.

A few minutes later, Sean steered his kayak toward the River Lodge dock. By the time George slid into the kayak launch, Sean already had his kayak stowed in the rack. He helped George with his kayak, and they walked around the River Lodge to the parking lot and climbed into Sean's golf cart.

Sean zipped down River Drive, turned into his neighborhood, and made his way to George's house.

"Are you still up for tonight?" George asked as Sean pulled into George's driveway and spun the cart around in front of the garage door.

Sean removed his baseball cap, ran his hand through his thick brown hair, and wiped the sweat from his forehead. "As long as your lovely wife isn't plotting to play matchmaker again."

George got out of the passenger seat and punched a code into his garage door opener. "Beth just wants you to be as miserable as all the other married men in the neighborhood." George grabbed his fishing pole and vest and set them inside the garage. He returned to the cart and collected the empty Styrofoam cup from where he had left it when Sean picked him up earlier that morning. "We don't want to pressure you, but we all think it would be okay if you started dating, even if it's just to get laid."

It had been almost a year since Sean's wife died. It seemed like forever ago yet just yesterday at the same time. "Make sure Beth knows that if a single woman mysteriously shows up tonight, I'm leaving."

George gave him a thumbs-up, and Sean eased his golf cart out of the driveway and down Blue Heron Lane. The wind on his sweaty skin made the blistering heat of the South Carolina Lowcountry feel almost cool for a moment.

As he passed the intersection with Cormorant Court, he saw a community security vehicle, an ambulance, and two SUVs with Campbell County Sheriff's markings parked across the street from his house. Police vehicles inside the gates of the development were a rarity. Except for an occasional domestic disturbance or traffic collision—normally an elderly resident who ran his golf cart off the road when driving home from the country club after too many cocktails—crime was mostly nonexistent. But medical emergencies were common, certainly due to the advanced age of many residents in the so-called *active adult community*.

Sean let up on the accelerator and crept down the street. A uniformed deputy stood on the front porch of Ken and Nancy Russo's house speaking into his radio's shoulder mic. The Russos were both sixty-five, not exactly elderly, and Sean wasn't aware of either having any major health issues.

Sean pushed the button on his remote and the small garage door rose. It took some getting used to when he moved down here and discovered many houses had a smaller garage door specifically for a golf cart next to the overhead doors leading to a typical two-car garage. He pulled his golf cart into the garage alongside his SUV. A few neighbors were huddled together several houses down. One thing he hated about living in a retirement community was too many people had too much time on their hands and filled it by gossiping about everything. Sean hoped his life would never become so empty that he would have to fill it with concern over the minute details of his neighbors' lives. He closed the garage door and went into his house, looking forward to a shower, followed by a lunch with a huge glass of iced tea. He was certain that Beth and his other neighbors would know all the details of what happened by the time he met them for dinner tonight.

2

The tropical breeze blowing off the Atlantic Ocean did little to cool the outdoor deck of the Sandy Feet Bar. Detective Sergeant Charlotte "Charlie" Nash shifted her chair to chase the shade of the large canvas umbrella and held up her empty water glass to a passing waiter. She dipped another piece of breaded flounder into tartar sauce and popped it into her mouth as Jimmy Buffet sang about Margaritaville over the outdoor speakers.

The Spartina Island beach was packed. Children splashed in the warm water close to shore, teenagers on body boards bobbed on swells farther out waiting for a worthy wave, and sun worshipers from young to old lazed on towels and beach chairs up and down the white sand beach.

Charlie scanned the crowd of people around the bar and surrounding tables for the umpteenth time. Not that she expected to spot a telltale bulge of a gun tucked into the swim trunks of a sunburned man bellied up to the bar or notice a group of young partiers begin to eye the cash register suspiciously, but she'd been a cop long enough to know shit could happen anytime and anyplace. If anything, as the only woman wearing a pantsuit among the lunch crowd dressed in swimsuits, shorts, and tee shirts, she was the one who looked out of place.

A volleyball net stood in the soft sand between the restaurant and beach. A crowd of spectators surrounded the court occupied by two four-player mixed teams. "Six service ten," yelled a darkly tanned girl with long brown hair as she tossed the ball and smacked it to the other side.

The ball sailed low over the net. A boy wearing yellow board shorts crouched and bumped it up with a forearm pass, where a girl in a pink bikini set it high to her left. A tall, lean boy leaped high in the air and spiked the ball with his open hand across the net and into the sand at an opponent's feet.

"Great shot, Spencer," yelled some of the teenagers ringing the court.

Charlie fought the urge to scream her own praise, but the last thing her seventeen-year-old son needed was his mother embarrassing him in front of his friends. Although it had been twenty-six years since she played volleyball in that exact same spot with her friends the summer before she left for college, she still remembered spying her father on the bar's deck watching her. If he hadn't disappeared ten years ago, she was certain he'd be sitting alongside her right now gushing with the same pride she felt for the young man Spencer had become.

Spencer's team rotated positions, and a bikini-clad college-aged girl served the ball over the net just as Charlie's phone rang. She pulled it from her pocket, glanced at the screen, and frowned. "Hey, lieutenant, what's up?"

A half hour later, Charlie Nash tucked a loose strand of blonde hair back into her low bun and crept closer to the body sprawled in front of her. Nancy Russo—white female, sixty-five, blonde hair, brown eyes—lay naked in a pool of partially dried and congealed blood on the porcelain tile floor in front of the shower. The killing had all the earmarks of a domestic murder, Charlie thought, except for the absence of a grieving, blood-covered husband standing in the doorway mouthing his remorse when the first units arrived.

A bloodstained butcher knife rested on the cream-colored floor beside the victim. A stab wound in the back and a gaping wound in the throat were the only two injuries she could see without rolling the body or stepping into the blood. A black knee-length negligee and black panties lay in a pile nearby, as if the victim had just undressed and dropped them there. A neatly folded towel hung over the side of the whirlpool tub just outside the shower.

Charlie sidestepped the bloody shoeprints made by firefighters and paramedics' boots on the floor to get a view of the body from the other side. Damn, she knew the emergency responders' priority was rendering medical aid to a victim, but did they really have to tromp through the blood and track it all over the place?

Deputy Hicks, one of the department's crime scene technicians, stood against the far wall fingering his Nikon. He was five-foot-six and combed his long strands of thin hair over his bald dome. Hicks loved his job working day shift as a tech. To avoid having to return to regular patrol duty and write traffic tickets and deal with family fights, he'd probably mop the floor if Charlie asked.

Charlie caught his eye. "You finished with photos in here?"

"Yes, ma'am." Hicks grinned, showing tobacco-stained teeth. "I'll take some more pictures when the coroner gets here and starts pickin' up Mrs. Russo, but I got plenty for now."

"You'll do a rough diagram for me?"

"Yes, ma'am. Can't have you waiting around for SLED to send you their work."

The Campbell County Sheriff's Office wasn't large enough to have their own full-service crime scene unit, so on major cases they relied on SLED, the South Carolina Law Enforcement Division's investigative services team. The downside was waiting a few hours for them to respond from Columbia and then several days for even a preliminary report and crime scene photos.

Charlie heard her name called and made her way through the house to the foyer, where one of her three detectives was speaking with a petite woman with short brown hair. Javier "Jay" Garcia was the youngest detective in her squad but the one she relied on most. After four years in the Marine Corps and two years of college, he'd joined the sheriff's office seven years ago and was promoted to detective after five years in uniform.

"I was about to follow Mrs. Keller home and take her formal statement, but wanted to see if you'd like to talk to her first," Jay said. "In summary,

Mrs. Keller told me she came to Nancy Russo's house to pick her up for an exercise class scheduled for twelve-thirty. She rang the doorbell, but there was no answer, so she entered through the unlocked front door. She called for her friend and headed toward her bedroom, where she figured Mrs. Russo was still getting ready. She found her on the bathroom floor and called nine-one-one. The call came in at twelve-fifteen."

Charlie introduced herself to Mrs. Keller and said, "I'm very sorry for your loss."

Debbie Keller was a fit-looking woman in her early fifties wearing black yoga pants and an oversized tee shirt. She nodded and wiped her tear-streaked face with the back of her hand.

"You just let yourself in when there was no answer?" Charlie asked.

"All of our friends do," Debbie said. "As long as you're expected it's okay."

"Has Mrs. Russo mentioned having problems with anyone?"

"Not at all. She's one of the nicest, sweetest ladies in the neighborhood."

Charlie was tempted to ask her what she knew about Nancy's husband and what she thought of him, but she trusted Jay could better ease into that line of questioning once he got her away from the crime scene and comfortable in her own home. "Thank you, Mrs. Keller. Detective Garcia will take you home now."

Once Jay left with Mrs. Keller, Charlie took in the house. It was an open design with high ceilings, common in new construction in the Lowcountry, the coastal region of the state from Myrtle Beach in the north to the Savannah River in the south. A formal dining table was to the left of the door, and beyond that was a modern kitchen with a large granite center island and stainless-steel appliances. Oversized and overstuffed sofas and chairs filled the living room area atop a glistening hardwood floor. Everything spoke of a financially comfortable retired couple who entertained and no longer had to worry about the wear and tear a family of kids caused to a house.

Not wanting to forget anything on her first major scene, Charlie ran through her mental checklist: crime scene tape strung and deputies securing the perimeter of the house; her other two detectives and several patrol deputies doing a door-to-door canvass, hoping someone saw something or knew something; the department crime scene tech taking integrity photos and a rough sketch; the reporting person being interviewed; her boss making the notifications to higherups in the department; SLED and the coroner notified and on their way.

The final item on her checklist was media relations. The area was considered to be a media desert with only one small daily newspaper, but a small army of freelance reporters, mostly retirees, filled the void. The security officer at the gate to Sea Island Plantation would prevent the press from flooding the area as they commonly did at major crime scenes in larger cities. Nevertheless, they'd soon bombard the sheriff's office with inquiries and pepper the gated community's office with questions. She knew the calm that existed at the scene right now didn't mean the media storm wasn't brewing on the horizon.

3

Sean sat on the screened porch at the back of the house finishing his lunch, a salad with slices of chicken breast overflowing with wedges of fresh tomatoes he picked up at the farmer's market on Saturday. Annie, his yellow Lab, lay on her dog bed with one eye open, alert for any squirrels venturing into the backyard. Annie had never caught a squirrel, but that didn't stop her from chasing them back into the trees where she figured they belonged.

Beyond his yard flowed the Spartina River, a tidal river that opened into the ocean sound at the south end of the island. At low tide, the river was only a hundred feet wide, but at high tide, the salt marsh looked like a lake stretching a half mile across. The marsh had its own beauty even at low tide, its forest of cordgrass, known as Spartina, growing out of the pluff mud, and swaying in the breeze. Herons, egrets, cormorants, and other shore birds searched for food along the bank, while an occasional dolphin swam by upriver and bald eagles and osprey soared overhead.

This had been Lauren's favorite spot. They'd have their morning coffee out here during the summer and often sit on the porch with a glass of wine in the evening. Sean remembered complaining during their first winter here how the stalks of the Spartina grass turned brown in December. Lauren reminded him the cordgrass was essential to the salt marsh ecology, providing food for insects and fish and a protected habitat for small fish to grow. It helped prevent erosion of the shoreline and filtered pollution from the water, which made the tidal river water some of the cleanest in the nation.

The Spartina grass had to die off, Lauren had said, so it could decompose into the silt that became the pluff mud, which would nourish the growth of new grass in the spring and supply food for the fish and oysters, which would in turn become food for larger fish, birds, otters, dolphins, and other animals. Maybe Sean had worked Homicide for too long, but he was unable to see the same hope for rebirth after death that Lauren had seen. And after Lauren's death, Sean saw nothing in death but the end of life.

The doorbell rang, and Annie jumped up and barked.

Sean made his way through the house and opened the front door. Jason "Stretch" Andrews stood there next to a heavy-set woman in her sixties with short brown hair. Annie rushed forward and nosed Stretch's hand until he petted her. Sean had met Stretch at his first meeting of the Island Retired Law Enforcement Officers Association, a group of fifty former cops who had made their post-career homes in the Spartina Island vicinity. He was in his early sixties and had retired from the Vermont State Police where he had worked the major crimes unit for the last two decades of his career. He was around six-two, but probably didn't weigh much more than 160. His fellow state troopers had given him the nickname Stretch as a rookie and it stuck.

"Sean, this is Denise Sheppard, retired FBI. Spent the end of her career on the organized crime task force in Chicago."

"Hey, Denise." Sean held out his hand, which she shook firmly.

"She's known as Feebee among us cops," Stretch said. "Not that the FBI is real police."

"The FBI is the nation's premier law enforcement agency," Feebee said.

"Only according to the FBI," Stretch said.

Feebee grinned. "Your envy is apparent when you locals are in the presence of the FBI."

"Anyway," Stretch said, "we stopped by to bring your cold case team gift."

When he moved down here, Sean had declined an invitation to join the group of retired detectives that volunteered their time to examine unsolved homicides for the sheriff's office. There was nothing worse than a retired cop who didn't know how to retire. He knew guys back in Oakland who'd been retired for twenty years, yet couldn't stay away from the department. When a member of the cold case team, a retired Detroit detective, passed away a few months ago, Stretch and a few others subjected Sean to a recruiting pitch to join the team. Although a lot had changed in his life in the past year, he still declined.

Feebee pulled out a metal button from her pocket and handed it to Sean. It was the size of the Obama-for-President buttons that everyone had seemed to wear in the Bay Area when Sean was working homicide with Oakland PD. This button had a cartoon-looking dead body lying in the pluff mud alongside what looked just like the Spartina River and the words, *Mudflats Murder Club*.

"I already told you," Sean said, "I have no desire to sit around playing Sherlock Holmes with a bunch of old guys."

"You mean with fellow old guys," Stretch said.

"Your buddy Lieutenant Green said we need to fill the open slot and suggested we ask you," Feebee said.

"And the team got together and voted to accept you," Stretch said.

"What's going on across the street?" Feebee asked.

Sean looked past them toward the street. The ambulance was gone but a half dozen sheriff's department cars remained. A uniformed deputy stood on the front porch of a neighbor's house talking to the couple that lived there. A slender man dressed in a white shirt and tie plodded up the walkway to another house. His belt held a holstered handgun, handcuffs, and sheriff department star. Detectives didn't normally conduct a door-to-door canvass, so something more serious than a stolen flowerpot or missing cat must have occurred, Sean surmised.

Sean shrugged. "When I got back from fishing a half hour or so ago, there was an ambulance and a couple of cars. Figured some kind of medical call. I've been eating lunch on the back porch and haven't been paying attention."

"Looks bigger than that now," Feebee said.

The early afternoon sun was beating down on the front porch. "You guys want to come in where it's cool?"

Sean offered them something to drink, but both declined. He invited them into the living room, but they stood in the dining room and looked out the large front window.

"What do you think?" Stretch asked.

"Could've been a burglary," Feebee said. "That would explain the neighborhood canvass."

Stretch rubbed his gray crewcut. "Then why the ambulance?"

"Last month, a mope head bogarted his way into an LOL's house in a plantation on the other side of the island," Feebee said, referring to a little old lady. "When she said she had no money in the house, he made her drive to her ATM and withdraw the max allowed."

"That could explain the ambulance," Stretch said. "Old people victimized by crime could have a heart attack or something."

"Old people, like us?" Feebee said.

"We're just older," Stretch said. "We've got another twenty years or so before we're old."

Feebee pulled a chair away from the dining table and sat down facing the window. "An ambulance showing up to check a victim would make sense."

As the two jabbered back and forth, Sean wondered if stopping by to drop off the murder club button and pitch him to join the team was just a pretext to look into the police activity on his street. He guessed he should feel honored that they felt so comfortable that they made themselves right at home in his house.

"Still, with all the cars there, I bet it's more than just a residential burglary," Stretch said.

"If we wanted to be like those folks we despised when we were working," Sean said, "we could go over there, flash our retired ID, and ask what's going on."

"If I did that, I'd have to go home and slap myself," Stretch said.

Feebee nodded while keeping her eyes on the street.

Sean pinned the cold case team button on his golf shirt and looked down at it. Cute, but silly. "You don't really wear these things do you?"

"Only when we're drinking together or when we want to piss off the captain," Feebee said.

"Drinking and pissing off Captain Clinton Cannon the Third are two things the team does really well," Stretch said.

"One of our guys made up the buttons last year," Feebee said. "That led to our team being nicknamed the Mudflats Murder Club. But I liked the old nickname better."

"The Spartina Island Murder Club?" Stretch said. "You gotta be kidding me."

"It's where we live—this tropical paradise."

"Mudflats Murder Club has a tougher, more dangerous ring to it," Stretch said.

"We're old and retired now," Feebee said. "We don't have to be tough anymore."

"Although it was before I was on the team, the nickname was based on the first cold case the team looked at," Stretch said. "The media coined it the mudflats murder."

"Before my time too," Feebee said, "but I saw the crime scene photos. An old guy shot multiple times around thirty years ago and probably dumped in the river. Weeks later, the body was found in the mudflats at low tide, most of his face eaten away by crabs and whatever."

"A couple of the old timers on the cold case team really dug into that murder," Stretch said. "Causing a few sheriff's deputies to call them the Mudflats Murder Club."

"I will admit," Feebee said, "as silly as it is, the name Mudflats Murder Club has grown on me."

"What happened to that cold case?" Sean asked.

"It went nowhere, a prime example of why most cold cases we look at were never solved in the first place. Anyway, last year we decided to make up the buttons and resurrect the old nickname."

That was normally Sean's experience with cold cases. The easy murder cases were solved within days. After a few weeks, or months sometimes, most of the obvious leads had been followed and led nowhere. Occasionally, a tip would come in years later, often by someone arrested for something and deciding to snitch on someone to lessen his own jail time. Or an advance in forensic science would pop out a suspect's name, like on one of his unsolved Oakland cases when DNA was discovered on the rope used to hang a prostitute twenty years earlier.

"You'll get to meet all the other guys tomorrow," Feebee said. "I hear they're going to present the case of a woman who was murdered while vacationing down here thirty some years ago."

"I don't know," Sean said.

"Come on, brother," Stretch said. "Give it a try. If you don't like it, you just quit. We're all just volunteers after all, so you just stop volunteering."

Sean nodded. "One meeting."

"Since Sean is the rookie," Stretch said, "shouldn't he have to bring the donuts?"

"Nah, I better bring them," Feebee said. "Look at his waistline. Bet he doesn't know shit about buying donuts."

4

Charlie had just returned to the bathroom and was standing over the body when she heard yelling outside the house, followed by a primal scream and the front door banging open. She rushed through the bedroom into the great room. A gray-haired man dressed in a tee shirt and shorts pushed his way through the doorway, half-dragging Detective Darryl Pickett. Charlie rushed toward the foyer to assist her detective, but Darryl was able to grab the man's wrist and apply an arm bar.

The man yelped as Darryl jerked up his wrist to increase the pressure. "I just want to see my wife," the man screamed.

Darryl continued torquing his arm upward, forcing the man to his knees. He then pulled his handcuffs off his belt.

Charlie held her hand up to signal Darryl should hold off cuffing him. "Are you Ken Russo?" Charlie asked.

"Where's my wife?" Sweat ran down his face as he choked out his words.

"What's your name, sir?" Charlie asked calmly as Darryl relaxed the hold a bit, while still maintaining control.

"Ken Russo." He lowered his head and rubbed his sweaty face on his shoulder. "I want to see my wife."

"This is a crime scene, so that's not possible," Charlie said softly.

"This is my damn house," Russo yelled. "You have no right to…"

Charlie stood there quietly as Russo began slapping the floor with his free hand and kicking his feet like a child having a temper tantrum. Soon, his rage diminished, and tears filled his eyes. "Mr. Russo, if you can remain calm, I'll have Detective Pickett let you up."

Russo sniffled and said, "Okay."

Darryl helped him to his feet.

"What happened?" Russo asked. "Why would someone…?"

"That's what we're trying to determine," Charlie said. She then chose her words carefully to avoid future problems with Miranda. "What can you tell us?"

Russo wiped his nose on his tee shirt. "I was at the beach when our neighbor, Debbie, called and said I needed to come home because Nancy was dead. Someone killed her."

Charlie studied the man's face, searching for telltale signs of deception. When he met her eyes with a steely glare, she said, "Mr. Russo, we'll be in your house for most of the day. We'll need to do a thorough search for evidence, and you can speed this up if you give us written permission to do so."

Russo continued to stare at her.

"Otherwise, we'll be here even longer while we wait to get a search warrant before we can begin to do our job."

"Anything to help you figure out what happened," Russo said.

Darryl pulled a consent-to-search form from his notebook and pointed with his pen to where Russo needed to sign.

"Meanwhile, I'd like you to go with Detective Pickett down to the station," Charlie said. "I'll see you there in a little while and we'll talk more. And Mr. Russo, I'm very sorry for your loss."

After Darryl led Russo from the house, Charlie returned to the bathroom where Hicks stood looking at his clipboard. "You finished with the diagram?" she asked.

Hicks handed her a metal clipboard with a pencil sketch of the room filled with measurements. She studied it, shifting her gaze back and forth from the diagram to the body in front of her. The tightness in her stomach turned into a knot. The victim's right foot, with its freshly pedicured red toes extended twelve feet, seven inches from the edge of the vanity on the north side of the room, according to the measurements done by Hicks.

Perfect hair without a hint of gray roots. Immaculately manicured nails painted the same color as her toes. A bathroom measuring sixteen by twelve with a ten-foot ceiling. His-and-her vanities at opposite sides of the room, a separate toilet room, jetted tub, and a walk-in shower large enough to bathe a small horse.

That's what bothered her. If Nancy Russo had bottle-blonde hair, do-it-yourself nail polish, and had been lying on a linoleum floor of a tiny bathroom where her feet touched the single sink in the room and her head rested against the toilet on the other side of the room, Charlie's stomach wouldn't feel so twisted. It's not that any of that made a difference to Charlie—to her every victim mattered equally. But the murder of a well-to-do retired woman in Sea Island Plantation, an affluent gated community on Spartina Island, meant the entire world—or at least her South Carolina Lowcountry piece of the world—would expect nothing less than the speedy identification and arrest of the killer.

Charlie handed the clipboard back to her crime scene tech. "Now that we have the search consent, have you gone through the rest of the house?"

"I done finished checking all the doors and windows," Hicks said in his slow drawl. "Didn't nobody break and enter or force their way into this house."

"What about the murder weapon?"

"I checked like you asked. It's the same brand as the other ones in the knife block on the kitchen counter. And the big one's missin' from there, so I betcha dollars to donuts that butcher knife lying right there came from Mrs. Russo's kitchen."

"What are you doing now?" Charlie asked.

"Taking pictures of everything in the house. Then I'll go outside and do the same."

"Sounds good."

Charlie jotted a few notes in her steno pad as Hicks shuffled down the hall. Maybe the anxiety she felt was unnecessary. Despite his returning to the scene with a display of anger, grief, and shock, the husband was most likely responsible. Maybe he was dumb enough to be still wearing the clothes he had worn when he stabbed his wife. Maybe the neighbors will be able to recount occasions of fights between them, maybe some threats he made. With a little physical evidence and prior history to confront him with, Ken Russo might even confess.

Charlie's phone buzzed. She pulled it from her pocket and looked at the text: *The club wants me to play a doubles exhibition Saturday night as my final match before leaving for college. Love, Spencer.*

Charlie responded: *OK with me. Who's your partner?*

Spencer: *I'll check with Madison, but she might have a family thing.*

Madison and Spencer had been friends since sophomore year. His girlfriend, as far as Charlie was concerned, but Spencer insisted they were just friends. They didn't date, but rather *hung out*, because their generation didn't really date, as Spencer often reminded her.

She texted back: *I'm sure you'll find someone. BTW, I'll be working late. Sorry.*

A murder the week before her son left for college was certain to screw up her plans. Times like this she wondered why she ever became a cop.

No problem, Mom. Bye.

Charlie put her phone in her pocket, took a deep breath, and tried to focus. She heard footsteps approaching and turned to see her supervisor striding down the hallway from the master bedroom.

"Coroner and SLED crime scene team's ETA is forty minutes," he said. Standing six-two and weighing nearly three hundred pounds, Lieutenant Billy Green filled the doorway. He smiled at her with the same toothy grin he had given her the day she hit the streets as a brand-new deputy ten years ago. As if he could feel her anxiety and read her mind, he said, "You've got this, Charlie."

Charlie prided herself on never showing uncertainty around her coworkers. The men in the department could spot weakness in a heartbeat, and just as a wolf would single out the weakest deer in a herd, the men could identify any deputies—especially female ones—who didn't meet their required police standard of toughness and confidence. But as a Black man, Billy had experienced his own struggle being accepted when he came on years before Charlie, and he was one of the few people she felt comfortable lowering her guard around.

"I know." She sighed and lowered her eyes.

"I don't care that this is your first homicide as the team sergeant. You've worked murders before as a detective, and if you weren't up to it, we wouldn't have given you the position."

They'd had this conversation when the new sheriff promoted her to sergeant two years ago, and again, when after a stint in uniform, she was assigned a few months ago as the first woman in the history of the department to lead a detective squad. She gave Billy a confident nod and half smile.

He clasped her shoulder with one of his huge, meaty hands and grinned. "I'm gonna leave you to finish up things inside before the coroner gets here. I'll be out front keeping the sheriff and captain out of your hair and making sure the uniforms aren't just jacking their jaws under a shade tree."

5

Stretch and Feebee left after spending ten minutes filling Sean in on the other members of the cold case team. Sean went out to the garage to clean his fishing gear and replenish his supply of fishhooks and other essentials in his vest.

He opened the garage door to let some air in and saw three people huddled in front of the Russo's house, a Lowcountry-style stucco home directly across the street. A community security officer wearing a polo shirt and a uniformed deputy with sergeant chevrons on his sleeves listened intently to a stocky Black man the size of a refrigerator, who was dressed in a black suit, white shirt, and tie.

The Black man looked over his shoulder and lowered his sunglasses on his nose. "Yo, Sean, it's about time you show your face."

Sean had met Billy Green twenty-five years ago when he vacationed on Spartina Island with his wife and kids for their first time. After an exhausting day of keeping up with a two and four-year-old on the beach, Sean and his family had been browsing through some shops on the way back to their rental unit, when their four-year-old daughter disappeared. One moment she was there and the next she was gone. Sean and his wife had frantically searched the tee shirt shop they were in, the stores next to it, and the walkways throughout the shopping plaza.

After ten long minutes of fruitless searching, Sean was preparing to call 9-1-1, when across the shopping plaza, he saw Rachel's tiny head above the crowd. Even though she was a few hundred feet away, Sean swore he heard her squeal in joy as she pointed at him. Sean and his wife had pushed through the throng of people to see Rachel perched upon the shoulders of a huge Black man dressed in a deputy sheriff's uniform.

The deputy had hoisted Rachel off his shoulders into Sean's arms and said, "I was down the way at the snack bar drinkin' me a sweet tea when I feel this tug on my pant leg and see this little creature lookin' up at me. I crouch down, and she says, 'My daddy told me if I ever need help, I should find a police officer. I need help to find my mommy and daddy. My daddy's a policeman too.'" Billy had eyed Sean up and down, as if he were evaluating his fitness for police duty and then said, "My name's Deputy Billy Green. What's yours, Mister Policeman?"

Sean left his garage and crossed the street, passing two twenty-foot palms that stood sentinel in the Russos' front yard. He stopped in the shade of a crepe myrtle, the clusters of deep red flowers hanging just over his head in the thick, still air. He smiled and thrust out his hand. "What's going on, Billy?"

Billy shook his hand and gave him a half hug with his left arm. Every year since that day they met, Sean had gotten together with Billy during his family's summer vacation on the island. They swapped cop stories, and Sean followed Billy's career as he advanced to detective, sergeant, and lieutenant, and finally to his present assignment with the sheriff office's CID, or criminal investigation division.

"You know the couple that lives here?" Billy asked.

Sean knew it must be serious for Billy to dispense with small talk so quickly. "We did some social things, dinners, parties, and other neighborhood stuff with them when Lauren was alive. The women got together more. Card games, lunch, shopping, and that sort of thing."

"Any idea who'd want to hurt her?" Billy kept a straight face, giving away nothing, the same as Sean had done thousands of times in his career.

Sean shrugged. "Is she dead?"

Billy nodded.

"Homicide?"

"Looks like it."

Except for his first few years on the job, Sean had always lived in the suburbs. There had been a few residential burglaries and car thefts on his street and even an occasional robbery nearby, but never a homicide in the neighborhood where he lived. One reason people moved into a gated community after retirement was for the security. Having a murder occur within their midst would rattle the world of his neighbors.

"How well do you know her husband?" Billy asked.

When a married woman was murdered, the first person detectives looked at was the husband, so the question didn't surprise Sean. "Not exactly my best friend, but I know him pretty well. He used to play golf with a group of us."

"Used to?"

"He had a knee replacement a few months back. I see him walking and bicycling, but not golfing again yet."

"Anything else?"

Sean knew Billy was asking the obvious. "Do you mean is he the kind of man who could kill his wife?"

Billy nodded. "You've dealt with a bunch more murderers than me."

"Nice guy. Good neighbor. Quiet. Never even seen him raise his voice. But in my experience," Sean said, looking Billy in the eyes, "everyone is capable of murder."

6

"A detective might need to take a formal statement later," Billy said. "But lemme get the basics."

Sean knew the routine all too well. "Like what did I do today, did I see anything unusual?"

"Yeah, start at the beginning." Billy opened his notebook and pulled a ballpoint pen from his shirt pocket.

Sean glanced at his wristwatch. 1:32 p.m. "Got up at six, the same as every morning, made coffee, fed Annie, ate a bowl of cereal, took Annie for a walk—about a half hour long—then got ready to take my kayak out on the river."

"Did you see anyone, or did anyone see you on your walk?"

Billy was just doing his job, but it still felt funny having to be ruled out as a suspect. "When we left the house, it was getting light, so probably about six-forty."

"Any lights on in the Russo's house?"

"Not that I recall but could've been. We walked right past their house to the cul-de-sac at the end of Blue Heron Lane."

"Any vehicles parked on the street?"

The community rules prohibited overnight parking on the street, and service vehicles weren't allowed in until seven. "No, I would've noticed."

"Where'd you walk to?"

Sean detailed his walk. Down the path to the River Lodge, around the pool, and to the end of the dock.

"Anyone there?"

High in the sky three black vultures slowly orbited around the neighborhood, lazily dipping and rising on the thermal layers. Sean was always amazed at the speed they would arrive, often a dozen or more, to a roadkill site. Although he knew logically they could not know something was dead in the house in front of him, their presence still gave him shivers.

Sean shook his head. "We waited at the end of the dock for the sun to rise over the river. You can check, but I think sunrise is around six-fifty." He described his route through the neighborhood that brought him back home around 7:10 a.m. "I recall a car parked in the lot by the lodge. Sometimes people go there early to fish or crab."

"The car in the parking lot?" Billy asked.

"A light-colored SUV, I think. Parked on the right side of the lot by the lagoon. But we weren't close enough to see if it was occupied or not."

"Make or model?"

"Jeez, Billy. I'm not even positive it was an SUV. My coffee hadn't fully kicked in yet and I was on autopilot."

"That's not much help. Half the folks on the island drive SUVs." Billy looked up from his notebook. "Sorry, buddy, just venting."

Sean wished he *had* noticed a suspicious person or vehicle, but nothing had struck him as out of the ordinary. "I got home, had my second cup of coffee, changed, and picked up my neighbor, George Laughlin, at his house about seven-thirty. We took my golf cart to the River Lodge parking lot, carried our fishing gear and vests to the end of the dock, got our kayaks from the rack and put them into the water. We probably paddled off upriver a few minutes before eight."

"Did you see anyone suspicious on the way there or around the dock?"

Sean thought for a minute. Before he retired, he always looked at people twice. It was the nature of being a cop. But in the last year, he'd lost his edge. Maybe he was finally relaxing and no longer seeing the world and everyone in it as threats. He shook his head.

"What then?"

"A little before noon, George and I paddled back to the dock, put our kayaks up, and I dropped him off at his house. On my way home I saw an ambulance and a couple of units out front but decided not to be a nosy neighbor. So, I went inside and made lunch."

Billy closed his notebook.

"Did Ken do it?" Sean asked.

"He showed up at the house all distraught. We'll interview him at the office later."

An old Chevy pickup pulling an open trailer filled with landscaping equipment rumbled down the street. A white man got out of the driver's side and three Hispanic men eased out of the crew cab. A uniformed deputy strode toward them with his pen and clipboard in hand.

"But you have your doubts."

Billy shrugged his shoulders. "If you're not busy, you care to walk through, take a look?"

"I'm retired, remember?"

"I'm sure it's like riding a bike. You probably see things we local yokels miss."

"You love putting on that dumb southerner act, but I know better." Sean chuckled, knowing the Campbell County Sheriff's Office paid near the top in the state and attracted some of the best cops in the area.

"I've got two kinds of detectives, the smart ones that came on in the last decade or so but still lack experience, and the older ones who were hired because they were good ole boys and friends with one of the previous sheriffs."

"And then there's you."

"Back then they needed a few more token Negroes, and I was the first one they found who could read and write."

If they were sitting around drinking a beer, that would've called for a friendly punch in the arm. Even if the department's motive were to increase diversity or meet a quota, Billy was more qualified than most of the white males that made up the department back then. "I'd love to help you out, Billy, but this isn't my jurisdiction. Besides, how'd it look having some civilian wandering through your murder scene?"

"You passed the background and completed the security training, so you're an official department volunteer."

A few months ago, Billy asked Sean to review a murder investigation on which the local prosecutor refused to file charges. As a favor to his friend, Sean agreed, but to be permitted access to law enforcement records, he had to conduct online training required by the state and sign forms swearing he wouldn't disclose law enforcement information to others.

"That was just to look at some paperwork and give you my take on it."

Billy pulled out his phone and tapped on a text message, holding it up for Sean to see. "I understand you've accepted a position on the cold case team."

Damn, Sean thought. Stretch and Feebee must've fired off a text to Billy the moment they left his house.

"I only agreed to give the cold case team a try," Sean said. "I didn't sign a contract or anything."

Billy had tried to recruit Sean to join the team when he first moved here, but Sean figured he had investigated enough murders to last ten lifetimes and wanted to focus his time and energy on his marriage, restoring his health, and adjusting to retirement. But everything in his life had changed after Lauren died.

"I'm only asking you to do a quick walk-through. You'd be helping out the department, which is what volunteers do."

"You've handled murder scenes before," Sean said.

"Yeah, but we don't normally get ones like this. Most are...well, you know."

Yes, he did know. They were like most murders he had handled in Oakland, where the victim was into drugs, gangs, or prostitution. Homicides where the newspapers ran a two-inch article on an inside page, and two days later, no one but the assigned investigators seemed to care. "Are your people processing the scene?" Sean asked.

"SLED's bringing in their crime scene team, but one of our guys is doing preliminary photos and a diagram."

"I don't want to get in their way."

"You'll be in and out before SLED even gets here."

7

Charlie was in the Russos' master bathroom trying to visualize how the murder occurred when Hicks approached and told her he'd finished taking photos of the interior of the house. "I'd put my money on the husband," he said. "Old, retired folks together in the same house day after day. She burns dinner one too many times, and bingo, he flips."

Charlie knew theories were easy to come by. Evidence proving them was what counted. She heard the front door open and Billy's voice. Her heart skipped a beat, fearing SLED was here already.

She made her way to the living room, expecting a couple of Tyvek-suited crime scene technicians lugging in cases of equipment. Instead, Billy stood in the doorway next to a civilian who bent over and removed his sneakers. The man set his shoes outside and stepped onto the thick Oriental rug in the foyer next to Billy. He was dressed in tan knee-length shorts, a blue golf shirt, and black ankle socks. He removed a blue and white Callaway golf hat from his head and placed it by his shoes on the front porch.

Standing beside each other, the men looked like two retired football players, Billy an offensive lineman, and the other man, a few inches taller than Billy, could've been a tight end. He had the broad shoulders and narrow waist of someone who was an athlete when younger, yet still frequented the gym. His dark brown hair transitioned to iron gray at the temples and was just long enough to require a comb. He appeared to be about her age, but at second glance, she saw the creases on his ruggedly handsome face that indicated a longer life—a life fully lived.

"Charlie, this is Sean Tanner," Billy said. "He's retired from the Oakland police department and lives across the street. And Sean," Billy continued, "this is Sergeant Charlotte Nash, the B squad team sergeant. She's the lead investigator on this case."

"California?" Charlie asked.

He looked at her with his deep brown eyes, studying her for a few counts. He smiled slightly and nodded. A pleasant face—but one accustomed to hiding his thoughts and feelings.

"What did you do there?"

"Patrol and special operations as an officer and sergeant, but mostly I worked investigations." He spoke softly for such a large man, obviously having learned that a loud, deep voice coming from a man his size could overwhelm and intimidate many people.

"Sean spent sixteen years working homicide," Billy said. "Over two hundred cases as the lead investigator, some that they wrote books about and use as case studies at the FBI academy."

Charlie raised her eyebrows even though she meant to maintain a neutral expression. Oakland's reputation for violent street crime and tough-as-nails cops was well known in law enforcement circles. "And you moved here when you retired?"

"About two years ago."

She looked at her notes. "We show you as the resident at number twenty-four. What's your date of birth, Mr. Tanner?"

He crossed his deeply tanned arms across his chest then quickly lowered them, obviously aware of what that body language conveyed. She noted a tarnished gold band on his left ring finger and felt a tinge of disappointment. Tall, dark, handsome, and married—the story of her life.

"I already interviewed Sean and have all of his information," Billy said.

Charlie turned to her boss, wanting to say, *then why the hell did you bring him into my crime scene.* "Okay, lieutenant, was Mr. Tanner able to offer anything of value?"

She listened as Billy summarized Sean's timeline for the day and his knowledge of Nancy and Ken Russo. Sean stood there passively without adding anything. The answer was no, she thought when her boss finished.

"I asked Sean to do a walk-through of the scene," Billy said. "See if anything jumps out at him."

She glared at her lieutenant in bewilderment. He was the one who was adamant that access to a major crime scene should be limited to essential personnel only. He stressed that the old days, where every command officer from the sheriff on down ducked under the crime scene tape just to look around, were a thing of the past. She fought to hold her tongue, but her tongue won the battle. "No fucking way. We don't allow civilians in a murder scene."

Sean lowered his eyes, showing he wanted nothing to do with their disagreement.

"Sean just became a member of the cold case team," Billy said calmly. "They finished his background check and he's been fully vetted and cleared."

Charlie had sat in on several cold case team meetings. A bunch of old men and a woman second-guessing the actions of cops who had done their best under difficult circumstances with limited resources. She often wondered if any of them could've done any better back when they carried a badge and gun for a living. They occasionally came up with promising ideas, one of which helped solve an old murder case, but mostly they were a bunch of arrogant old pricks who thought modern policing only existed on the other side of the Mason-Dixon line.

"He's still a volunteer and not a sworn law enforcement officer," Charlie said.

"We'd be escorting him and he's only here to observe and provide insight."

"I don't like it," she said. What bothered her even more than some former hotshot California homicide dick entering her crime scene was that Billy thought she needed the help. That he didn't trust her to solve the case.

Charlie glanced at Sean, who stood there quietly, as if he didn't care one way or another.

Sean pursed his lips and said, "Billy, maybe this isn't such a good idea.

I'd feel the same way as Sergeant Nash if a boss wanted to bring an outsider into my scene."

Billy looked at her. Waiting. Leaving it up to her. She knew where he stood. If she dug in her heels and the case turned out to be a whodunit, people would say that her refusing help allowed a killer to escape justice. Stubborn and prideful were some of the words she'd heard people in the department use to describe her. She didn't need to supply them with additional ammunition to solidify that assessment of her.

"Okay," she said reluctantly.

"I'll take a look," Sean said. "But I'm no Sherlock Holmes, and I usually end up with more questions than answers from a crime scene."

8

Charlie handed Sean a pair of booties and nitrile gloves. It still pissed her off that Billy thought this man possessed some sort of magical power to interpret a basic murder scene—some ability she didn't have.

"I won't touch anything," Sean said as he donned the booties and gloves, "but if it comes up in court, you can document I was gloved up."

Damn straight! Even though she thought the world of Billy, if asked, she'd testify that bringing an outsider into her crime scene wasn't her decision.

Sean asked, "Any signs of forced entry?"

"The neighbor who found the body said the front door was closed but unlocked," Charlie said. "So, we figured either the husband did it or someone else who had a key."

Without even acknowledging her answer, Sean slowly walked through the living room, his head on a swivel. "Did Ken Russo say anything yet?"

Charlie followed Sean, glancing where he looked to make sure she hadn't missed anything during her initial walk-through. "Only that he left at around seven and went to the beach, where he remained until a neighbor called and told him his wife was dead."

Sean nodded and walked around the kitchen island, looked in the sink and studied the knife block on the counter. He sniffed inside the coffeepot. He walked past the breakfast nook and bent over to examine the lock on the door that led to a screened lanai. "Was the back door locked?"

That was basic police work, Charlie said to herself. Of course, they'd carefully document whether doors were locked or unlocked. She struggled to keep her tone polite. "The responding deputies said it was unlocked when they arrived."

Sean crouched down and studied the floor by the door. "Have any of your people used this door?"

"A deputy went out the door and into the backyard to look around," Charlie said.

Sean looked over his shoulder at Hicks, who was following him like a little puppy dog. "Make sure you get some photos of the dried grass on the floor."

Charlie made some notes and bit her tongue. As if none of his California patrol officers ever tracked debris into a murder scene. Cops did that all the time, especially during the initial response when they were still figuring out what was going on, whether the victim was alive or dead, and if a suspect might still be present. All of that took precedence over protecting the crime scene.

Billy, Hicks, and Charlie followed Sean as he retraced his steps through the kitchen and into the laundry room, where he opened the door to the garage. A Toyota Avalon was parked in one of the two stalls. "The husband drove up in a Lexus SUV," Charlie said. "We'll impound it and process it later."

Sean nodded but didn't say a word. He could have acknowledged she was thinking ahead, she thought, and taking proactive steps to search for blood and other evidence that the husband might've transferred to his car.

Sean made a quick loop through the guest room and bath then walked across the living room, stopping to look at a dark blue afghan and two throw pillows on the floor in front of the sofa. He continued through the living room and into the powder room. "Are all the lights in the same condition as you found them?" he asked.

"The only lights that were on were those in the kitchen and the master bathroom," Charlie said, hoping the responding deputies were honest and exact when they had assured her they hadn't touched any light switches in the house.

"Can I borrow a flashlight?"

Hicks pulled a full-size Streamlight from his belt and handed it to Sean. He turned it on, shined it into the toilet bowl and the sink, and swept the white light across the hand towel hanging next to it. He turned off the light, handed it back to Hicks, and stepped into the master bedroom without saying a word. He stood in the doorway for a minute, taking it all in. Then he slowly walked around the room. He got onto his knees and looked under the bed. "Was the ceiling fan going like this when you arrived?" he asked as he walked to the front of the room.

"The first deputies on the scene said they didn't change anything." She was getting tired of repeating this.

He studied the corner of the room where sheets and pillowcases were rolled up in a ball on the floor. He walked back to the bed and examined the bare mattress cover.

"I don't know what this means," Charlie said. "If the husband didn't kill her, I guess it's possible an intruder came in and murdered her in her bed. He might've gathered up the sheets to dispose of them because they contained his DNA."

"I'm sure you'll have the lab check for any foreign DNA," he said as he walked into the short hallway and stood outside the walk-in closet.

She was about to reply, *of course, we're not stupid*, but then decided a half smile was the better response. Sean stared at the rows of clothes neatly hung in the closet for a few minutes and looked inside the wicker laundry basket. He leaned over it and sniffed several times.

He stood at the entrance to the bathroom, studying the body, blood, and knife. His face showed no sign of disgust or repulsion, emotions Charlie had to suppress when she walked into the bathroom and saw the body for the first time. He crept toward the victim, taking tiny steps, and looking at his feet as if he were crossing a minefield. He crouched down, looked some more, and moved around to different spots and did the same, apparently trying to view the corpse from as many angles as possible while remaining outside the pool of blood.

After a few minutes, he walked gingerly to the clothes on the bathroom floor, squatted down, and took several short sniffs. He stood up and asked, "Did the neighbor who found her touch anything in here?"

"One of my detectives is taking a statement from her right now."

Sean nodded and walked through the bedroom and back to the front door. He pulled off his gloves and booties and stuffed them into his pocket.

9

"Any thoughts?" Charlie asked.

"It looks like your victim began undressing to take a shower and that's when she was attacked," Sean said. "Your medical examiner will have a better idea once he gets her on the table, but from what I could see, there are two stab wounds, one coming from the right and above that entered her shoulder and back area. I suspect that was the initial attack. The victim probably responded by turning and facing her assailant, who then stabbed her with a thrusting motion into the throat. The spray, appearing as low-velocity blood spatter that we see on the floor, is likely from the arterial bleeding when the carotid was severed. But she quickly collapsed, which limited the extent of the spray. A blood spatter expert may be able to tell you more, but the droplets just outside the pool of blood indicate she was stabbed where she now lies."

"I imagine the suspect was a relatively strong man to be able to drive the knife into her back," Charlie replied.

"The medical examiner can determine the depth of penetration, but the weapon is a Henckels Professional S series chef knife with an eight-inch blade. It's part of the same set in the knife block on the kitchen counter. It's heavy, strong, and razor sharp. A child could bury it halfway to its hilt with ease. The suspect used his right hand, so was probably right-handed."

"How can you tell?" Charlie asked.

"The wound was high on the shoulder, close to the neck. If the suspect used his left hand, the victim's head would've blocked an overhand stabbing motion. Unless he swung the knife backhand, which would've been unnatural."

Charlie asked, "Someone taller than her to make the overhand stab?"

"Pathologists and detectives who determine the height of an attacker based on the trajectory of bullets or angle of knife wounds in a victim are only guessing. And if they guess wrong, you could eliminate the real killer." Sean glanced at Billy then returned his attention to Charlie. "If we assume the victim was standing fully erect, which may or may not be correct, someone as much as a foot shorter than her could've inflicted those injuries. And even though I used *he* when I described the attacker, I wouldn't rule out a woman."

Charlie scribbled a few comments in her notebook.

"And she had sex recently, probably this morning."

"What?" Charlie said, surprised. "Really?"

"I detected the odor of semen in her underwear on the bathroom floor."

Charlie didn't know whether she should be impressed or grossed out that old homicide detectives sniffed dirty laundry for clues.

"Is this looking like a sex crime to you?" Billy asked. "Was she raped and murdered?"

"Her husband could've had sex with her this morning, got angry over something, and killed her. He could've had sex with her and later went to the beach as he said. After which, she could've gone in to take a shower and been killed by a stranger. Or she could've been raped and murdered by a total stranger. Or she could've had consensual sex with a lover…"

"I get it," Charlie interrupted. "If the DNA in the semen matches the husband, it tells us nothing."

Sean shrugged. "If it *isn't* his, it says quite a bit. If the medical examiner sees indications of vaginal trauma, it points you in one direction. If there's no sign of forcible intercourse, it tells you something else. And if it is the husband's—an older couple having morning sex—well, that's certainly interesting if nothing else."

Sean smiled slightly. It was the first time Charlie had seen any expression on his face since he began examining the scene. It was also Sean's first hint of humor, something that she'd found the grimness of a murder often required.

The possible scenarios churned through her head. Every different DNA result opened up various different possibilities and a wide pool of potential suspects. The only one that would provide an immediate answer would be a DNA hit on a suspect with a criminal history who had no legitimate reason to be in her house.

"The absence of forced entry to the house doesn't tell us much," Sean continued. "People living here get complacent and many never lock their doors. Ken's initial statement about leaving at seven might be the truth. I've seen him drive off around then a number of times when I'm out for a morning run or walking my dog. But I didn't see him this morning."

"Maybe other neighbors will know his routine," she replied.

"There was dried dribble on the floor in front of the toilet in the powder room. Could've been anyone, but it wouldn't hurt to swab it for DNA. If this was a stranger, he might've used the toilet. And the toilet seat was down, so if the suspect lifted the seat, he could've left prints."

She had never thought of that. She just hoped none of the deputies was dumb enough to use the toilet and drip on the floor. If they identified one of their prints or DNA in there, she would never let them live that down.

"The fan running in the bedroom could be something," Sean said. "I sleep with my fan on but turn it off as soon as I get up."

"And I know people who leave fans running in every room in the house all day," Charlie said.

"My wife was that way." Sean's eyes lit up for a second then went blank. Charlie noted that he used the past tense when referring to his wife. Divorced, she figured. No man who spent thirty years as a cop would be easy to live with.

He continued. "Sheets rolled up on the floor is unusual. Although it could be the work of a stranger who did it to dispose of evidence, I've seldom encountered suspects in these kinds of murders who are that smart. Plus, this wasn't a planned homicide, as indicated by the murder weapon coming from the victim's house. Maybe your victim was just planning to wash the sheets, so she stripped the bed when she got up and left them on the floor so she wouldn't forget to wash them after her shower."

Charlie smiled slightly to hide her embarrassment. She felt stupid for having speculated aloud what she had been thinking. She didn't know why she felt the need to impress Sean. She knew better than to come up with a theory based on a few isolated pieces of evidence at a crime scene.

"The last thing I noticed was the shower was wet, but the victim's body wasn't. If I were going to the beach, I wouldn't take a shower first, so I'm guessing it wasn't from Ken. More likely, the victim was getting ready to take a shower. You may want to ensure the detective interviewing the neighbor asks if she touched anything in the house, turned on or off any lights, fans, water faucets."

She nodded to placate him.

Billy finally broke his silence. "Did the husband do it?"

Sean shrugged.

"Once we finish here, we'll interview him and see what he has to say," Charlie said.

Sean opened the front door and grabbed his hat and shoes from the porch. "Good luck."

"And if he doesn't confess, what would be your next step?" Billy asked Sean.

"Knock on doors and talk to people. Follow the leads," Sean said. "And get ready for a whole lot of community outrage when people realize Sea Island Plantation might not be the Shangri-La they thought it was."

10

Sean stepped out of the shower, his second one today. He had started sweating in the humid heat while talking to Billy outside the Russos' house. Besides, there was something about visiting a murder scene that demanded a shower. With its ten-foot ceiling and walk-in shower, his master bathroom was twice the size of the bedroom he had shared with his brother growing up in Pittsburgh. If he evaluated his life by his *stuff*, his life was about perfect—a large, beautiful house in a resort-like community, two cars in the garage, a pension that was more than he needed.

He lathered his face at his sink and rinsed his razor in hot water. Lauren's sink on the other side of the room loomed in his mirror, her trays of lotions and skin cleansers still adorning the countertop. Although his daughter had gone through her mother's cosmetics and clothing and taken those items she wanted, Sean hadn't touched anything since her death. He knew at some point he should clean out her vanity drawers and cabinet. But not today. He'd said that every day for nearly a year.

He pulled on a pair of navy-blue shorts and scanned the row of shirts in his closet. He selected a pale yellow button-front with a full cut and straight bottom designed to be worn untucked. Before going out at night, he used to stand behind Lauren as she did her hair and makeup. She'd glance at him in her mirror and either smile and give him a thumbs-up or send him back to his closet to try again. He thought she would approve.

He slipped on his well-worn boat shoes and grabbed his phone. It showed a voicemail from George Laughlin. He walked into the dining room and looked out the window as he hit "call back" without listening to the message. Three unmarked cars and the SLED crime scene van were still parked across the street.

"I guess you heard what happened," George said in a panic. He had been a dentist in New Jersey, where he grew a large practice and raised a family in one of the affluent towns within commuting range of New York City. He'd thought his life was perfect until seven years ago when he was served divorce papers at his office. He sold his practice, married Beth, a divorcee he'd been having an affair with, and moved to Spartina Island.

"Yeah, I've already talked with the detectives," Sean said.

"They came over here and grilled me and Beth. Are you okay?"

Sean doubted the detectives actually "grilled" George. They probably questioned him the same as Sean would've done himself with friends and neighbors of a victim. "Sure, why wouldn't I be?"

"They were asking whether you and I actually went fishing today, what time you picked me up, if anyone else saw us."

Annie ran to the back door, sat, and barked once. Sean opened the door and followed her outside, grabbing a poop bag just in case. "That's routine. They need to account for the whereabouts of neighbors and possible witnesses."

"They treated us like suspects. Beth was a mess even before the cops interrogated us. Losing her best friend like that…"

"That's right. They knew each other back in New Jersey, didn't they?"

"We were all members of the same country club, and Beth and Nancy were always together."

"I'm really sorry." Sean didn't know what else to say.

"They asked Beth what she did today, but she didn't go out or see anyone until the afternoon. She doesn't have an alibi."

"Don't worry. The only people who establish an alibi are those planning to commit a crime. Not having an alibi isn't against the law."

Sean followed Annie as she sniffed her way through the lush back yard.

She squatted in the pine straw under a sprawling live oak tree with clumps of Spanish moss hanging from its massive limbs.

"Do they know what time she was killed?" George asked. "They wanted to know if Beth and I sleep in the same bed together, what time we got up, if we went out anywhere before I left with you."

Sean was getting tired of repeating himself. "Those questions are routine, and they won't know the time of death until after the autopsy. Even then it'll probably be a wide range."

"So, they might not know if she was killed while we were fishing and can vouch for each other?"

Sean snapped his fingers to get Annie's attention and headed back to the air-conditioned house. "At least you have Beth as an alibi," he said, although he seldom gave much credence to spousal alibis when he worked a case. "All I have is Annie, and I doubt the detectives would consider her a reliable witness to my whereabouts."

The line was silent for a few counts. Finally, George chuckled. "Oh, Annie, your dog."

Sean regretted his attempt to lighten George's worry. Civilians could never understand the way cops could make jokes in times of tragedy. "Did you still want to go to dinner, or should we cancel?"

"Beth had a migraine earlier but insists we should go. She says neighbors should be together at times like this."

11

Sean was the last one to be picked up. One of the advantages of being tall was friends usually let him sit in the front. George waved him to the passenger seat, and Sean climbed in. He shook hands with George, who was wearing dark long pants and a blue oxford shirt with the sleeves rolled up almost to the elbows. Despite the casual attire in the Lowcountry, George insisted gentlemen should never wear shorts to dinner. Sean twisted in his seat to greet Beth and the Kellers sitting behind him in the Acura MDX's spacious back seat. Debbie Keller sat in the middle and was holding hands with Beth. They were both crying, and Sean immediately wished they would've cancelled their dinner plans.

Debbie and Jeff were fit, tan, and in their early fifties. Jeff was one of the few people in their neighborhood who still worked full-time, and although Debbie worked with him a few days a week, she mostly played tennis and golf and attended exercise classes. After vacationing on the island for years, they had started a mortgage company down here as a branch of their Ohio office about ten years ago. They bought the house two lots down from the Russos when Jeff turned fifty, which was the minimum age to buy a house in an active adult community. They then sold their company in Ohio and expanded their Spartina Island business. Because Debbie and Lauren were close in age, they had become friends, and after Lauren's death, Debbie tried to include Sean in their social activities. If Sean refused her invitations too often, she'd respond with, "Lauren would've wanted you to," to guilt him out of the house and away from his TV and stack of books.

Upon arrival at Benson's Seafood Restaurant, Beth and Debbie went straight to the ladies' room, while a hostess led the three men to an outside table. "The girls are a mess," George said.

"Understandable," Jeff said. "If we wanted to experience murders on our street, we would've stayed in Cleveland."

Sean didn't know how best to respond, so he just nodded and gazed across the harbor at the sun setting beyond the water. A large powerboat cruised under the bridge that connected the island with the mainland. The briny scent of the ocean filled the air.

The restaurant was located on the Spartina Island side of the Intracoastal Waterway and had its own fishing boat that brought in fresh fish every day. Its view and fresh seafood made it a favorite of tourists as well as locals. The temperature had dropped into the low eighties, but even with the breeze off the water, dining on the restaurant's deck was still a touch warmer than Sean thought comfortable.

Although Sean had spent plenty of summers in the south, first with the Army at Fort Stewart outside Savannah and later during their family vacations, he never thought he'd get used to the humidity. The air was so thick at times, it felt like he was draped in a wet blanket. Lauren had told him to think of the weather as tropical instead of humid, muggy, sticky, or the other adjectives that rolled off his tongue. People didn't complain about humidity in Hawaii or the Caribbean, she reminded him. An osprey soared above them, then dropped toward the water like a dive bomber. Just before it struck the water and whatever fish it had seen, the large bird fully extended his wings and swooped across the water before flapping his wings a few times to climb back into the sky. The fish were one up, but Sean knew the osprey wouldn't go hungry.

Beth and Debbie arrived at their table wearing fresh makeup. Nearly twenty years older than Debbie, Beth was an attractive, petite woman, with short chestnut-colored hair that perfectly framed her angular face. She wore slim white pants, white sandals with two-inch heels, and a tight, burgundy knit top.

"Did you all know that Nancy almost became a nun?" Beth said. "She went to Catholic school all twelve years, and her older brother died in Vietnam her junior year."

"Senseless deaths like that often turn people away from God," George said.

"Nancy was always religious," Beth said. "She and Ken were both council members of the Catholic church on the island."

"But she was never preachy about it," Debbie said. "She told me, too, about once wanting to become a nun. But then she discovered boys."

Everyone laughed. Sean remembered how fond Lauren was of Nancy. She had given Lauren decorating advice and showed her around to all the stores in the area when they moved here. "Nancy was the first neighbor to invite Lauren to a neighborhood get-together when we got here," Sean said. "It was just cards or something, but it meant the world to Lauren."

"She did the same when I moved here," Debbie said. "She didn't talk much about it, but she also volunteered four days a week at the Dufftown Self-Help. Did whatever was needed, somedays working in the thrift shop, others carrying in boxes of food and clothing and sorting it for the needy families."

Once their meals came, the conversation shifted to Nancy's death. After Sean ate his last piece of grilled grouper, he leaned back in his chair. Debbie mostly pushed her food around on her plate and appeared to be on the verge of crying during the entire time they ate. Finding your friend stabbed to death can do that to you, Sean figured.

Beth pushed away her half-finished plate. "I still can't believe she's gone."

Disbelief and emotional denial of the murder had been the crux of the dinner conversation. It reminded Sean of the countless times he had met with the families of homicide victims. Occasionally he gleaned information that would help his investigations, but most of the time he ended up as nothing more than a sounding board or the target of their grief, frustration, and anger. Sean understood talking about a friend's violent death was therapeutic, but he wondered if he had used up his allotted share of empathy years ago.

"I should've known something was wrong when Nancy didn't come to the door as soon as I pulled into her driveway," Debbie said. Although she had told the story of how she found Nancy several times, no one interrupted. "I rang the doorbell and went inside. Everyone knows that's the way it is down here. A friend's expecting you and the door's open, so you just go in. I yelled for Nancy to hurry up, that the class was starting in fifteen minutes. She was of that generation that had to put on makeup and fix their hair even if they're going out to get sweaty. I went to her bedroom door and was about to call out again, when I heard the shower running."

"You heard the shower running?" Sean asked. She hadn't mentioned that in her earlier versions of the story.

"I thought showering before exercising was obsessive even for Nancy."

"Did you tell the police that?" Sean asked.

"They didn't really ask."

Sean leaned forward in his chair. "What happened then?"

"I was going to give her grief about taking a shower, but I felt something was wrong, that she must've forgotten we had the class. When I stepped into the bathroom, that's when I saw her."

"And you turned the shower off?" Sean said.

She scrunched up her nose. "I guess so. Out of habit. You don't waste water."

"Was the water hot?"

She thought for a minute. "No, it was turned to hot, but it was running cold. I guess the hot water tank only holds so much."

"Did the detective you spoke with leave a card?"

"It's on the kitchen counter."

"You should call tomorrow," Sean said. "That might be important."

Debbie sighed.

Jeff popped a shrimp in his mouth. He had ordered the captain's plate, which was enough fish, scallops, and shrimp to feed two people. "You think you know someone when you live next to them."

George shot him an icy glare. "No one said Ken killed her."

"Everyone knows it's always the husband," Jeff said. "Am I right, Sean?"

The waiter came and began clearing their plates, giving Sean a reprieve. "Would anyone care for coffee?" the waiter asked.

George and Jeff nodded. The pony-tailed man turned to Beth, and she shook her head. "Just like Nancy, I never drink the stuff."

Once the waiter left, Sean's dinner companions turned their attention back to him. They weren't about to let him off the hook. "Under the circumstances, he'd be a likely suspect, but he's just as likely to be innocent."

"If this was your case, you'd interrogate him until he confessed, wouldn't you?" Jeff asked.

Sean hated the term interrogation because people associated it with coercion and threats. Besides, Sean had never entered an interview room looking for a confession. Getting the truth was his only goal. "If there was evidence that pointed at the husband, we'd push him to tell the truth. But if he didn't do it, he might also be able to supply useful information that would lead to the real killer. A good detective doesn't want to alienate someone who might be able to help solve the case."

"I guess we'll know if the cops bring him home tonight," Jeff said.

Sean didn't mention that just because the detectives released Ken, it didn't mean he was innocent. He'd released many suspects after interviewing them because there wasn't sufficient evidence at the time. Once lab results came in or additional witnesses were interviewed, he'd sometimes arrest a killer several days or even months later.

"I still can't believe she's dead," Debbie said again.

"Yeah, murdered by her husband," Jeff said.

"We must not forget that no matter what, Ken lost his wife today." Beth rose from her chair, threw her napkin on the table, and glared at Jeff. "He needs our support, and we shouldn't be judging the poor man and sending him to the electric chair before the facts are in."

Sean agreed in theory, but if he were a betting man, he'd still put his money on the husband any day.

12

Charlie opened the door and stepped into the interview room. Unlike the claustrophobic interview rooms in the former, antiquated sheriff's station, this room was about ten by ten, well lit, and clean. The walls were finished with textured cement board, which was more impervious to punched holes and scratched graffiti, and the floor was covered with the same industrial-grade carpeting as the rest of the building. A metal table was bolted to the middle of the floor and surrounded by four aluminum-framed plastic chairs too light to be effective weapons should an agitated suspect consider it.

She resumed her place in the same chair she had vacated an hour ago, Darryl sat across from her, leaving Ken Russo seated between them. Ken looked like he'd aged ten years since she first saw him at his house. The bags under his eyes hung nearly to the top of his sagging jowls. They had spent an hour and a half with him the first session, which she kicked off with tried and tested language that got them through the Miranda warning: *All of us in this room want to find out what happened to your wife, and any background information you can give us will be very helpful, but before we talk to you, we're required to advise you of your rights.*

Ken agreed to talk without an attorney present. Since he had no arrest record, they took his fingerprints and collected his DNA on a cheek swab.

She then casually conversed with him and gathered background information about him and Nancy. They were both born and raised in Newark, New Jersey. They met right after college when they both worked at PSE&G, the Public Service Electric and Gas Company. They dated for a year and married at twenty-five. They both advanced into the executive offices of PSE&G, he on the operations side, and Nancy through human resources. As their salaries increased, they moved to successively more expensive suburbs outside of Newark. They had three children, all of whom were now married and living with their own families in New Jersey.

Ken and Nancy took their first vacation to Spartina Island forty years ago. They later bought a two-bedroom villa on the island, which they rented out most of the year, and built their house in Sea Island Plantation ten years ago. They initially just spent vacations and holidays here, and finally retired on Spartina Island full-time five years ago.

"Mr. Russo," Charlie said as she opened her notebook. Although she preferred addressing possible suspects by their first names to establish an air of authority over them, she normally addressed people of an older generation by their title and last name. That's how she was brought up, and even in today's informal society, she still bristled when a kid addressed adults by their first names. "My detectives and I spent the last hour trying to verify your earlier whereabouts. You told us you left your house about seven and stopped at the McDonald's for coffee and an Egg McMuffin. They're one of the few businesses on the island with security cameras, which showed you pulling up to the drive-through window at seven-oh-six. We also spoke to the girl who worked the drive-through this morning. When we showed her your photo and that of your Lexus SUV, she remembered you. Seems you're a regular and she confirmed you were there this morning."

Ken smiled slightly and slumped in the chair, exposing a roll of flab between his *Sandy Feet Bar* tee shirt and the waistband of his green madras shorts.

"We tracked down a few of the lunch-time workers at the sandwich shop you said you stopped at some time before noon, but none of them recognized your photo. But here's the problem. Even if they did verify you were there, that still leaves a window from seven-fifteen until twelve o'clock where no one saw you. That's the time when your wife was most likely killed. You said you parked in the lot at town beach. There are no cameras there, and since the parking lot is only open to town residents with a sticker, there's no pay station like the other beaches that would prove when you arrived. You said you took your chair and towel to the beach and spent the day walking the beach, wading in the water, reading, and napping. You said hi to people who passed by, but none of whom you know by name."

"But you saw my swimsuit and towel were wet," he said.

"Sure," Charlie acknowledged. "You told us you returned to the beach, ate your sandwich, took a last dip in the water, and then changed back into your shorts at the beach changing rooms, getting ready to come home. That's when you received the call about your wife. But, if you had something to do with her death—you could've driven to the beach afterward, taken a swim, and waited for someone to find her."

They had no physical evidence linking Ken to the murder yet. It would take the state crime lab a while to process the knife for DNA and fingerprints, but unless they found Ken's full handprint and no others on the handle, it wouldn't prove much. The knives were in his kitchen, so a first-year law student could explain the presence of his prints. Charlie had already examined the clothes he was wearing, and although they'd collect them later and send them to the lab, whoever cut Nancy's throat should've been covered in blood. If it was Ken, he had changed clothes, and a swim in the ocean or a shower would've removed her blood from his body.

"Let's talk some more about your relationship with Nancy," she said.

"I don't know what more to tell you," he said. "We've been retired down here for five years now. We had quite a few friends. You already wrote down the names I gave you. We got together for dinners, parties, wine tastings, and other activities. We also did our own things. Nancy had her exercise classes and card groups with her girlfriends. I play golf and pickle ball with men and poker occasionally."

"I understand you haven't been able to participate in many activities for a while."

"I had a knee replacement seven weeks ago. I have physical therapy twice a week and I walk and bicycle. So yeah, it's a drag right now. That's why I spend so much time at the beach."

Darryl leaned across the table toward Ken. "Because you can't stand being in the house with your wife that much?"

Charlie glared at Darryl. She wanted to reach across the table and slap him. Prior to stepping into the room, she had explained her strategy and warned him about pushing Ken too soon. But that's the kind of detective Darryl was. He was fifty-three and had been with the department for thirty years, hired by one of the old-generation sheriffs, the local southern white men who were elected because of the favors they had done for people in the past and for the favors they promised in the future. That sheriff was the uncle of Darryl's wife, and back then, a family connection was about the only qualification you needed to become a deputy. Although Charlie's mother also traced her family roots in Campbell County back to the pre-Civil War days, that was about the only similarity between Charlie and Darryl's lineage.

"Have you been married for more than forty years, Detective?" Ken shot back.

Darryl's face reddened. Charlie could tell he was trying to control his temper, knowing that if he got sucked into a he-man/whose-dick-is-bigger challenge with a murder suspect, she'd have him standing tall in the lieutenant's office tomorrow morning. Darryl's outburst also placed her in an unwinnable predicament. She could embarrass him in front of Ken by telling him to shut up, which would also show they were not a team, or let him handle this on his own, which could push Ken into invoking his Miranda rights. She decided to give him a little more rope—and hope he didn't hang himself.

Darryl leaned back in his chair and rested his hands on his beer belly. "No, sir. I got married before I graduated high school, so it's been a bit over thirty-five for me."

"Then you probably know that you've already talked about everything you've needed to with your wife by now, and no matter how big your house is, you bump into each other if you're together all day."

"Yes, sir." Darryl smiled, showing a wide gap between his front teeth. "That's why on most of my days off I go huntin' or fishin'."

Charlie knew prodding a suspect just to piss him off in hopes he'll confess seldom worked. And when you have to back down, as Darryl did, it only added to their confidence. She gave Darryl a final stern look and turned back to Ken, hoping to draw his attention away from Darryl.

"I loved my wife," Ken said to Charlie. "She was my best friend and the person I planned to spend the rest of my life with. I admit I've been a grouch for the past few months. With my bum leg, I feel like an invalid at times, and she went from babying me to nagging me about doing my exercises and watching my diet, reminding me the surgeon mentioned more than once that had I not been carrying around fifty extra pounds, my knees might've lasted longer. But our disagreements were minor, and I would never lay a hand on her."

Ken had dug himself in. He found his story and was sticking to it.

Charlie's phone buzzed. She looked at the screen. "Let's take a little break," she said to Ken. "We'll be right back."

13

"What the fuck, Darryl!" Charlie said when they stepped into their squad room.

"Come on, Charlie. I was just trying to help. I feel about as useless as tits on a bull sitting there saying nothing."

When she first made sergeant, she had been tempted to jump the shit of any deputy who addressed her by her first name. But she understood the Darryls of the department grew up in a society where men were the bosses and women were secretaries and homemakers, and she wasn't about to change their culture by acting like the kind of hard-ass bitch they'd accuse her of being.

"Damn it, Darryl, I'm the lead investigator. I decide when we push a suspect. We're lucky he didn't lawyer up on us."

"I'm sorry. Just that this is a big case. Lots of folks'll be watching. We both know he did it, and if we can get him to confess, you'll look real good in the eyes of the sheriff and my cousin. Should be important to you, this being your first homicide case as the team sergeant and all."

Darryl seldom missed an opportunity to remind Charlie that Captain Clinton Cannon III, the commander of the criminal investigation division, was his cousin. The inference was that he was in a position to influence what the captain thought of her and maybe even if she kept her job.

"None of that changes the way we conduct interrogations. You don't interrupt me, and you don't take it upon yourself to decide when we confront a suspect."

"Yes, ma'am. You da boss." Darryl set his legal pad and pen on his desk. "I got time to step out for a smoke before we get back at him?"

"Yeah, go ahead."

Charlie looked at the text on her phone: *Hope you're cracking the case. Love, Spencer.*

She smiled and pressed call.

"Hey, Mom. Your murder is all over the news. All my friends are talking about it. So how's it going?"

"Just busy detecting like we detectives do," she said. "I wish I were home though. I wanted to spend time together this week."

"Mom, I'm just going away to college, not dying. What you're doing is really important, so don't worry about it."

"What are you up to?"

"Grandma made dinner and I'm just working on packing."

"Wish I could be there helping."

The phone was silent for a moment, and Charlie knew her son was deciding whether to remind her for the hundredth time he wasn't a kid anymore. "All my friends say I've got the most awesome mom in the county, so keep doing your cool detective stuff and don't worry about me."

She ended the call and was wiping her eyes when Darryl came back inside reeking of cigarette smoke. "You ready?" she asked.

They resumed their places in the interview room and Charlie locked her eyes onto Ken. She needed to nudge him out of his comfort zone. "I know this may feel intrusive, but I need to ask, how's your sex life?"

Ken raised his eyebrows in surprise. He met her gaze for a few beats then looked down at the table. "Fine."

"Mr. Russo," Charlie said, leaning closer to him, "I know it must be uncomfortable discussing this, but it's relevant to the investigation. How often did you and your wife have sexual relations?"

He met her eyes, unflinching.

"I need an answer," she said.

"Once or twice a week," he said softly.

"It sounds like you had a very healthy marriage." Charlie softened her voice even more. "When was the last time you and your wife had sex?"

Ken shifted around in his chair. "Why is that important?"

"It's relevant to the investigation," she replied.

"Was she violated?" Ken's eyes narrowed. "Was she raped?"

Charlie remained silent. Once Ken's breathing slowed and his face relaxed a bit, she said, "There's no indication of that. When was the last time you and your wife had sex?"

"Saturday night," Ken finally said.

"You're sure?"

He nodded. "The previous Saturday night we had our wine tasting group at the Nowaks' house and this Saturday we planned to spend the day together. Nancy said she had her heart set on finding a new outfit for an upcoming lady's luncheon, so I went with her to Charleston. We had an enjoyable day checking out all the shops on King Street. She found what she was looking for, and we had an early dinner and were home by eight. It was hot and sticky walking the streets, so we both showered when we got home, and well...you know."

"And that was the last time?" Even though doing it again Monday morning seemed unusually frequent for an older couple, it was important to pin him down.

He nodded.

"The state crime lab people should be finished at your house by now," she said. "They will have collected a vast amount of evidence, everything from dirt and fibers to fingerprints and DNA evidence and data from electronic devices." She watched his eyes carefully for a reaction as she laid out places where he might have left evidence.

She saw no change and continued. "The medical examiner will conduct an autopsy tomorrow. That will tell us how she died and provide clues as to who did it. Over the next few days, we'll talk to numerous people—friends, neighbors, people you and Nancy did business with. The lab will process the evidence and tell us whose DNA and fingerprints were in your house, even where a particular piece of debris came from that's so small the naked eye can't see it. We'll track people's cell phones—yours included—to tell us where they were at various times, who they called, texted, and emailed."

Charlie took a sip of water. Ken had been listening as intently as a star pupil does to a favorite teacher. It was time to ease into the final phase. "I've seen plenty of conflict between spouses in my career. I understand how emotions can flare between two people who still care for each other. Love is such a strong emotion it can quickly transcend into jealousy, contempt, and anger. And occasionally, in the blink of an eye, it can become physical. It's seldom intentional. Few men say, 'I'm going to hit my wife today.' One moment they're arguing, the next, he pushes her. Or maybe she pulls a knife in anger, and they struggle over it. So if something like that occurred, maybe a momentary lapse, or even an accident—"

Ken rose from his chair. "I would never, ever hurt my wife. If you're implying that I did this to her..."

Darryl stood, reacting to Ken's raised voice as men normally do—puffing up their chests to yell back. She grabbed Darryl's forearm and said calmly, "It's okay, Mr. Russo. Please sit down."

Ken dropped back into his chair and covered his face with his hands. Darryl returned to his chair.

"If something happened this morning between you and your wife," Charlie said, "Now is the time to tell us. Let's get out in front of this. No matter what happened, I'm sure there were reasons for it. Reasons many people can identify with."

Ken put his hands in his lap and looked at her warily.

Charlie spoke softly as she slid her chair around the table until her knee barely touched his. "There is a time in an investigation, once we have witnesses and enough physical evidence to tell us what happened, that any explanation by the responsible person becomes only self-serving. Now is the time to tell us your side of the story. Will you tell me what happened this morning, Mr. Russo?"

She let her facial expressions and eyes do the rest of the talking, displaying empathy, and conveying that no matter what he might say, she wouldn't judge him. They looked at each other for a full minute.

"I already told you what happened. When I left the house this morning, she was alive. When I returned, she was dead. And I didn't do it."

14

When Sean walked into the house, Annie was sitting on the rug just inside the front door waiting for him. He walked through the living room, opened the back door, and grabbed a flashlight and poop bag. Annie shot through the doggie door built into the screened porch and across the lawn, barking as ferociously as a Labrador retriever was capable of doing. Sean jogged after her and shined his flashlight at a sound of rustling in the bushes that led into the marsh. Annie stood at the edge of the lawn, the hairs on her back standing straight.

The rustling stopped and two eyes glowed in the flashlight's beam. A large raccoon stared at him for a moment then ambled off into the Spartina grass. Raccoons, squirrels, and opossums were frequent visitors to Sean's backyard, where they scrounged the seed below the birdfeeders that the birds knocked off during the day. Sean didn't feel bad about interfering with the raccoons' evening snack, for the marsh held a smorgasbord of food for them—crabs, oysters, lizards, snakes, insects, and even small fish that swam too close to shore.

The moonlight shone across the salt marsh. At low tide, the river was now just a narrow ribbon running through what appeared as a meadow of tall grass. With tides coming in and going out twice a day, the marsh was ever changing. At low tide, mudflats were exposed to sun and wind. Then the cycle would repeat. The tide would roll in and six hours later, the mud flats would be covered in seven feet of water.

Annie finished her business, and Sean grabbed a beer from the refrigerator and settled into a rocking chair on the front porch. He normally sat on the screened porch—or lanai, as people called them here—during the evening. It was not only bug free, but he preferred the privacy and solitude. Even when it was too dark to see the water, knowing the river ran just beyond his backyard was calming. But tonight he felt compelled to sit out front and watch the street. Maybe it was an unconscious need to guard the neighborhood or maybe he just wanted to be closer to people.

Sean cracked the beer, and Annie lay beside him on the front door mat. The only streetlights in Sea Island Plantation were lampposts at street intersections. They barely illuminated the streets below them, and few people even turned on their porch lights unless they were expecting visitors because all they did was attract clouds of bugs. Sean liked the darkness. It gave the neighborhood a casual, country feel, quite different from the harsh white lights shining down from giant light poles in big cities where residents needed light to ward off crime and create an illusion of safety.

An insect buzzed in his ear. Maybe a mosquito, but probably a gnat, which the locals called no-see-ums. He got up and flipped a switch inside the front door. Two ceiling fans whirled above him, creating enough of a breeze to drive the nuisance away.

A Dodge Charger, an unmarked sheriff's car, pulled into the Russo's driveway across the street. Ken climbed out of the back seat and slogged to his front door as the car backed out of the driveway and disappeared down the street. Sean sipped his beer. A few minutes later, Ken came out his front door and walked to his mailbox. Annie ran to the end of the driveway and barked. An invisible fence reminded Annie where her property line ended, and since she couldn't run across the street to greet her neighbors without getting a shock through her collar, she had learned to bark to invite them to her yard.

"What are you doing outside by yourself, girl?" Ken yelled across the street.

"Hey, Ken." Sean set his beer on a table by his chair and walked down the driveway. "We were just sitting out on the porch."

Ken crossed the street and Annie bounced up and down in excitement then flopped onto her back and rolled over. Ken squatted down and rubbed her belly.

"How ya doing?" Sean asked.

"Still in shock." He patted Annie's head and stood. "I just can't believe she's dead."

Sean had said those same words to himself for months after Lauren died. "I was having a beer. You wanna join me?"

"I have so much to do, so many arrangements to make." Ken's eyes dropped to the ground. "I don't even know where to start."

"I know the feeling," Sean said without thinking. That was the last thing a person wanted to hear when suffering a loss. But Sean *did* understand what Ken was going through, at least to a degree.

"I guess you do." Ken looked up. "I don't drink, remember."

"How about a Diet Coke?"

Ken followed Sean to his porch and dropped into the other rocking chair. Annie sat in front of him and rested her chin on his knee as Sean went inside. He returned and handed Ken a can of soda and a glass of ice and set down an ashtray with two cigars on the small table between them. Ken used to be a regular at the monthly poker games the men in the neighborhood held, and Sean remembered Ken hosted one on his screened lanai last year and brought out cigars.

Sean clipped the end of his cigar, lit it, and handed the cutter and box of matches to Ken. They puffed on their cigars and sipped their drinks in silence for several minutes. "The cops think I killed my wife," Ken finally said.

Sean was keenly aware the man sitting next to him might be a murderer, but in a strange way, it didn't bother him. He'd spent countless hours talking with killers over the years and didn't feel the least bit uncomfortable around them. A few were cold-blooded psychopaths, but most were relatively normal people who did something bad—horrendously bad. "Really?" he replied.

Sean listened as Ken vented about his hours in the interview room.

When he finished, Sean said, "I could be totally off base, but it sounds like the detectives handled this like I would've myself. Sometimes I had evidence the husband did it, but normally, I didn't know much early in the investigation."

"So maybe they weren't really trying to coerce me into admitting something I didn't do?"

Sean remembered how tough those interviews had been. Knowing he might've been interviewing a man who'd just lost his wife, yet he had to push him to confess when he wasn't sure if the man actually did it. He was glad that part of the job was in the past. "If you did it, it's their job to bring you to justice. If not, they move on to find the real killer. As long as you told them the truth, you'll end up okay."

Ken looked at him for several counts and slowly nodded his head. Sean could tell Ken was reflecting on what he had told the detectives, what he left out, the half-truths, and the outright lies. Sean had learned from interviewing thousands of people that just about everyone lied. Even those who hadn't committed a crime often lied about small things, such as financial issues, marital problems, infidelity. And those lies often swayed detectives to believe they were also lying about having committed the crime in question.

Ken took several gulps of his soda. "How did you get through it?"

Maybe that was the reason Sean invited Ken onto the porch. A chance to talk with a fellow sufferer. He didn't know, but he had felt a connection with Ken when he saw him trudging from the detective's car to his house with his shoulders stooped and his head hanging low. "Who says I have?"

"At least, you had the opportunity to..." Ken set his cigar in the ashtray and faced Sean. "I don't mean to imply it was easier with Lauren. I just wish I had the chance to say goodbye, to tell her how much I loved her, to tell her how sorry I was for...you know, all those things husbands have to be sorry for."

As difficult as it was to watch Lauren die, Sean would've never given up one second of that time they had together and the chance to say all those things to each other. She had finally told him she'd been having bad stomach pain in April. She first played it off as resulting from the stress of the move and all the physical activities in which she was involved: tennis several days a week, golfing with two women's groups, fitness classes, and long walks with Annie. But when it got worse, she finally saw a specialist who ordered a CT scan. The scan and a biopsy showed a tumor on her pancreas that encased the artery supplying blood to the intestines and colon. The only course of action was four rounds of chemo, with the hope it would shrink the tumor enough to operate. Eight weeks later, the tumor had grown, and the chances of recovery dropped from five percent to nil. They met with hospice, and two weeks later, she was gone.

The hospice nurse had said Lauren's death would leave a jagged hole in his heart. Over time, the hole might heal, but the scar tissue would remain forever. "I still miss her every day," Sean said to Ken, feeling his eyes begin to well. "I don't think we ever get over it. But we learn to function, to somehow live life, and maybe—just maybe—we might someday actually find happiness again."

15

TUESDAY

Charlie rushed down the grand staircase, through the entry hall and dining room, and into the kitchen. She dropped a pod into the Keurig, slid a travel mug in place, and pressed the start button. Her mother rose from the round table in the adjacent breakfast room, balancing her china cup on a saucer. Abigail Nash was sixty-five, but she looked younger thanks to her avoidance of the South Carolina sun and her regular peels, laser treatments, and Botox injections at the medical spa. She wore cream-colored linen slacks and a silk blouse, and her hair was perfectly coiffed and sprayed in place. "No tea this morning?" she asked as she refilled her cup from the hot water dispenser and dropped in a fresh teabag.

"Not enough caffeine." Charlie hadn't left the office until two in the morning, and although she slept in until seven—which meant forgoing her morning run or CrossFit workout—she needed an extra jolt to get going this morning. She opened the refrigerator and scanned the shelves.

"Did you eat last night?" her mother asked.

"Not really." Unless she counted a slice of cardboard pizza and a protein bar around midnight.

Abigail put a skillet on the six-burner stove and turned the gas to high. "Why don't you go dry your hair and I'll fix you some eggs and toast."

Charlie looked at her watch—7:35. "No time."

"Your breakfast will be ready in two minutes. The way I've seen you vacuum your food, you'll be to work with plenty of time. If you had an age-appropriate hairstyle, you would also have time to dry your hair before leaving the house."

Her mother had many rules for women over forty, including hair no longer than shoulder length, no shorts in public except when participating in specified athletic activities, and definitely no two-piece swimsuits. Charlie broke those rules and more. She took several sips of her coffee. "Have you seen Spencer yet this morning?"

"I heard him come in around ten, but his door was still closed when I came downstairs this morning."

Charlie had seen the crazy, high-risk behavior of other teenagers during their summer after high school graduation, but Spencer ran with a good crowd of kids that didn't drink, experiment with drugs, or race their cars. Her only worry was Spencer getting Madison pregnant. She was a tall, slender girl with a bright smile and the cutest Southern accent, which she turned on and off at will. Charlie was certain they were sleeping together despite Spencer's insistence they were just friends, and he consistently resisted her attempts to discuss safe sex and birth control. "Is he still going boating today?"

Abigail dropped a pat of butter in the pan, cracked two eggs over it, and put two slices of bread in the toaster. "He mentioned something about taking the skiff to the riviera to meet some friends."

The "Dufftown Riviera" was actually a large sandbar in the middle of the Cusseta River, which flowed past Dufftown, the town in which they lived, and into the ocean at the southern tip of Spartina Island. People moored their small boats and jet skis in the shallows by the tiny island or beached them and hung out and partied when the tides were right. "If I get off on time, maybe we can take the Hinckley to Benson's or the Harbor Inn for dinner."

"I think he'd like that as long as he can invite a few of his friends. What time should he tell them to be at the dock?"

Charlie was about to say six o'clock but caught herself. She knew better than to make personal plans in the middle of a murder investigation. In a few more days, Spencer would be off to college, and she'd be lucky to see him before Thanksgiving. She had planned to take a few days off this week to spend time with him before he left. "I wish I could commit, but…"

Abigail pursed her lips, scraped the scrambled eggs onto a plate, and set it on the counter in front of Charlie. Charlie braced herself for her mother's umpteenth reminder of her foolishness for leaving her urban planning career for police work. Although her mother had preached, *if you can't say something nice, don't say anything at all*, it never prevented her from hiding a dig within a compliment.

"Maybe Roger could take Spencer and his friends out tonight on his boat," Abigail said.

Charlie nearly spit out the piece of toast she was chewing. "Spencer is with me until he leaves. Period. No further discussion." Even though they'd been divorced for ten years, her mother still thought of Roger as her son-in-law. She continually hinted that Charlie should have stayed married even though her husband was cheating on her and had morphed into one of the slimiest lawyers in the county.

"I'm sorry, Charlotte. I'd forgotten how sensitive you were about the custody arrangement."

Like hell you did, thought Charlie. And whenever she reacted to something insulting her mother uttered, it was her fault for being too sensitive. In a few weeks, Spencer would turn eighteen and could make his own decisions about which parent to spend time with. No more being served with papers when she had to work late. No more Roger claiming Spencer was left home alone, even though he knew damn well Charlie's mother was there. Despite her flaws, no one could claim a child was neglected or in jeopardy when Abigail Nash hovered over him.

"I could see if James is free," Abigail said. "I'm sure Spencer would like to see his uncle before he leaves."

Spencer adored Charlie's youngest brother, and Charlie trusted him fully piloting the big boat, no easy feat when returning up the river after dark when the tides and wind could create treacherous currents. "Thanks, Mom, and if this investigation allows, I'll be there."

"Both the Charleston and Savannah stations led their local news with this terrible tragedy. The Spartina Island mayor says the public should not panic, that the death appears to be an isolated event. But people are saying it's the work of a serial rapist murderer. He's got to be a real sicko to be targeting older women."

Charlie knew better than to respond, because whatever she said would be repeated to every member of the Cusseta Country Club by noon. She shoveled two forkfuls of eggs into her mouth, grabbed her travel mug, and headed to the door.

"Aren't you going to dry your hair before you go out?"

"I'll drive with the windows down. It'll be dry enough to put up by the time I get there."

16

The Campbell County Sheriff's Office was housed in a modern building on the mainland, two miles from the bridge to Spartina Island. With all the new development in the region and a long-term contract to provide police services for the Town of Spartina Island, the county was able to afford a sheriff's office facility that not only met the current needs of the department, but also allowed for future growth in years to come.

After working out of the cramped sheriff's office in the old courthouse and an annex consisting of modular office trailers, Charlie was thrilled to move into the new building eight years ago. She could not fathom working as a detective in their old facilities. In addition to private offices for the captain and two lieutenants, the criminal investigation division's wing included a conference room, break room, interview rooms, and space for crime analysts, juvenile detectives, narcotics and gang investigators, and three detective squads. One of the detective squad rooms would remain empty until the county's population grew and justified increased police staffing.

Charlie grabbed her desk phone on its second ring.

"Good morning, Sergeant," said Detective Jay Garcia.

"Are you enjoying the beach?" Charlie asked. She had sent her three detectives home around ten last night after giving them early morning assignments. She had assigned Jay and Sherman Todd, the other detective in her squad, to get to the beach parking lot by 7:00 a.m. to search for beachgoers who might have seen Ken Russo. She tasked Darryl with leaving the station at the same time for the long drive to MUSC, the Medical University of South Carolina in Charleston, which would get him there just in time for the nine o'clock autopsy of Nancy Russo.

"Frankly, ma'am, I'd be more comfortable in shorts and flip flops, but I'm proud to serve. I'm calling because we just located two witnesses who saw Ken Russo park his car in the lot shortly after zero-nine-hundred hours yesterday."

"Positive ID and time?" Charlie asked.

"We've been showing the subject's photo to people as they pulled into the lot with negative results for two hours. Just after nine, Sherm and I both got hits. The woman I spoke to recognized him from the photo and then described the SUV she saw him offloading a beach chair and tote bag from. She says her morning routine is to leave her apartment at nine most days and drive to the beach. Her apartment is less than a mile away, so she's certain about the time—plus or minus five minutes."

"You got her statement?"

"Yes, ma'am. And she's willing to come to the station later if you think we need to videotape her. Sherm spoke to a man who was walking a dog from the beach into the parking lot. He remembered Mr. Russo because Russo was walking to the beach carrying a chair and towel and stopped to pet the man's dog. He positively IDed the photo. This witness walks his dog off-leash every morning on the beach. He was sure of the time because he sets his phone to alert him at nine because that's when the town beach ordinance requires dogs to be on leashes. He says he immediately leashes his dog and walks to the parking lot, which takes just a few minutes."

"Sounds like Russo lied to us about going straight to the beach after his stop at McDonald's," Charlie said. "Can you guys handle the heat out there for another hour or so?"

"No problem. We've got water and there's shade in the parking lot. You want us to head over to the sandwich shop when they open for lunch?"

"Yeah. Let me know if you turn up anything else." With a few hours of work, they already blew Ken's alibi to pieces. Unless the medical examiner determined the time of death was after nine, this meant he had opportunity. Means was a given—the knife from his kitchen. Motive could be inferred—they were married after all, and everyone wants to kill his or her spouse at one time or another. And lying to investigators was universally accepted as consciousness of guilt.

Charlie had returned to the pile of reports and statements from the neighborhood canvass when her phone rang again.

"Hello, I'm calling about the murder of Nancy Russo." The voice, undoubtedly that of an elderly woman, cracked as she spoke.

It was the twelfth call she'd received in the two hours she'd been at her desk. She was beginning to regret sending all of her detectives into the field the morning after the murder. She'd worked the phones on high profile cases before and knew 99% of the calls turned out to be worthless. "How may I help you, ma'am?"

"I'm not one to gossip, but my husband and I saw them at the pool Sunday afternoon arguing."

"Who are you speaking about?"

"Ken and Nancy Russo. They live the next street over?"

"What Sunday was this?"

"The day before yesterday about five o'clock. It was a real doozy of a fight. She cursed at him. He grabbed her, shook her a couple of times, and pushed her under the water."

Charlie copied down her name and address. "Don't go anywhere. I'll be right there."

17

Sean stepped out of the golf cart as Stretch Andrews stopped in the middle of the fairway. Stretch checked his GPS and quickly selected a club. Sean normally played three days a week. Two days a week were with a neighborhood group, but Tuesdays were with his retired cop buddies, usually two foursomes with some sort of team competition between them. Everyone on the losing team had to pay the winning team a dollar, and then the winning team had to buy a round of drinks for the losing team. Of course, their winnings didn't cover the bar tab.

Stretch had been playing golf since he was a teenager, but he had several vertebrae in his back and neck fused ten years ago following a serious on-duty injury with the Vermont State Police. Although he could only drive the ball 180 yards or so these days, every shot was right down the middle. Stretch took a practice swing, waggled his club, and hit his ball. It sailed straight toward the flag, landing just short of the green. Sean knew that he'd likely chip it up from there and single putt it in for a par.

"Great shot." Sean slid into the golf cart and Stretch drove down the right side of the fairway.

"There was a day when I could hit the center of the green from this distance with a seven iron, now I need a fairway wood and I end up short. Don't get old, Sean."

When Sean retired from Oakland PD, he was considered one of the old guys, but here he was one of the youngest. He liked being considered young again, even though he didn't feel that way.

Stretch drove through the stand of pine trees that separated the right edge of the fairway from the back yards of the houses on Egret Way. He crept slowly across the pine straw and stopped next to a Callaway ball sitting about two feet from the white stakes that marked out of bounds. "Almost got it in my backyard," Stretch said. "Helluva drive. Close to two-hundred-fifty yards."

"Too bad it wasn't straight," Sean said. "This is your house?"

"Looks different from the back, huh?"

"Ever have your house hit by hackers like me?"

"We occasionally get a few balls in the yard, but the house is set back far enough to be safe. Also gives us plenty of privacy, even when the course is busy."

The other two golfers in their foursome were looking for one of their errant drives in the trees on the other side of the fairway. Looking that way, Sean recognized the back yard of the Russos' house. "Looks like you're right across from Ken and Nancy's house."

"Yeah, but with a fairway between us, it's not exactly like we're neighbors."

Sean's GPS showed it was a bit over a hundred yards to the green. He selected his pitching wedge and approached his ball. "Ever notice anything unusual over there?"

"Too far away to see much. People are sometimes out trimming bushes and puttering in their yards. Don't specifically know if that was the Russos or not. Don't pay much attention."

Sean stood behind the ball. The loft of his pitching wedge could send the ball high enough to hit the lower branches of a tree in front of him, so he returned to the golf cart and grabbed his six iron. "So not much activity across the way, huh?"

"Didn't say that. Even though they're not supposed to, people walk along the course in the mornings and evenings. Golfers never make it to the fourteenth hole before nine, and it's rare to see anyone playing through here after five, so no one cares if people are walking as long as they're not interfering with golfers. Our houses are closer together than those of you rich folks on the marsh, so it's not unusual to see the wives walking through the back yards to visit their neighbors."

"When I grew up, all your friends came around the back and only company used the front door."

"Me too," Stretch said. "The cart path on the other side makes a nice little walkway for the folks living over there. I'll now shut up so you can hit your ball."

Sean had to keep the trajectory low to stay under the tree, so his plan was to punch the ball out into the fairway and then chip onto the green. With luck, he could bogey the hole, which for Sean was a good score. Sean swung his club and hit the ball thin. It ran across the fairway and into the sand trap next to the green.

Two hours later, Sean pulled his car into the driveway of a small house in a new development on the mainland, a few miles from the bridge to Spartina Island. He rang the doorbell, and a young attractive brunette opened the door. "Hey, Dad."

"Hey, Rachel, how's my favorite daughter?"

"Your only daughter?"

"That too." They hugged and Sean followed her through the great room to the kitchen where she poured him a tall glass of iced tea. Lauren had been the one who stayed in closest contact with their children. She and Rachel talked every day, and Lauren kept Sean informed about their daughter's life. With Lauren now gone, he gave Rachel a lot of credit for calling him every day or so and meeting for lunch or dinner every week, even though he seldom had much to say.

Sean sat on a bar stool at the kitchen counter while Rachel cut up slices of smoked turkey and divided it between two salads. "Getting ready for the new horde of third graders?" he asked. Ever since Sean could remember, Rachel had wanted to be a teacher like her mother. She attended Georgia

Southern University, just like her mother. There, Rachel fell in love with the Southern lifestyle and had no desire to return to California, so she got a job at Spartina Island Elementary when she graduated.

She set a salad in front of Sean and sat on the stool next to him. "Taking care of personal stuff this week, like a doctor's appointment this afternoon."

"Is everything okay?"

"Just routine female stuff. What's new with you?"

Sean knew better than to pry when women mentioned female stuff. "Played golf this morning."

"How'd you do?"

"I broke a hundred."

"Is that good?"

"No, but I still had fun." Sean glanced toward the living room. "Looks like you got some new furniture."

"Ever since we've been together, we've wanted to replace the old sofa and loveseat Austin's mother gave us. We finally saved up enough."

When Rachel and Austin got married four years ago, they lived in an apartment on the island not far from the beach. Although they loved living there, they eventually wanted their own house, and like many young couples, they couldn't afford a decent house on the island. A year ago, they bought this house in a new family-oriented development, and although it was on the mainland, it was only a fifteen-minute drive to Rachel's school and Sean's house. "You know if you ever need some help…"

Rachel kissed his cheek. "I know, Dad, but Austin and I are fine. Anything else new in your life?"

"Went out to dinner with some neighbors last night."

Rachel was quiet for a few counts. "I heard on the news about the murder. They said it was on your street."

In all his years as a cop, Sean never talked about the horrors of the job with his kids. He still wished Rachel lived in a bubble and hadn't heard about the murder. "Nancy Russo. I'm sure you've met her."

"Oh, yeah. A real nice lady. Lived right across the street. That's so sad. Do they know who did it?"

"Not yet."

"That's not supposed to happen in Sea Island Plantation."

"Don't worry. It's not like two warring drug gangs shot up the neighborhood."

"Okay, but I still worry about you."

Sean wondered at what stage of a child's life it became normal for them to start worrying more about their parents than their parents worried about them. He doubted Rachel would worry about him if Lauren were still alive.

Rachel chewed a forkful of salad and swallowed. "Have you found a lady friend yet?"

"Still culling through the casserole brigade's roster."

The very day after Lauren's funeral, the women of Sea Island Plantation began their invasion. Dozens of widows, alone or in pairs, ranging in age from sixty to ninety, showed up at his door armed with hot dishes in clear Pyrex or white CorningWare and plates of cookies, pies, and cakes. They were accompanied by offers of a home cooked meal when he was up to it.

"Dad!"

The image of Charlie popped into his head. Young, tall, skinny, conceited, and stubborn. Too stubborn to realize she didn't know everything about investigating murders, yet too arrogant to admit it. If she ever smiled, she might even be attractive, he thought. "Haven't been looking."

"I'm gonna sound like a broken record, but remember, Mom wanted you to date and not turn into a recluse."

Sean remembered some of Lauren's final words to him: *Enjoy life—you sacrificed for the country and city you served, so now it's time to be selfish, take care of yourself, and do what you enjoy. Don't be a hermit—get out and socialize with people. Be open to love again—you do much better with a woman by your side.* "Maybe I'll hook up with one of the eighty-year-old widows down here."

"Dad, that's not funny. I'm sure there are a few single women in the plantation your age, and there must be loads of women more your age outside the gates. Take Annie to the beach—I guarantee she's a chick magnet."

Sean looked at Rachel and smiled. It was uncanny how much she looked like her mother when Lauren was Rachel's age. "Okay sweet pea, I'll get right on it."

Rachel grabbed one of his hands in both of hers and looked up at him. "Do you think we'll ever get over missing Mom?"

Sean felt his eyes begin to moisten. Then he smiled and said, "I'm not sure why we'd want to."

18

Charlie sat at the Strozewskis' round kitchen table with her notebook and recorder in front of her. A giant fake flower arrangement sat in the center of the table, forcing her to bob her head to either side of it depending upon which person was talking. She was tempted to move it out of the way, but Marge Strozewski seemed like the sort of lady who would take great offense to anyone touching her decorations. The couple was in their mid-seventies. Their white hair looked especially bright against their sun-bronzed skin.

"This was at the Riverside pool, not the main one at the racket and fitness center, right?" Charlie said.

"That's right," Marge said. "They were right up in each other's faces, yelling at each other."

"What were they arguing about?" Charlie asked.

"We were at the other end of the pool, so we couldn't hear," Marge said.

"Were there other people in the water or nearby that maybe could've heard?"

"I'm sure there were, but we weren't paying any attention to them," Marge said.

Charlie poked her head around the flower centerpiece to look at Dick. He shrugged his shoulders. It was obvious Marge did the talking in this family.

"Okay, what happened next?"

"He grabbed Nancy by the arms and sort of shook her."

"Did she do anything to precipitate that?" Charlie asked.

"Not that I saw, but then she kicked at him under the water."

"You could see that from where you were at?"

"You could tell, the way she leaned back and kicked," Marge said. "Ken sort of yelped, like she got him. Then he shoved her. She lost her balance, went under the water, and got her hair all wet. She was pissed."

"What happened next?"

"She called him some nasty names, and he just got out of the pool, grabbed his shirt and towel, and left."

"What did she call him?"

Marge tightened her lips but said nothing. Finally, Dick spoke up. "She said, 'you're an asshole, a real fucking asshole.'"

Marge nodded. "Yeah, that's what she said. After Ken was gone, Nancy went to the chair her stuff was on, wrapped her towel around herself, and left."

"Who else was there when this happened?"

"Can't think of anyone by name," Marge said quickly.

Charlie knew she was lying as people often do when they didn't want to involve others. She glanced at Dick, but he silently pursed his lips. She decided not to push it. "If you think of anyone or talk to anyone who was there and heard what the argument was about, give me a call."

Charlie handed them her card, turned off the recorder, and thanked them for their time as she walked out the door. Just because a man argues with his wife and shoves her, it doesn't mean he killed her, Charlie thought. But Ken lied to her last night when he said they never had any major disagreements and would never lay a hand on his wife. They'd already caught him in his second lie. And the investigation was still young.

Charlie drove down Wood Stork Lane and made a left on River Drive. She remembered driving through this area more than twenty years ago with her father, shortly after she graduated from Clemson and got a job with the regional planning commission. The land was part of an old plantation that grew Sea Island cotton, the most valuable cotton of the old South. Then the Civil War changed the South's economy forever. She had bounced down the old, rutted roads in her father's Mercedes G-Class SUV, across long-ago-collapsed irrigation ditches, and through thick maritime forest and wetlands that had taken over the land. Her father had stopped at the site where the River Lodge currently sat, and they looked out at the river and the hundreds of snowy egrets, ibises, herons, and wood storks foraging for food in the shallows.

Her father had told her about his plans to buy the land and develop it into an active adult community that co-existed with the environment. Maintaining the ecology and the natural beauty of the land would be his top priority. He'd build no more than three hundred homes on the one-thousand-acre plot, keeping large swaths of forest and wetlands intact. It took years to get the necessary approvals, arrange financing, and begin development. He started with the riverside tract, the area where the Russos and Sean Tanner currently lived. He plotted out streets and lots for a hundred homes, all of which sold quickly. Then came the recession, and high-end new home sales dried up. Her father's partner wanted to increase the density from two hundred to eight hundred houses on the remaining land and build smaller tract homes which could sell for much less. But her father refused to budge on his vision. Then he disappeared and his partner got his wish.

Charlie crossed the creek along the causeway and entered the new part of Sea Island Plantation. She had cried when she saw the bulldozers knocking down thousands of trees and filling wetlands ten years ago. Roads going in, followed by lines of red stakes marking the lot boundaries, as many as six houses per acre. Over time, the landscaping matured, homeowners added personal touches to their houses, and the cookie-cutter appearance so common in new developments faded. Although Sea Island Plantation was much nicer and more open than the scores of active adult communities in Florida and the rest of the sunbelt, where compact houses were crammed next to each other, there was still a lot less nature and more asphalt and stucco than her father had envisioned.

19

Charlie's three detectives glanced up when she entered the squad room. She dropped her leather tote bag on her desk and scanned the surface for phone messages or new reports. She remembered working in this same office as a detective a few years ago, watching her sergeant at the large U-shaped desk in the corner of the squad room, dreaming someday it would be hers. *Careful what you wish for,* her father had often warned her, but if he were still around, he'd be as confident as Billy that she was up to the job.

Charlie rolled her chair to the small conference table in the middle of their office. "Let's huddle and talk about what we know so far," Charlie said.

The three men spun their desk chairs around, slid to the table and flipped through their notes. Charlie began by summarizing the crime scene details. She was halfway through detailing the results of the interrogation with Ken Russo when Billy entered their team room. He quietly sat in a chair against the wall. Knowing Billy's style was to listen and observe without interfering, Charlie continued and summarized her interview with the Strozewskis. She then turned to Sherman Todd.

Sherm was a soft-spoken, methodical investigator who had spent ten years in uniform before making detective five years ago. "I ran the neighborhood canvass. Along with a few patrol deputies, we spoke to thirty residents and eight service people—landscapers, a housekeeper, and an electrician—who were in the area. The victim was universally loved by everyone. No one had anything negative to say about her or her husband. No one was aware of any issues between them or with anyone else. I'm going through the notes and statements to compile a list of her closest friends so we can contact them."

"Did you have time to talk to security?" Charlie asked.

"They have plans to install security cameras at the front gate, but currently there are none anywhere in the plantation. They issued more than a hundred visitor passes the day before the murder—about average for a Sunday—and thirty-five on that day up to the time the incident was reported. They're making a list for me." Sherm flipped through his notes. "They also have three hundred annual commercial passes for landscapers, housekeepers, delivery companies, and repair and service companies, so the number of people authorized entry in addition to the residents is staggering."

"Is the entry of vehicles recorded?"

"It's an older system with a sort of barcode on vehicle decals," Sherm said. "The barcode triggers the gates to open for residents, but there's no database that collects the entries. Guests and commercial passholders are waved in by security when they see their passes."

"As time permits, chip away at the list of guests and commercial passes to see if any names show up in the system, but I doubt we'll identify our perp this way," Charlie said then pointed at Darryl.

His chair creaked as he leaned forward, rested his elbows on the table, and paged through his notes. "The pathologist verified the two stab wounds exactly as you and that California detective suspected. He said the depth and width match the Henckels knife found on the floor. The lady had some bruises on her upper arms that he thinks were done by somebody grabbin' her a day or so before, but the doc said older people bruise easily, so it don't mean it had been an assault. He found semen inside the vagina, meaning she had sex within a few hours before she died, but he didn't find any sign of vaginal trauma or defensive wounds. So it could've been a rape or maybe not. He thinks Mrs. Russo died roughly between six and nine a.m."

"Any hairs, fibers, or other evidence on the body?" Charlie asked.

"The doc did the normal pubic combing and clipped the nails in case she scratched the assailant. They're sending everything to the crime lab. I wrote up and submitted the examination requests."

"Jay," Charlie said.

"I already told the sergeant, but for everyone else, Todd and I found two witnesses that put Mr. Russo arriving at Town Beach just after zero nine hundred. Both were credible and were accurate about the time. We couldn't verify whether the subject was at the sandwich shop or not; however, if the time of death was between six and nine, his whereabouts later may be irrelevant."

"SLED gathered quite a few latents from the house and Mr. Russo's car," Charlie said, referring to latent fingerprints. "They also swabbed likely places for possible DNA. We all know how long it might take for anything to come back, so we're not going to wait for lab results to point us in the right direction." She spun around in her chair. "Lieutenant, anything I missed or any questions?"

"Y'all done a bang-up job here. I know there's still a lot more that needs to be done, but I have faith in this team." Billy stood. "Charlie, I got a text from the captain a few minutes ago. He wants to see us."

Charlie spent fifteen minutes briefing Captain Clinton Cannon III on the progress of the investigation, while he sat on the other side of his desk and jotted down a brief note every minute or so.

When she finished, Cannon said, "The citizens of Campbell County and our elected officials expect a quick arrest and resolution of this matter. It looks to me that Mr. Russo did it. We all know it's normally the husband. This here knife attack looks personal and in the heat of the moment, which also points to the husband. Only a guilty man lies to law enforcement, and we caught this boy in two lies already. I think if y'all talk to his friends and neighbors, we're gonna find some more things he lied about, and probably learn that their marriage wasn't all peachy."

"Charlie's team is planning to do exactly that," Billy said.

"Absent an eyewitness or physical evidence that directly ties him to the murder, all we have is circumstantial evidence at this time," Charlie said. "We need something from the lab or other evidence before we try to interview him again."

"Are we in agreement he did it?" Clinton asked.

Charlie glanced at Billy sitting there quietly and quickly said, "My gut says he did, but without evidence to prove it, a gut feeling means nothing."

"Well then, young lady, you best find that evidence." Clinton glared at her for several beats. He then turned on his phony charm and smiled. "Don't forget, we have the cold case meeting this afternoon."

"You've got to be shitting me!" Charlie exclaimed. "We're in the middle of a murder investigation. And you want me to—"

"Now, Charlotte, your momma always said you'd argue with a fence post. You know the cold case team is important to the sheriff. Our program is getting statewide attention." Clinton smiled again, showing the same bleached teeth that had graced his campaign posters when he unsuccessfully ran for sheriff two years ago. "You should have your presentation all prepared, and I don't hear you sayin' you're all ready to go out and arrest that fella this very moment."

Charlie was preparing to fire back when she felt Billy's meaty hand gently touch her arm. "We'll take care of it, captain," he said. He rose from his chair and winked at Charlie to do the same.

Once they were inside Billy's office with the door closed, he said, "That's a battle not worth fighting. When Captain Clinton was assigned as the point person for the cold case team, he saw it as another opportunity to increase his visibility in the community. He's not about to delay the chance to add another bullet point to his resume for his next run for sheriff."

"This is total bullshit," Charlie said, trying to keep her voice low enough that the captain wouldn't overhear her through the adjacent wall. "Everyone in our team drops everything, their other cases, their family life, and their sleep when we have a major case, but we're supposed to find time to make the captain look good?"

"Who'd you assign to work up the old case?" Billy asked.

"Darryl."

"Keep it to an hour and then pass out the murder books. If Darryl gets too long winded, cut him off and get back to what's important."

"Can I still bitch about it?"

"Darlin'," you know my door's always open for bitchin', complaining, and venting. But when you're done and feelin' better, you need to put on your big girl pants and be the kind of detective sergeant the community and your team expects you to be."

Charlie stood and grabbed the thick leather belt that held her Sig Sauer, handcuffs, spare magazine, and badge. She hiked it up and smiled. "Big girl pants have been on all day."

20

Sean parked his Corvette in a visitor's slot at the sheriff's office. He still felt strange driving the car. Throughout their marriage, Lauren drove the family car, a newer minivan or SUV. He always had an old compact pickup, something that would get him back and forth to work when he didn't have a homicide take-home car and to use for weekend runs to Home Depot and the dump. After they moved to Spartina Island, his wife took his truck one morning—to pick up potting soil she said—and returned with a pristine, ten-year-old dark blue Corvette convertible. "You sacrificed during our entire marriage," she had said, "driving an old piece of junk so the kids and I could have the new car. Now you get your dream car."

Sean had stopped dreaming of owning a Corvette the day he learned Lauren was pregnant with Rachel. When Carson was born two years later, Sean knew raising a family in the Bay Area on a police officer and teacher's salary would never allow for luxuries like a sports car. But throughout their marriage, he never thought he sacrificed. Rachel was in first grade when Sean was accepted into the homicide unit, and Lauren mostly took care of the house and raised the kids so that he could work the long, crazy hours required in homicide. She made sure bills were paid, setting aside money for their children's college and their retirement. She ensured the kids were fed, clothed, and shuttled to their events, while also guaranteeing the house was clean and comfortable and all family and social obligations were met. Somehow, she did it while working full-time, and always with a smile and sense of gratitude. And he mostly worked, tried to be the best dad he could be, and mowed the lawn and fixed things around the house when needed. But Lauren was the glue that held the family together.

Sean told the civilian sitting behind the front desk he was here for the cold case team meeting, and she buzzed a door and told him to follow the hallway to the department's briefing room. It was a large, bright space with four rows of tables and modern video screens on the front wall. Wanted posters and crime alerts covered two bulletin boards, and a coffee machine and cubbyholes holding various report forms lined the back wall.

Five men and one woman sat at the tables closest to the door. They stopped talking when Sean entered. Stretch Andrews and Feebee Sheppard nodded to him. Sean recognized two of the others, probably from one of the retired law enforcement officers' functions.

A thin man with wispy white hair on the sides of his head rose, grabbed his cane, and stalked across the room with his hand out. "Frank Martin. You must be the FNG," he said with an unmistakable Brooklyn accent.

It had been a long time since Sean had been considered a rookie or the fucking new guy. He shook Frank's hand, surprisingly firm for a man of his age. "Sean Tanner," he replied.

"Yeah, we knows all about you," Frank said.

And Sean knew all about him, too. From what Stretch and Feebee had told him and his own internet research on the cold case team members, Sean knew that Frank Martin was eighty years old and spent twenty years as an NYPD detective. After he retired, he worked as an investigator with the Manhattan DA's office. He was then hired to set up a program for the New York State Police similar to the FBI's Behavioral Science Unit and ViCap—the unit that studied and profiled serial killers and rapists and assisted local police departments with serial crimes.

The other men stood and introduced themselves, and Sean matched the names with the backgrounds he already knew. Bernard "Doc" Henderson was in his late sixties and had worked as a forensic pathologist for the Franklin County Coroner's Office in Columbus, Ohio. "Irish" John

O'Shea was a retired detective from Boston P.D. and in his early seventies. Marvin Johnson had a striking resemblance to the actor, Morgan Freeman. He had joined the Philadelphia District Attorney's Office right out of law school and spent the last half of his forty-year career prosecuting murder cases. Stretch had told Sean they called him the team legal beagle, and the nickname, Beagle, had stuck.

"I saved a seat for you, kid," Frank said, nodding at the empty chair beside him.

Sean was tempted to respond with, "Thanks, Pops," but being the FNG, he thought it best to just smile and take the seat.

The door opened and a forty-something-year-old man dressed in a blue pinstripe suit and white shirt entered, followed by Billy, Charlie, and a short, heavy-set man wearing khaki slacks and a cheap-looking blue blazer.

The man in the pinstripe suit went to the podium at the front of the room. "For retired Sergeant Sean Tanner, the newest addition to our team, I'll introduce myself. I'm Captain Clinton Cannon the Third, the commander of the sheriff office's criminal investigation division and the coordinator of the cold case team. My family's lived in Campbell County for nearly two hundred years, and I'm a fourth-generation law enforcement officer. My daddy was sheriff for twenty-five years, until his retirement two years ago. My granddaddy was sheriff for the twenty years before that."

Cannon looked at a sheet of paper in front of him. "Let me tell y'all about Sergeant Tanner. He spent thirty years with the Oakland, California, police department, working as a homicide detective sergeant for most of it. If you don't know much about Oakland, I can tell you they have plenty of crime, especially murders, and their detectives carry a caseload two to three times that of other departments. He was the one who solved the Coffee Girl Murders, a series of close to twenty homicides by a coffee bean wholesaler out of Nicaragua. The investigation was presented at the FBI academy and other conferences and written about in a best-selling true crime book. So, welcome Sean."

Sean nodded. He didn't need the accolades, especially when they focused on the serial murders and the killings of rich or famous people he had solved. The cases he was most proud of were the innocent bystanders caught in gunfire between warring drug dealers, and the street prostitutes killed by their pimps. Those were the victims no one spoke for. They didn't get their five minutes of fame—even in death—on the six o'clock news. Those were the cases Sean and his partner worked alone, without the benefit of task forces or police brass pushing to expedite lab work. DA's weren't willing to charge suspects in those cases until he accumulated overwhelming evidence.

"I'll explain how the cold case team operates," Cannon said.

Doc whispered, "Mudflats Murder Club," loud enough that all the members could hear. Frank gave him a stern look.

Cannon stared at the group like a teacher would when he overheard someone talking in class and then continued. "This is mostly for Sean, but it's a good refresher for you veterans of the cold case team. One of our two investigative teams, B team, in this instance, pulls all documentation on a cold case and presents the case to y'all. We give you two murder books, three-ring binders containing all relevant reports and documents. One member of the cold case team is assigned as the case coordinator, and he keeps one murder book. The other one is reviewed and passed around to the other team members. Y'all send your recommendations for further investigation to the case coordinator, who prepares a report with recommendations to me, and I'll forward it to the assigned investigation team sergeant. If you have questions, you ask the case coordinator, and he'll check with me."

"Yo, Captain," Irish said, "we've always been allowed to call or email the assigned investigator or the detective sergeant with questions and stuff. Are you saying we can't do that?"

Cannon stiffened. It was obvious to Sean the captain was trying to control the investigation. Informal communication and information sharing between investigators was vital to a successful investigation, and when a command officer insisted everyone funnel information through him, it was a recipe for failure.

Cannon cleared his throat. "No, it's fine to talk to the detective and sergeant, but that should be done by the case coordinator, so in a sense, he's kind of the primary investigator for the cold case team. But, still, we don't want to inundate poor Sergeant Nash or her detectives with too many calls, now do we?"

"That's how we've been doing it," Beagle said, "and it's been working fine."

"Glad that's settled." Cannon smiled. "This month, Frank Martin's the coordinator, and I'd like Sean Tanner to tag along with him to learn the ropes. I'll now turn this over to Sergeant Charlotte Nash."

21

Sean watched Charlie stride to the front of the room. Instead of the black suit she wore yesterday, she was wearing a dark gray one over a light blue shirt. Sean had worked with dozens of female investigators during his career, and he could tell a lot about them by the way they dressed. Some wore form-fitting pantsuits or even skirts. They mostly stayed in the office where they could avoid any risk of conflict. When they did leave the office—usually to go to lunch—they pulled their handguns from a desk drawer and placed them inside their outfit-coordinated handbags.

The others dressed like Charlie in a pantsuit consisting of a loose-fitting jacket and what the women in the department called man-tailored pants—pants with wide belt loops for a substantial belt that would support a holstered gun and other necessary equipment. A functional pantsuit seldom flattered a woman's figure. It needed to fit loose enough to allow freedom of movement and conceal a pistol worn on their person. Charlie's functional clothing conveyed the female detective meant business and could run down a suspect and wrestle him into handcuffs when necessary.

"Assisting in the presentation is Detective Darryl Picket, who pulled this cold case together for us today," Charlie said as the man in the blue blazer stepped to a laptop situated next to the podium. "Excuse me if I seem a bit hurried as we talk about a three-decade old murder, but my team picked up the murder of Nancy Russo yesterday, and that's foremost on my mind."

Charlie's eyes darted to the back of the room where Cannon sat. Sean admired the balls of the sergeant to jab her boss in a group setting. He glanced back at Cannon, who nodded at him and smiled with the same kind of grin he'd seen in the countless Oakland command officers who had given him bullshit assignments when he was in the middle of working a case.

Darryl hit a key on the computer, and the black-and-white image of a dark-haired woman appeared on the large monitor at the front of the room. "Thirty-eight years ago, on July fourteenth, Theresa Goldberg, age twenty-seven, was vacationing on Spartina Island with her husband, Aaron," Charlie said. "She told her husband she was going out for cigarettes, and several hours later, she was found dead with a GSW to the head near the Spartina Harbor public boat ramp. According to her husband and the other two couples that they traveled down here with from their homes in New Jersey, it was not unusual for Theresa to leave alone at night and walk the beach or go to a bar."

An image of a corpse lying on the grass appeared on the monitor. "She was found by two teenagers about an hour after she was killed. Her wallet and ID were missing and never recovered. We identified her when her husband called later that night to report her missing. Deputies canvassed the area with negative results. There was an outdoor bar at the harbor that had music playing that night, but no one heard a gunshot."

The monitor showed an image of a naked woman on a stainless-steel autopsy table with a gunshot entrance wound just above her nose. Charlie continued. "No ballistics evidence was found at the scene, but a nominal thirty-eight caliber round was recovered from the victim's skull. It's been entered into NIBIN, the National Integrated Ballistic Information Network, but got no hits."

"Her husband was at their rental villa watching a baseball game on TV with the other men," Charlie said, "so he had a strong alibi, and there were no indications of difficulties between Theresa and Aaron or with the other two couples. According to the two detectives who worked the case, it appeared to be a robbery gone bad." Charlie stepped to the side.

Darryl brought up two mugshots of Black men in their early twenties on the monitor and said, "A week later, a man vacationing from Pennsylvania was mugged and shot outside the marina general store, the same store we believe Ms. Goldberg bought a pack of cigarettes from that night. Deputies found a nine-millimeter shell casing at the scene, but the slug that traveled through the victim's arm was too badly deformed for typing. These two suspects, Tyler and Joshua Jefferson, were arrested for the robbery a short distance away. Additional nine-millimeter ammo was found in their car, but no gun. They lawyered up, but were convicted of the mugging and sent to state prison for fifteen years.

"The detectives were convinced the Jefferson brothers killed Ms. Goldberg based on the MO, the same caliber shell casing at the scene as the ammunition in their car, and the proximity of the crimes to each other, but there was insufficient evidence for the circuit solicitor to file on them for her murder. Since then, both fellas have been in and out of prison for assault, drugs, burglary, car theft and just plain raisin' cane throughout the county."

"That's not much evidence to say they did the murder, too," Irish said.

Darryl shuffled his feet and Billy cleared his throat from the back of the room. "Things were different back then," Billy said. "You have to remember that the first bridge to the island had just opened a few years before this murder. Before that, you needed to take a ferry to get on and off the island. The population of the island was around a thousand, with maybe another two thousand visitors at any given time during the summer. The Black population was about two hundred and most lived in the freeman district, the area where the original Gullah people settled after being freed during the Civil War. That's where I was born and raised. Black people didn't mingle much with the white folk back then, and with that small a community, everyone pretty much knew who the troublemakers were."

Sean remembered stopping at the Gullah Cultural Center on the island with Lauren and the kids during one of their summer vacations years ago. They saw a display of baskets, hats, and other items woven with Spartina grass by descendants of the original Gullahs, who still lived on the island. They fought to hold on to their heritage even as beachfront resorts and housing developments were devouring their land. Lauren had bought a small basket, and Rachel adopted it as her easter basket when she was seven years old. Sean wondered if she still had it.

"So, when a crime occurs, you round up the usual suspects, and they happened to be the Jeffersons," Feebee said.

"Maybe a bit simplistic," Billy said, "but murders and armed robberies were pretty rare on the island back then. When two happen within a week, it's natural to conclude it's the same folks responsible. We included the report from the mugging in the murder book, and I believe you'll conclude there was a lot more evidence to show they committed the robbery than merely deputies rounding up the nearest Black men."

Charlie handed two three-ring binders to Frank and said, "I regret that there's not a whole lot in the murder books. We have the crime report and some reports by the detectives and the file on the subsequent armed robbery, but most of the detectives' notes and handwritten statements were destroyed in the flood of eighty-eight. The rain from a tropical storm left a foot-deep layer of mud and water in the annex where the detectives were working back then, and a number of case files were lost. But maybe y'all can find something in what remains that we've been missing all these years."

22

Charlie was sitting at her desk going through the reports on Nancy Russo's murder later that afternoon when Billy called and asked her to meet him in Captain Cannon's office. Billy was already sitting in one of the guest chairs in front of his boss's desk. Charlie stood behind him with her arms crossed.

"Sit a spell, Charlie," the captain said.

She'd already spent much more time with the brass today than she needed to and didn't need any more *guidance*. But she sat down next to Billy to avoid antagonizing the captain any more than she already had.

"I think the cold case meeting went well," Cannon said. "I know you're not too pleased about us not rescheduling, but I appreciate you not pitchin' a fit in front of those gentlemen."

Charlie bit her lower lip.

"Do y'all think they'll come up with a way to have the Jefferson brothers pay for their crime?" Cannon said.

Charlie looked at Billy, having decided when she entered the office to do her damn best to keep her mouth shut.

"The cold case team investigators are a whole lot brighter than me," Billy said. "If they see the Jeffersons as the killers, they'll either find the evidence or come up with a strategy to prove they did it. But it'll be a hard row to hoe with a case this old and most of the file gone."

Cannon nodded. "I've been talking with the circuit solicitor about the Russo homicide. Seeing that the media is all over this, he's as interested as we are in a speedy arrest and prosecution. One of his investigators found a report showing Mrs. Russo visited St. Joseph's in Savannah last year with a broken wrist and contusions on her leg. The examining doctor in the ER thought the injuries were suspicious, so the hospital notified the police, even though both the missus and her husband said she fell in the shower of their hotel room. The police investigated, did a report for possible spousal abuse, and sent a copy to the South Carolina Department of Social Services."

"Did the Savannah police make an arrest?" Charlie asked, knowing the police would err on the side of arrest in cases of domestic violence, especially when the victim was old enough to meet the criteria of elder abuse.

"They noted in their report there was insufficient evidence to show a crime occurred, but the solicitor and I both agree it's more than a little suspicious. We think this might be the pattern we've been looking for. Combined with the fracas in the swimming pool and the fella lying to us, the solicitor says he'll file murder charges on Mr. Ken Russo."

"You're kidding, right?" Charlie said, unable to contain her surprise. "There's not a jury in the state that would convict a man of murder based on that."

"The solicitor knows that there's more work to be done, but says there's sufficient probable cause to make an arrest. He's got a judge signing the arrest warrant as we speak. And he's hoping that when you arrest him and confront him with his lies and all, he'll confess. The solicitor's also been on the phone with SLED's crime lab. They're prioritizing this murder, and we're confident they'll find plenty more to prove Mr. Russo's guilt before his first court date."

"And if he doesn't confess?" Charlie asked.

"If the Lord's willin' and the creek don't rise, the lab will connect him to the killing," Cannon said. "And there's gotta be additional people out there who know about more fighting going on between them two."

"I'm a bit confused here," Billy said. "We take cases to the circuit solicitor's office time and time again with more than enough evidence, and they turn us down, always demanding more evidence or additional witnesses.

They require a slam dunk case they can't lose in court, but here, they're getting a warrant without any direct evidence or witnesses to the crime."

"You've got to understand the big picture," Cannon said. "The TV and papers are saying we have a killer on the loose, a man who comes into a gated plantation and brutalizes a nice woman who retired up north and moved down here for all the island has to offer. Safety and security rank right up there with our beaches and reasonable cost of living. Folks will be cancelling hotel reservations and homebuyers will be telling realtors they're having second thoughts about moving here."

Charlie threw up her hands. "So we arrest a man who might be innocent, just to show the world there isn't a maniac out there randomly raping and killing older women."

Cannon leaned across his desk. "You think he did it?"

Charlie shot back. "I don't know for sure."

"Well, Missy, you don't have a law degree, and the man who has one says there's enough to arrest the husband. So, you go put that boy in handcuffs, bring him down here, and get him to tell you why he murdered his wife."

23

The fitness center at Sea Island Plantation was geared toward the more senior residents of the community. There were two rows of cardio machines—treadmills, elliptical machines, bicycles, and rowing machines—and a full set of weight machines, where you could purportedly work every muscle group. But Sean missed the free weights at the Oakland PD gym. He had begun lifting seriously when he joined the SWAT team as a young officer thirty years ago. By the time he was promoted to sergeant and left the team four years later, he was a lean but muscular 220 pounds and could bench press and squat 350 pounds.

However, he had been forced to give up heavy free weights after his left shoulder was shattered by a protester who dropped a hunk of concrete on him from an elevated part of the freeway during a demonstration more than ten years ago. It had taken more than a year of surgeries and rehab before he regained enough use of his shoulder to return to full duty. These days, he was satisfied with finishing three sets of twelve reps with two hundred pounds on the Smith machine at the community fitness center. Sean was setting up the cable weight machine he used for curls when he spotted Frank Martin, dressed in gray gym shorts and an NYPD tee shirt, hobbling toward him on his cane.

"Nice to see you keeping fit," Frank said. "Too many of us old farts retire and spend our days lying on the couch watching sports."

"You live here in Sea Island?" Sean asked, even though he'd fully researched the man and knew exactly where he lived.

"Left the snow and high taxes eight years ago. That was a nice intro the captain gave for you."

"It felt like I was being buttered up before being pitched a timeshare."

"Yeah, that's Clinton Cannon the third, or just Cannon number three, as we call him," Frank said with a wry smile. "He thought he was the natural heir to the job of sheriff when his father retired. He'd been working the county's good-ole-boy network and was certain he had the election in the bag until another man retired from the state police, moved back to his hometown of Dufftown, and decided to run. He promised to end corruption and professionalize the department. The new business owners backed him, and he got the vote of just about everyone who moved down here in the last ten or twenty years."

"So did he?"

"End corruption and professionalize the department? I think the new sheriff's doing his best, but some things are deeply entrenched down here. Business is largely based on relationships, many of which are generations old. One of the old-time developers might've donated to Cannon's election, not as a bribe per se, but maybe because Cannon's father let the developer's son skate on a driving drunk charge thirty years ago."

"I've always stayed out of politics," Sean said.

"An especially good philosophy down here. So, what do you think about the cold case team?"

"Lots of experience among the members," Sean said as he stuck the pin in the eighty-pound mark and did ten reps to warm up. "The case presentation on that old murder seemed rather sketchy. Not much to go on."

"Yeah, that was Charlie's first cold case as the team sergeant, and I think she's up to her eyeballs in yesterday's murder. But she's good police."

"I guess I'll see if there's any potential leads they missed when I review the murder book." Sean upped the weight to a hundred and did eight reps.

"What are you doing tomorrow afternoon?"

"Nothing I can think of right now."

"Good, I'll be done with the murder book in the morning and bring it over to your house around one."

Before Sean could think of a reason to object, Frank hobbled across the gym to the leg machines.

Sean finished his upper body workout and drove home, where Annie met him at the door wagging her tail so hard it was as if she hadn't seen him in months. After taking a quick shower, Sean grabbed a novel he had been reading—a series featuring an ex-military government agent who saved the world in every book.

One thing Sean had loved when Lauren was alive was the rhythm of their days in retirement. Since she died, he couldn't find a routine that felt right. Sometimes he wandered around the house aimlessly, as if he were looking for something he'd misplaced or a chore that needed to be done. A cardinal and two Carolina wrens were splashing around in the fountain in his backyard. He picked up three plastic containers from the screened porch and filled the birdfeeders—two that held different mixes of seed and a shallow one that was for mealworms. A bluebird sat in a nearby tree waiting for him to finish.

He came back into the house, tossed three of the throw pillows off the sofa onto the floor and propped the remaining one against the armrest, then stretched out with his book.

He looked at the pillows on the floor and pulled a business card from his wallet. After five rings, it went to voicemail. "Sergeant Nash, this is Sean Tanner. A couple of thoughts came to me on the Russo murder. The pillows and afghan on the living room floor might indicate that one of them slept on the couch Sunday night. Maybe that means something—maybe not. And one of our cold case team members who lives across the fairway from the Russos said people living on the golf course visit each other through the back yards. Also, I had dinner with some neighbors last night, and Debbie Keller said she remembered the shower was running in the Russo's house when she entered the bathroom. She turned it off. I asked her to call your detective, but in case she didn't.... Don't know if any of that might be useful, but if you have any questions, give me a call." Sean left his phone number and hung up.

Sean hoped Charlie would view his tidbits of information as helpful rather than an annoyance. Back when he worked Homicide, a few of his fellow investigators were sometimes rude and abrupt to people supplying tips, but Sean recorded every single one and thanked the callers. You never knew what tiny piece of information might turn out to be the nugget that solved the case.

24

Charlie entered the interview room, followed by Darryl. She was still pissed about the way the captain spoke to her, pissed that he was calling the shots on her case, and pissed that she needed Ken to confess to stay out of the captain's shithouse.

Ken Russo was rubbing his wrists. "Were the handcuffs really necessary?"

"Sorry, that wasn't my call," Charlie said as she took a seat across from him. "Before we talk again, I need to remind you of your rights."

Ken was dressed in a clean polo shirt and cargo shorts, but his haggard face showed he hadn't gotten much sleep since she saw him last night. "You could've just called, and I would've come down."

"Boss's orders," she said and read him his Miranda rights.

"The two detectives who brought me here said I was under arrest."

"An arrest warrant has been issued for you," Charlie said.

"Why? I already told you I'd never hurt Nancy."

Charlie leaned back in her chair. "What can you tell me about Nancy's broken wrist in Savannah last year?"

"You've got to be kidding." Ken chuckled—a nervous forced laugh. "Nancy and I went to Savannah for her birthday weekend. Stayed at one of the boutique hotels near Columbia Square. We had reservations at a romantic restaurant in the city that night and she was getting ready. I hear a crash. I come into the bathroom and see her getting up from the shower floor holding her wrist."

"You weren't in there with her?"

"I was nowhere near her. She was in a lot of pain, so I drove her to the emergency room. Next thing I know, two cops are there questioning me. The doctor gave Nancy some pain meds, so she was mostly out of it that night. The next morning, we laughed about it—that they thought I was a wife beater and broke her wrist."

"Did you know they sent a report for suspected elder abuse to social services?"

"That's ridiculous! I told the orthopedic surgeon we went to for follow-up about the police coming, and he even said the break was typical of a fall. If it was a spiral fracture, one that's caused by violently twisting someone's arm, that might make him think possible abuse, but he sees these kinds of fall injuries all the time."

Charlie paused for a moment and watched Ken's demeanor. "Tell me about the fight you two had on Sunday at the Riverside pool."

"Jeez, you guys are really reaching for straws. That was nothing. Just a disagreement."

"It was something. Witnesses said you grabbed her and threw her down into the water."

"People are exaggerating."

"You told me you've never hurt your wife, and I've learned you manhandled her the day before she was killed."

"Look, we've had a difference of opinion concerning a family issue for a while. She brought it up again when we were in the pool. She was getting loud and causing a scene, so I put my hands on her shoulders. I asked her to keep her voice down and suggested we continue this conversation when we got home. And she kicked me in the leg. The one I had surgery on. I pushed her away and she lost her balance and went underwater. All that got hurt was her pride."

"You grabbed her hard enough to leave bruises on her arms."

Ken took a deep breath and shook his head. "You're looking for something that didn't exist."

"What were you arguing about?"

"I told you it was a family matter."

"I need you to be more specific," Charlie said.

"What we argued about has nothing to do with Nancy's death."

"I'm sorry, Mr. Russo, but I'm the one who needs to make that determination. That's the way murder investigations work. Now, what was the argument about?"

"It's personal."

Charlie stared at him. She knew whatever he was hiding was important. She didn't know if it was relevant to the murder, but his refusal to talk about it made her think he was hiding a lot more. Rather than continue to press him on it, she decided to hit him with all of the facts, one by one, and come back to this again if he didn't break by then.

"When we spoke yesterday, you said you left the house at seven, went to McDonald's, and then went to the beach."

"Yeah, so?"

"You went straight to the beach after McDonald's, is that right?"

"That's what I said."

"How is it that we've found several eyewitnesses, all upstanding citizens with no reason to lie, who saw you arrive at the beach a few minutes after nine o'clock?"

Ken met her stare. His lips tightened. This was it, she thought. He realized he'd been caught. She just needed to maintain eye contact with him, show him she wasn't going to let him go until he broke.

It took less than a minute for him to take a deep breath and speak.

"This is bullshit!" he blurted out. "You're inspecting every inch of my life and every word Nancy and I might've said to each other to try to make it fit into your little theory that I killed her. Is that what you really think, detectives, that I killed my wife?"

Ken looked at Charlie, then to Darryl, and back to Charlie.

She said softly, "Yes, Ken, I do."

His eyes were close to tears. His face showed defeat.

"Tell me what happened?" she said softly.

He took a breath. His expression changed instantly from defeat to defiance. "You think I killed my wife. Then I better speak to an attorney."

25

Sean turned onto Blue Heron Lane and continued his stroll with Annie heeling on his left side. The sun had just dropped below the trees, and the horizon glowed red, orange, and blue. He and Lauren had taken Annie for walks every evening when they first moved here. Within a month, they had met nearly everyone that lived in the Riverside neighborhood, the hundred homes on this side of the creek and wetlands.

They marveled at how beautiful, peaceful, and safe it felt. All the houses were meticulously landscaped, the lawns manicured. The Sea Island maintenance crews kept the public areas immaculate, trees and shrubs trimmed, and fresh flowers planted around the clubhouse and along the main road coming in. Street sweepers came through weekly, and a piece of litter on the street was an anomaly.

Sean had concerns about moving into an "active adult" community, known as a fifty-five-plus community for the federal law that allowed adult communities as an exception to housing discrimination laws. The communities could restrict owners to people over fifty-five, although a small percentage of new buyers could be as young as fifty. Before they moved in, Sean had visions of hordes of senior citizens playing shuffleboard and hobbling down the streets on walkers. What he found was that despite their gray hair and wrinkles, the residents were more active and full of life than those half their age in his old suburban neighborhood.

Retiring and moving here after his thirty years with Oakland was not part of Sean's life plan. He was set to take a job as an investigator with the DA's office, and Lauren planned to continue teaching to max out her pension. But Sean failed the pre-hire physical. Although Lauren had known his health was deteriorating, he was in denial. His weight had dropped drastically since his previous physical two years earlier and his blood pressure and cholesterol were both at high-risk levels. When pressed by his doctor, Sean also admitted to frequent headaches, neck pain, and sleep issues. Stress, the doctor had said, sixteen years working homicide will do that to just about anyone.

Despite being rejected because of the medical report, Sean was still set on working for the DA's office. Some other retired homicide investigators had gone there and loved it. The salary was similar to that of a sergeant at Oakland, although there was no overtime pay. But the hours were generally nine to five, Monday through Friday. Investigators were given an unmarked car that they could take home, and the work was low stress compared to working homicide. And when they added their OPD pension to their salary as a DA inspector, they were making very good money.

Sean worked his last day with OPD and fought to get his health back so he could retake the physical in a few months and start his second career with the DA's office. Ever cognizant of the toll his job had taken on him, Lauren queried a realtor friend and crunched some numbers. Thanks to the skyrocketing Bay Area housing market, their suburban tract house had more than doubled in value to well over a million dollars. Meanwhile, a South Carolina realtor found their dream home in Sea Island Plantation. It was a thousand square feet larger than their California house and set on a much larger lot overlooking the river and salt marsh. With the equity from their Bay Area home, they could buy it with cash. With no mortgage, property taxes a third of what they were paying, and a lower cost of living in South Carolina, Lauren figured they could live quite comfortably on their pensions and savings.

A flock of white ibises flew overhead, probably on the way to their nightly roosting spot. Sean waved at a car and continued down their street.

During their walks, Lauren had often joked that everything was so beautiful and everyone so happy and friendly, that Riverside reminded her of the opening scene in the movie, *The Stepford Wives*, where everything seemed perfect. And it had been, Sean thought. Until the murder across the street shattered that fantasy, much like when the sinister undercurrent in the fictional Stepford community rose to the surface.

Sean approached his house and spotted George standing in front of the Farmers' house. Dorothy Farmer and her husband lived next door to Ken and Nancy but normally visited family in Ohio for most of July and August. "What's going on, George?" Sean asked as Annie nosed George's thigh, begging for a pat on the head.

"Just waiting for Beth, as I do much of my life." George grinned. "She waters Dorothy's plants for her while they're away."

"It's neighbors like Beth that make Riverside such a great place to live," Sean said, but when it came out, it sounded like Lauren was speaking.

"Do the police have any leads on Nancy's death?" George asked.

"I don't have a clue."

"I hear they took Ken down for questioning again."

"Really?"

George nodded. "I think I might be in trouble."

"For what?"

"Well, when the police questioned me and Beth, I told them I was home with Beth until you picked me up to go fishing."

"And that's not true?"

"Not exactly. I always get up around six, and Beth normally sleeps in. I close the bedroom door, so I don't disturb her with the morning news on the TV. And I sometimes sneak out and get breakfast."

"I don't think leaving the house for breakfast is a crime."

"I had a stent put in a clogged artery a few years ago, and Beth would be really pissed if she knew I went to the gas station mini mart and bought two sausage and egg biscuits. I pulled into the garage a minute or two before you came by in your golf cart."

"Sounds like Beth assumed you were home and that's why she told the police you were there."

"Yeah, and I didn't want to contradict her and admit where I was."

"Ya know, George," Sean said, "when I worked a murder case, I always stressed to people the importance of telling the truth about everything. When people lie about even trivial things—like eating a sausage and egg sandwich—it makes detectives think they're hiding something a lot worse."

"If I call and correct my statement, do you think they'll tell Beth?"

"I think they have better things to do than snitch a man off for not adhering to his diet."

26

Sean was awakened by his cell phone vibrating on his nightstand. His bedside clock read 11:34. He pulled the phone off its magnetic charging pad and looked at the screen—*Campbell County*. "Hello."

"Sean, this is Ken Russo. I'm so glad you answered. No one seems to answer their phones at night."

Sean threw the covers back and sat up. Annie rose from her dog bed near the door and stretched. "Where are you? What's wrong?"

"I'm in jail. The detectives arrested me for murder."

"I'm sorry to hear that." Sean sure hoped that Ken wasn't expecting him to post bail for him.

"I messed up big time. I lied to them about my whereabouts, and they caught me. Combined with some other little things, they're convinced I killed Nancy."

"Shouldn't you be talking to a lawyer about this?"

"I don't know any lawyers, and I sure don't know any who answer their phones at night. I need a big favor."

"You really should get a lawyer."

"They're pretty sure Nancy was killed between seven and nine. I told them I left the house just before seven, went to McDonald's and straight to the beach. They verified I was at McDonald's, but they found out I didn't get to the beach until nine."

Sean felt like he was repeating the same advice he had given to George last night. "It's not normally a good idea to lie to the police."

"I was trying to protect my private life and keep other people out of this," Ken said. "I didn't want everyone in Riverside to know, but I'm an alcoholic and attend AA meetings."

"That's nothing to be ashamed of and certainly not a crime."

"I know, but it was private, and I didn't think it was anyone's business. Besides, I thought they'd need some hard evidence before they could arrest me, and since I didn't do it, there couldn't be any."

"Are you saying you were at a meeting at that time?"

"I was. The meeting runs from seven-thirty to eight-thirty, and I got there early and left late."

"Why don't you just give the detectives the names of some people who were at the meeting? They can go there and verify your alibi."

"They call it alcoholics *anonymous* for a reason. You don't talk about who you saw there."

"Ken, I've had friends in the program. I understand the anonymity stuff, but it's not like you're revealing the identities of people in witness protection."

"I know, but I still can't just sic a bunch of cops on them. Besides, I only know most by their first names. I tried calling a few of them, but no one's picking up, and they're about to put me in a holding cell and I don't know when I'll be able to use a phone again."

"Tell me the names you know and where the meeting is. I'll pass it on to the detectives. I'm sure they'll be discreet."

"You know where the old Methodist church is on Island Road?"

"Yeah, on the left heading toward the beaches?"

"Yup. Pete Burdette is there every morning, and he and a bunch of other old-timers shoot the breeze outside the church hall after the meeting's over. Pete's my sponsor, and he can verify my alibi. And Sean, please go there yourself. Pete can ask others if they're willing to get involved, but I don't want to out anyone without their permission."

Sean promised to do what he could, without agreeing to go there himself. He hung up and tried to go back to sleep but lay there awake thinking about Ken. Was he innocent or guilty? What did the police have on him beyond his lying about his whereabouts? Why did Ken think Sean would get involved for him?

Sean knew the answer to his last question. People trusted him. As long as people didn't break the law, they liked having a cop in the neighborhood. Throughout the years, neighbors came to him with questions about the workings of the criminal justice system. Why'd the cop ticket me for a stop sign violation when it was a rolling stop and no one was coming? Why'd they give me a speeding ticket—aren't they supposed to give you a ten-mile-per-hour leeway? How can I get out of jury duty? Are the murders in San Francisco and the one in Oakland yesterday the work of a serial killer? And they sometimes asked for favors, like fixing a ticket.

Still, he wasn't comfortable helping create an alibi for a suspect who his brother and sister officers had arrested. He knew from experience that most alibis were bullshit, friends and family lying to protect someone. But good detectives would rather hear about alibi witnesses early in an investigation than be surprised by them in court.

Plenty of suspects in his cases claimed they had alibis for the time of their murders. They probably thought he'd just let them go after a quick phone call. But once confronted, few people were willing to go to prison themselves for being an accessory after the fact for lying to the police. So, he'd bring the alibi witness downtown and into an interview room. Make sure they knew the interview was being recorded and then tell them the penalty for lying to protect someone who committed a crime.

Occasionally the alibi checked out. The alibi witness was an upstanding citizen who wasn't lying. In those cases, Sean would release the suspect he was holding and begin his search for the real killer. But most of the time, alibi witnesses had been asked to lie by the murderer.

He'd call Charlie first thing in the morning. Even if she was initially angry for having to deal with what might be a bullshit alibi, she should prefer that to being blindsided by it during trial. Or even worse, to be holding the wrong person, which meant the real killer was still running free.

27

WEDNESDAY

Annie let Sean sleep in until 6:10, at which time she stuck her cold nose against his neck. He pulled on a pair of shorts and tee shirt and poured a cup of kibble into her dish. She inhaled her food as he ground the beans, poured water into the coffee maker, and hit the start button. He followed her into the backyard and watched as she did her business and sniffed around the perimeter of the yard to determine what uninvited creatures had invaded her territory last night. By the time she was finished, his coffee was ready, and Sean settled into a cushioned chair on the screened porch with his first cup.

Dawn was just starting to break, and birds began calling to each other. The air was still and heavy but perfumed by the lush vegetation in his backyard. More birds sang, and Sean saw a titmouse land on the birdfeeder.

The phone call last night had interrupted his sleep, and he tossed and turned the rest of the night. He wasn't used to feeling groggy in the morning. Back when he was working, he ran for days with just a few hours of sleep a night. Now, he'd become accustomed to a full night's sleep and couldn't imagine going back to the way he had lived.

He called Charlie's direct number and left a voicemail then called the detective division's main number. It rolled over to communications. The dispatcher said she'd contact Sgt. Nash and pass on the message.

When he didn't get a callback by the time he finished his second cup of coffee, he grabbed the leash and took Annie for her morning walk. He took their short loop and didn't let Annie sniff as long as normal in the spots the other dogs in the neighborhood frequented.

Still no return call by the time they got back to the house, so he phoned again. Once again, he got Charlie's voicemail. After leaving another message, he called the main number. A woman who sounded like a civilian admin assistant said Sergeant Nash was in a meeting but would have her call him as soon as she got out.

He skimmed the morning newspaper halfheartedly while watching the clock. When she still hadn't called by 8:15, Sean scrolled to Stretch's number on his phone and tapped his name.

"We didn't have a tee time this morning, did we?" Stretch asked.

Sean told him about Ken's call last night and his attempts to reach Charlie.

"And you're thinking about going to the church and talking to this Pete guy?"

"Isn't that what a normal citizen would do if his neighbor asked for help?" Sean said. "Or am I thinking like a cop?"

"Shit, man, you and I will never think like normal people. We were cops too long."

"You're probably right."

"If you're going out there, you shouldn't go alone," Stretch said.

"I'm not really afraid of being mugged in a church parking lot in broad daylight."

"It's not that. If you were still on the job and going to interview a possible witness, would you take your partner along?"

"Sure, as a second set of eyes and ears, or in case the witness says something and tries to recant it later," Sean said.

"Right. Always good to have the word of two cops."

"If you're not doing anything, you wanna meet me there?"

"I'm on my way."

Sean got in his car and drove to the church. It was a wood-sided building with a steeply pitched roof and requisite steeple. Behind it was a more modern stucco building with a sign that read *Church Hall.*

About twenty cars were parked around the main door of the church hall under old shade trees. Sean backed into a slot where he could watch the door. His car thermometer read eighty, but the dew point felt just as high, so he kept the engine running and air conditioner on. He suspected Charlie might not be pleased that he drove out here. He imagined she was still harboring resentment over him walking through her crime scene.

A few minutes later, Stretch drove into the parking lot and pulled his car alongside Sean's, driver door to driver door. They both lowered their windows.

"I couldn't just sit home and pretend leaving the message for Charlie ended my responsibility," Sean said. "If Ken really was at an AA meeting when Nancy was killed and no one was available to contact his alibi witnesses this morning, Ken would have to sit in jail for another day."

"That wouldn't be right," Stretch said. "You do realize you're thinking like a cop, don't you?"

"Guess we can't help it, huh?"

A few minutes after 8:30, the door swung open, and people streamed out. A young woman holding a toddler by the hand, two men dressed in shirts and ties, a group of women ranging from twenty to seventy, and lastly a group of six men who looked to be of retirement age.

Sean and Stretch got out of their cars and approached the men, who had stopped to talk halfway down the walkway. Two lit cigarettes. One looked at Sean and said, "If you're looking for the meeting, it started at seven-thirty."

"Actually, we're looking for Pete Burnette," Sean said. "I'm a friend of Ken Russo."

"I'm Pete," a hunchbacked man in his late seventies said. "We heard about his wife and been trying to call him, but he's not answering."

"He called me from jail last night and asked me to come and talk to Pete."

"He's in jail?" Pete said.

"They arrested him for murder," Sean said. "According to what the police told Ken, his wife was killed around the time Ken said he was here, but he didn't want to tell the police due to AA's anonymity policy."

"That boy is sure dumb," a tall, lanky white-haired man said.

"He's new," another man said. "What's he got, a couple months?"

"Ken will get his nine-month chip the end of the month," Pete said then turned to Sean. "We're anonymous, but we're not a secret society. Ken was here the entire meeting and stuck around after the meeting just like we're doing today."

"The police would want to talk to some people who can verify that."

"Hell, we'll all go down there right now," the white-haired man said.

"Probably be best if you called first to set it up," Stretch said. "Make an appointment."

"Anyone in particular we should call?" Pete asked.

Sean recited Charlie's office number, and Pete entered it into his phone. "We'll take care of it," Pete said.

Sean and Stretch walked back to their cars. "Leaving it up to strangers to follow up with the police feels awkward," Sean said. "If this was my case, I would've at least gotten every man's name and contact information."

"Maybe taken statements from a few of them right here and then driven one or two to the station for recorded statements," Stretch said.

Sean opened his car door. "But this isn't our investigation, and we're just civilians now."

"You got it, brother."

28

Charlie stomped out of the captain's office. She knew she should take deep breaths to calm down, but she didn't want to *fucking* calm down.

She'd spent the last hour feeding reports and other documents to the assistant solicitor assigned to the Russo murder case. The prosecutor continually asked for additional evidence that didn't exist and then acted surprised when she said that was all there was. He had been sent to the captain's office by his boss, the elected circuit solicitor for the judicial circuit that included Campbell County. The same man who agreed with Cannon yesterday there was sufficient probable cause to arrest Ken Russo.

But the assistant solicitor was more politically astute than Charlie was and obviously knew better than to openly complain in front of her or Captain Cannon about the stupidity of filing charges prematurely. He probably knew the captain would pick up the phone the second he left and tell the solicitor he had a malcontent on his staff. So, when he had every report that existed on the case, he smiled, thanked the captain, and headed out the door, leaving Charlie with a head shake and eye roll.

She stomped down the hall toward her office when she heard the detective division's admin called out, "Sergeant Nash."

"What!" She spun around and jammed her free fist onto her hip.

"I'm sorry," Gladys said apologetically. "But this man's been calling for you and says it's very important."

Charlie immediately felt like a bitch for snapping at Gladys. The person that kept the section humming smoothly. The person that kept her calm demeanor when all the detectives were stressed. The person that answered the phone with a voice that dripped of Southern hospitality, even when four lines rang simultaneously. "No, I'm sorry. It's been a rough morning."

"Don't fret, honey," Gladys said. "Plenty of that going around today."

Charlie took the message and saw Sean Tanner's name on it. Her frown almost changed to a smile when she recalled his presence at the cold case meeting yesterday. It was nice seeing someone on the team who hadn't retired from their law enforcement career before she started high school.

"Did Tanner say what he wanted?"

"Only that it was important and timely. I think it might have something to do with the four older gentlemen who are sitting in the lobby asking to see you."

"Just what I need."

"I told Detective Garcia, and he's out there talking with them."

Charlie entered her squad room just as Jay was coming down the hallway. "We have four men here who all said they saw Ken Russo at an alcoholics anonymous meeting Monday morning at seven-thirty. I put them in separate interview rooms. I figure we'll talk to them one at a time and get their statements."

"You think they're all lying?"

"No, ma'am," Jay said. "These guys are all righteous citizens."

"Okay, I'll take one. Where are Sherm and Darryl?"

"In the coffee room. I'll round them up. You probably want to take Pete Burdette. I put him in interview room number one."

Charlie grabbed her notebook, flipped the switch outside the interview room door to turn on the video camera mounted on the wall near the ceiling, and stepped inside. The man stood, extended his hand, and said with a smile, "My name's Pete Burdette."

"Sergeant Nash," she said and sat across from him. She gathered the necessary biographical information: 79 years old with an address in the new part of Sea Island Plantation, a retired CPA from Connecticut, lives with his wife of the same age, and has four children, eight grandchildren, and two great grandchildren.

"I understand you think Ken killed his wife," Pete said.

"Evidence points that way," Charlie said. "Are we wrong?"

"Well, I'm sure you do a fine job at what you do, so all I can tell you is what I know. I was at my morning AA meeting at the Methodist Church on Monday. I go there Monday through Friday. I always get there fifteen minutes early. That would be seven-fifteen. I have a number of sponsees. Do you know what an AA sponsee is?"

"Not exactly."

"In AA, people who've been around for a while act as sponsors for new people. We sort of guide them through the program and help them out. I've been sober and going to meetings for over forty years. I met Ken when he came to his first meeting and agreed to be his sponsor. He and I have a standing meeting before the meeting on Monday mornings, so he was there waiting when I came in at seven-fifteen."

"You're sure about the day and the time?"

"It was only two days ago. I can remember that far back."

"Did he stay for the meeting?"

"Sitting right beside me. Meeting finished at eight-thirty. The guys smoked and joked outside for another fifteen minutes after the meeting, and then I drove off. Ken was still there with a few of the fellas, but they probably broke up a few minutes later."

"Are you sure it was eight-forty-five when you left?"

"See here," he said, pulling out his phone and opening an appointment on his calendar app. "My wife and I only have one car these days, and she needed the car at nine to go to her volunteer work at the hospital. To make sure I don't get carried away yakking with the boys, I set up a ringer. The bell went off at eight-forty-five, and I left."

Charlie smiled. Pete reminded her of her father—disciplined and exact about everything in his life. "How did Ken seem that morning?"

He shrugged his shoulders. "Definitely not like someone on his way to kill his wife, if that's what you're asking."

"Has he mentioned any problems with his wife?"

"No more than most men."

"What does that mean?" Charlie asked.

"Sergeant, I know what you're looking for. But it's not there. That isn't Ken. He has struggles like everyone, but what someone says in an AA meeting stays there. Nevertheless, if someone talked about killing his wife, and then his wife turned up dead, I'd tell you."

"Fair enough," she said. "When did you last see Ken or talk to him?"

"That time just after the meeting on Monday. When I heard the news about his wife's death, I tried to call him, but only got his voicemail. After he didn't show up at the meeting Tuesday, a bunch of the people at the meeting said they'd try to call him, too."

Charlie wondered if all those people had been calling Ken's cell phone, which she seized as evidence after they finished questioning him Monday night. "By the way, what prompted you to come down here?"

"When the meeting got out this morning, a big man—name of Sean—was waiting outside with another gentleman. Sean said Ken called him last night from jail and asked him to get ahold of me."

29

Sean stopped at the local grocery store on his way home from the church. Although he liked the selection in the larger Kroger and Publix, an independent grocery was in the shopping center right outside Sea Island Plantation, and he could get in and out a lot faster than he could at the big supermarkets when he only needed a few items.

He grabbed a small shopping cart and rolled it to the dairy case in the back. He checked the expiration dates on the milk and chose one with ten days still to go. He rolled his cart to the bakery section and had the guy behind the counter slice a loaf of whole wheat bread. He put five apples in a bag and continued through the produce aisle, looking for vegetables on sale that looked good.

Sean stopped by a bin with green beans and ripped a plastic bag from the roll. An elderly man was pulling out string beans one at a time and examining them before he put them into his produce bag. Sean was tempted to reach around him, grab a handful of beans, and shove them in the man's bag, telling him that he could sort through them at home like everyone else. Before he could act, a memory of shopping with Lauren came to him.

They had just moved here, and Sean was still moving at California speed. He was showing his impatience with the many retirees who frequented the local grocery store, blocking aisles with their shopping carts while they labored forever over a decision between different brands of peanut butter. Lauren just smiled and reminded him they were no longer in a rush to do everything, and that someday, they would be the elderly people, where their big event for the day was going grocery shopping.

"Hey, Sean."

He turned to see Denise Sheppard pushing a shopping cart toward him. She was wearing flip flops, shorts, and a shapeless top that reminded Sean of a shortened muumuu. "How ya doing, Feebee?"

She gave him a stern look. "It's okay to call me Denise when we're in public."

"Yes, ma'am. Since I'm the FNG, I'll address you however you wish."

"I see you're a smartass just like the rest of the Mudflats Murder Club," she said.

Sean scanned her shopping cart: Coke, beer, an apple pie, white bread, potato chips. If he knew her better, he'd bust her chops about her food choices.

She must've read his mind. "I'm starting my diet and workout program tomorrow."

"I'd never judge."

"No cops ever do."

They both laughed. Sean glanced at the old man still picking green beans. "Do you live in Sea Island Plantation?"

"Bought a place down here about six years ago, shortly after my husband and I retired. One of the neighborhoods near the activities center. I could walk to the fitness center in five minutes if I were so inclined. Our house is nothing like your custom house on the river, but it's plenty for us."

"Was your husband in the bureau too?"

"Hell, no. That's too cliché—young female agent marries studly male senior agent." She laughed. "Maybe even more cliché—I was a second-year in law school, taking a night class on tax law, and he was the professor."

"Ah, yes, the naïve coed seduced by the esteemed professor."

"Not exactly. He was an adjunct, teaching one class a semester, and we never even went out until I graduated."

"I wasn't judging."

"Of course not. Cops never judge one another." She smiled. "The only reason I went to law school was to get into the FBI. That had been my dream ever since I watched the old TV show with Efrem Zimbalist, Jr. as a kid. I figured law school was the surest route for me."

"It worked."

She nodded. "Did you always want to be a cop?"

"My father and grandfather were both police. I respected what they did and never imagined doing anything else."

"Not many people get to work a career with such purpose."

Sean smiled slightly and nodded. His career and family had been his purpose for thirty years. But the job and Lauren were gone, and his grown kids didn't need him anymore. Playing golf a few times a week, fishing, and taking Annie for walks was all he had left. "I'm not ready for the rocking chair and watching the grass grow."

"I'm sure you put in as many hours in your thirty years wearing a badge as most people do in a normal career spanning forty or fifty years. We earned the right to retire early and enjoy life."

Enjoying life was something he had never really thought about until he retired. He just did what he was supposed to do. Some of it he enjoyed, some of it he just did because it needed to be done, like mowing the lawn, sweeping the garage, painting the house. He enjoyed the satisfaction of a job well done. He enjoyed watching his kids when they were on sports teams and when they opened presents on Christmas morning. But he never had time to pursue hobbies or other activities just for fun. He was still trying to figure out what he enjoyed doing.

The older man shuffled away from the green bean bin, and Sean said, "I better finish up my shopping."

"Nice chatting with you, Sean. I'll see you later."

Feebee wandered toward the bakery section, and Sean grabbed two handfuls of string beans, stuffed them into a plastic bag, and dropped them into his cart.

He was looking forward to Frank's visit and digging into the cold case. Although he didn't expect to find some long-ignored or neglected lead that would solve the old murder, working it would at least be more meaningful than sitting in his recliner watching TV or reading another book.

30

Within moments of Charlie sitting down at her desk, Jay, Sherm, and Darryl filed into the office. Each detective reported their witness said much the same as Pete. There was little doubt Ken was at the AA meeting between 7:15 and 8:45 on the morning of the murder.

She marched down the hall to Billy's office. His door was open, and she walked in and dropped into the chair in front of his desk. Still miffed that she'd been left alone with the captain and solicitor, she asked, "Where have you been all morning?"

Instead of jumping her shit for speaking to him like that, he slowly removed his reading glasses and said, "I hear you had a rough time with the boss this morning."

She nodded, quickly feeling like a jerk for taking her frustration out on Billy.

"I was out with the other team on a rape that occurred last night."

Charlie cringed. Although others might consider it sexist, her team normally got all the sexual assault cases since she was the only female detective in the division. Although many of the male detectives were just as skilled and empathetic as she was—maybe more so on her bad days—the reality was most rape victims felt more comfortable talking to a woman. "How's the victim?"

"About how you'd expect," he said. "Woman meets a man at a bar and goes back to his hotel room."

"I don't like where this is going."

"Yeah, lots of alcohol involved."

"Any injuries?"

"Nothing visible, and the doctor doing the rape exam found no signs of physical trauma."

"Let me guess—the man said the sex was consensual."

Billy nodded.

Charlie hated he-said-she-said acquaintance rapes. The woman would likely bear some emotional scars for years, maybe for the rest of her life. But absent witnesses or physical evidence to show there was coercion or force, no jury would convict the man and therefore, no prosecutor would file charges. She hoped the other detective squad would find something to corroborate the woman's story.

"What's new with your murder?" he asked.

Charlie told him about her meeting with the solicitor and the four witnesses who just gave Ken Russo an alibi for the time when the murder occurred.

"How certain is the doc on the time of death?" he asked.

"I didn't talk to him myself, but they usually give a conservative window."

"Have you done a timeline yet?"

"Only in my notes," she said.

Billy rolled a whiteboard from the wall and handed her a marker. "Humor me."

Charlie paged through her notes and began writing on the board as Billy returned to the reports on his desk. When she finished, she turned the board toward Billy.

0600 Earliest TOD per ME
0700 Ken Russo leaves house
0701 Nancy Russo calls Debbie Keller to confirm exercise class
0706 Ken seen on McDonald's security camera
0715 Ken arrives at AA Meeting
0845 Ken leaves AA Meeting

0900 Ken arrives at beach
0900 Latest TOD per ME
1215 Debbie Keller arrives at Nancy's house to pick up Nancy for class, calls 9-1-1
1220 Deputies, ambulance, fire arrive. Vic pronounced.
1302 Debbie calls Ken, tells him Nancy's dead
1315 Ken arrives at house

"Let's go through this," Billy said. "How'd you come to the time Ken Russo left his house?"

"It's based on his statement and the latest he could've left to arrive at McDonald's by seven-oh-six without driving so recklessly he'd attract attention."

"And the call from Nancy Russo to Debbie Keller?"

"Debbie told this to Jay. Jay verified it by looking at her phone."

"Which means our vic was alive at seven-oh-one. That cuts the time of death window down considerably." Billy scratched his chin. "How long's it take to drive from the church where the AA meeting was located to the beach parking lot?"

"Seven minutes if he hit all the lights perfectly and there's no traffic. Maybe double that with morning traffic."

"But still, seven minutes minimum."

Charlie nodded.

"And those who saw him on the beach, was that exactly nine o'clock?"

"Both saw him a few minutes after nine," Charlie said. "One when Ken was getting stuff out of his car in the lot, the other witness when Ken was walking onto the beach."

"What about that call by Debbie Keller to Ken just after one? We were already at the scene and had her in tow, didn't we?"

"We lost control of her," Charlie said. "Jay took her to her house to get her statement. She used the restroom, and when she was in there, she took it upon herself to call Ken."

"I don't like that at all."

"We didn't see anything out of the ordinary during the initial interview, but we could talk to her again," Charlie said. "Are you thinking Ken might've done it and she aided him?"

Billy leaned back in his chair and stared at the ceiling.

"That would mean they planned it and Debbie stayed at the scene to fake the call from Nancy's phone," Charlie said. "Everything about the scene indicates it was spontaneous."

"Unless they wanted to make it look that way. Anything going on between Debbie and Ken?"

"I can't imagine so," Charlie said. "Calling a neighbor to tell him his wife is dead doesn't seem unusual. I don't buy a conspiracy between them."

"You're right. What about any other calls or texts from Nancy or Ken Russo's phone?"

"Hers has a password, which Ken says he doesn't know, so we've done a search warrant on the cellular company. Ken refused to give up his phone voluntarily, so we seized it as evidence. But same thing—password protected and search warrant."

"Seven to ten business days for results from the phone company, right?"

Charlie nodded.

"Okay, let's say we have a window of as much as twenty minutes for Ken to have committed the murder, and that's if we assume the witnesses at the beach are off a bit with their times. Is it possible to drive from the church, park and enter his house, kill her, return to his car, and then drive to the beach in that time?"

"Only at three in the morning with no traffic and driving like a maniac," she said. "And even then, it would leave no time to commit the act."

"I take it neither witness at the beach mentioned Mr. Russo had blood on his clothes or appeared frazzled or out of sorts."

"Nope, just a man leisurely taking a chair from his car and walking to the beach."

"Unless we're missing something here or someone is lying to us, there's no way Ken Russo could have murdered his wife."

"That was my conclusion. Should I go tell the captain?"

"No, it's my job to take his abuse," Billy said. "You should get back to work and figure out who *did* kill her."

31

When Sean got home and unpacked his grocery bag, he sprinkled the green beans with olive oil, roasted them in the oven for fifteen minutes, and ate half of them with two pieces of fresh bread slathered with almond butter for lunch.

The doorbell rang at exactly 1:00 p.m. Annie barked twice, ran to the door and sat, her tail wagging in anticipation of a visitor. Sean opened the door and saw Frank standing on the porch with a briefcase in his hand and a sour look on his face. "I'm still a New Yorker at heart and we don't like dogs," he said and stepped inside.

Annie followed him, wagging her tail even harder and nosing Frank's empty hand. "Annie doesn't care," Sean said. "She even likes people who don't like her."

Frank patted her head once then wiped his hand on his pants. "Where's your office?"

"We could sit at the dining room table," Sean suggested, following him as he hobbled on his cane into the great room and looked around.

"Nice house. Lots bigger than mine. Just you and the dog, huh?"

"Yeah," Sean replied.

"Lots of wasted space. Sorry about your wife," Frank said, followed quickly by, "Detectives don't do real work at dining room tables. Your office?"

Off the foyer was a small study with glass French doors that opened to the great room. Lauren had decorated it with a cherry writing table with curved legs, matching bookcase and file cabinet, and a Queen Anne upholstered chair next to a small table and reading lamp. She used the room to pay bills and work on her laptop, which she always closed and put away when guests arrived so that the room looked like a page out of a home design magazine. Sean knew better than to invite Frank to work there.

He led Frank up a set of stairs between the kitchen and laundry room. Annie ran up the stairs ahead of him. Sean had never before had an office. In their California house, they had turned the tiny fourth bedroom into a combination guest room and office. Lauren was the only one who used the compact desk pressed against a wall, mostly for grading school papers and handling the family finances. At work, Sean had an old metal desk in an open squad room during his first tour in Homicide and a laminate workstation on his last tour in the same open squad room. He had preferred the old desk.

Sean waited at the top of the stairs as Frank hobbled up by placing both feet on each step before climbing to the next one. The room was called a bonus room or F.R.O.G. by the realtor, a front room over the garage. It had a full bath and closet and could be used as a fourth bedroom, but with two guest rooms downstairs, they certainly didn't need another one. Lauren had envisioned their grandchildren would someday sleep there on air mattresses when visiting on holidays while Sean's son, daughter, and their spouses filled the two guest rooms downstairs. Another of Lauren's dreams that would never come to be.

Lauren had furnished the room as Sean's man-cave and office. An L-shaped desk as large as the deputy police chiefs in Oakland had in their offices sat next to the window that overlooked the driveway and street. On the other side of the room were a leather sofa and two leather recliners facing a large TV mounted on the wall and bracketed by two bookshelves. A coffee table was covered with books that Sean had read since his retirement but was still contemplating how to arrange on the bookshelves. Sean would occasionally sit with a book in one of the recliners next to the window overlooking the back yard and the river.

Frank scanned the room and whistled. "If I had this office, my wife would never see me."

"With just me in the house, not much reason to come up here anymore."

"Now that you work cold cases, you have a reason." Frank pulled a three-ring binder from his briefcase and set it on Sean's desk. He then lowered himself into a leather recliner and grabbed the remote. "You mind if I watch the news?" He powered on the television and began surfing channels before Sean could reply.

"You're gonna wait while I read all of this?"

"Not like I got anything else to do." Frank punched up Fox News. "I figured we could discuss the investigation when you're finished."

Sean sat at his desk and opened the murder book. Annie curled up on her dog bed in the corner of the room where she kept one eye on Frank. The TV didn't bother Sean. Actually, the different political pundits arguing with each other sounded a lot like the constant din of the homicide office he had worked in for much of his career.

Sean first read the patrol deputies' reports, from which he was able to piece together a rough synopsis of the incident. Deputies had responded to a call at the marina general store at 11:30 p.m. and met with Jerry Larson and Dana Whittle, both seventeen and residents of Spartina Island. They had waited by the pay phone from which they made the call. They led the deputies through the dirt parking lot to the public boat ramp about two hundred yards away. The victim was lying about five feet from the high tide line.

The teenagers said they were just looking for a place where they could be alone to talk—which Sean knew meant to make out, drink, use drugs, or have sex—when they saw the body. The deputies checked for signs of life and determined she had been dead for some time. They called for a supervisor, detectives, coroner, and crime scene technicians.

The remaining patrol supplemental reports didn't say much. The deputies interviewed about thirty people who were at the bar next to the general store, but no one heard or saw anything. They knocked at doors of houses on the road that led to the harbor and some houses north of the boat ramp, but no one heard or saw anything unusual. It was a typical warm, humid summer evening, and most residents were inside their houses with the windows closed and air conditioners running.

Sean turned to a report by the SLED crime scene technician. He was called out from home and arrived at the scene about 2:00 a.m. He shot two rolls of 35 mm film of the body and the scene. He searched the area for evidence and collected two cigarette butts—Marlborough Lights—near the body, one of which appeared to have lipstick on it. He wrote in his report that he could not ascertain if they were connected to the crime, although they appeared to be fresh. The crime scene technician searched the scene again after sunrise with a metal detector to try to locate shell casings or bullets, but found nothing of evidentiary value.

The voices on the TV changed when Frank switched to MSNBC. It was much the same as Fox—three or four people sitting at tables talking over each other and voicing outrage about everything the opposing political party did.

Sean turned to the lead detective's report. The first two pages consisted of the standard crime scene summary—he and his partner arrived, were briefed by the uniforms, looked and observed, and interviewed a few people who had nothing of value to say. The report contained nothing significant until dispatch notified the detectives of a missing person call at the Island Beach and Racquet Resort. The lead detective, accompanied by a patrol deputy, drove there and met with Aaron Goldberg. He said his wife, Theresa, had left around nine o'clock to take a walk and get some cigarettes, but never returned. Aaron said he spent the evening in his rental unit drinking beer and watching a baseball game with Tim Early and Steve Nowak, friends from New Jersey with whom they were vacationing. The detective showed Aaron a Polaroid photo he'd taken of the victim, and Aaron positively identified her as his wife.

The detective spoke to Tim and Steve. Both confirmed they were drinking and watching baseball with Aaron from seven o'clock until around eleven. Lizzy Early, the wife of Tim, said she was disappointed the men wanted to sit home and watch baseball, so she went to the nearby beach bar by herself. She came home and went to bed around midnight.

Sandra Nowak, the wife of Steve, said she stayed in her unit reading a paperback novel in bed and fell asleep sometime around eleven. All five of them said Theresa had no enemies and was not into any high-risk activities, such as drug use. The detective wrote in his report that he took written statements from all of them.

The detective's report continued with other routine activities until he attended the autopsy the following day. The pathologist recovered a nominal .38 caliber slug from the victim's skull and noted tattooing around the entrance wound. Sean knew that tattooing—unburnt gunpowder particles embedded in the skin, indicated the gun's barrel was close to the victim's body when fired, probably within a few feet. The distance could vary depending on the caliber and type of cartridge. A nominal .38 caliber projectile could mean any bullet with a diameter that size, including a .38 Special, .357 Magnum, 9mm, or .380. Sean hoped there would be a lab ballistics report that would tell him more about the bullet. Sean made a note on a legal pad to check on the ballistics report and another note to have the cigarette butts resubmitted to the crime lab. With advances in DNA technology every few years, trace amounts of DNA could be found on items today that were not visible in the past.

No other injuries were found on the body. That told Sean there was probably no struggle between the victim and assailant before the fatal shot.

Sean was preparing to read the next part of the detective's report, which detailed the Jefferson brothers' arrest and connection to Theresa Goldberg's murder when his phone buzzed. He looked at the screen—a local number he didn't recognize. "Hello."

"Mister Tanner, this is Sergeant Nash, the detective whose murder investigation you're sticking your nose into."

32

Charlie tried to maintain her professionalism, but she was sick and tired of other people running her investigation—first Billy bringing in Sean, then Captain Cannon forcing the premature arrest of Ken Russo, and now Sean running around and finding witnesses to send to the station.

"I tried to call you," Sean said.

"Well, I'm in the middle of a murder investigation, so excuse me for not waiting at my desk for your phone call."

"We asked the men to call first and not just show up," Sean said.

"Well, they didn't."

"I thought you'd want to—'"

"What I want is for people to pass information to me so I can decide the appropriate action, not run my investigation and drag me along trying to catch up."

"I tried but—"

"You now have my cell phone number, so you've got no excuse for not calling before playing detective on your own."

"I'm sorry but—"

Charlie pressed the red hang-up icon on her cell phone and dropped it on her desk. She threw her half-eaten sandwich in the trash and picked up the list of residents Sea Island security had given them. With Ken ruled out as the suspect, they were back to square one. Jay and Sherm were going through the list of business and service people with access to the plantation, and Darryl was handling the tip hotline and random calls that came into the detective division.

Darryl timidly approached her desk, obviously a bit apprehensive after overhearing her telephonic ass chewing of Tanner.

"One of the phone tips might've panned out," he said. "A caller said he was riding his bicycle around the Riverside neighborhood Monday morning and saw a truck with an *Island Screen Porches* logo stop at the house next to the Russos'. The driver, a Hispanic man dressed in khaki pants and white long-sleeved tee, got out and jogged to the back of the house."

"What time was that?"

"He said around seven-thirty or so."

"Did he see the man do anything else?"

"No, he just kept riding," Darryl said. "And he couldn't provide any further description."

She pulled her marked up map of the neighborhood from a folder and pointed at the house to the right of the Russos' house.

"That's the one he indicated," Darryl said. "Dorothy and Ed Farmer. There was no answer there when we canvassed Monday morning."

"Well, let's go knock at the door again," she said.

Twenty minutes later, after ringing the doorbell and walking around the house, Charlie and Darryl returned to her car. She started the engine and cranked up the AC. Darryl flipped through the resident directory and found a mobile number for the Farmers.

Dorothy Farmer answered, and after introducing herself, Charlie said, "A company called Island Screen Porches was at your house Monday morning. Can you tell me what they were doing there?"

"Are you the detective investigating what happened to Nancy?"

"Yes, ma'am. About the screen porch company?"

"I haven't stopped crying since I heard about it. Do you know when the service will occur?"

"No, ma'am. We're just the ones responsible for finding out what happened."

"Nancy was just the nicest person. I can't imagine why anyone would do such a thing. I heard there might be a serial rapist running around on Spartina Island."

"From whom did you hear that?"

"You know—just talk."

"About the screen porch company?"

"Oh, yeah, I'm sorry about jabbering on," Dorothy said. "We're in Ohio visiting the kids and grandkids for the summer. I called them to repair the screen on our back porch after a tree branch punctured it during a windstorm last week."

"You were out of town when this happened?"

"We've been away since the beginning of July. A neighbor waters our plants when we're away and she noticed it and called me up here, so I called the company. They did the repair last Friday according to my neighbor."

"Do you have any idea why they came back Monday morning?"

"No idea," Dorothy said.

"What's the name of the neighbor who waters your plants?"

"Beth Laughlin," she said and rattled off Beth's phone number.

When Charlie hung up, Darryl said, "Beth and George Laughlin live at number five Blue Heron, about ten houses down from the Russos. I talked to them on Monday. She was home all morning, and George was the fella out fishing with your California ex-cop friend."

"Friend, my ass," Charlie mumbled. She called Beth Laughlin, who confirmed she had called Dorothy about the damage to the screened porch and checked on the repair after they finished the work on Friday. She had no idea why the company returned Monday.

Charlie found a number for the screen porch company on the web and called. A man said one of the company's three crews spent an hour at the Farmer's house on Friday, but he showed no service calls on Monday at that location. He gave Charlie the location where that crew was currently working.

Charlie drove across the bridge from the island with Darryl riding shotgun and continued west on Spartina Island Road. With the island constrained by water on every side, Dufftown and the unincorporated area surrounding it had seen a building boom in the past few years. Huge swaths of land were being razed, and housing developments, business parks, and shopping plazas were popping up everywhere. She sighed as she remembered the rural nature of the area where she had grown up.

A few miles past the turnoff to Old Town, the original one-square-mile Dufftown, Charlie turned right on a road that took them north for a mile. In front of them were two bulldozers and an excavator working a huge field of reddish-brown dirt. Two dozen finished houses already had well-established lawns with two tiny saplings planted in each front yard. A few cars were parked in driveways, and a small boy pedaled a tricycle on a sidewalk under the watchful eye of a young woman. Beyond the completed homes were twenty more at various stages of construction.

Charlie spotted a white crew-cab pickup with the Island Screen Porches logo on its side parked in front of a house under construction. She pulled in behind it. Men were on the roof laying shingles, others were fitting pieces of PVC pipe together in what would become the irrigation system for a front yard, and one man was carrying a roll of nylon screen from the truck around to the back.

"Excuse me," Charlie said. "I'm with the sheriff's office."

"No Habla," He pointed in the direction he was walking. "Foreman."

A brown-skinned man climbed down from a ladder as Charlie and Darryl approached. "We're with the sheriff's office," Charlie said as she swept her jacket back to show her badge. "Are you the foreman of the screen porch workers?"

"Yeah. Did my guys piss in front of the residents again instead of using the porta-john?"

Charlie shook her head. "I was wondering if you fixed a torn screen on Friday over in Sea Island Plantation."

"Yeah. We screened the porch a few years back and a tree branch fell on it. We replaced a panel. Last job of the day. Took maybe twenty minutes."

"Did you return Monday?"

The foreman shook his head in frustration. "We showed up at this job site Monday at seven all set to start, and one of my guys says he left his cordless drill at our last job on Friday. So I give him the truck and tell him to go get it and get his ass back here and get to work."

"We'd like to talk with him," Darryl said as he eyed the two Hispanic workers.

"He doesn't work here anymore."

"No?" Charlie asked.

"After he gets back with his drill, we're working on one of the new houses, and he swings a ladder around and busts a big window. I had to tell the boss and he fired him on the spot. Two strikes and you're out."

"What's his name?"

"Armando Cabrera."

"Do you have a date of birth and address on him?"

"No, the owner has all that stuff."

Charlie jotted down the name and direct number for the company owner and she and Darryl returned to their car.

Once the air conditioning was blowing, Charlie called the owner. She introduced herself and said, "I need the full name, date of birth, and home address for a former employee. Armando Cabrera."

"Sergeant, we comply with all state and federal laws on hiring and check their documentation carefully before we hire anyone."

"Sir, we have absolutely no interest in his immigration status or your hiring practice. I just need to identify and locate him for an investigation I'm conducting."

"Hang on a second."

A moment later he came back on the line and gave Charlie Cabrera's information. She had Darryl call the station for a record check on Cabrera as she drove toward his address. She tried not to get her hopes up, but it was hard not to when you discover a man just happened to be in the vicinity of the murder at the time it occurred. Of course, he may be uninvolved in the crime, in which case he might've seen something.

Charlie drove through the historic old town of Dufftown. Tourists strolled the streets past antique stores, over-priced boutiques, and trendy restaurants that had taken over many of the old historic houses. Charlie grew up in this area and had seen enormous change over the years.

"Hang on a minute," Darryl said to his phone and turned to Charlie. "Cabrera was arrested for sexual battery last year. He grabbed a woman's breasts and tried to force himself on her."

"Have them pull the detective's report and find out what the final disposition was. I'd like to know why he's not in prison."

Darryl nodded and continued his conversation with the records clerk as Charlie got on the radio and requested a uniform to meet them at Cabrera's address.

33

Sean stared at his phone. Frank muted the TV and turned toward him. "Sounds like that went well."

"Sergeant Nash," Sean said.

"She's a spitfire, but a damn good detective," Frank said. "You don't want to get on her wrong side, that's for sure. She forgets her Southern manners real fast if someone gets between her and solving a case."

Sean told him about Billy requesting his help at the scene of Nancy Russo's murder.

"I can see where she'd feel threatened. The detectives down here are already over supervised. The sheriff's office only has two general investigation teams of one sergeant and three detectives each. The sergeants are working sergeants, so I won't count them fully as bosses. Then there's a three-man gang and narcotics squad and a juvenile investigator, which makes twelve workers. And they have two lieutenants and one captain over them. That's two command brass too many."

Sean agreed. In Oakland, a captain commanded their CID with eighty investigators, and lieutenants had units with upwards of thirty investigators and sergeants.

"I didn't realize you lived right across from that murder," Frank said. "It's hard not to get involved."

"I'm not trying to, but I hear and see things I feel I need to pass along."

"Don't worry about Charlie. If she doesn't like you, she just ignores you. So from the way she's treating you, she must think you're okay."

"I read all through the cold case," Sean said, changing the subject. "All but the robbery investigation because I don't want to jump to the same conclusion as everyone else that those suspects are good for the murder."

"What do you think?"

"There's not much there."

"Back in those days, detectives down here wrote a formal report to document the crime in the first week or so after the incident. After that, they recorded their investigative activity in notebooks. If they solved the case and arrested someone, they typed up a formal investigative report for the prosecutor from their notes. Since there was no arrest, the case file would've mostly contained pages of handwritten notes. All of which was lost in that flood."

"I wonder if the detectives who worked it could remember anything," Sean said. "Maybe some hunches or feelings about the husband or witnesses or that they thought the killing was over."

"They only had two detectives back then. Both of them were in their fifties and died years ago."

"What about requesting lab work to examine evidence with new science that wasn't around back then?"

"I don't know why there's nothing documenting it, but detectives submitted the two cigarette butts for DNA analysis a while back. One matched the victim. The other one had no hits in CODIS. We should probably have them run it again. Maybe the profile will hit with a recent addition to the DNA registry."

"And the slug the pathologist dug out of the victim?"

"SLED should still have it. I already made a note to have it reexamined."

"I'd like to talk to the husband and those friends," Sean said. "Something about a woman walking alone to a bar a mile or more away doesn't sound right. My gut tells me something else was going on."

"Like what? You think she was out scoring drugs? You know, back then marijuana was still treated like a hard drug in South Carolina."

"Could be," Sean said.

"We've set up phone interviews with old witnesses before. The cold case team and an active detective did conference calls with witnesses."

"That sounds cumbersome," Sean said. "What about crime scene photos?"

Frank reached in his briefcase and pulled out a stack of photographs. "SLED still had the negatives, so they made copies for us."

"I'd like to scan them and see if I can maybe enhance them."

"You can do that?"

"It's not rocket science. I have a good scanner and printer, and my wife had bought an advanced Photoshop program when she joined the photography club down here."

Frank handed him the photos. "Knock yourself out."

"I'd also like to make a copy of the murder book and set up my own case file."

"We're not supposed to copy reports according to Captain Cannon."

"Can I borrow it for a day or so to go over it again?"

Frank gave him a crooked grin. "Sure, just don't let the captain know there's another copy floating around. I didn't see you take much of any notes while you were reading."

"I have a pretty good memory," Sean said.

"Really?"

Sean nodded.

Frank pulled a legal pad filled with notes from his briefcase. "Who found the victim?"

"Jerry Larson and Dana Whittle," Sean replied.

"Where did they live?"

"Jerry was at 182 South Harbor Road. Dana lived on Cotton Lane, but there was no house number, only a post office box listed as the mailing address."

"Impressive," Frank said. "A photographic memory?"

"Just good recall," Sean said, pleased that he passed Frank's test. "So, what are your thoughts?"

Frank stretched his bad leg and rose from the chair. "I'd like to continue with the direction the original detectives were heading. They thought the Jeffersons were good for it, so we should pursue that. I can get presentence reports and prison records on those two, from which I can create a criminal profile. This might be the work of a serial killer. I can profile the crime and contact my buddies at the FBI to check for similarities with unsolved murders and see if the profile I work up on the Jeffersons matches anything on file."

Sean didn't have much faith in profiling as a means to solve a murder. In his experience, most criminal profiles were done after the fact, when the suspect was already identified through old-school detective work. "I guess it couldn't hurt."

"What would you recommend?"

"Start from scratch, especially since we're missing much of the original investigation. Do background on the victim. Find out who she really was. Do the same with her friends. Maybe one of them was into something that could've led to Theresa's death. Motive might point us toward the killer."

"What would be your first step?" Frank asked.

"Just like with every murder, I'd go to the crime scene."

34

As Charlie approached the address, she spotted a marked sheriff's patrol SUV parked alongside the road under a canopy of trees. A stocky deputy with short, spiky blonde hair sat behind the wheel with the door open and one booted foot propped up on the doorsill. Jane May exited the car and approached Charlie's car as she pulled in behind her.

Charlie got out of her car and gave Jane a hug. She had gotten to know Jane when Jane was struggling to make probation as a rookie deputy four years ago. Even though Jane had passed the weaponless tactics portion of the academy, she failed several times to subdue resisting suspects on the street. Not willing to let another female wash out without a fight, Charlie offered to help. She listened to Jane complaining about how the department was picking on her because she was a woman, then told her bluntly, "Your sergeant and fellow deputies are picking on you because they see you as a liability. The bad guys could care less about your gender, and they're not going to give you an inch because you're a woman. Male or female, if you lose a fight on the street, you might lose your life. And no deputy in the department, male or female, wants to get themselves killed protecting you."

Jane had surely been given a similar talk by men in the academy and at the sheriff's office, but when Charlie said it, she didn't argue and agreed to follow her suggestions. Charlie took Jane to the CrossFit gym that had toughened her when she was considering a law enforcement career years earlier. Over several months, Jane got into amazing physical condition through the CrossFit program and the gym's martial arts classes. It also gave her an aura of confidence that conveyed Deputy Jane May would kick the ass of any suspect who wanted to fight her. With her new attitude and skills, she passed probation and became the deputy others wanted to work with.

"Hey, girlfriend, I missed you up in the mountains this summer," Jane said.

Charlie's family had a cabin in the North Carolina mountains that they normally frequented to escape the summer heat, and she often ran into Jane, who rented a place nearby in Flat Rock for a few weeks every summer. "It's Spencer's last summer before college, and he wanted to spend it here with his friends."

Jane rested her right elbow on the butt of her duty pistol. "What brings you to my beat?"

Charlie filled her in on Armando Cabrera, and Jane entered his information into her car's mobile data terminal, or MDT. "Twenty-five years old, five-nine, one-ninety, brown and brown," Jane said. "Shows the same address you have for him."

Charlie and Darryl leaned into Jane's car and looked at the DMV photo on the computer screen.

"How you wanna handle this?" Jane asked.

"Right now, we just want to talk to him. Maybe take him downtown for an interview. But the sexual assault history raises my hackles because our victim might've been raped." Charlie pictured Cabrera lurking in the backyard next to the Russos' house Monday morning, watching Nancy through the window, finding the back door unlocked, and entering. "Even though we don't have enough to arrest him, he could be involved in the murder, so don't let your guard down. I guess you and I should go to the front door and Darryl can take the back in case he rabbits."

They followed Jane's marked unit to an old apartment complex consisting of three single-story cinder block buildings arranged in a U-shape around an asphalt parking lot. Each building had eight units, and Cabrera's apartment was on the far right side of the rear building.

They parked and Darryl jogged around the back. Charlie and Jane walked past two toddlers in diapers splashing in an inflatable wading pool next to a swing set surrounded by dirt and weeds. A Hispanic woman in her early twenties watched the two deputies warily as they approached Cabrera's front door.

Suddenly, Charlie heard a crash from around the back, followed by Darryl yelling, "Stop! Sheriff's office!"

Charlie sprinted around the building with Jane on her heels. As they rounded the corner, Darryl was getting up from the ground and starting to chase Cabrera, who now had a twenty-yard head start on him.

Charlie took off across the weed and litter-strewn lot that surrounded the complex. At the corner of the last building, Charlie overtook Darryl, who had fallen even farther behind Cabrera. She heard Darryl wheezing as she passed him.

Cabrera turned into a stand of hundred-foot-tall southern pines and weaved through the widely spaced tree trunks. Cabrera was pumping his arms as he ran, and she could see his hands were empty of weapons. He wore jeans, sneakers, and a white sleeveless undershirt, termed a wifebeater on the streets. His long brown hair flowed behind him.

Charlie glanced over her shoulder to see Jane nearly matching her pace, about ten steps behind her, and Darryl slowing to a labored jog fifty yards back. She yelled, "Sheriff's office! Stop," even though she knew it was futile.

Cabrera came out of the trees onto a dirt road, crossed it, and ran toward a ramshackle wood house with a sagging roof. He stumbled for a second in some high weeds then continued running. Charlie began pacing herself, taking deep breaths and falling into a rhythm of long, easy strides. She felt her skin begin pricking with sweat. She hoped her physical conditioning would win out over the adrenalin that was probably fueling Cabrera.

Cabrera looked over his shoulder and cut right, heading diagonally across the front of the shack and toward another house in the distance. Charlie cut the angle and continued her pursuit. Cabrera slowed and looked over his shoulder again. He was running out of steam.

He suddenly stopped and turned. Charlie didn't slow. Cabrera shuffled right and left, like a punt returner trying to evade a tackle, but Charlie continued directly at him. At the last second, Cabrera twisted to the left, as if he were going to start running again. But he was too slow, and Charlie was on him.

She grabbed his shoulders and pulled. They both fell to the ground. Cabrera got up, but Charlie grabbed one of his legs. Cabrera was still struggling to break free from Charlie's grasp when Jane hit him with her shoulder like a linebacker. Cabrera's body smacked the ground with a thud, and Jane tumbled past him and rolled.

Charlie grabbed one of his wrists, jammed a knee between his shoulders, and torqued his arm behind his back. Jane yanked his other arm behind his back and cuffed him.

35

Sean had locked the back door and grabbed two bottles of water from the refrigerator by the time Frank hobbled down the stairs from his office. "You're driving," Frank said.

Sean wasn't about to argue, even though he didn't like the way Frank said it. Having spent a lifetime in military and paramilitary organizations, Sean was accustomed to taking orders from superiors. But they were both retired and volunteers, and Frank sure as hell wasn't his boss. Sean raised the garage door, opened the door to his Corvette, and started to slide in when Frank said, "If I could somehow get into that thing, there's no way I could get out."

Sean nodded toward the Highlander. "Would this be better?"

"Unless you wanna drive my car."

Sean looked at the old Ford Taurus with its sun-faded gray exterior parked in his driveway. "No, we'll take the SUV."

Frank set his briefcase in the backseat and climbed into the passenger seat. "You snazzy California cops must all be on the take. Able to afford a mansion on the marsh and a fancy sports car in retirement."

Sean was about to explain that his retirement was based on his police salary, which might seem exorbitant to cops in the rest of the country, but with the high cost of living in the Bay Area, it was all relative. Then he noticed the twinkle in Frank's eyes.

"Just busting your balls, kid," Frank said. "By the way, the wife and I also have a brand-new Buick SUV, but I been driving this old thing for twenty years and know where all the buttons are."

"With a pension from NYPD, the DA's Office, and the state police, I didn't think you had to do your grocery shopping at the food bank."

"You forgot the social security checks the wife and I get every month." Frank buckled his seat belt and grinned. "Do you follow baseball?"

Sean shook his head, but that didn't stop Frank from talking about the Yankees nonstop during the fifteen-minute drive across the island. He pulled his SUV into the parking lot and waited as Frank exited the passenger side with his cane.

South Harbor had continued to grow in the twenty-five years since Sean had first visited the island on vacation. It now encompassed the largest marina on Spartina Island, with more than a hundred slips, some able to accommodate yachts as long as a hundred feet. Located two miles upriver from the open waters of the Atlantic Ocean, it was also the oldest harbor on the island. Prior to the Civil War, Sea Island cotton was loaded onto ships in this harbor, and supplies were offloaded for those who lived and worked on the island.

Once the first bridge to the island was constructed forty years ago, the harbor reinvented itself as a recreational boat marina. Barges were no longer needed to transport vehicles, construction materials, and supplies to the island, and the ferries that shuttled people back and forth to the mainland ceased operation overnight. Most of the fishing and shrimping boats remained, and soon the slips were filled with recreational powerboats and sailboats owned by the wealthy visitors who began making the island their vacation spot.

Sean walked toward the large building that faced the parking lot. It was still called the Harbor General Store, but like much of the island, it had morphed with the times. Today, it contained beach and resort wear, touristy knickknacks, and an upscale grocery area, where visitors could stock up on everything they'd need for a weeklong stay at one of the nearby rentals. Past the general store and overlooking the water, the Harbor Inn and

Restaurant offered four-star accommodations and some of the best—and most expensive—seafood on the island. The harbor village sat on the far side of the marina and housed an assortment of shops and smaller restaurants catering to the tourists.

Sean stepped out of the blazing sun onto the covered porch and pulled the stack of photos from his pocket. "This must be where the payphone was that the teenagers called from," he said to Frank.

Frank studied the photo and nodded his agreement. "Can't tell for sure from this, but I'll bet the bar where everyone was listening to music was where the harbor restaurant now sits."

"If it becomes necessary, we can probably find old photos and maps of the harbor at the library or historical society." Sean and Frank walked along the water's edge toward the boat launch. Seagulls and terns skimmed over the water, occasionally screaming as they flew by. A brown pelican sat perched on a wood piling jutting from the water. They passed fishing boats with signs offering charters and dolphin-watching cruises. Two large sailing yachts big enough for people to live aboard were tied up to a dock that extended into the tidal river.

They walked through a parking lot filled with pickups and boat trailers. They were both sweating by the time they reached the concrete boat ramp that extended into the water. Sean thumbed through the photos again. He continued past the boat launch to a small park with a nicely kept grassy area and several picnic tables under the shade of ancient live oak trees.

Frank wasted no time sitting down at a picnic table. Sean spread the photos in front of him. Frank studied the photos and looked around for several minutes. "This little park didn't exist back then," he finally said. "Although the reports described the scene as the public boat launch, the victim was actually located over there." Frank pointed to a spot near an old live oak where a picnic table now sat.

Sean looked at the photos and walked to the location Frank indicated. "I think you're right. People apparently hung out and partied here long before it was designated as a park." Sean studied a live oak tree with a massive branch bigger in diameter than his torso that grew horizontally from the trunk a few feet above the ground. He returned to the table and thumbed through the photos until he found the one he was looking for. A blue bicycle leaned against the horizontal branch in the photo.

"Whose bike?" Sean asked.

"Good question," Frank replied. "It's less than thirty yards from where the victim was found, but there's no mention of it in any reports. The detective's report said our victim walked to the store to get cigarettes. Maybe she rode a bike."

"Or maybe the killer did," Sean said.

36

Charlie and Jay entered the interview room. Cabrera had pulled a chair into the corner and sat there rubbing his knee, which had an oozing abrasion visible through his torn jeans. Jay said something to him in Spanish and Cabrera slid his chair to the table and sat down. After another short conversation, Jay said, "It's just a skinned knee from when you tackled him, and he said he doesn't need medical attention."

Charlie nodded.

Jay and Cabrera conversed back and forth in Spanish for a minute, until Jay finally said, "Bullshit!"

Cabrera raised his hands, palms up, and said, "Okay, I speak English."

"He thought that if he pretended he didn't speak English, we would just let him go as cops sometimes do."

Charlie grinned. "I guess he wasn't expecting you."

Charlie took over the interview and asked him the standard background questions. Cabrera came to the US as a teenager and had actually attended Dufftown High School for a few years before quitting and getting his GED. He'd worked at various unskilled jobs, mostly for landscapers and contractors, and had been with the screen porch company for three months before they let him go.

"Right now, you're under arrest for resisting law enforcement officers by running from us," she said. "We just wanted to talk to you, but you made the decision to make this into something bigger."

"I thought you were immigration or something."

"Are you undocumented?" Jay asked.

"I'm a Dreamer and I have a work permit and all other DACA paperwork."

"Then why run?" Jay asked.

Cabrera shrugged.

Charlie read him his rights, which he waived. "Let's talk about the screened porch you repaired in Sea Island Plantation on Blue Heron Lane."

"That was last Friday," he said. "What about it?"

"Why'd you go back Monday?"

Cabrera took a deep breath and sighed. "When we were packing up on Friday, Jose—that's our crew boss—was yelling to hurry up, that we were cutting into his Miller time. So we threw the stuff in the truck and left. But when we got to work Monday, I realized I left my drill there."

"And you went back and got it?" she asked.

"Jose gave me the keys to the truck."

"How long were you there?"

"Just a minute. It was right where I left it next to the barbeque grill on the patio."

"Did you go next door? Maybe peek in a window?"

"Hell no! Is that what this is about—you think I'm a peeping tom?"

"Just answer the question," Charlie said.

"I grabbed my drill, got back in the truck, and drove back to the job site."

"You didn't make any other stops?"

"When I started working there, Jose laid out the rules. We can't use the truck for any unauthorized business, can't speed, and have to be on time everywhere we go. The company has GPSs in the trucks and the owner can monitor where we are at any given second."

Charlie and Jay exchanged looks. Charlie returned to her desk and called the owner. While he was accessing the truck's GPS information, she looked over at Darryl, sitting at his desk and typing on his computer with two fingers. His face was streaked with dirt and sweat. His tie was undone, and his white shirt was covered with reddish brown dirt. "Why don't you go down to the locker room and get cleaned up?"

He nodded and limped out of the office. She knew he'd be sore tomorrow. His short sprint was probably the most exercise he'd had in months. But she was sure that it was his ego that was more bruised than his body.

The owner came back on the phone and rattled off locations and times, which she copied into her steno pad. The truck left the job site at 7:11 a.m., traveled directly to 23 Blue Heron Lane with no stops other than typically expected for traffic signals. It arrived there at 7:29, departed two minutes later, and returned directly to the job site.

She thanked him and hung up, then pulled up the arrest report on Cabrera's sexual battery on her computer. It said pretty much what Darryl had told her. She clicked to the investigator's report and skimmed down the screen until she came to the detective's follow-up interview with the victim. The victim said she had never wanted to make the complaint, but her boyfriend insisted. She was at a party and flirting with Cabrera to make her boyfriend jealous. When her boyfriend accused her of trying to seduce Cabrera, she told him that Cabrera grabbed her breast and was coming on to her. Her boyfriend called the police, and she went along with the story because she didn't want to admit she was the instigator.

Back in the interview room, Charlie said to Cabrera, "Everything you said checked out. Did you see anyone around the house or the one next door when you were there Monday?"

"I just grabbed my drill and left."

"How about anyone in the back yards?"

He shook his head again.

"Did you hear any yelling or screaming?" she asked. "Any raised voices?"

"That's where that murder happened that was in the news?"

"That's why it's important if you saw anything at all," she said.

"If I did, I'd tell you."

"If you think of anything or hear anything, call me." She handed him her card. "If we let you go, can you get yourself home?"

"You're not sending me to jail?"

"We'll talk with the solicitor about this, and if he decides to file charges, they'll send a notice in the mail. Don't ignore it, or else deputies will come out and arrest you again."

"I'll show up in court if I get the notice. But no matter what, don't come out with that other lady cop. I'd hate to admit I got my ass kicked twice by a couple of girls."

37

Sean scraped stir-fried chicken breast, string beans, and rotini from a skillet onto a plate and set it on his kitchen counter with a large glass of milk. While eating, he opened an old map of Spartina Island. With a yellow highlighter and red pen, he marked various locations: South Harbor, the villas where the Goldbergs had stayed, the Jeffersons' address, and the few stores, bars, and restaurants that he knew existed back then.

After he and Frank had finished examining the original crime scene, Sean wanted to drive to the villas and retrace the route Theresa would've taken that night to the harbor. But Frank nixed that idea, saying that doing so was a waste of time. Frank returned home to begin his profiling work, and Sean went upstairs to his office. He scanned the photos and documents from the murder book and printed copies of the reports to set up his own case file. He started an activity log on a yellow legal pad to document everything he did. If he was going to work a murder case, he intended to do it right.

Once he finished eating, he loaded the dishwasher and called Stretch. "What're you doing right now?"

"Headed out to dinner with my lovely bride in a few minutes," Stretch said. "What's up?"

Sean told him about his trip to the cold case murder scene with Frank and Frank saying that following up at the condos where the victim was staying was unnecessary.

"You think you'll learn something there?"

"You never know if you don't knock on some doors and ask some questions," Sean said.

"My wife would be pissed if I cancelled on her. Why don't you call Feebee?"

Sean thanked him and pulled the team roster that he'd been given at the meeting from his notebook. At the top of the page, it read, *Mudflats Murder Club*. He found Feebee's number and called.

"Hey, Feebee, this is Sean Tanner, are you busy?"

"Just sitting here watching some stupid TV show with my husband."

He told her about visiting the crime scene with Frank and calling Stretch, who suggested he call her.

"I'm game, but that place, like most on the beach, has a security guard, and since we don't carry badges anymore, they won't just let us in to wander around."

"You don't mind a short walk on the beach, do you?"

"I like the way you think," she said. "I'll meet you there."

Sean tucked the murder case packet under his arm and headed to the door. "Annie, you wanna go for a ride?" She bounced up from her dog bed and ran after him. He opened the hatch of the SUV and she leaped into the back.

Twenty minutes later, Sean and Feebee were walking along the wet, hard-packed sand of Island Beach, and Annie was running through the water, chasing seagulls and other shorebirds. The town permitted dogs off leash after five o'clock as long as they were under voice control, and Annie always—well almost always—ran back to his side when he called. She leaped through the water and over the small breakers until she could no longer touch the bottom. She swam out for a minute or so, and finally circled back toward shore. All he could see was the top of her head, her nose just above the water. Her otter-like tail trailed behind, acting like a rudder as she paddled toward him. When her feet touched sand, she ran toward him, stopping by his side to shake a gallon of water onto him.

"Thanks for the shower, girl," he said as a sunburned couple with three small children paused their beach stroll to laugh. The sun was low in the sky and the beach was mostly deserted.

"When we first moved here," Feebee said, "my husband and I came to the beach all the time."

"When Lauren was alive, we'd come out here a lot too, watch the sunset and let Annie frolic in the water."

"How'd she die?"

"Cancer. It was quick."

"I'm sorry."

Sean nodded, glad Feebee had not said anything more. He didn't need to hear anyone else talk about their own losses, or how time would heal his grief. He recalled his strolls on the beach with Lauren where they reminisced about being there years earlier while their two children played in the sand and shallow waters. And now, those memories of him and Lauren recalling memories of their children were his most cherished memories. They continued along the shore until they came to the Island Beach and Racquet Resort.

The complex wasn't much of a resort by modern standards, but when it was built forty years ago, luxury hotels were only being envisioned by developers. The wood-sided two-story building faced perpendicular to the ocean, which gave all units a slice of ocean view from their tiny balconies or patios. Even though it only occupied two hundred feet of oceanfront, the complex would've been replaced by luxury condos years ago had each unit not been individually owned.

Sean snapped on Annie's leash, slipped on his sandals, and walked up the weathered boardwalk to the pool area of the complex. Although the driveway coming in from the main road had a security guard to keep out unauthorized people, resorts didn't control access from the beach. With Annie at heel, they skirted around the pool, where a dozen small kids splashed while their parents sipped drinks in nearby lounge chairs.

"What's your plan?" Feebee asked.

"Don't really have one. We look like a couple vacationing down here with our dog, so I figured I'd just act that part."

"So we're retired law enforcement with no police powers, pretending we're working undercover as a husband and wife to gather information on a cold case that we're not really supposed to be doing active investigative tasks on."

Sean looked at her. "When you put it that way..."

"As long as we don't impersonate police officers, I've got no problem with it," Feebee said. "Besides, I was the work wife to many of my male partners over the years."

"You mean working undercover as a husband and wife team?"

"No, I mean acting like their wife at work. Telling them to clean up after themselves in the break room and nagging them about the way they drove and them bullshitting about sports when they should've been working."

Sean chuckled and climbed the exterior stairs and opened the door to the second-floor hallway. They made their way across well-worn carpeting to unit 210 and knocked. A woman wearing shorts and a pink scoop-neck tee shirt with a bright yellow palm tree on the front opened the door. "Nice dog," she said and patted Annie on the head. "She's all wet."

"She loves the water," Sean said. "I'm sorry to bother you, but we were wondering if you have the name of the owner of this unit?"

"We go through a vacation rental company. Hang on a minute." She left the doorway and returned a moment later with a pamphlet. "This company manages half the villas in the complex. They're all pretty much alike."

Sean had rolled his eyes when he first vacationed here and heard people refer to a small condo as a villa. He had always pictured a villa as a huge estate in Italy or Spain, but he eventually accepted it as another real estate marketing term in the Lowcountry. "All one-bedrooms?"

"Sort of..."

Sean sensed hesitancy in her voice. He would've felt the same if two strangers showed up at his door asking questions, but he was glad to have Feebee with him. Her presence probably made them appear less threatening. Still, he was accustomed to flashing a badge as an introduction. "I'm sorry," Sean said, making up a lie on the fly. "This must seem weird, but an old friend of ours rented this unit thirty years ago with his girlfriend at the time. They got married, raised kids, and are finally able to take a vacation alone again. He wants to surprise her by bringing her back here. I imagine they've changed a lot in that time."

The woman laughed. "I doubt it. The décor and furniture look at least that old to me."

Sean pulled out his phone and flashed his best disarming smile. "I don't want to intrude, but would it be possible for you to maybe snap a photo for my buddy?"

"My husband will be back in a minute, but come on in."

Sean ordered Annie to sit and stay. He dropped the leash, and he and Feebee followed the woman inside. "Your dog's okay there?"

"She won't move until I return," Sean said.

Inside the door to the right was a small bedroom, barely large enough for the single dresser and the king bed pushed against the opposite wall. Built into an alcove on the left side of the hallway were two bunk beds. Beyond the bedroom was a small bathroom. The hall ended at the main room, consisting of an efficiency kitchen, large enough to make a quick meal, but not much more. Next to the kitchen was a round dining table with four chairs, and beyond that was a sofa and two upholstered chairs facing a TV mounted on the wall. Beach scene framed photographs and painting reproductions adorned the walls, and a sliding glass door opened to a balcony with two plastic chairs and a table.

"It's not much," she said. "But it's the cheapest place on the beach with a kitchen and a bed for our son."

Sean snapped a few photos with his phone. "Reminds me of where we stayed with our kids when we first visited the island."

Feebee gave her best work-wife smile. "Yes, very similar, honey."

Sean pictured three men sitting in the living room years ago drinking beer and watching a baseball game on an old-style picture-tube TV, and a wife slipping from the bedroom through the front door unnoticed.

Sean thanked the woman and continued down the hallway with Annie. He counted the doors—twenty on each side of the hall, forty per floor, eighty total in the building. They went down the stairs on the other side of the building and into a parking lot.

"It was nice to get a feel for what the rentals looked like," Feebee said. "Not sure it tells us anything though."

"You never know when some tiny piece of information will end up being the missing piece of the puzzle." Beyond the parking lot were four asphalt-surfaced tennis courts and a small children's playground. They walked past them and down the driveway, which led to a guard shack, where a sixty-something man in a gray uniform sat. Just outside the guard shack was a bicycle rack with twenty light blue beach bikes with fat tires and *Island Beach & Tennis Resort* stenciled on their frames.

"Can any of the guests use the bikes?" Sean asked the guard.

"Just need to see your guest ID." The guard pulled out a clipboard. "When you bring it back, I check you off the list."

Playing along like they were guests, Sean asked, "What if someone doesn't bring it back?"

"We notify the rental company you went through. They charge you five hundred for the lost bike."

"But they're marked with your name, so you must get them back," Feebee said.

The guard grinned. "The locals know there's a hundred-dollar finder's fee for lost bikes they return."

Pretty good scheme, Sean thought, the resort gets the bike back and a four-hundred-dollar profit. "Has the resort always had bikes for guests to use?"

"I've been working here part-time for twenty years. At least that long."

Sean and Feebee turned right on the road and headed back to the parking lot where they left their cars. He now knew where the bicycle in the old crime scene photo came from. But he didn't know if the victim rode it there, or if the killer did and was also staying at the beach resort. They passed by several old motels, which, like the Island Beach and Racquet Resort, hadn't changed much in thirty years. Between the motels stood monstrous beach houses and modern condos. On the other side of the road were larger complexes that catered to the lucrative tourist market.

They stopped at Feebee's car. "Thanks for getting me out of the house tonight," she said.

"I'm glad you were available."

"I think you're gonna be a great addition to the Mudflats Murder Club."

"We'll see," he said. "I haven't agreed to anything beyond this case."

"We'll talk tomorrow," she said, as she pulled her door shut and drove off.

Sean wasn't ready to go home and sit in his house alone. He walked back toward the beach and a few minutes later, he grabbed a table on the outside deck of the Sandy Feet Bar. Annie lay beside his chair. Although now part of the Sand Dune Inn, the Sandy Feet Bar and Grill was originally the only place to get a meal and a drink on the beach side of the island. Back then, it was surrounded by a dozen beach cottages and a few rustic motels, but it took a ferry from the mainland and a shuttle along a dirt road to get there.

A server brought him a beer and a bowl of water for Annie. A golden retriever eyed Annie from the other side of the outdoor bar, but Annie ignored him. Half the tables and barstools were empty, but Sean knew the place would soon be packed once those inside the inn's restaurant finished their meals and the band started playing outside. Until then, he'd enjoy the sound of the surf and the soft breeze.

He called his daughter. "How'd your doctor's appointment go?" he asked.

"Everything's fine," Rachel said. "It was just a routine visit. What are you doing?"

"Having a beer with Annie at Sandy Feet Bar."

"Is she old enough to drink?" Rachel giggled. "Any single ladies there?"

"I hadn't noticed."

"Just sit there and look handsome. They'll come to you."

"I doubt it. My chick magnet went swimming and smells like wet dog."

"What else have you been up to?"

He told her about the cold case team and the bare basics of the thirty-eight-year-old murder.

"It's wonderful that you've found something meaningful to do..."

"But?"

"Well, you know how you can get obsessed with a case."

"Not to worry," he said, taking a swallow of beer. "It's just a hobby. A bunch of old guys like me lending our experience and trying to bring closure to some families."

"You're not old, Dad."

"Thanks, honey. Love you."

A few minutes later, Sean drained his beer and put a five-dollar bill under the glass. "Come on Annie, time to go home."

38

After Charlie escorted Cabrera out of the station, she pulled Darryl into an interview room and gave him a royal ass chewing. "Had you fully reviewed the report about Cabrera's sexual assault, we might've realized he wasn't a sexual predator. And therefore was likely nothing more than a possible witness to the murder. And maybe we might've approached him differently. And avoided the foot chase and wrestling match."

Darryl cleared his throat, but before he could get a word out, Charlie said, "I don't want to hear it." She looked at her watch. The only positive resulting from this fiasco was she could still make it to the going-away-to-college party she was supposed to be hosting with her ex-husband for Spencer and his friends. "I want you to write the report," she said to Darryl, "documenting every single action we took from the moment you received the phone tip about the screen porch company until Cabrera left the station."

Darryl hung his head. "Yes, ma'am."

"And I want it sitting in my in-box before you go home." She pivoted and stormed out the door before Darryl could plead for a tomorrow deadline.

She was still pissed during her drive home, maybe a bit at herself for hoping Cabrera was the killer so they could wrap up the investigation. She left her car in the driveway and jogged up the stairs to her bedroom. She peeled off her filthy suit, pinned up her hair, and showered off the sweat and grime from the day. She slipped into a colorful sundress and a pair of wedge sandals, knowing Roger would be there and hated it when she stood taller than him. She inspected herself in the mirror, and then added a sexy plunge bra. She needed all the help she could get in the cleavage department, and all the better if other parents looked at her and thought Roger was an idiot for having ever cheated on her.

A half hour later, she stepped into a banquet room at the Sand Dune Inn on Spartina Island. The room quieted and the eyes of twenty parents and ten soon-to-be college students looked her way. She smiled and glided across the room to her table.

Charlie made the rounds and thanked the other parents for coming then took her glass of wine to the back of the room and looked out at the ocean. Although the waiters had already brought out the dinners by the time she had arrived, she still had to endure an hour of boring small talk punctuated by Roger pontificating about his take on the world. Once everyone finished eating, she had waited for a pause in the conversation so she could leave the table without appearing too rude.

Before long, Charlie's mother came her way with her after-dinner drink in hand, oblivious to the hint she wanted to be alone. "I don't know why you let him get to you like that," Abigail said.

"Who? You mean that pompous ass ex-husband of mine?" Roger was in his element surrounded by other equally pompous parents of Spencer's friends. This was supposed to be the dinner that they hosted for Spencer and his friends. It was supposed to be about them. But Roger made it about himself as usual, how successful he was, how big his boat was, how low his golf handicap was, and how big his new girlfriend's boobs were. She was all of thirty, closer to Spencer's age than Roger's. And her boobs weren't even her own. Charlie remembered her as a twenty-two-year-old paralegal when she started work at Roger's law firm. Now, with a two-cup-size breast enhancement, collagen lips that looked permanently ready to kiss everything in sight, and sharing a bed with the senior partner, she probably thought she was at the pinnacle of her life.

"Do I sense jealousy that Roger's moved on and found someone who makes him happy?"

"Right, Mom. I sure regret I couldn't be that adoring Southern belle who bats her glued-on eyelashes every time Roger passes gas."

"It wouldn't hurt you to be a little nicer to men."

"And embrace the role of a proper southern lady—look pretty, smell nice, and please her man?"

"Those were your aunt's words, not mine." Abigail took a sip of her Martini. "You look very nice this evening, especially considering you had no time to get ready."

She ignored the comment about having no time to get ready, obviously another dig about her having a job with an unpredictable schedule. But her mother was right. She did look damn good—especially for a mother of a college-age son. And she had to admit it felt great to notice the eyes of the men in the room follow her as she worked the room.

Abigail circulated back to the group of parents near the bar of the restaurant's private room, and Charlie glanced at the kids laughing and joking around a table near the door. She knew better than to intrude and put a damper on their conversations, but she also had no desire to join the cluster of parents by the bar, where most of the men were talking about their careers as lawyers, doctors, and CPAs, and the women about redecorating their house for the umpteenth time or their latest charity fundraising event. If she joined them, they'd ask about the recent murder. Not that people really wanted to hear the gritty details. They just wanted a glimpse of a detective's life, sort of like visitors sticking their toes into the ocean in December, wanting to get a taste of the icy water, but scared to take the plunge.

Cindy, Madison's mother, came her way cupping a drink in an old-fashioned glass. "I wanted to thank you for hosting this dinner and inviting us," Cindy said.

Charlie had known Cindy since high school. She was part of the clique that had teased Charlie for being the tallest and skinniest girl in their class. Beanpole, Twiggy, and Giraffe were some of their nicknames, as she was the only freshman girl who still had boy hips and a flat chest. Until then, it had never bothered her. She was a tomboy as a kid, more comfortable playing sports and hanging out at the river with the boys than doing boring girl stuff. Her mother tried to influence her, constantly telling her, "Put on some decent clothes and paint your toenails," but then her father would offer to take her crabbing or hunting.

"I hope we'll still see each other now that our kids aren't around to provide the excuse," Charlie said.

"Maybe at the club," Cindy said. "If I spent more time in the exercise rooms there and less in the dining room and lying by the pool, I might see you."

By the time they all started having kids in their twenties, Cindy and her friends had put on weight, especially around their middles, and warned that Charlie, too, would lose her figure when she had Spencer. But thanks to great genes, a high metabolism, and her running and gym routine, Charlie was back to wearing her old clothes before Spencer's first birthday and still wore the same size today.

After chatting about her current diet, the shoes she wore, and her planned Christmas vacation in London, Cindy wandered back to the group of parents. All the other parents seemed so comfortable in social settings, but Charlie felt like an outsider.

She wished she were on the other side of the glass, on the sand-covered deck of the Sandy Feet Bar. Not worrying that she was going to trip in her heels or slip out of her push-up bra if she bent over. Through the window, she saw a large man rise from a table outside. Dressed in cargo shorts, leather sandals, and a loose-fitting polo shirt over a broad chest, he weaved his way through the crowd with a dog at his side. Sean Tanner. Her heart skipped a beat. She wanted to push open the door that led to the deck and say hi. Apologize for treating him like a jerk on the phone this morning. Tell him about the shitty day she had, knowing that he'd understand.

"Charlie," a voice said behind her. She turned to see the dermatologist dad of one of Spencer's classmates.

"Why don't you join us?" he said. "We're talking about the crime wave that recently hit the island."

39

THURSDAY

The digital clock in Charlie's unmarked sedan read 5:45 as she parked at the end of Blue Heron Lane's cul-de-sac and turned off the engine. She grabbed her Surefire flashlight and notebook and exited the car. The neighborhood was quiet in the early morning except for the hum of an air conditioner across the street. Newspapers lay on every other driveway. A lawn sprinkler came on down the street. She walked past the Russos' house. It was dark inside, the same as the previous two houses she had passed. A light was visible through the front window of the Farmers' house next door. Probably a lamp left on to make the house appear occupied.

She continued up the street, noting two houses with lights on inside. They weren't very bright, probably nightlights, she figured. Crossing the street, she trudged back the way she had come. A light came on in 20 Blue Heron. She jotted the time, 5:53, and address in her notebook. Probably the kitchen light. Although that house was across the street from the Russos' house and three doors down, they might be early risers. They might've seen something Monday morning.

Charlie made the loop around the cul-de-sac and headed down the street again. At six o'clock, a light appeared at 24 Blue Heron, glowing through the blind-covered window at the left side of the house, the side opposite the garage. She'd been inside enough of these houses to know that was probably where the master suite was located. The bedrooms were normally at the back of the house and the master bathroom or large closet at the front. She copied the details in her notebook and remembered that was Sean's house.

A few minutes later, she noticed a light shining through the front window. With the home's open layout, the light could be coming from the living room, dining room, or kitchen area. She imagined Sean brewing coffee and maybe fixing breakfast in the kitchen.

She continued down the road, noting lights as they came on. She planned to review the statements taken during the canvass when she returned to the office to get a better idea of the morning habits of the residents. Through follow-up interviews, maybe one of the early risers would recall having seen or heard something Monday morning.

She heard a door open down the street behind her, followed by a man's voice. "Fetch the paper."

She turned to see Sean silhouetted in his doorway and his dog bounding down the driveway. The dog stopped at the newspaper and looked directly at her with its ears back. The tail stopped wagging. Charlie froze in the darkness, feeling like a voyeur.

"Come on, girl, fetch the paper," Sean said. "There's nothing out there, let's go."

The dog gave one final look her way, grabbed the paper in its mouth, and ran back to the house. Charlie looked at her watch, jotted a notation in her notebook, and made another loop to the end of the street and back.

The sky began to lighten about six-thirty. She'd recorded four houses on the street with signs of activity so far. A woman dressed in slippers and bathrobe two houses from the intersection with Egret Way had come out to get her paper. Probably too far from the Russos' house to have seen anything, but Charlie would still add her to the list of people to be re-interviewed. As Charlie was walking back toward the cul-de-sac, she spotted Sean walking her way with his dog.

Sean stopped ten feet away. The dog immediately sat by his left leg. "Returning to the scene at the same time of day," he said. "Good practice."

"What's your dog's name?"

"Annie." Her ears perked up at the sound of her name.

"Can I pet her?"

"Annie, go say hi to Charlie." He dropped the leash and Annie bounded over to Charlie, her tail wagging so hard her butt shook from side to side. She rubbed her head against Charlie's leg as Charlie scratched her behind the ears.

"Didn't picture you as a dog person," he said.

"We had Boykin Spaniels growing up. Sammy then Lucy. My dad got them for bird hunting, but they were mostly family pets. My mother hated the dog hair in the house, so after Lucy passed, we only had cats." She brushed the hair off her black pants. "I paid attention to your message about people walking on the back side of the houses. Thought I'd take a look myself."

"We were just going for a walk. I'll show you the way if you'd like."

She followed Sean and Annie to the end of the cul-de-sac, down a walkway that led to the River lodge, through the parking lot, and along a golf cart path that passed through a stand of pine trees. A wood stork stood at the edge of a man-made pond that extended along the back of the putting green, looking into the water for its breakfast to appear. Charlie spotted an alligator's nostrils and eyes just above the surface of the water near the shore. Especially in the early morning light, people sometimes mistake them for a floating log, but Charlie could tell by the size of its head, that alligator was at least eight feet long.

Although real estate marketers called the fabricated ponds lagoons, they were part of an intricate flood control system land developers like her father installed to collect runoff from tropical storms that could dump a foot or more of rain in a few hours. The lagoons also made developments such as Sea Island Plantation special. They doubled as water hazards on the golf courses, created water views for many of the houses that backed onto them, and instilled a tropical atmosphere to the area.

"I was taken by surprise when all those AA men showed up," she said as they walked. "But I'd never want to see an innocent man sit in jail."

"I've had to release a few people I'd arrested myself over the years."

"We should've never arrested Mr. Russo in the first place."

"Oh?"

"Political pressure."

"I've been there," he said.

"Nevertheless, it wasn't right for me to have taken it out on you." She wanted to say she was sorry—she was wrong—but if you admit you were wrong in the macho world of policing, people will remember it forever. "It's just that everyone wants a quick arrest, and they don't want this to be the work of a serial rapist killer."

"No matter what the brass and politicians want, a murder is what it is. But this wasn't the work of a serial rapist."

"How can you be sure?"

"You were at the scene. Did it feel that way to you?"

She nodded, understanding he was telling her to trust her instincts. They walked in silence for a while and she felt like she needed to say something to fill the void, but Sean didn't seem like the type for idle chitchat. She often found it easy to pinpoint a person's dominant emotion. Some were generally happy, others angry, some content. Sean's dominant emotion seemed to be sadness. She noticed he limped slightly on his left leg. She wanted to ask about it, but figured it was an old injury from the job. Most cops wanted to forget the scars their profession left them with once they retired. If that was his only injury, he was probably lucky to have survived thirty years in Oakland with nothing worse.

"I'm sorry about your wife."

He glanced at her and nodded.

"Billy told me," she said.

He stopped and, once again, Annie sat. "This is the Russo's house."

Beyond the cart path was a stand of pine trees about fifty feet wide that bordered a decent-sized backyard. She recognized the house.

"It's against the community rules to walk on the course unless you're golfing," Sean said. "But if people do it early in the morning or in the evening when no golfers are out, no one normally cares."

She looked across the fairway to the houses on the other side. "If residents across the way look out their back, they could see people coming and going over here."

"That was my thought. Some of the older people living here have too much time on their hands. They'll watch a birdfeeder for hours. Some have a sitting room in the front of the house and watch people coming and going on the street. When we first moved here, an older lady mentioned to my wife that I had worn the same light blue shirt when walking Annie three days in a row."

Charlie laughed. "And your wife was embarrassed that people thought you never changed your clothes."

Sean nodded. "The point is there are people in a retirement community who know everything happening."

"I just need them to talk to us."

"You might have to drink a lot of tea and listen to stories about grandchildren and doctor visits, but if you're patient, knock on the right doors, you might learn something useful."

She told him about the notes she'd taken of residents' morning routines.

"Smart detective work."

She didn't need his approval, but it still felt nice coming from someone with his experience.

"I've been doing some work on the cold case," Sean said.

After she left the presentation, she'd put that old case out of her mind. With the fresh homicide to deal with, a cold case was nothing but a distraction.

"Not much to go on, was there?"

"I visited the old crime scene and the villa where the victim stayed. I'd like to do some more background on the victim and those she vacationed here with."

"We normally get more involved with the cold case team when we assign a case, but to be honest, I've got more important things on my plate."

"I totally understand. I just don't want to step on your toes again."

"As long as you're doing background, I don't see a problem. If you interview people who might end up being a witness in court, a defense attorney will destroy us at trial for allowing civilian volunteers to conduct a criminal investigation. That is if it's ever solved, which we both know is doubtful."

"Understood," he said as they began walking back. "And I'm sorry about your divorce."

She gave him her best *what-the-fuck* look.

He grinned. "Billy told me."

"Did he also say my ex is the biggest asshole lawyer in the county?"

"I don't know what it's like in your department, but I was an anomaly at OPD for being married only once, especially considering all the years I worked homicide."

"We divorced before I came on, but even if we hadn't, there's no way his ego would've allowed him to be married to a deputy. There aren't many decent men down here who want to be in a relationship with a female law enforcement officer. The South is not as progressive as California, and most men feel threatened by a woman who carries a gun for a living. I tried dating within the profession, but that didn't work either, especially in a small department where you'll eventually end up working alongside someone you dated."

She glanced his way and noticed he was listening intently as they walked. She felt embarrassed for venting her dating frustrations on someone she hardly knew.

"I can only imagine how tough it is."

They walked back to the lodge parking lot in silence. "That path will take you to your car." He pointed toward the cul-de-sac. "Annie needs to do another half hour, so we're going the other way."

"Thanks for being my guide. And for...you know...listening," she said. "You have my cell number if you turn up anything else."

40

After Sean finished walking Annie, he changed clothes and ran the mile and a half to the fitness center, where he did a weight workout followed by a yoga class. If he had told his brother cops in Oakland that he was doing yoga, he would've been laughed out of the police station. But after his failed physical exam, his family doctor sent him to a physical therapist for his back and neck aches. Among other things, she recommended yoga.

Sean discovered yoga was a lot tougher than he had imagined, but it did wonders for his ailments and helped dissolve the stress that had built up inside him over the years. After a while, he began staying for the optional ten-minute meditation, the first time in his life he had ever tried quieting his mind for that long. Yoga, meditation, and the other life changes he'd made since retirement slowly began restoring his health. A year after his failed pre-employment physical for the DA's office, his blood pressure and cholesterol had returned to normal levels, and his weight was back to 220 pounds. That was the same that he weighed when he was on the SWAT team in his twenties and probably in the best physical condition of his life.

Sean jogged the mile and a half back home in the ninety-degree heat, showered, and sat down at his desk. He labeled file folders with the names of people connected to the cold case: Theresa Goldberg, Aaron Goldberg, Tim and Lizzy Early, and Steve and Sandra Nowak. Since most of the paperwork had been lost in the flood, he didn't even have the personal information—birthdates, addresses, and phone numbers—of the people connected to the case, so Sean started from scratch.

If he were still at OPD, he'd tap into the department's automated records and could find any police contacts on them, even as insignificant as being a witness to a house burglary five years ago. He'd then run them in state DMV, which would reveal their current and recent addresses, moving violations, and cars registered to them. He'd run them in the county criminal history system, which would show arrests going back fifty years. He could expand the search to state level and the FBI, which would show arrests and convictions anywhere in the country.

When Sean started with OPD, law enforcement had the most comprehensive computerized records on people, but as the internet matured, he had found there was a wealth of information available to the public. He started with Aaron Goldberg and continued until he had searched each name on various websites. He then filled each folder with pages of printouts and notes.

His phone buzzed with a text from Feebee: *Check your email.*

He clicked on the icon and saw three from her. The first one included a link to a shared document and instructions on how to access it. The next one, sent an hour later, included the same link with a message indicating there were changes to the document. Sean clicked on the link, which brought up a running chronology, beginning with a detailed summary of the cold case written by Frank. This was followed by another entry by Frank detailing their trip to South Harbor yesterday and his observations and theories. Feebee made an entry documenting their visit to the victim's vacation rental last night and stated she was beginning to do backgrounds on the Goldbergs, Earlys, and Nowaks. Doc Henderson wrote that he'd made several phone calls to request a copy of the autopsy report and was waiting for callbacks.

The last email said Frank Martin called a team meeting for today at noon at Bubba's Shrimp Shack. Sean's watch showed 11:40. He stuffed all his paperwork into his case packet and rushed downstairs. He slipped on his well-worn boat shoes, patted Annie on the head while promising he'd be home long before dinnertime, and grabbed a baseball cap on his way to his car.

At the stop light outside the main gate, Sean lowered the convertible top of his Corvette. When the light turned green, he made a left turn and sped across the bridge, heading toward Dufftown. The midday sun was hot, but as long as he was moving, the heat was bearable, and the wind on his face felt wonderful. A sailboat trailing the northerly wind passed under the bridge, and Sean saw four people on the deck waving to a pair of jet skiers that were overtaking it.

A mile past the road to Old Town Dufftown, Sean made a right turn on Kelly's Landing Road. He recalled driving this road for the first time early one evening when he and Lauren first moved here and excitedly explored the area. They had traveled through a few miles of forest, passing an occasional house lining the road and several dirt roads leading into thick woods. Then the forest ended into what looked like miles of grassland that reminded them of the savannahs they saw in movies taking place in Africa. They had expected to see a giraffe stick its head out of the grasses or a herd of zebras thundering across the grassland. As they'd continued driving, they realized they were passing through a huge salt marsh at low tide, and the vegetation was miles of spartina and other grasses common to the Lowcountry wetlands.

A broad tidal river soon appeared through the windshield of Sean's Corvette. A rusty shrimp boat was docked alongside some smaller fishing and pleasure boats on a pier that jutted into the river. He pulled into a dirt parking lot, put the top up on his car, and walked up the wooden stairs to the restaurant. Weathered board construction contributed to the rustic appearance of the building. During his first visit here, Lauren had asked the owner if he was Bubba. The sixty-something man with a shaved head and weathered face gave a big belly laugh and said he and all his staff were Bubba, as were all of his regular customers. He then whispered that his real name was William, and he'd spent his life captaining a shrimp boat. After seeing the movie *Forrest Gump*, he'd decided to open the shrimp shack restaurant and name it after Forrest's friend in the movie who had wanted to buy a shrimp boat after he returned from Vietnam.

William was behind the counter when Sean opened the door. He grinned and said, "Hey, Bubba."

"Hey to you too, Bubba," Sean replied.

The inside of the restaurant was small, just six tables inside, but the outside deck held eight picnic tables that could fit ten people each. Sean saw around thirty people but no one he recognized.

"Looking for the Mudflats Murder Club?"

"Yeah."

"Outside," William pointed toward the door leading to the kitchen. "Employee break area."

Sean passed the restroom and entered the compact kitchen. A man was lowering baskets into a large deep fryer, while a woman was laying pieces of fish onto a grill. They didn't even look up as he passed. Sean pushed through the door to a smaller deck that hung over the water and was hidden from the customers' outdoor deck by a plywood wall.

Stretch, Frank, Feebee, and Beagle sat on plastic chairs around several tables that had been pushed together. Frank looked at his watch and said, "Glad you could make it."

"I just saw the email about the meeting."

"Sorry, Sean," Stretch said. "I should've told you that it's customary to get together a few days after a cold case team meeting. I guess you figured out the document sharing system."

It would've been nice if Frank had told him about this instead of droning on about baseball yesterday, Sean thought. "Yeah, I'll get the hang of it."

A plump woman wearing shorts, a Bubba's Shrimp Shack tee shirt, and an apron came through the door from the kitchen. "You must be the FNG," she said. "What'll ya have to drink?"

He saw beers in front of Feebee, Frank, and Stretch, while Beagle was nursing a tall glass of something with ice. "How about iced tea?"

"Sweet tea?"

"Unsweet, please."

"Must be a northerner, huh?"

"From California," he said. "My name's Sean."

"Sean, huh? They'll give you another name once they get to know you." She pointed at the name tag on her chest. "I'm Bubbette."

"Of course you are," Sean said.

"Away from the shrimp shack, I go by Gwen. My husband's with the sheriff's office, so if you try to pull any shenanigans on me, be forewarned, I've already seen it."

Sean smiled. He liked her.

"Okay, then, the police special today is the shrimp basket or the fresh fish of the day, which is grouper."

Three of them ordered the shrimp basket, and Frank ordered the grouper. "How's the grouper come?" Sean asked.

Bubbette rolled her eyes. "Fried, in a basket with hushpuppies and fries. But I could do it grilled if you insist."

"I'd preferred grilled."

She winked at the other four then said, "And I'll bet you'd like coleslaw instead of fries."

"I would."

"Damn Northerners." She winked. "And I'll bring three more beers."

Once she left, Feebee set up a laptop at the end of the table, and Doc Henderson's face appeared on the screen. "Nice seeing everyone," he said. "Where's Irish John?"

"Had a doctor's appointment." Frank pulled out a steno pad and said, "I'm still going to look into the two mutts the original detectives focused on, but what Sean said makes sense. We should investigate the case all over again. From the beginning. Assume the initial investigation got it all wrong. You want to add anything, Sean?"

Sean was shocked to hear Frank agreeing with him. "It would be one thing if we had detailed reports, taped recorded statements from all witnesses, and the kind of thorough crime scene investigation that we'd expect today," Sean said. "But policing wasn't done that way forty years ago, and much of the documentation is missing. Most of it we won't be able to recover. Witnesses have died and the memories of those still around will have faded over time. But sometimes, people's loyalties and morality change as they age. Not that this is necessarily drug related, but if it were, people often leave the game as they get older and get good jobs and raise families. Maybe someone felt it necessary to lie to protect a friend back then, but later, they realize justice is a higher value."

"I started trying to locate the surviving members of the three couples who had come here on vacation," Feebee said. "I searched the old phone number listed for the Goldbergs on the crime report. It came back to another name with an address in New Jersey. I called the number, and the woman who answered the phone said she had had that phone number for twenty years and never heard of the Goldbergs."

"I spent a few hours searching each name—Goldberg, Nowak, and Early." Sean pulled the file folders from his case packet. I found several Aaron Goldbergs in New Jersey. One of the names showed a man about the right age with an address in Short Hills. It was near where they had lived thirty-eight years ago. I googled Short Hills, and found it was an affluent community about ten miles west of Newark. If I were a betting man, I'd bet this is the Aaron Goldberg who was married to our victim."

Bubbette appeared with their food, and the conversation turned to talk of who had the worst landscaping crew, why the main pool in Sea Island Plantation remained closed for two days after a resident's three-year-old grandson pooped in it, and whether politicians in New Jersey were more corrupt than those in Chicago.

Once they finished eating, Sean said, "I'd like to call the number I found for Aaron Goldberg."

41

"We can't do that." Frank said.

Sean set his glass of iced tea down. "Why not?"

"First of all, because Captain Clinton said phone interviews are outside our authority. Secondly, what if the case is solved and goes to trial and something he says becomes direct evidence, or worse yet, he blurts out that he killed her?"

"First of all, Clinton made that rule because he wants to control everything we do so he can take credit if we solve it," Feebee said. "The Bureau is probably the strictest agency around on rules and regulations, but we allow our analysts, who aren't sworn law enforcement, to make phone calls to people all the time."

Sean was distracted by a small boat motoring up the river. It drifted into the dock and tied up, and a middle-aged couple got out and walked toward the shrimp shack.

"What if he all of a sudden confesses?" Frank said.

All heads turned to Beagle. He was silent for a moment. When he spoke, it was slow and measured. "It wouldn't be the ideal confession, but as long as we don't commit a crime ourselves, such as impersonating a law enforcement officer, I'd have no problem getting it admitted in court, if I were the prosecutor. Would any of you be reluctant to testify in court if it came to that?"

Everyone shook their heads.

"I ran into Sergeant Nash this morning when she was recanvassing my neighborhood over the murder of Nancy Russo," Sean said. "She said she was too busy with that murder to worry about this cold case right now."

"That leaves us with the fear of pissing off Clinton," Stretch said. "I've got no problem with that. How about you guys?"

Everyone but Frank shook their heads. "I don't like it," Frank said. "We've never done this on our own."

"You're the lead investigator on this case," Feebee said. "So, technically, you make the decisions."

"Even if we all disagree with you," Stretch added.

"It's against my better judgement," Frank said. "But okay."

Feebee drained her beer. "It was Sean's idea, so he should get the honor."

Sean put his phone on speaker and dialed the number, while Feebee set her phone beside it and started the record app.

A male voice answered with a hesitant, "Hello."

"My name's Sean Tanner. I'm working with the Campbell County's cold case team and looking into the murder of Theresa Goldberg," Sean said. "May I ask who I'm speaking with?"

"Who's this?"

"Sean Tanner. I'm trying to locate Aaron Goldberg."

"That was a long time ago. Do you have new information?"

"Is this Aaron Goldberg, the former husband of Theresa?"

"Yeah. You the police?"

Sean ignored his question since he didn't want to misrepresent himself nor admit he was nothing more than a civilian volunteer. "Mr. Goldberg, we've reopened the investigation and I'm contacting everyone listed in the case file to see if we missed anything back then." Sean hated cold calls such as this when he worked homicide. People were justifiably suspicious, and he often ended up answering more questions than he asked. And now, not being a real detective, he hated being evasive about his identity.

"I heard you arrested two African American men back then but had to let them go."

"There was insufficient evidence to show they killed Theresa, so we're looking into other areas. I'm wondering if you could tell me about that day when Theresa left the villa and was later found by the boat ramp."

"What about it?"

"I understand you, Tim Early, and Steve Nowak were watching a baseball game on TV in your unit. Is that right?"

"Yeah."

"You remember what time the game was?"

"I don't know. Probably started around seven or eight."

"And what time did Theresa leave?"

"I don't remember. The game had been on a while. She was doing something in the kitchen and said she was going out for cigarettes."

"Did everyone stay until the end of the game?"

"Sure. The other guys went back to their villas a few doors down from ours and I went to bed."

"Did you wonder where Theresa was? Why she wasn't back yet?"

"Look, detective, we were young and partiers back then. We'd been drinking all day around the pool and on the beach and then while watching the game. The girls were doing the same. They weren't interested in baseball, so they did their own thing. For all I knew at that time, Theresa was with one of the other girls, or she stopped at a bar to listen to music, or whatever."

"Okay. So at what point did you worry about her and call the police to report her missing?"

"I have no idea who killed Theresa or why. If I knew, I would've told your detectives back then."

"When she wasn't in the bedroom when you went to bed, did you check with the other ladies to see if she was there?"

"I don't like what you're insinuating."

"I'm not insinuating anything," Sean said. "I'm just trying to create a timeline of Theresa's activities that day."

"That was the worst day of my life. It took me years to get over losing my wife. But I eventually did so by putting it behind me. Now you want to dredge it up again. It's over and done with."

"Mr. Goldberg..." Sean looked at his phone and saw the call had been ended. Goldberg had hung up on him.

"That sure went well," Frank said.

Back at his desk in his home office, Sean spent the next half hour typing his activity over the last day into the shared document. He had never worked a homicide case as a team, where it was incumbent upon everyone to keep the others up to date to avoid a duplication of effort or conflicting actions. Back at Oakland, he'd take notes of his activities during the investigation. When there was a lull in the investigation, sometimes days later, he'd sit at his computer and update his investigative follow-up. The only person he needed to coordinate with was his partner. His lieutenant was busy managing a dozen investigators, so investigators didn't bother him with anything but major developments.

Sean looked at the vacation rental pamphlet the woman had given him last night and called the number on the front. The company gave him the name and number of the owner of the unit where the Goldbergs had stayed years ago. Sean called him. The man lived in New York and said he bought the unit as an investment when the complex was first built forty years ago. For years, he rented it out to people he knew and through word of mouth. He finally went with a property management company twenty years ago.

"Sure, I remember the death," he said. "It's not every day one of your guests is murdered. It was the second year the Goldbergs rented my unit. They came down with some other couples from New Jersey who rented other units in the building."

"Do you remember the names of the other couples they vacationed with?" Sean asked.

"The Nowaks vacationed with them at times."

"Any other names you can remember?"

"I can't remember what I had for lunch yesterday."

Sean chuckled. "You wouldn't happen to have any records from back then, would you?"

"That would've been with my tax records, which I purge after seven years."

"Did Mr. Goldberg rent from you again?"

"I never heard from him, but the Nowaks began renting my villa during that same week every year. Their friends probably rented other units in the building."

"Every year? For how long?"

"Jeez, fifteen, twenty years maybe. I heard they eventually moved down there. Into that active adult community."

"Sea Island Plantation?"

"Yeah, that's it."

After Sean ended the call, he brought the Sea Island Plantation online directory up on his computer. He found the Nowaks lived in one of the newer houses near the activities center.

He typed what he had discovered into the team shared document and called Frank and told him what he uncovered.

"Sean, we can't go out and interview people face-to-face as members of the cold case team. We're not cops anymore."

"Talking to people on the phone is okay, but not in person?"

"It sounds more like you're conducting telephone interviews rather than gathering background. That's a gray area, but a physical interview of a potential witness is definitely crossing the line."

"We both know a physical interview is a hundred times more effective than a phone conversation, so why should we call people when we can visit them?"

"Sean, you're doing great work. Write up everything you've done and your recommendations for follow-up. I'll pass it on and let the sheriff's detectives run with it."

If Sean had been holding a heavy desk phone receiver instead of his cell phone, he would've slammed it down.

42

Sean got up from his desk and stretched his back. He went downstairs and pulled a diet Coke from the refrigerator. His phone buzzed with a text: *Hi Dad. How R U? Hear you're working murders again.*

Like many kids these days, Carson thought texting qualified as conversation. He'd text every week or so to try to initiate a back-and-forth messaging process that seldom revealed anything. Sean glanced at the clock: 3:42. Back in California, Carson was probably on his lunch break. He called.

"What's new, Dad?"

"I guess you've been talking to your sister."

"Yeah, she says some lady was killed across the street from you and you're investigating a cold case and you're taking Annie out to bars to pick up girls."

"Yup, all of that, plus playing golf and fishing."

"You're living the dream. No matter what Rachel thinks, I think it's cool for you to be working again. You were too good a detective to not use your skills."

"I appreciate your support, but I'm just a volunteer on the cold case team, not a working cop anymore."

"About the picking up girls thing…"

"That's Rachel urging me to start dating, not me actually doing it."

"Okay..."

Sean knew Carson was still not over his mother's death, and probably thought his dad should mourn for at least ten years before he even spoke to another woman. "What about you?"

"With girls? I have some friends I do stuff with, but nothing serious with any particular one."

"How's work treating you?" Carson had moved from Spartina Island to Mountain View, California, and taken a job at Intuit two weeks after Lauren died.

"Really well. Looks like I might be made a team leader for a new project next month."

"That's fantastic. Big raise?"

"Things are so friggin expensive here. If I get the position, I'll have enough to rent a decent place of my own and get out of this animal house I'm in."

Even though Intuit paid well, the most Carson could afford when he moved to the Silicon Valley area was a room in a four-bedroom house with three other guys, whom he described as a cross between nerds and frat boys. "You know if you need anything—"

"Dad, I appreciate it, but Rachel and I both want you to spend your money on yourself. We are both fine. I gotta go. Love you."

Sean put his phone away and looked down at Annie. "Guess that means I've got more money to spend on your dog biscuits." She looked up at him and wagged her tail.

Back at his desk, he saw an email from the cold case team with the subject line *Here's a recent change*. He clicked the link, which brought up the shared investigation chronology. Irish John had written a long entry saying he went online to the county property tax website, located the address for the Island Beach and Racquet Resort, and attached a list of the property owners. It showed the addresses of the property owners where the county mailed the tax bills, mostly in New York, Connecticut, and New Jersey.

John wrote that they needed to trace ownership back thirty-eight years to discover who else was staying there at the time, and suggested they could mail a form letter to the owners requesting they call the sheriff's office. He also said he'd try to visit the county offices to see if their deed records showed property ownership history going back that far. He acknowledged that although either route would be a time-consuming process, if some of the old owners had names of their renters back then, they might come up with a witness or two who knew something. Sean had worked cold cases at OPD when he was injured and remembered how laborious and time-consuming it was to locate witnesses after so much time had elapsed.

Sean sent a group email to the team. *Great work, John. Excellent plan to visit the county offices.*

He opened the folder he had created on Tim Early. The White Pages printout showed a 67-year-old man with a previous address in Short Hills, New Jersey, the same place Aaron Goldberg lived, and a current address on New York City's Upper Eastside. He googled Tim Early and got pages of hits on a man who managed a medium-sized Wall Street investment fund. Sean knew he'd never get through the corporate gatekeepers by phone. If he were still working, he'd call NYPD homicide, where someone would know the security director at the investment firm—probably retired NYPD or FBI—who could connect him with Early. Sean figured that Frank would know someone at NYPD that could help, but he didn't want to talk to him and hear another reason they should not pursue this lead.

He had a hunch that Early might've become an investor in the villas, so he clicked the link Irish had embedded in the shared document for the county tax records. It didn't show him owning any property at the Island Beach and Racquet Resort, but instead listed him as the owner of property appraised at six million dollars on MacCrain Island. He entered the address on a real estate website and found the house sat on five acres of beachfront property in the exclusive Marta Point development.

A few months after Sean had moved to Spartina Island, he and Lauren took the public ferry to MacCrain Island, rented bicycles, and toured the 2000-acre island. A tidal creek and low-lying marsh separated the island from the mainland, so the only way to get there was by boat. Many of the island's two hundred full-time residents lived around the harbor on MacCrain Creek, where hundreds of visitors disembarked from the public ferry every day to enjoy the beaches and quaint isolation of the island. Sean remembered the striking contrasts aboard the ferry, the super wealthy residents of Marta Point carrying shopping bags from Spartina Island boutiques sitting alongside day laborers and workers lugging cases of equipment and boxes of groceries and supplies.

He located Irish's phone number on the Mudflats Murder Club's roster and called. "This must be Sean Tanner," Irish said.

"How'd you know?"

"Cell phone with a California area code," Irish said. "We detectives call that a clue."

"You're doing some great research on your computer. You feel like getting out of the office and talking to some people?"

"Hell yeah."

Sean grabbed his sunglasses, slipped on his sandals, and took the fifteen-minute drive to South Harbor. He spotted Irish parked in a Toyota Camry nose out in the back of the parking lot. Sean's sunglasses immediately fogged over as he exited his air-conditioned Corvette and shook Irish's hand. He was around five foot eight and heavy set, like he enjoyed eating more than exercising. He put a New England Patriots hat on his bald head.

"You called me instead of Frank to join you?" Irish said.

"I didn't want to hear more of why I shouldn't step foot out of my home office."

"You got balls for the murder club rookie. But don't be too hard on Frank. He and I were the two original members who worked out our procedures with Cannon. It was a heated discussion, and it's still a work in progress. Personally, I'm pleased to see youngsters like you with new ideas. What's your game plan?"

"Just look around, talk to some people, and see what we can learn about Tim Early." They made their way to the ferry ticket counter in the muggy heat. The clerk at the general store doubled as the ferry ticket agent. She told them residents and regular workers on MacCrain Island typically bought a monthly pass, allowing them to use the ferry whenever they wanted, while other people usually bought a round-trip ticket for twenty dollars, or just handed the boat's first mate a ten-dollar bill when boarding each way.

If he had a badge to flash, Sean would've asked the woman to check her credit card receipts to see if Tim Early had recently bought a ticket or monthly pass. Instead, he bought a cold diet soda for himself and a regular Coke for Irish and wandered around the marina. A few people lounged on their boats, but he and Irish were the only ones walking around in the mid-afternoon heat. "How long have you been down here?" Sean asked.

"Fifteen years. Best decision we ever made."

Sean hadn't recognized the address Irish listed on the team roster. "I noticed you don't live in Sea Island Plantation like a lot of the guys."

"We lived in an older house a few blocks from the beach for years," Irish said. "But my wife had some back issues, which several surgeries couldn't fix."

"Sorry to hear that."

Irish waved his hand. "One of those things life can throw at you. When the doctors told us she'd never walk again, we moved into a continuing care facility. We have a small independent living apartment where there's help to get her into her wheelchair and stuff."

Sean wondered if that was what was awaiting him—independent living, assisted living, nursing home, then death. Although a continuing care facility seemed like just a few steps from death, he would've been willing to go to any lengths to still be with Lauren. "I lost my wife last year."

"I heard. Despite her physical limitations, I'm grateful we're still able to be together. She's not bedridden or anything, and she insists I get out and do things and don't just hang around with her all day."

They spotted a man with unkempt gray hair and skin the color and texture of leather sitting on a beach chair outside a shack next to two gas pumps. "You work here?" Sean asked.

"I guess you can call it that." The man looked to be in his seventies, but his eyes had the sparkle of a kid on his first trip to Disney World.

"Are you the harbor master?" Sean asked.

He laughed. "Heck no, the harbor master's the boss and mostly sits inside where it's air conditioned. I'm what they call a dockhand. I pump gas or diesel into people's boats, help them tie off when they come in, and sit on the dock enjoying the water the rest of the time."

"Sounds like a tough job," Irish said.

The man took a swig from a can of generic cola. "Ten years ago, I sailed down the coast on vacation. I stopped here one night, and the harbormaster offered me a job working four days a week for minimum wage and a slip for my boat. Went home, retired, sold my apartment, and been living the dream ever since. Where you from?"

"I live here now, but I'm from California." Sean sensed the dockhand could talk about the weather for hours if given the opportunity. "I'm trying to locate a man who has a place in Marta Point. Wondering if he might have a boat here."

"You a PI or something?"

"We're retired cops," Sean said, "doing volunteer work with the sheriff's cold case team."

"The man got a name?"

Sean stepped into the narrow slice of shade next to the dock shack. "Tim Early."

"He visits occasionally. Doesn't own a boat, but he came in two days ago. Said he's staying for a week."

"You talked to him?"

"Lots of the folks that own the big houses don't want the hassle of the ferry. Me and some other fellas make extra money running a sort of taxi service. I wasn't working at the dock that day, so I ran him out to the Marta Point private marina myself. Couple hours before, I saw Marybeth buying groceries and getting on the ferry. She lives on the island and does housekeeping for the rich folk like Mr. Early in Marta Point. My guess—she was stocking his place for his visit."

"Would you happen to have a local phone number for Mr. Early?" Irish asked.

"Better than that. I have his cell number."

A few minutes later, Sean was back in his air-conditioned car with a yellow pad propped on the steering wheel. Irish sat in the passenger seat beside him. "You know Frank would not approve of this?" Irish said.

"Yeah," Sean said and dialed the number the dockhand gave him.

"This is Tim."

"Mr. Early, my name is Sean Tanner. I'm working with the sheriff's cold case team and looking into the murder of Theresa Goldberg."

The phone went silent. "Mr. Early?" Sean said.

"I guess I shouldn't be surprised the police would find me after the recent murder."

There was only one recent murder he could think of. "You mean of Nancy Russo?"

"The past seems to be repeating itself," Tim said.

Sean had to bite his tongue to keep from asking, *What do you mean?* He needed to interview Tim face-to-face. The man might know something important or have relevant background that needed to be fully discussed and recorded. "My partner and I would like to sit down with you and talk. When are you available?"

"I'm expecting another visitor soon, someone who might help me put the old pieces together. So, any time after five would be fine."

"Let me talk to my partner and I'll call you back."

"I'm more than willing to come to your office," Tim said. "But I'd have to check the ferry schedule or arrange for a boat. Maybe tomorrow would be best."

Sean had learned the worst thing a detective can do is set up camp for the night when the trail leading to a killer was fresh. He could probably get the dockhand or one of his friends to take him there. He'd pay out of his own pocket if necessary. The question was whether Irish would agree to go with him. "I think we can come to you. I'll call you back as soon as I can."

Irish shook his head. "As much as I'd love to sail off to Marta Point and interview this witness or take his confession if he's the killer, we'd be way over the line. Plus, he alluded to our cold case being connected to the murder on your street. The sheriff's office is handling that, and they'd be rightfully pissed if we interfered with their investigation."

Sean knew Irish was right. And he knew Frank would tell him he should just document the call and he'd pass it on to the sheriff's detectives. But this couldn't wait. He called Charlie.

43

Charlie sat at her desk with piles of reports, computer printouts, and handwritten notes spread out in front of her. She had spent three hours walking the Riverside neighborhood and talking with more than a dozen residents, mostly LOLs—little old ladies, as the cops in the department called them. As Sean had predicted, she sipped a lot of tea, nibbled on plenty of cookies, and returned to the office with pages of notes. Although the information consisted primarily of rumors and gossip, she knew that even gossip was often rooted in truth, and some of it could mean something in the future, especially as they developed more background on people. Fitting all the pieces of a puzzle together required first collecting all the pieces.

She learned that Bert peed on the viburnum shrub in his backyard before bed every night, ninety-year-old Fred flirted with all the younger women in the neighborhood and told dirty jokes at parties, and Phyllis walked to the street to get her paper every morning braless and dressed in a sheer robe. The residents also told her stories of a creepy house painter who no one would hire anymore, a man on a landscaping crew who stuck his hand down his pants to "readjust" himself every few minutes, and housekeepers, dog sitters, and carpet cleaners suspected of stealing jewelry or money, although the residents conceded the valuables were possibly just misplaced.

Frustrated with the mass of seemingly irrelevant pieces of information in front of her, Charlie picked up her phone and called Spencer. "What time are you leaving?" she asked.

"They should be picking me up any minute." Spencer and four of his friends were going to a concert at the Charleston Music Hall and wouldn't be home until well after midnight.

"Did you eat already?"

"There's a pizza joint near where we park," Spencer said. "We'll get something there."

"It sounds like a wonderful time. I'm sure you'll have fun." Charlie wanted to remind him to make sure his friends drive safely and don't drink, because that's what mothers were supposed to say, but she knew that Spencer and his friends were responsible drivers and all of them pledged to abstain from drinking until they were twenty-one—and actually abided by it. "I won't wait up," she said, although she knew she wouldn't be able to fall asleep until she heard him come in.

"What will you be doing?"

"We have a million leads to run down on this case. I have plenty to keep busy."

"Don't stay too late, Mom. I'll text you when we get there and when we're on our way home."

She ended her call at the same time Darryl hung up his phone and twisted his chair toward his computer. "Something promising?" she asked.

Darryl had spent the day working the tip hotline, returning calls to more than thirty people. He would ask those who had information even remotely relevant to come in and give statements. If they were unable to come to the station, Jay and Sherm drove to their houses and interviewed them. "Another crank caller," Darryl said. "She thinks her ex-husband might've killed Nancy Russo because he's an asshole and the kind of person who'd do such a thing."

Charlie turned back to the list of people with guest and commercial passes to Sea Island Plantation. She was running a criminal history and records check on the next name on the list when her cell phone rang.

"I'm finding names in common between the cold case I'm working and Nancy Russo's murder," Sean said without any preliminary greeting.

"What do you mean?"

He told her about the Nowaks, who had vacationed with Theresa Goldberg thirty-eight years ago and now lived in Sea Island Plantation, and his conversation with Tim Early, who had vacationed with the Goldbergs thirty-eight years ago and now owned a house on MacCrain Island. "Tim Early said the past seems to be repeating itself," Sean said.

"What's that supposed to mean?"

"I told him we were looking into the murder of Theresa Goldberg, and he said that with the recent murder of Nancy Russo, the past seemed to be repeating itself."

"He didn't say he knew anything about them, right?" Charlie said. "He could just be theorizing. Any other time, I'd be glad to interview him. But I have to give a fresh murder priority over a cold case."

"Yes, I know. The murder of Nancy Russo, which he was referring to. He also said someone was visiting him who might help him piece together what happened."

"Did he say who that person was?"

"I didn't ask because—"

"I know, because you're only supposed to do background." She hated smartasses who used her own words against her.

"I know you're busy," Sean said. "I've been there myself. If you give me the okay, I can go out and talk to him myself with someone from the cold case team. If he has first-hand information showing the murders are connected or that requires a formal statement, I can call you."

She stared at the piles of paper on her desk, hundreds of potential leads that would probably go nowhere, and considered the prospect of sitting behind her desk well into the night. "He thinks the cold case might somehow be connected to Nancy Russo's death?"

"He certainly implied that."

"Give me his name and particulars," she said. She copied everything down and told Sean to standby for her return call.

Charlie called dispatch and inquired about the status of ECU. The environmental crimes unit consisted of two regular deputies and a half dozen reserve deputies. With two boats, they were responsible for patrolling the county's waterways for criminal activity, boater safety, and illegal dumping. Since the only way to get to MacCrain Island was by boat, they were also responsible for all law enforcement activities there.

Charlie listened to the tapping of a keyboard and muffled radio traffic for a minute. Then the dispatcher came back on the line. "One boat's on duty and they're working an illegal commercial shrimping operation in the north county with DNR," the dispatcher said, referring to the state Department of Natural Resources. "They can break if it's an emergency, or I can try to call out some reserves to get the other boat."

Charlie couldn't justify her shuttle run to MacCrain as an emergency and didn't want to wait the two hours it would take to find two unpaid volunteers willing to come in and get the department's smaller boat operational.

"No, that's okay," she told the dispatcher and called Sean back. "Can you meet me at my house in a half hour?" She gave him the address.

"Give me forty. I need to go home and change first."

"We're taking an open boat, so this isn't a coat and tie affair."

"I'm just in shorts and tee shirt now, and I'd never interview a witness dressed like that."

Charlie smiled. Although Sean was a pain in the ass, he was a true-blue cop who oozed professionalism.

44

Thirty-five minutes later, Sean parked in front of the largest antebellum house in Dufftown's historic district. Like probably thousands of other visitors that passed through the area, Sean had long wondered who lived in the beautiful old house. When Charlie had called him back and asked him to come with her to interview Early, he was afraid Irish would feel left out. Instead, he was more than happy to go home and spend the evening with his wife. He also agreed to say nothing to the other members of the Mudflats Murder Club.

Sean unfolded himself from the Corvette, hiked up his khaki pants, and instinctively tugged on the straight tail of his light blue shirt to ensure it hadn't ridden up over the Glock he wore in an inside-the-waistband holster on his right side. He opened the wrought iron gate, crossed through the front garden along a brick walkway, and climbed the steps to the wide front porch.

The front door opened before he touched the doorbell, and a striking, sixtyish woman wearing a yellow flowered dress appeared on the other side of the threshold. She had thin lips that barely turned upward as she smiled. "You must be Mr. Tanner," she said with a discernible Southern lilt. "I'm Charlotte's mother, Abigail Nash."

She held out her hand limp-wristed, almost as if she were expecting him to kiss it while bowing. Sean shook her hand gently. "Call me Sean."

She smiled again slightly and stepped back. "Very well, Sean. Please come in. Charlotte should be down momentarily."

Sean stepped into the foyer, which he imagined was likely termed an entry hall by the original occupants of the house. A thick Persian rug covered the center of the marble floor, and two curved stairways of dark, hand-carved wood ascended to a second-floor landing.

"Would you like to wait in the parlor?" Abigail motioned to a large room filled with dark furniture and thick rugs over a hardwood floor.

Sean was ready to step into the room when he heard a door slam upstairs and saw Charlie at the top of the stairs. Instead of one of the various shapeless pantsuits he'd seen her in previously, she wore white jeans, a blue and white striped shirt that screamed nautical, and canvas boat shoes. "I didn't hear you arrive," she said as she slipped on a light cotton blazer and descended the stairs. Sean pictured her descending the same staircase decades ago in a debutante gown or prom dress as a young suitor stood below.

"I just got here," Sean said, as Charlie made her way down the stairs and grabbed a leather shoulder bag off a table in the foyer.

"Good, so my mom didn't have a chance to get you into the living room and start serving sherry and hors d'oeuvres."

"The parlor, dear," Abigail said. "And if you were delayed, I would've offered Mr. Tanner tea since I fully realize this is not a social call."

"Thanks, Mom." Charlie kissed Abigail on the cheek and said to Sean, "We'll go out the back." She led the way through a formal dining room with a banquet-size table of gleaming cherry wood under two giant chandeliers, and then into a commercial-grade kitchen and out the back door.

"Your mother seems charming," Sean said.

Charlie laughed. "For someone who thinks she's still living in Scarlett O'Hara's era."

They followed a gravel path through a park-like backyard graced with centuries-old oak trees and a lush carpet of grass to a single-story building matching the colors and style of the main house. She pushed through a door into a six-bay garage filled with five vehicles: a boxy G-Class Mercedes

SUV that looked like a Jeep on steroids, a Cadillac, an Audi sedan, Charlie's unmarked Dodge Charger, and an old blue Toyota Prius. She threw her bag in the backseat of the Prius and slid into the driver's seat.

Sean waited while Charlie grabbed a pair of running shoes, a baseball cap, and water bottle from the passenger seat and tossed them in the back then brushed an assortment of food wrappers and scraps of paper onto the floor. He climbed into the passenger seat as the garage door opened. They made a right onto an alley, which Sean figured was an old carriage lane in an earlier era.

"I didn't see you as a Prius owner," Sean said as he reclined the seat so his head wasn't pressed into the roof.

"After college, I worked for the regional planning commission, trying to maintain a balance between the explosion of new development in the area and the environment. Not driving a gas guzzler seemed like the right thing to do."

She sped through Old Town, braking hard at the first stop sign and then accelerating as fast as the hybrid power plant would move the car. When she reached the next stop sign, she did the same thing. Sean wondered if she ever got anywhere near the Prius' advertised gas mileage driving the way she did. "That's a big career change from regional planning to cop."

She made a left and accelerated to at least twenty over the speed limit on the main road. "It's a long story, but at thirty-four I had an early mid-life crisis and entered the academy."

Sean studied Charlie's face. Smooth skin with a strand of sun-bleached hair that had escaped from the tight bun containing the rest of her hair. Billy had told him she'd been on the department for ten years, which would make her around forty-four.

"I know." She glanced at him out of the corner of her eye as if she could read his mind. "I don't look my age. Nor act it according to the department brass and my mother."

She made a hard left into the entrance drive of the Cusseta Country Club, the oldest and most prestigious country club in the region. Two long rows of old oak trees, their branches growing above and over the road, created a tunnel they drove through. "They have a deep-water marina on the Cusseta River where our family berths our boats."

They drove past a polo field, horse arena and stables, and a clubhouse that resembled an old southern mansion. A man and woman dressed in colorful golf outfits strolled along a perfectly manicured fairway followed by a caddie carrying their golf bags. The road continued past several tennis courts and a swimming pool to a parking lot with a sign reading *Cusseta Yacht Club*.

Charlie caught his eye again. "It's not all it's cracked up to be—growing up like this."

Growing up in a southern mansion with yachts, polo ponies, and golf courses with caddies was totally foreign to him. He was raised in a small house in a working-class neighborhood in Pittsburgh, where his father was a cop, as was *his* father. After a stint in the Army, Sean prepared to follow the family tradition, but with most of the steel mills closed, Pittsburgh's economy was dying. His father urged him to look elsewhere, and he found Oakland was hiring and had the best pay, benefits, and training in the country.

Charlie grabbed her shoulder bag and a duffle from the trunk of the car and headed toward the marina. She didn't resist when Sean took the duffle bag from her and carried it. She stopped at a small fiberglass boat almost hidden among the bigger fishing boats, sailing yachts, and custom pleasure boats. She stepped aboard, stowed the bags into a compartment under a seat and started the engine. Sean untied the lines and stepped aboard.

"This is a Carolina Skiff," she said. "Has a flat bottom so you can take it up the tidal creeks where there's only a few inches of water. Very stable in flat water, but you don't want to run offshore or in rough waters."

She directed him to sit in the seat directly in front of the console to best balance the boat and maneuvered out of the marina. She sped up a bit when they reached the middle of the river. Once they passed the Dufftown public pier, located at the end of Wharf Street, she pushed the throttle forward and the bow rose until the boat finally planed and skimmed over the water.

Sean turned to see Charlie standing behind him at the console with a huge grin on her face. "Ninety horsepower engine," she yelled over the wind and engine noise. "It'll do forty miles an hour."

Sean nodded and faced forward again to keep the wind from ripping his sunglasses off his face. She followed the winding river, staying well clear of a long sandbar in the middle of a bend where people waded in the shallows around anchored boats. Soon the mouth of the river widened, and the southern tip of Spartina Island appeared ahead. She throttled back the motor. The skiff settled back into the water and turned into MacCrain Creek. They motored slowly down the wide tidal creek with salt marsh on both sides. A few wooden docks jutted into the water from small houses on the island.

A marina containing more than thirty small boats soon appeared ahead. Charlie reversed the engine and coasted up to a dock as the sixty-foot public ferry pulled away. When Charlie's boat touched the dock bumper, she wrapped a rope around a dock cleat and tied it off. Sean picked up another rope, stepped onto the dock, and tied off the front of the boat. They walked down the dock, past an outdoor restaurant and bar filled with people, and continued toward the largest building in the small harbor area. Signs on the front read, *General Store, Lodging, Rentals, Post Office*.

They continued past a rack of bicycles and a row of faded golf carts and through a dirt courtyard surrounded by a dozen small cottages built of weathered boards. Charlie punched a code into a keypad on a large metal building. An overhead door rose. Inside was an old fire truck lettered with *MacCrain Island Volunteer Fire Department*, two rusty pickup trucks, and a Chevy Tahoe with Campbell County Sheriff's markings.

"We prepositioned this here for deputies to use when they patrol the island or for emergency calls," she said. "But the residents here know that if something happens, help is a long way off, so they're pretty self-reliant."

They drove through the old village of weathered houses, many of them not much more than shacks, and turned onto the main road that ran the length of the island. By the time the truck's air conditioning cooled the interior, they had passed through an open gate set between two stone pillars. "My father bought half of this island thirty years ago," Charlie said. "His plan for Marta Point included three hundred houses, a club house, golf course, and other amenities. About half the lots were sold and fifty houses built when he...when he died."

It was infuriating the way Charlie tossed out snippets of her past. Each one posed a million questions, and Sean didn't know whether he should inquire further or just nod and let her reveal more when she felt ready. "I didn't know your father was a developer."

She continued through a forest so thick it felt like they were in a jungle. The dense vegetation finally gave way to a salt pond. The Atlantic Ocean loomed in front of them. "He was the original developer for Sea Island Plantation, several of the other residential plantations on and off the island, and a lot of the commercial developments."

"How'd he die?"

She looked straight ahead and gripped the steering wheel harder. "He disappeared ten years ago under suspicious circumstances and was declared legally dead a few years ago."

Sean wondered if his disappearance was the crisis that propelled her into a law enforcement career.

She turned onto a road that paralleled the beach. Gigantic houses lined both sides. "But that story is for another time," she said. "We're here."

She pulled into the driveway of a two-story beach house standing ten feet above the sand on thick pylons that resembled telephone poles. "I'll take the lead in the interview," she said. "I don't mind if you interject as long as you follow my lead. When I finish with my questions, I'll give you an opportunity to ask whatever you want."

Sean nodded. That was the way he always worked with a partner. The primary investigator took charge of interviews, and the partner never interrupted or initiated a different direction or strategy. Even though it was her jurisdiction and her case, it still felt uncomfortable being told what to do by a detective with a fraction of his experience.

They climbed the steps to the front porch and rang the doorbell. No answer, so Charlie knocked at the door. Still no answer. She pulled out her phone and called Tim Early's number. When it went to voicemail, she said, "Mr. Early, this is Sergeant Nash. We're at your front door. You said you'd be home."

They walked down the steps and waded through loose sand to the back of the house. Waves broke offshore beyond a wide deserted beach. The nearest house was more than a hundred feet away, and there was not a human being visible on the beach as far as he could see. Although Sean enjoyed solitude, he wasn't sure if living in a luxury beach mansion on one of the most beautiful stretches of beach in the country would overshadow the isolation of this place.

They passed an outdoor shower, climbed the steps to an expansive deck, and peered in through the glass sliders that extended the length of the house. Behind an ivory-colored sectional sofa in the great room lay a man in a crimson pool of blood.

45

Charlie snaked her hand under her jacket, grabbed her Sig Sauer P365 subcompact 9mm from its SOB—small-of-the-back—holster, and pulled it out. She noticed Sean was already holding a mid-sized Glock at a low ready position. Although she had never inquired if he still carried after retiring, at this moment she was glad he did.

Standing in front of a wall of glass, they were completely exposed to a possible killer inside. Her pulse jumped as adrenalin coursed through her body.

They couldn't remain where they were. They could either run for the steps and get off the deck, or rush inside and find cover. She pointed to the sliding glass door in front of them and Sean nodded.

She tried the door. Unlocked. She quickly slid it open. She shivered once from the blast of cold air inside the house—or was it from fear?

She stepped inside and rapidly scanned the right side of the room. Out of the corner of her eye, she saw Sean scanning to the left, his gun and eyes moving as one. The old, retired homicide cop was no amateur, she thought.

"Cover me," she whispered as she moved toward the body and pressed a finger against the man's neck. The body was still warm, but there was no pulse. She looked at Sean and shook her head. He nodded and crept toward her, still holding his gun in both hands at a low ready while his eyes continued moving around the room.

"We need to clear the house," Sean said. "The suspect could still be here or there might be other victims."

"As soon as I notify dispatch and get back-up on the way." She pulled out her phone. When the dispatcher answered, she identified herself, gave her location, and said, "We were here to interview a witness on a homicide case, but found him dead. Body's still warm. I don't know if the suspect has fled the scene, so we'll be searching the house. We need expedited back-up and the works for a murder scene."

"We?" the dispatcher asked. "Do you have another deputy with you?"

"Only a civilian volunteer from the cold case team."

"Roger that. I'll get ECU en route. ETA will be twenty at best. And I'll initiate a call to the volunteer fire department. Most of them boys have guns, so you'll have some friendly faces with you until we can get there."

She thanked the dispatcher and said to Sean, "Stay with the body while I search the house."

"I don't know how you do police work down here, but where I come from, officers don't search houses for murder suspects alone."

She was ready to pull rank on him—regular sergeant to civilian—but he was right. She needed to stop thinking of him as a civilian who needed to be protected and kept out of harm's way. "Okay, but I'm point."

"It's your jurisdiction." He closed and locked the sliding door to the back deck. "Don't want anyone sneaking up on us from behind."

Charlie shuffled around the right side of the room, taking small steps to maintain a stable shooting platform should a threat appear. She peered around furniture and into the dining area. Sean did the same along the left walls. They met in the kitchen. She opened a door that led to the basement and garage after noting it had been locked. She relocked it. "We'll save this for last."

She moved into the foyer and pulled open a closet door as Sean scanned it. "Clear," he said. They did the same with a powder room.

She checked the front door, noting it was unlocked, and twisted the deadbolt to prevent anyone from coming in. If they had a full team, she could leave officers to guard doorways and areas they'd cleared, but with only two of them, they had to protect their six the best they could.

They swept through the master bedroom, checked under the bed and through the closets, and continued into the bathroom. No one present and no sign of a struggle or search. If this had been a home burglary gone astray, she knew the master suite was the first place a thief would search for valuables. They moved on to a guest suite at the other end of the house and searched it in the same manner as they had the master. They found nothing amiss and returned to the main room.

Charlie slowly crept up the stairs to the second level, her eyes and gun facing forward, while Sean walked backward, his eyes and Glock pointing upward toward the landing behind them. He pressed his back against her as they climbed slowly, one step at a time. Although she knew this was a tactic SWAT members used to keep contact with a partner when their eyes needed to focus elsewhere, the warmth of his body conveyed a strong feeling of safety and security.

They reached the landing at the top of the stairs and cleared a large rec room containing a pool table, bar, furniture, and flat screen TV. She led the way down a hallway, where they searched and cleared an office and two more bedrooms. She relaxed a little as they retraced their steps and descended the stairs to the ground level garage, which held a BMW SUV, golf cart, bicycles, and other recreational equipment.

They reholstered their guns and returned to the first floor. Charlie took a deep breath. Her shirt clung to her sweaty back despite the air conditioning, and she felt her pounding heart begin to slow.

Sean looked as calm and relaxed as when they were walking along the golf course earlier that morning. She pulled her cell phone from her shoulder bag, which she had left next to the body when they started their search. She had five missed calls. She called back Billy first.

"Are you okay?" he asked.

Not *what happened, who was murdered, what are you doing out there*, as many bosses would've asked. She loved having Billy as her boss. "I'm fine. We searched the house, but the killer's gone."

"Is Sean with you?" he asked.

"Yeah." Her voice still quaked as the adrenalin seeped from her system.

"Good. Now I *know* you're okay. The ECU boat is stopping at the marina to pick up three deputies. They should be on ground in fifteen minutes. Can you arrange for transportation to get them to your scene?"

"I'll figure it out."

"What have you got there?"

She gave him the condensed version of what led them to Tim Early's house and what they had found so far.

"I'll have one of your detectives start on the search warrant. It should be quick. I'll get the coroner and SLED's crime scene unit on the way and bring in more people as soon as I can scare up the boats to move them. Do you need anything else at this time?"

"Not that I can think of."

"I'll head that way too as soon as I can. The captain and sheriff will want to know if this is linked to Nancy Russo's murder."

"That's what we were hoping Tim Early might've told us," she said.

After Charlie ended the call, she studied the body for the first time. He was dressed in beige linen shorts and a Tommy Bahama tropical print silk shirt. A small hole was directly under his right eye. Although the back of his head was resting on the hardwood floor, the pool of blood surrounding it told her there was a significant exit wound she couldn't see.

Sean was standing at the end of the room, staring at the wall. "You didn't happen to see any ID in the house, did you?" she asked.

"There's something in his back pocket, but I'd wait for the coroner before I searched the body," he said. "I remember his photo from his company's website. This is Tim Early."

"Looks like he was shot right where he fell," she said. "But from the blood spatter on the glass coffee table, he might've been facing the other way."

"I'm no expert, but I think that's blowback, caused by blood escaping from the entrance wound as a bullet enters at a high velocity. There's a lot more blood, probably front splatter, which came from the exit wound, on the other side of the body."

"For not being an expert, you sound pretty certain."

Sean winked. "While you were on the phone, I looked around. Check under the white chair to your right."

Charlie crouched down and saw a brass shell casing under the chair. "Remington three-eighty."

"Most guns throw casings to the right and backward," Sean said. "Assuming the victim fell where he was shot, which the blood indicates, the shooter was probably standing just in front of the other upholstered chair or sitting on it. Our victim was standing just in front of the couch when shot. Less than ten feet away."

"That's a lot of assumptions from a casual observation of blood splatter."

Sean pointed to a small hole in the wall. "I'll bet this hole was caused by the bullet."

Charlie laughed. "So, you made a line from the bullet hole in the wall to the body and you determined where the shooter stood."

"Pretty much." Sean grinned. "What conclusion can you draw from this?"

"That the victim knew the shooter and invited him in."

Sean nodded. "Are you planning to wait for a warrant before you go through the house?"

"We obey the Constitution down here."

"We rushed through the search of the house pretty quick. We might've missed looking under a bed or behind clothes in a closet. I'm thinking it might be a good idea for me to take another look. If I see anything that might be relevant to the investigation while double-checking for other victims we might've missed, there's nothing wrong with making note of it."

"Go ahead," she said. "Just don't later tell me you looked in a desk drawer because you thought a suspect might've been hiding there."

Sean disappeared into the master bedroom as the doorbell rang. Charlie opened the door to two men in their forties dressed in jeans, work boots, and tee shirts. One held a long-barreled shotgun in his hands and the other had a revolver tucked in his waistband. "We're with the fire department," the taller one said. "We heard you needed some help."

Charlie shook their hands. "Thanks for showing up, but we're all secure here. I guess you can cancel the call."

"We don't just fight fires, ma'am. On MacCrain Island we all mobilize whenever there's a need. Tell us what the island folk can help y'all with and we'll see to it."

46

It was after seven o'clock when Sean finally took a break and stepped under a canopy the citizens of MacCrain Island had set up in front of the house. They were cooking hamburgers and hotdogs on two large grills and handing out water bottles and sodas to all of the law enforcement officers working the scene and the scores of citizen volunteers assisting. Others were shuttling people back and forth to the marina in their cars and golf carts. When they learned law enforcement and support personnel were waiting for boats to bring people and equipment to the island, some fired up their personal boats and made runs to the mainland.

A tall man in his late sixties with a high forehead and pointed chin flipped hamburgers on a grill. "Are you hungry, deputy?"

"I'm actually a civilian assigned to the cold case team."

"I guess that means you're one of the investigators."

"Sort of."

"The name's Glenn. I'm the president of our homeowner's association. Have you figured out what happened?"

"Not really. Other than someone was murdered."

"Tim was a very nice man," Glenn said. "We spoke just this morning."

"Really?"

"I walk through the point every morning. Down the roads and back along the beach. Tim was having his coffee on his deck, so we chatted."

"What about?"

"The weather, that kind of stuff." Glenn lifted burgers off the grill with a long spatula and flopped them onto a plate. "He said he'd be here a week this time."

"Is that unusual?"

"He only gets here once a month or so. Poor guy still works. Often gets here late Thursday or Friday and leaves Sunday. That's typical for the part-timers."

"You a full-timer?"

"Out of the hundred houses at the point, about thirty of us consider this our primary residence."

"Do you have a list of the residents with phone numbers and stuff?"

"Sure. You want me to send it to you?"

Sean gave Glenn his email address. Glenn poked at his phone, and a moment later, Sean received an email on his phone with an attachment. "Do you know who's here as of today?"

"I have a pretty good idea. People usually let me know when they're coming and going. I send it out to all the homeowners, so we can keep an eye on each other's places."

"You didn't happen to see if Tim had any visitors today?"

"Afraid not. Another deputy asked me that, too. I live a few houses down along the beach. When you live on the ocean, you don't spend much time looking toward the street to see comings and goings."

When Sean had done his second walk-through of the house, he hadn't noticed any indications of theft or a search, not even a sign the killer had been anywhere in the house outside the great room. "Is there much crime on the island?"

"Hardly any. Occasionally a resident living outside the gate gets into it with his wife, or a drunken visitor causes a ruckus at the bar by the marina, but I've never heard of any problems inside Marta Point."

Sean remembered Tim Early telling him on the phone that he was expecting another *visitor*, someone who might help him piece together the murders of Nancy Russo and Theresa Goldberg. The Spartina Island chamber of commerce refers to tourists—people who don't reside there—as visitors, and locals have picked up the usage. Sean wondered if Tim meant visitor as someone from off the island or as someone visiting him. "Assuming the killer doesn't live on the island, how'd he get here?"

"Most likely the ferry. It makes a run every two hours in the summer and can carry close to two hundred people. On a lovely day like today, it's often full. If they had their own boat, they could tie off down at the public marina. Occasionally an unauthorized boat docks at our marina, but someone usually notices them and shoos them away or lets me or the staff know."

"I noticed bicycles and golf carts by the general store. I take it visitors rent them to get around."

"That or they just walk or hitchhike. Nothing is more than a few miles from the harbor, and locals are happy to give visitors a lift."

"I'll take you up on that hamburger," Sean said.

He called his neighbor, Beth Laughlin, while he was eating and asked her to feed Annie and take her out. He didn't know how late he'd be, and Beth had taken care of Annie before when he and Lauren planned to be gone most of the day. He gave her one of the temporary codes he'd inputted into the digital door lock, and reminded himself to delete it when he got home. Although many of the neighbors trusted Beth with their house keys, the cop in Sean didn't feel comfortable knowing someone could just walk into his house anytime they wanted.

Sean headed back toward the house to tell Charlie what he'd learned. He reached the top of the stairs as Charlie, Billy, and Darryl Picket exited the front door. "A LIDAR scan is in session," Billy said.

Sean was impressed that SLED had a laser imaging, detection, and ranging machine. The system used laser beams to measure the distance and direction of thousands of data points, allowing it to create an extremely accurate three-dimensional crime scene diagram. It was especially valuable when trying to reconstruct bullet trajectories at shooting scenes. Although it could be operated while personnel were moving around the crime scene, it was much faster and more precise when no one other than the operator was present.

Sean told them what Glenn said.

"All of the deputies and two of my detectives are still canvassing the Marta Point development," Charlie said. "It might be a few hours before we can expand out to the rest of the island."

"I'm sure Glenn would be happy to be my guide," Sean said. "I could go out to the general store and see what they can tell me about any visitors who came through today."

Charlie was quiet for a moment as she thought about it. "Go ahead, but take Darryl with you." She faced Darryl, "Let Sean take the lead since he has a better feel for the case, but you're responsible for taking detailed notes and writing up a report documenting everything you did."

Darryl frowned, obviously not happy being relegated to scribe duties for a civilian. Sean wondered if Charlie's decision had more to do with her faith in his abilities or her lack of trust in Darryl.

"Yes, ma'am," Darryl said. "You da boss."

The thumping beat of a helicopter filled the sky, and they all looked upward to see a maroon Bell helicopter with *News 12* on the side streaming toward them from the north. A half mile out, it swung westward and began orbiting their location.

"Fuck!" Charlie said. "The entire country will see the MacCrain Island beaches on the news tonight."

"And wondering why another well-to-do senior citizen was murdered in paradise," Billy added then turned to Sean. "I'm sure I don't need to tell you, but the only information we're sharing with the public is that there's been a murder. We won't release the name until the coroner advises the next of kin's been notified."

A few minutes later, they were bouncing down the road in Glenn's electric golf cart. Sean sat in the front beside Glenn, who talked non-stop about life on the island. Darryl sat behind them in a rear-facing seat, trying to hold on as Glenn swerved around potholes in the road.

Glenn parked in front of the general store and introduced Sean and Darryl to the heavy-set woman with dreadlocks behind the counter. She explained that visitors who rented golf carts had to fill out a waiver form and leave a credit card deposit, but if people paid cash to rent a bicycle, they only needed to leave their license or a credit card as collateral, which the store returned when the visitor brought the bike back. She made them copies of all credit card invoices for the golf cart and bike rentals for the day as well as the waiver forms for golf cart rentals.

"How many people you think rented bikes with cash?" Sean asked.

"Cash is five dollars less than using a credit card, so most of them."

"How many would that be?" Sean asked again. "I'm not the IRS and could care less what your cash business is."

"Normally around fifty a day. Some folk ride to the beach and keep the bikes all day, but most only go out for an hour or two. That's plenty for visitors who ain't used to our heat down here."

Sean and Darryl headed over to the bar where they collected copies of the bar's credit card receipts for the day. Sean then left Darryl to record the names of everyone eating and drinking at the bar, while he wandered over to the marina to see if anyone with a boat transported someone off the island just before he and Charlie arrived.

47

FRIDAY

Charlie stood next to the sheriff during the 9:00 a.m. press conference at the station. He was his normal professional self, reading a prepared script of the limited details they could release without hampering the investigation. It was a delicate balance, feeding the press enough to satisfy their hunger without being devoured in the process. He then introduced Charlie and stepped away from the podium. She'd anticipated the reporters' questions and rehearsed her answers.

"Are you looking at any particular suspects or persons of interest?"

"Not at this time."

"How many times was Tim Early shot?"

"I can't reveal that information without jeopardizing the investigation."

"Is this murder related to the murder of Nancy Russo?"

"We're investigating that possibility."

"It seems to me they're related," a Charleston reporter with a spray-tanned face said. "Both are senior citizens. Both are transplants from the north. Both live in exclusive gated plantations. Both are well off—one downright wealthy. They were murdered within days of each other." His camera operator focused on him asking the *hard* questions, making him more of the story than the non-committal response he surely expected. "Are you denying the similarities?"

"We're investigating all of that plus more."

After she'd given the same response a third time, Captain Cannon edged his way to the podium and took over the microphone. He hinted to the room of journalists that the same person did the murders, and he—the captain stressed *he*—and his investigators were close to an arrest. Charlie felt the slime from her captain beginning to drip onto her and slipped out of the room. She doubted he even noticed.

She sent a text to Darryl: *Anything interesting yet?*

Darryl: *Single GSW to the head. No defensive wounds.*

Charlie: *Let me know when done and en route back?*

Darryl: *OK*

She'd sent Jay and Sherm back to MacCrain Island this morning with a list of tasks that would keep them busy all day. She could count on them to report in when they learned anything important. She didn't feel as comfortable depending on Darryl to attend the autopsy, but since he only had to observe and report, there was little he could screw up. She grabbed her third cup of coffee and sat at her desk. She'd already drunk more coffee during this investigation than she did in a typical month. Her brain felt fuzzy after having left the Island at 3:00 a.m. and getting no more than three hours of sleep before heading to the office.

Despite what she had told the reporters, there was no doubt in her mind the murder of Tim Early and Nancy Russo were connected. But she wasn't as convinced as Sean about the link to Theresa Goldberg's thirty-eight-year-old murder. Sure, Tim had been part of the group vacationing with Theresa when she was killed, but Charlie couldn't fathom a motive for a killer to wait nearly four decades between killings, unless—

Unless Tim was successful in connecting the pieces. What if Tim figured out who killed Theresa? What if he started asking questions, and it got back to the killer?

She found the evidence log from the MacCrain Island murder in a pile of papers on her desk. It listed a cell phone collected from Tim's body at the scene. Even if the phone wasn't password protected, they'd still need a warrant to access it. She located Tim's next of kin, his wife Susan Early, and called her number. No answer. Charlie left a message in the hopes that

Susan knew her husband's cellular account password and would give them legal consent to view his call log.

She looked at the background information they had on Nancy Russo. She and her husband had lived in Short Hills, New Jersey, before moving to Spartina Island. Sean said that was where Tim Early and Theresa Goldberg also lived. But a lot of people who knew each other up north ended up moving south. All three victims knowing each other was a solid connection, but that didn't lead her any closer to the motive or the killer's identity. Too many questions swirled through her head. She needed to return to gathering facts and hard evidence.

She suspected Tim Early's killer didn't live on MacCrain Island. She looked at the stack of credit card receipts from the ferry office, the general store, and the bar and grill. Maybe the killer was dumb and used his credit card. She started with the first receipt and ran the name in the department's database.

She'd been at it for more than an hour before she got a hit. Two different people with addresses in Sea Island Plantation bought two ferry tickets each. Their names hadn't previously come up in the investigation, but Charlie wondered if they knew Nancy Russo or Tim Early. It was a long shot to interview potential suspects without knowing in advance if they even knew the victims, but she couldn't just sit at her desk all day drinking coffee. She grabbed her car keys and headed out the door.

An hour later, Charlie climbed back in her car after striking out at the second house. Neither couple said they knew the Russos or Tim Early. They had just taken the ferry to walk around and have lunch on MacCrain Island. Charlie believed them. She started driving back to the station when the police radio broadcasted a deputy being dispatched to a check-the-well-being call a few streets away. Charlie recognized the voice of her friend, Jane May, acknowledging she was around the corner. Her backup was fifteen minutes away, so Charlie decided to roll by and cover Jane until the other deputy got there.

Charlie and Jane pulled up to the pale yellow single-story house at the same time.

Jane swung out of her patrol car and crossed her arms, reminding Charlie of a miniature sumo wrestler. "Did you catch that one on MacCrain yesterday?"

"Yeah, another whodunit," Charlie said. "Whatcha got here?"

"Nothing that requires super detective Charlie Nash."

"Remember when I was a patrol sergeant and I constantly reminded you guys that any call can go sideways?" Charlie said. "Yet still *some* deputies think they're bulletproof and don't wait for backup?"

Jane grinned. "It's probably nothing. A woman from Ohio called dispatch and said her elderly mother phoned her from this house requesting help. The phone was then disconnected. Medical's been here before for an LOL who fell and couldn't get up."

"Why'd she phone someone in Ohio?"

"The caller in Ohio said her sister lives nearby and her mother normally calls her, but she's away for the weekend."

"How I miss being a patrol deputy," Charlie said sarcastically. "Shall we?"

They heard a loud TV blasting from inside the house before they made it halfway to the front door. Jane knocked and rang the doorbell, but there was no answer. They went around the back, peered in through the window, and knocked at the back door. Still no answer, but the TV was even louder. Jane tried the door. Unlocked. She pushed it open and entered.

They walked into the main room and spotted a man, who had to be in his nineties, sitting in a recliner watching TV. He jumped when he saw them and fumbled with something on the table beside his chair. He inserted his hearing aids, while Jane clicked the TV off.

"What're you doing in my house?"

"Your wife called," Jane said. "Where's she at?"

The man shrugged.

"I'm in here," a woman yelled from down the hall.

Jane opened the bathroom door, and Charlie saw a woman lying on the floor, wedged between the toilet and the wall. Jane helped her to her feet and pulled her pants back up for her. The woman shuffled down the hall behind her walker to the living room and dropped in the chair beside her husband.

"You stupid old goat," she said. "I was screaming for you to come help me."

"I didn't hear you."

"You took out your goddamn hearing aid again, didn't you?"

"Yeah, well, I told you a million times they feel like someone's poking their fingers in my ears."

Charlie and Jane smiled at each other. "I guess we're no longer needed here," Jane said.

The woman pointed a bony finger at Charlie. "We've seen you on TV saying Ken didn't kill his wife. Have you questioned the grandson? He's a drug addict, you know."

"Do you know the Russos?" Charlie asked.

"Not really. They're part of the rich snobs that live over in Riverside. Even though we live here in the poor rent district, we can use their swimming pool."

"What do you know about their grandson?" Charlie asked.

"Only what Ken and Nancy were saying. Or yelling, more like it. They were going at it last Sunday at the pool. Nancy said she wanted to cut Trevor off, that he's a no-good junkie. Ken wanted to pay for rehab so the boy didn't end up homeless or in jail."

"What else did they say?"

"That's about it, because she splashed him, and they started fighting in the water."

Charlie turned to the husband. "What did you hear?"

"Don't wear my hearing aids in the water. Even if my wife was nagging me, I couldn't hear it."

48

Charlie swung by the community management office on her way out the gate. A pleasant woman with a strong Southern accent punched Trevor Russo's name into a computer and found he had a guest pass valid for a month. She called her office and asked Gladys to run him out. Trevor had some minor charges related to drugs and petty theft, but nothing significant.

Charlie drove to the Riverside neighborhood and stopped in front of Ken Russo's house. Ken answered the door dressed in knee-length gym shorts and a tee shirt.

"I'm sorry I had to arrest you." Reopening dialogue with someone you placed in handcuffs and threw into jail was not easy, but Charlie had learned long ago that a smile and an apology could reopen a lot of doors. "It wasn't my idea."

"I shouldn't have lied to you. I probably gave you no other choice."

"May I come in?"

"Sorry about the mess," he said as he gathered up newspapers and dirty dishes from the sofa and coffee table.

She sat across from him on the sofa. "You didn't tell me the argument at the pool was over Trevor."

He shook his head. "Sorry. Trevor has my disease, but instead of booze, he feeds his addiction with opioids."

"That must be hard to watch."

"Especially when you're sober and know there's a solution."

"When did you last see him or talk to him?"

"He came by the house the day before Nancy and I argued about him at the pool. I talked to him about his addiction, rehabs, and AA."

"How'd that go?"

"About how you'd expect. He's in denial, just as I was for years. But he said if he couldn't get clean on his own, he'd consider rehab."

"I remember you telling me you had three children, and they all still live in New Jersey."

"Yeah. Trevor left home when he turned eighteen earlier this year. He said his father—my son—was too strict. We invited him to come down and stay with us."

"Did he?"

"He got a job bussing tables at Benson's Seafood. I'd been going to meetings for a while, so I was clearheaded for the first time in years. I noticed he was always either overly subdued or super agitated. Nancy and I confronted him, and he admitted he had an opioid habit. When we told him we couldn't have that in our house, he moved out."

"Where's he living now?"

"I have no idea. I've told him he's welcome to visit when he's not high, and he comes by a few times a month. I left a number of messages on his cell to tell him about his grandmother's death, but he hasn't called back."

"Do you know any of his friends?"

"He's brought friends by, but I don't remember any of their names. They all work in the restaurant business together."

"We never had the chance to ask for your help in finding the killer—"

"Because I started out lying to you. I don't blame you for treating me the way you did. The truth is Nancy was really angry after what happened at the pool. I slept on the couch that night and left the house for my meeting in the morning without even seeing her."

"Do you think you could get me a list of everyone who's been in your house over the past—let's say—six months?"

"You mean like friends, repair companies, that sort of stuff?"

"Exactly. People often go through their calendars and checkbooks to jog their memories." She handed him her card with her email address on it.

"Do you think it was someone I knew?"

"We're looking at every possibility."

Back in her car, Charlie called Darryl's cell phone. "Where're you at?"

"Pulling into the station in a few minutes."

"I asked you to call when you left the autopsy."

"I thought I was only supposed to call if they found something unexpected."

She didn't have the energy to argue with him. "I guess they didn't discover anything else significant."

"No, ma'am."

"The second you walk in the office, I want you to run out a Trevor Russo, age eighteen, and text a photo to Jay. Then meet me at Benson's Seafood with a hardcopy of the photo. I'm on my way there now."

Charlie hung up and called Jay. "Finding anything interesting yet?"

"We pretty much finished talking to the residents of Marta Point that were missed last night. No one saw anyone around the victim's house, and no one knew anything about any visitors our vic was expecting."

"We deserve a break in this case," she sighed.

"We're heading to the harbor area soon to talk to people there."

"Darryl will be sending you a photo of an eighteen-year-old named Trevor Russo. Show the photo around. See if anyone saw him there."

"Russo? As in Nancy and Ken Russo?"

"He's their grandson."

"Are you on to something, sergeant?"

"Maybe. Just let me know if you get a hit on him."

Benson's lunch operation was in full swing when Charlie arrived. The hostess buzzed the manager, who led Charlie to the back office. He pulled Trevor's employment file and punched some keys on his computer. "His address is 25 Blue Heron Lane," he said.

"That's his grandparents' address, but he's not living there anymore," Charlie said. "Does he pick up his check here or do you mail it?"

"Everything's direct deposit these days."

"What's his work schedule?"

"It varies every week." He hit a few keys and the printer spit out a sheet of paper.

Charlie studied the printout, which showed Trevor was off yesterday and today. He had worked the dinner shift of 5:00 p.m. to closing the previous four days, which meant he was not working at the time of Nancy's and Tim's murders. "Who's his closest buddies here?"

"Is Trevor in trouble?"

Charlie didn't like causing problems for people at their jobs unnecessarily. "His grandmother was the woman killed in Sea Island Plantation on Monday. We just need to see if he knows anything."

"Jeez, he never mentioned it," the manager said. "When Trevor and Rory, another busboy, are on the same shift, I often see them leaving work together."

"Is Rory working now?"

"He's on the same schedule as Trevor this week, so they both report back tomorrow for the dinner shift."

With a copy of Rory's employment record, she trudged across the parking lot to her car, feeling the heat radiating off the asphalt through her shoes. Darryl was waiting by her car holding a booking photo of Trevor in his hand.

"Ride with me," she said. "We're going to a house where a work friend of his lives."

Ten minutes later, they knocked at the door and a young, thin man with dirty blond hair and a scruffy beard answered the door. "Are you Rory?" Charlie asked, sweeping back her jacket to show her badge. She looked past him into the house and saw a very pregnant-looking woman sitting on a sagging sofa watching TV.

He nodded and stepped outside, closing the door.

"We're looking for Trevor."

"Trevor who?"

"Don't give me that Trevor-who crap. We know you work together and are friends."

"Yeah, we work at Benson's together and sometimes hang out after work, but he's not really a friend."

"His grandmother was killed a few days ago, so we need to talk to him."

"He never mentioned anything about that." Rory made a tiny sign of the cross. "I'm sorry for his loss."

"People say Trevor is having some problems with drugs."

"I don't know nothing about that." He turned the inside of his arms to face her. "I don't do no drugs. I'm about to have a baby and can't be wasting money on shit like that."

Charlie understood friends lied for each other, but she didn't think it was worth the time and effort to drag Rory downtown just to make him admit he knew about Trevor's drug use. If something materialized later showing Trevor was involved in the murder, she could always come back.

"Where's Trevor staying?"

Rory began to shake his head.

She stepped toward Rory until her face was only inches from his. "Don't lie to me."

"I don't know the address, but I can tell ya how to get there."

49

Although the fishing on the river was often best at low tide, when Sean took his tandem kayak out at 7:00 a.m., he left his fishing gear at home and took Annie instead. When they had moved to Spartina Island and bought the tandem kayak, Lauren wasn't sure if Annie would ever be comfortable in it. The first time they put her inside, the kayak rocked from side to side as Annie moved around and she tried to jump out. Annie had been swimming plenty of times, and she loved going into lakes and rivers in California, but she seemed to prefer solid ground to sitting in a long, narrow piece of plastic that swayed every time someone shifted their weight.

Sean had his own reservations. If Annie jumped out and tried to swim to shore, she'd likely end up in the marsh's pluff mud. Although it supplied essential nourishment for Spartina and other grasses, which in turn, was necessary for the very life of the marsh, it could act as quicksand to people or animals that stepped in the wrong place. If the pluff mud didn't get her, Sean envisioned Annie cutting her feet to ribbons on sharp oyster shells, or an alligator, which occasionally ventured into the saltwater river, grabbing her.

But Lauren had sat in the front seat and held the sixty-pound lab in her lap as Sean slowly paddled around the dock. After a half hour, Annie stopped shaking and began looking around and even wagging her tail as they passed other kayakers. It seemed as though she realized she had no business swimming in the river that ran through the salt marsh, but sitting in the front of the kayak while Sean did the work was just fine.

Sean rolled the kayak down the launch, and Annie jumped in, taking her place on what used to be Lauren's front seat. Sean climbed in and pushed off. He paddled downriver with the current of the outgoing tide. The river was narrow during low tide. A sandbank ran along one side, and egrets and other shore birds stalked through the shallow water, occasionally dipping their beaks into the water. Spartina grass grew out of the pluff mud that extended to the water's edge on the other side of the river. Carolina wrens and other small birds sat on the stalks of cordgrass and flew off to new perches when the kayak got too close.

The sun finally crested the trees to the east, and a wood stork soared from the trees and glided past them. Next to the great blue heron, the wood stork was the largest American wading bird. Once nearly extinct in the US, they were now a common sight around Spartina Island. Annie stood up in the bow of the boat and watched the bird with its five-foot wingspan until it landed in the shallow water a hundred yards away.

Sean had thought about sleeping in this morning, but Annie nudged him awake at six o'clock. Even though he had less than five hours of restless sleep, he got up. As he sipped his morning coffee, he realized he had nothing planned for the day. His cold case was no longer cold, and since it was connected to the active murder Charlie was working, he knew better than to interfere. The weather forecast and tide charts showed it was a great day to kayak, so he ate a quick breakfast and headed to the dock.

Sean paddled leisurely for a while, enjoying the light breeze and warm sun. A few miles downriver, he spotted a fin speeding through the water in front of him. Then a second and third one. Then a dolphin's nose came out of the water and disappeared again. He stopped paddling and kept his eyes on the water. For the next hour, he watched a pod of four dolphins hunt fish in the shallow waters of the river. They swam back and forth, corralling hundreds of small fish toward the shore. Some of the fish jumped onto the shore to escape the hunters, but the dolphin flopped onto the bank, plucked the fish out of the mud, and wiggled their way back into the water.

Sean and Annie sat there and watched the dolphins until they disappeared down the river, having either eaten their fill or decided to move to a better fishing hole. The sun and rhythmic motion of the kayak was so relaxing, Sean started to doze. He was no longer used to working long nights and then getting up early. When he had gotten home last night, he sat behind his computer and documented in the cold case team's shared file his investigative activities: discovering Tim Early had a home at Marta Point on MacCrain Island, talking to the dockhand who knew Early's phone number, and then calling and speaking to Early. He kept the synopsis of the conversation brief, only mentioning that Early said he had been expecting police contact after Nancy Russo's murder because the past—the murder of Theresa Goldberg—appeared to be repeating itself. To justify not calling Frank, Sean wrote that since this appeared to be a lead on an active case being investigated by Sgt. Nash, he called her instead.

Sean then summarized their travel to Tim Early's house and finding him dead. He didn't include the details of the search of the house or the murder scene because Charlie would include all of that in her report. He had learned over the years that two officers writing reports about the same activity was an unnecessary duplication of effort and only led to problems. Defense attorneys loved to point out any differences in police reports to a jury, even when they were minor and insignificant, to try to show the cops were either lying or incompetent.

Sean held the kayak's paddle and was taking a deep drink from his water bottle when his cell phone vibrated. A text from Stretch: *Frank called an emergency meeting of the Mudflats Murder Club for 0900 to talk about YOU. I take it you weren't invited.*

Sean began typing a reply when another text popped up, this one from Feebee: *Frank wants us to come to a meeting at 9 AM at the Sea Island Plantation to discuss your recent investigation. I think it's b.s. that you aren't on the distro list. I think you should show up anyway.*

It was political crap like this that Sean hated the most about policing. He was tempted to just say *screw it* and quit the team. He didn't need this.

But he did. He'd felt more alive in the last week than he'd felt since Lauren's death. Besides, it was obvious there were at least two members of the team on his side. He sent a text to Stretch and Feebee: *I'm on the river in my kayak. It'll take me some time to get there.*

It was 9:45 a.m. by the time Sean walked into the club house's casual restaurant next to the golf pro shop. Unlike the formal restaurant and bar upstairs, there was no dress code in the lower level, but people still eyed him as he strode in dressed in a yellow long-sleeved performance tee, knee-length river shorts, and sandals.

Frank, Feebee, Stretch, and Irish John sat at a large round table covered with empty plates and full cups of coffee. Frank's eyes widened, but the other three smiled when they saw Sean. Sean grabbed a chair from a nearby table and slid it between Feebee and Stretch.

Stretch raised his hand for a high five. "The FNG solves the first cold case he looks at."

Sean slapped Stretch's hand. "It's a long way from solved."

Frank's brow furrowed. "We'll be lucky to still have a cold case team after this."

"What the fuck, Frank," Irish said. "Sean handled this like any good cop would."

"That's the problem," Frank said. "We're not cops anymore."

"Once a cop, always a cop," Stretch said.

"If it was just a normal lead on a cold murder, I'm sure Sean would've just written it up," Feebee said. "But this was different. Sean was asked to help on the murder of that lady on his street from the beginning. He recognized the tie in between our cold case and the active one and appropriately notified Sergeant Nash."

Frank leaned forward in his chair. "If he didn't place a phone call to a potential witness on his own, without running it by me or the rest of the team, he wouldn't have had to get Sergeant Nash involved and go running off to MacCrain Island like…"

"Like a real cop?" Stretch said, finishing Frank's sentence. "If he didn't take the initiative and make that call to Tim Early, the sheriff's office probably wouldn't've found his body for a week, and they'd have no idea Early was meeting with someone connected to our case."

Frank reminded Sean of some of the lieutenants he had worked for at OPD—so risk averse the officers under them were afraid to do anything for fear of making a mistake. No one ever got in trouble because they never arrested anyone. "I'm sorry if what I did caused problems for the team. That's the last thing I was trying to do. I guess I was just trying too hard."

Sean saw Stretch grin. He probably used that same apology when he worked—being guilty of trying too hard.

Irish turned to Frank. "You and I were the first two members of our little Mudflats Murder Club. We've looked at lots of cases and haven't really accomplished shit on most of them. All we do is read old reports and try to think of some outrageous crap the sheriff's detectives should do to solve them. On this one, we decided to start from the beginning and reinvestigate it. And look what it got us. Besides, I was with Sean when he made that phone call, and I was in agreement."

"And we need to start doing something other than read old reports and play on our computers," Stretch said. "My former detective boss used to see a bunch of detectives sitting at their desks and yell at them to get off their asses, go knock on doors, and talk to people. Maybe we should be doing more of that."

Sean looked at Frank, waiting for him to say something. Feebee spoke up. "Don't worry Sean, we settled this before you arrived. We all agreed Frank was being a dickhead for not calling you about this meeting and worrying too much about what Captain Cannon might think."

"So, what's our next step?" Stretch asked.

Everyone looked at Sean. "As much as I hate standing down on our cold case, that's the right thing to do. It's clearly connected to the active murders that Sergeant Nash is handling, so anything we do might interfere with her investigation. We should forward her our activity report, and if we come up with anything else, let her know right away."

"I need to tell Captain Cannon something," Frank said.

"Why?" Irish asked.

"Cause he's our boss," Frank said.

"Bullshit," Feebee said. "I'm retired, so I don't have a boss anymore."

"I agree," Stretch said. "Sergeant Nash is up on all of this. It's her job to brief her lieutenant, and his job to brief the captain."

Irish looked at Frank. "I guess if you feel a need to kiss the captain's ass, you can send him a copy too."

"You guys are just like my old NYPD detective squad," Frank said. "Busting my balls just for the sport of it. I'll forward our report to Sergeant Nash and cc the captain. Then we wait for their response about anything else we can do to help."

"In the meantime," Feebee said, "I say we continue with the research we were doing and pass anything we discover directly to Sergeant Nash."

Everyone but Frank nodded in agreement.

50

Charlie and Darryl drove past the entrance to Sea Island Plantation and followed West Road as it curved left and headed toward the southern tip of the island. The road ran halfway between the Intracoastal Waterway, a mile to the west, and the Spartina River, a mile to the east. They entered a part of the island where development had not yet made its way. Old cement-block houses, manufactured houses, mobile homes, and dense trees lined the road. She turned onto a dirt road that jutted west and stopped in front of a mobile home set on a foundation of cement blocks in a row of four other trailers nestled under towering pines and century-old live oak trees. A rusty Honda Civic sat in front of the house.

"Let's low-key this," Charlie said. "He's an addict and probably runs with other druggies who could be our suspect. These murders could be burglaries or home invasions gone wrong, so I'd like to convince Trevor to come back to the station with us voluntarily for an interview."

"You think he's our man?" Darryl asked as he stepped from the car.

"Nothing points directly at him, but when there's a user in the family who has access to the victim's house, it's a possibility. If nothing else, he's someone we need to talk to."

They walked across a carpet of pine needles to the trailer. Although its siding was probably white at one time, mold and mildew that hadn't been power washed off in years had turned it a muted green. Thick humid air hung over the trailer park. Air conditioning units groaned to cool the metal shells in the August heat.

The door of the trailer cracked open as they reached the back of the Ford. Charlie's phone buzzed.

"Hang on," she said to Darryl and looked at the screen. It was Jay.

"Make it quick," she said to Jay. "We're approaching Trevor's house."

The door of the trailer opened, and Trevor appeared in the doorway. He was medium height and skinny, wearing jeans and a dirty tee shirt.

"Trevor was here yesterday," Jay said.

"What?" Charlie said.

"Let me see your hands, young man," Darryl yelled to Trevor.

"He was on MacCrain Island," Jay said. "Positive ID of him renting a bicycle."

In a heartbeat, Trevor's status changed from witness to possible suspect.

Charlie stuck her phone in her pocket without even ending the call and drew her pistol.

Darryl swept his coat aside and fumbled for his gun.

"Hands up," Darryl yelled as he pulled his gun.

"Darryl, back off," Charlie yelled. "Let's wait for backup."

Darryl brought his gun quickly to eye level and yelled, "Drop it! Drop the gun!"

Hanging loosely from Trevor's right hand was a large black revolver.

"Rory called," Trevor said. "Told me you were coming. I'm not going to jail."

Charlie shuffled backward and sidestepped behind the Ford.

"Darryl, pull back," she yelled. She crouched behind the car to make herself a smaller target.

Darryl froze in place. "Drop it. Drop it. Drop it," he screamed repeatedly.

Trevor descended the two steps from the trailer, the gun still at his side.

He was no more than twenty feet away. The revolver wasn't blue steel as were most Colt or Smith & Wesson revolvers, but instead looked almost like it was coated in black paint. It was huge—at least a six-inch barrel.

Darryl hadn't budged from his spot directly in front of the door. He stood ten feet from Trevor, his gun still locked in a two-handed grip. He continued to yell for Trevor to drop the gun.

"Darryl, walk backward to me," Charlie said as calmly as she could. "Behind the car."

Trevor swayed from side to side at the bottom of the cinderblock steps. His eyelids drooped. If he hadn't been holding a gun, Charlie would've thought he was ready to fall asleep.

"Leave me alone," Trevor said softly. "I won't go to jail."

"Drop it. Drop it. Drop it," Darryl yelled.

"I can't do this anymore," Trevor said. "I won't survive in jail."

Charlie tried to talk to him, but Darryl's yelling drowned her out. Darryl continued to yell until his voice turned hoarse.

Darryl's voice changed. No longer commanding a man to drop a gun, it sounded like he was pleading with him—begging him.

"Darryl," Charlie yelled. "Come here. Walk back to me."

Darryl ignored her. She'd seen it before during especially tense situations. He couldn't hear her. Through his tunnel vision, he saw and heard nothing beyond Trevor and the gun in his hand. She inched around the back of the car—leaving her place of cover—and crept toward Darryl. Slowly, so as not to startle Trevor.

She needed Darryl to lower his gun and back off. Deescalate the situation.

She was pretty sure Trevor didn't want to shoot them. And she didn't want to shoot *him*.

"Trevor, go back in your house," she said in between Darryl's commands. "We'll leave. It's gonna be okay."

They could let him go back into his trailer. They could back off and call out the SWAT team and negotiators.

Darryl continued to yell at Trevor to drop the gun. Trevor focused on him, as if he were the only person there.

Another step and she could reach out, grab Darryl's gun, and lower it. Maybe snap him out of his hyper-focus on what he viewed as an imminent threat. She didn't want to startle him, but she had to get his attention.

She took another step just as Trevor raised the gun.

Darryl fired once and quickly again. Charlie felt the muzzle blast on the side of her face as the gunshots exploded a few feet from her head. It felt like her eardrums ruptured.

Trevor slumped to the ground. The revolver tumbled to the ground beside him.

"Holster your pistol," she yelled.

Darryl looked at her in shock. As if her presence surprised him.

He slipped his Sig Sauer into his holster.

She rushed forward and handcuffed Trevor. Then rolled him over to check his wounds. Two expanding blotches of blood on his tee shirt. One on either side of his sternum.

He looked up at her, and she saw the life ebbing from his eyes.

She looked down at the gun and immediately recognized it was a BB gun. Just like the Crossman BB pistol her brothers and friends plinked with as kids.

She sat on the ground and held Trevor in her arms until he took his last breath.

51

SATURDAY

Sean sipped his morning coffee on the screened lanai with the *Island Gazette* on his lap. Even though it was only 6:20, a half hour before sunrise, the temperature already hovered around eighty. The paper said the high would reach ninety-five today. With the humidity, it would feel like well over a hundred.

But it wasn't the weather that had his focus. The headline read, *Police Kill Armed Man on Spartina Island*. Sean read the article a second time.

Two detectives with the Campbell County Sheriff's Office went to the home of a man on Wilson Lane on Spartina Island yesterday at 1:15 p.m. as part of an investigation into two murders that had occurred earlier this week. The eighteen-year-old man, who sources close to the investigation termed a person of interest in the homicides, stepped from his residence with a firearm in his hand.

Despite repeated commands to drop his weapon, the man raised it, and a detective fired multiple shots. The victim, whose name is being withheld pending next of kin notification, was pronounced dead at the scene.

The South Carolina Law Enforcement Division (SLED) is leading the investigation, as is protocol for all officer-involved shootings in the state. A spokesperson at SLED stated they do not comment on active investigations, but would issue a statement upon conclusion of their investigation.

Captain Clinton Cannon III of the Campbell County Sheriff's Office identified the detective involved in the shooting as Darryl Pickett, a 30-year veteran of the department. Pickett and his supervisor, Sgt. Charlotte Nash, a 10-year veteran, went to the location to question the man.

Pickett was placed on paid administrative leave, as is departmental policy following officer-involved shootings, pending the results of the investigation. Cannon stated he could not provide any details of the shooting since SLED was the investigating agency.

The article went on to rehash what the paper had already reported over the past four days about the murders. Sean had investigated dozens of officer-involved shootings when he worked homicide and remembered how emotional the aftermath of the shootings was for everyone involved. Protests often sparked in the neighborhoods where the shootings occurred, normally fed by rumors that had little basis in the facts.

He also remembered the emotional toll the shootings took on the officers. An officer who had to use deadly force in the line of duty was often not the same afterward. Sean had changed after the first time he pulled the trigger. He had been a young patrol officer conducting a traffic stop on a red light violation. As he approached the car, the driver leaped out with a gun in his hand and started shooting. Sean had no recollection of what happened in the next few seconds but recalled standing there afterward with his empty .357 magnum service revolver in his hand and pain shooting through his bloody right thigh where he'd been hit by a bullet from the driver's gun. The driver, a parolee who had just been released from prison, lay dead by his open car door with four of Sean's six rounds in his upper chest.

Sean still recalled the conflicting emotions he felt as the scene flooded with officers, paramedics, detectives, and reporters. He was angry. Angry at the man for trying to kill him. Angry at the man for forcing him to shoot him. Yet he also felt intense joy. Joy that he was alive. Joy so great that he wanted to jump up and down and hug every officer he saw. He suddenly realized that a man is never so happy to be alive as when he looks death in the eyes and survives.

Although Lauren had never asked him to leave the job, he felt her worry. His daughter had just been born, and Lauren was afraid she might have to raise her alone. But being a cop was who he was, and Lauren would never have taken that from him. Sean remembered his grandfather saying policing was a job, better than working in the steel mills. Sean's father referred to it as a career, but one filled with purpose. To Sean it was even more than that. To him, law enforcement was a calling.

Sean had survived two more shootings after that. He saw the worry in Lauren's face for weeks after each one, but she continued to support him. When his doctor presented him with the physical and emotional toll his career had done to him and Lauren showed him they could fully retire, he gladly moved to Spartina Island. Lauren had supported his dream for thirty years. The least he could do, he thought, was support hers.

But then she died. She deserved to live her dream for the next thirty years. He felt guilty for joining the cold case team, because if she were still alive, he would've never done that to her. He also felt guilty for loving every second of the last week he spent investigating homicides. Although no sane man would hope for someone to be murdered, Sean became energized working a fresh homicide. And he felt more alive on Thursday searching a house for a possible suspect and working a murder with Charlie than he'd felt in a long time.

Sean wondered how Charlie was doing following the officer-involved shooting. Sean had finally left MacCrain Island just before midnight on Thursday. He offered to stay as long as Charlie remained, even though there was nothing useful for him to do, but finally, she and Billy insisted he take the next boat home. He kept waiting for her to call yesterday, even checking his phone every hour in case he somehow missed her call or text. He didn't want to accept the reality that she had three regular detectives under her and didn't need his help. When he saw the flash on the nightly news, he understood. They had picked up a lead on a suspect and were hot on his trail.

Sean wanted to call Charlie or Billy to get the real scoop. The paper said the eighteen-year-old was a person of interest. He hated that term. It was something the media coined to categorize people when law enforcement agencies refused to call them suspects. Person of interest had no legal definition and only meant someone the cops were interested in—maybe interested in talking to as a witness, or someone they were interested in knowing more about. Sean knew he was an old-timer when he realized the phrase, person of interest, had not yet been popularized when he entered law enforcement.

Although Sean knew they were too busy with the officer-involved shooting on top of the murders to call him with an update, he sure wished they would. He wanted to be part of the team.

52

Charlie stood in front of a huge floor fan in the corner of the CrossFit gym. She had finished the workout of the day without dying, although she felt like it near the end. Today, it was three circuits of pullups, deadlifts, box jumps, overhead squats, and clean-and-jerks, with a lap around the gym between each exercise. The gym was nothing fancy, just a light industrial building with a cement floor. No mirrors on the wall. No fashion-statement dress code. It was filled with weights and other equipment designed to leave the CrossFit athletes soaking wet and gasping for air after every workout.

Ray Mitro, the co-owner of the gym, threw a towel at her. She caught it and wiped the sweat from her face and arms. A certified CrossFit trainer and martial arts black belt, Ray was in his sixties but had the physique of a much younger gym rat. Shortly after her father's disappearance, she had begun talking to friends and family about joining the sheriff's office. Ray invited her to his newly opened gym. Although she had considered herself an athlete after playing tennis, basketball, and volleyball throughout high school and college, she needed a harder regimen if she was going to succeed in the police academy. She found it in the CrossFit box and the separate room where Ray and his partner, a retired Marine Corps officer, also ran a martial arts program.

"Haven't seen you in a while," he said.

She remembered the day she showed up for her first class dressed in yoga pants and a sports bra, the same attire she wore for her Zumba and aerobics classes at the country club. Ray had tossed her a baggy tank top two sizes larger than she'd normally wear with a picture of a muscle-bound woman doing squats and the words, "Real Girls do CrossFit." Although she had appreciated the energy of aerobics and the calming and relaxing mental benefits of yoga, she felt they would be a detriment to the transformation she'd need to make to succeed as a cop, where she had to become stronger, tougher, and more aggressive—not more serene. "Been pretty busy," she replied.

"I read the paper. What the hell's going on in our tropical paradise?"

"I don't know," she said. "Maybe we need some of your former friends to help me figure it out."

Ray grinned. It was their inside joke, although Charlie believed there was a lot of truth to it. He had shared tiny bits and pieces about himself over the years she had known him. He majored in chemical engineering in college and worked as an energy consultant for various companies, some in Washington and others throughout the Middle East and Europe. There were also stints of government service with the State Department and Department of Energy, although he was never clear whether he was a consultant or a government employee. After a particularly tough workout one evening, she said, half in jest, that she believed he worked for the CIA and the energy companies were merely his cover. He'd just smiled.

"Even if I had those kinds of friends, you don't need them. You're smart and mentally tough enough to bring these cases to their rightful conclusion."

Ray and his partner had drummed the concept of mental toughness into her and the mindset of never quitting, never giving up. "But there's just been so much happening." She told him briefly about the murders and the work Sean had done on the cold case that showed a clear connection between it and the other cases.

"The way you talk about that cold case investigator sounds like he is quite an asset."

She didn't realize she had said that much about Sean, but Ray must've picked up on something. "Sean has been more of a pain in the ass than an asset."

"Why?" Ray asked. "Because he relies on instincts honed from years of experience? Or because he focuses on the objective and moves toward it without asking for permission?"

"At least you didn't say I have a problem with him because my fragile ego feels threatened."

He smiled. "Is this cold case team something that might reopen the investigation into your father's disappearance?"

Although seeing Ray always brought back memories of her father, the thought of the unresolved mystery of his disappearance came flooding back to her. Ray and his partner had been there for her after her father went missing, listening as she vented her feelings of grief and anger and her subsequent suspicions. In some ways, Ray had become a sort of father figure to her—listening when she needed a sympathetic ear, offering encouragement when she had lost her confidence, and sharing his experience, strength, and hope when she needed someone to believe in her and tell her she was okay exactly the way she was. "The department considers it closed, so there's nothing to investigate unless new information surfaces."

"And no new information will surface unless someone looks for it," Ray said, finishing her thought.

She nodded.

"Hang in there, kiddo. Like I told you years ago, all you need to do is work through your feelings, focus on the mission, and trust your instincts and the honorable people around you. When this is all over, you need to come over for dinner. Jackie would love to see you and catch up."

As she was driving home, she kept replaying the shooting in her mind. She had kept her formal statement to SLED last night factual and left out her personal feelings. There was no doubt Darryl ordered Trevor repeatedly to drop the gun and Trevor raised it up. She had no inkling the gun was not real until she saw it lying on the ground after the shooting. Those facts alone would lead an officer to fear for his life, making the shooting justified. The investigators from SLED had kept professional open minds, but it was obvious they were thinking the incident had all the markings of a suicide-by-cop. Trevor had used Darryl to kill himself.

What she didn't say to the investigators was the shooting never needed to happen. She had recognized Trevor was high on opioids and desperate. They could've retreated, surrounded the house, and waited for the SWAT team to secure the premise and negotiators to talk him down. She told the investigators that she tried to tell Darryl to back off, but he apparently didn't hear her. All of that was true. What she didn't say was that Darryl froze. Whether it was from fear or stress-induced tunnel vision she didn't know, but he froze.

After she gave her statement, Billy told her to take the weekend off and check in on Monday to see if SLED had issued a preliminary finding. Although she wasn't the one who shot, being the supervisor on the scene made her partly responsible for the outcome. He could've formally placed her on administrative leave as he did with Darryl. She dialed Billy's number.

"Hey, Charlie, how ya feeling?"

"Fine. Why wouldn't I be?"

"You went through a traumatic incident. Feeling a bit shaken up would be normal."

"I guess," she said. "But I'm fine. Can you tell me the results of the shooting investigation?"

"You know SLED's running lead on it. We helped them last night interviewing witnesses and retracing the steps that led you to Trevor. This is my opinion, and if you repeat it, I'll deny I said a word, but everything you did was by the book. You didn't know Trevor was a likely suspect until you were there, so it was reasonable to approach someone who seemed to be nothing more than a witness without calling for backup."

"Is the brass seeing it another way?"

"We'll have to wait for SLED's finding, but I don't think the captain or the sheriff view this as anything other than a tragic case of a desperate young man using law enforcement officers to commit suicide."

"When can I return to work?"

"SLED promised they'll have a preliminary finding to us by Monday. After that."

"What about my murder cases?"

"Do you trust me to shepherd Detectives Garcia and Todd and take the lead on your cases during your absence?"

"Of course, lieutenant," Charlie said. "I seem to recall you were once a damn good detective."

"It'll be fun getting back into the trenches again, even if it's just for a few days," Billy said, his excitement over the prospect of actively investigating a major case obvious. "We've been up all night, and most of us didn't get much sleep the night before, so I'm just about to send everyone home. Jay and Sherm will meet me here tomorrow morning and we'll see what we can do on the homicides while you're away."

"I don't think Trevor's the killer."

The phone was silent for several beats, and Charlie could picture Billy thinking how best to respond. "We have him present at Marta Point that day," Billy said. "He obviously had access to Sea Island Plantation and his grandmother's house. She wanted to cut him off financially. He's emotionally troubled. He thought you were arresting him for murder—showing consciousness of guilt—and decided to die instead."

"You sound like Captain Cannon instead of Billy Green."

"I don't disagree with the captain's assessment. A mentally unstable man who had means and motive."

"It's easy to pin a murder or two on a dead man," Charlie said. "But we can't let them do that without proof."

"Charlie, trust me. I'll do the right thing."

53

Charlie used her key card to enter the back door of the station. The only people normally working on weekends were uniformed patrol, and except during shift change, the station was often vacant. She went through the back hallway of the investigations division to her squad room.

Both homicide case packets were on Jay's desk. She could always count on him to keep a case file in order and up to date. She turned on her computer and brought up the murder of Tim Early. The last entry Jay had made was just past midnight, about the time she sent him and Sherm back on the boat with Sean.

She opened the accordion folder and checked Jay's handwritten log, finding no additional entries. Knowing Darryl was always delinquent in typing up his log, she pulled his notes and her own log and walked to the copy machine across from Gladys's desk. She could access all the computerized reports and typed investigators' follow-up reports through the department's website from her computer at home, but if she were going to stay current on the cases, she needed logs and notes that had not yet been typed. Although she had faith in Billy to properly work the investigation over the weekend, they were still her cases. She put the pages in the feeder and pressed the button.

As the machine spit out printed pages, she looked beyond Gladys's desk and noticed the captain's office door was ajar. She peeked inside but it was empty. It was not like Captain Cannon to leave his door unlocked, but like everyone else in the division, he had worked two long nights in a row, and sleep deficit often made people sloppy. She returned to her desk and went through the case files again to make sure she had everything.

Thinking about what Ray had said, she pulled a folder from her desk titled, *Missing Person—Henry Nash*. She had read the report a hundred times. According to the report, her father received a phone call at home that evening ten years ago shortly before nine o'clock and told her mother he was going out for a quick meeting with a business partner. When he wasn't home at midnight, she called the sheriff's office.

Although the department would not normally take a report until an adult was gone twenty-four hours, they made an exception because her father was a prominent man in the community. Deputies checked the local hospitals and jails with negative results and put out a missing person alert. That morning, deputies found his car in the parking area on the mainland side of the bridge to Spartina Island. Detectives were notified, and Detective Sergeant Clinton Cannon III responded to the scene.

Charlie turned to the report written by the man who was now her captain. Cannon wrote that he examined the vehicle and found the victim's cell phone and wallet in the glove box but no signs of foul play. He spoke to Charlie's mother who gave him permission to access her father's cell phone log. Cannon found the last call was to Boyd Moretti, her father's partner in the Sea Island Plantation development. According to the report, her mother said it was not unusual for the two to meet halfway between their houses (Boyd lived on Spartina Island) after dinner to smoke cigars and discuss their business ventures.

Cannon interviewed Moretti, who acknowledged talking with her father over cigars in the parking area. Moretti left after thirty minutes, and her father said he was going to take a walk on the bridge. Cannon later spoke to her mother who agreed it was not unusual for her husband to walk along the pedestrian and bicycle path on the bridge, often stopping at the halfway mark to admire the view of the island to the east and the mainland to the west. Cannon's final entry was a month later, writing that he'd spoken to numerous people, handwritten notes of which were in his case file, but no one could offer any leads as to the victim's whereabouts or a clear motive for his disappearance. Cannon wrote that he suspected the victim may have fallen from the bridge, either accidentally or as an intentional act; however, since no body had been found, the case would remain open as a missing person.

Charlie had one more report in her slim file, this one written by Darryl Pickett and dated three years ago. Darryl wrote that he was assigned the missing person report when the department received a court finding, which stated that after her father had been missing for seven years, he was declared dead in absentia. Darryl then officially retitled the case as an accidental death and filed it pending additional leads.

Charlie remembered the upheaval her father's disappearance had created in her family. Her two brothers, both of whom worked in her father's company, took over the day-to-day operation of the developments and commercial real estate management, while her mother assumed the helm as president and CEO and made the major decisions. People in the community talked. Many thought he committed suicide. Although he'd been recently diagnosed with prostate cancer, it was at an early stage and his doctor recommended only watchful waiting. No reason to take his life. Besides, her father was a fighter and loved life too much to check out. The recession had affected real estate prices and development, but her father understood real estate was cyclical. He'd been through it before and always came out ahead when things rebounded.

Charlie had looked for the case file in the records section after she became a deputy, but the records supervisor told her that there were about a hundred sensitive case files maintained in locked file cabinets in the CID commander's office. She once asked Billy if she could see the file, but Billy told her the captain refused because it contained sensitive information, was still an open investigation, and because she was family and personally involved.

Charlie walked down the hall and stood in front of the captain's open door. She stepped inside. Sitting on his desk next to two paper coffee cups half-filled with old coffee was a key ring containing five keys. She carried it to the row of file cabinets along the front wall, one of which was fitted with a locking bar and heavy-duty padlock. She opened the padlock, slid the bar free, and pulled out the top drawer. It contained employee files on everyone in the division. The second drawer contained criminal offense investigations on current and former members of the sheriff's office.

She then opened the third drawer. Inside were file folders arranged in chronological order. One labeled *Nash, Henry* was near the back of the drawer. She scanned through the handwritten notes and chronological log and stopped at one entry. Two days after her father was discovered missing, Cannon interviewed a second man who admitted being with her father and Boyd Moretti that evening in the parking area at the foot of the bridge. The man was Moretti's attorney, Charlie's ex-husband Roger Medcalf.

She carried the file to the copy machine, placed all the pages in the feeder, and pressed the start button.

54

Sean pulled his SUV into his garage and opened the hatch. One o'clock and it was a scorcher already—ninety-three degrees with the heat index well over a hundred. He grabbed several bags of groceries and lugged them into the house. When he returned for the rest of them, a four-door sedan that reeked of rental car pulled into Ken's driveway across the street. Two men in their forties got out and stretched.

The word that Ken's grandson was the eighteen-year-old the police shot yesterday had spread around the neighborhood like wildfire. Nancy's memorial was now postponed. According to a neighbor Sean spoke with on his morning walk and another neighbor he ran into at the gym, Ken's two sons—one of them Trevor's father—were flying in from New Jersey to arrange for Trevor's body to be brought back home.

The driver of the car looked a lot like Ken. The other man not so much. Although Sean wondered what Ken thought about Trevor's connection to the murders, now was not the time for him to ask, nor was he the person to do the asking. He had to let go and trust the sheriff's office to handle the investigation.

After he unpacked his groceries, he dragged the laundry bag from the bedroom and loaded the washer with his dirty clothes from the week, mostly golf clothes and workout attire. He spent the next few hours channel surfing between NASCAR, baseball, and golf, while attending to the laundry whenever the washer or dryer beeped.

A little after three, the mail truck passed by, and he and Annie went out to the mailbox. The heat was even more oppressive. The sky was darkening in the distance. Back inside, Sean dropped the mail on Lauren's desk in the study and returned to the sofa and TV remote. He felt restless and bored.

Thunder rumbled in the distance. A few minutes later, thunder cracked nearby, and the sky got so dark it looked like dusk. More thunder and lightning. Then the rain. First came large heavy drops, followed by a torrent of rain as the sky opened wide. Sheets of water rolled over the gutters and splashed on the driveway.

Thirty minutes later, it stopped. A few minutes after that, the sun came out. Typical summer thunderstorm in the Lowcountry.

Sean stepped outside, raked the mulch that had washed away back into the flowerbed at the front of the house and picked up a few small branches the wind had snapped off his trees. The temperature had dropped at least fifteen degrees, and the air smelled fresh and clean. He sat on the back lanai and checked his email on his phone. When Lauren died, he had set up her account to forward her emails to him. As the months passed, he deleted more and more without reading them.

An email addressed to all tennis players at Sea Island Plantation just came in, saying the courts would be dry and the *Duel at Dusk* tennis match against Cusseta Country Club would be played as scheduled this evening.

Although Lauren had last played tennis recreationally in high school and college, when they moved to Sea Island Plantation, she joined the tennis club and started playing again. Several of Lauren's tennis girlfriends had called Sean several times after she died and invited him to matches and parties. Although most of the women Lauren played with were married, the thought had entered his mind that if he were ever ready to date again, the tennis club might be a good place to meet fit and active single women his age.

Annie rested her chin on his knee and looked up at him. Although the whole concept of dating felt incredibly uncomfortable, he had enjoyed watching matches with Lauren.

"Do you feel like seeing some tennis tonight?"

She wagged her tail.

The tournaments had been going on for an hour when Sean parked his golf cart at the Sea Island sports center. The building housed the fitness center and rooms for many other activities that drew retirees to the development. Tennis, bocce ball, and pickleball courts and a resort-style pool with snack bar surrounded the building.

Sean had attended the *Duel at Dusk* with Lauren a number of times and found it more social than regular, highly competitive tournaments. Tennis clubs from around the area played each other weekly during summer evenings in short matches that only lasted an hour, allowing three matches on each court. He and Annie walked behind the tennis courts and stopped when he recognized some of Lauren's friends watching a doubles match.

A short brunette woman whose name Sean didn't remember gave him a warm embrace. "It's awesome seeing you, Sean. Our gals are up two matches."

He smiled and pretended he cared that the Sea Island teams were winning.

"I want you to meet Yvonne," she said, and pulled him by the arm to a woman about his age wearing a pink tennis dress. "Yvonne, this is Sean, Lauren's husband."

Sean smiled. From the way she introduced him, it sounded as if Lauren was still alive. At least he wasn't introduced as Lauren's ex-husband, as others had done, which sounded like they were divorced.

He equally hated the term widower. He hated all of this. Being reminded of Lauren. People introducing him to single women. The expressions on their faces that said they felt sorry for him. "I'm gonna grab something at the snack bar," he said. "Nice meeting you."

He ate a grilled chicken sandwich and chips alone at a table by the pool. It felt like everyone was looking at him, wondering why he was alone, what was wrong with him, and why he didn't have a wife sitting with him. He had felt pressured to talk with Yvonne. She was probably a perfectly nice woman, but he had no idea how to proceed. Do you start with small talk about the weather and where you're from? Or jump right into asking what she expected from him—dinner, sex, eventual marriage? Should he immediately lay his cards on the table, so he didn't waste her time?

He was definitely not ready for this. Maybe he never would be.

He decided to walk around for a few minutes with Annie to appear social and then get the hell out of this place. Thank goodness he had Annie with him. They strolled toward court one where the largest crowd congregated. Sean recognized the older couple playing on the near side of the court as a husband and wife from Sea Island Plantation who'd been playing tennis club tournaments together for fifty years.

Two women who Sean recognized as tennis pals of Lauren came up and said their hellos. "See the mixed double team they're playing against," the taller of the women whispered. "The kid just turned eighteen, and this is his last match playing with Cusseta before leaving for college."

The tall, athletic-looking kid tossed the ball in the air and delivered a blistering serve. The older man on the Sea Island team returned it with a smooth forehand. They volleyed back and forth a few times until the woman on the Sea Island team, playing the net, was able to intercept the ball and put it away.

"Who's his partner?" the shorter woman asked her friend.

"It was supposed to be some girl from his high school, but there was a last-minute substitute," the taller one said quietly as the kid served.

The Sea Island woman returned the serve, but the kid's female partner was at the net and smashed it down the sideline where the Sea Island team had no chance of getting it. Since her face was hidden behind sunglasses and a baseball cap, Sean couldn't judge her age, but she carried herself with more confidence and less bounce than a high school girl. Wearing a white tennis skort and red razorback tank, she was tall and slender, with tanned and toned legs and arms. Her long blond hair was threaded through the hole in the back of her baseball cap and extended halfway down her back.

"She reminds me of Maria Sharapova," the shorter woman whispered as the kid double faulted.

"She's not that tall," said her friend. "More like Caroline Wozniacki or Ann Kournikova."

Although Sean didn't watch women's tennis, every red-blooded male knew who those tall blonde tennis players were. He glanced at the scoreboard. The Sea Island team was up by one game.

"Thirty-forty," the kid said as he served. The Sea Island team returned it and the Cusseta woman stretched to reach it but made poor contact and hit the ball just outside the line.

"That's game and match," Lauren's friend said.

The Cusseta female player trotted toward her opponents, her blonde ponytail swinging back and forth in cadence with her steps, her long, lean legs traversing the court effortlessly. She shook the man's hand and hugged her female opponent.

Sean began walking back to his golf cart with Annie. Behind him, he heard his name called. He turned and saw the Cusseta tennis player removing her hat and glasses and wiping the sweat from her face with a large towel. It was Charlie.

55

Charlie finished toweling herself off and loaded her racket into her bag as Sean walked her way. She crouched down to greet Annie, taking her head in her hands to rub behind both of her ears simultaneously.

"I didn't know Annie liked tennis," she said.

Sean smiled. A nice smile that she hadn't thought he was capable of. "My former wife used to play with the Sea Island team, so I came out to watch her friends."

"I wonder if we ever played together."

"I doubt it. She was just getting back into it and not at your level."

"I hardly play anymore." Charlie slung her tennis bag over her shoulder and stepped away from the court so the next team could warm up. "I missed a lot of shots I would've nailed when I played regularly, but still, we were just plain outplayed by more experienced players."

"I guess tennis is a sport where experience can trump the athletic ability of youth."

Charlie wasn't sure if he was only referring to tennis. "If Spencer's normal doubles partner had been able to play, they would've beat them. She's going to Clemson on a tennis scholarship."

"Spencer?" he asked.

"My son. My tennis partner in that match. He's a natural athlete—baseball, lacrosse, tennis. He was offered several athletic scholarships but decided to focus on his academics."

"I didn't know you had a son."

She was tempted to say there was a lot he didn't know about her, but resisted being a smart ass, for once. Her mother would be proud. "He leaves for college tomorrow. Duke, majoring in biophysics."

"Impressive."

She glanced at Spencer, who was surrounded by a few of his friends on the other side of the bleachers. "He's headed over to court two where their friends are playing, so I've got an hour to kill."

Sean shuffled his feet. She smiled inwardly at his nervousness over how best to respond to her obvious hint. Finally he said, "I can stick around if you want to go over to the pool snack bar and get a soda or something."

"Do they have beer?"

A few minutes later, Sean brought two large plastic cups of beer back to a poolside table where she waited. "I didn't picture you as a beer drinker," he said.

Another item on a long list of things he didn't know about her. "I'm full of surprises."

He blushed. She enjoyed making him nervous. He had given her a quick once over when he put the beers down, and she remembered the surprise from other men at work when they saw her in civilian clothes for the first time. Although she technically wore civilian clothes at work now, her suits were far from flattering.

"I read in the paper about the officer-involved."

She noted how quickly Sean changed topics to one he was more comfortable with. "The brass wants to pin both murders on Trevor, the kid that was shot."

"And you don't think he's responsible?"

She told him about the leads that had led them to Trevor and the final tip that he'd been seen on MacCrain Island the day Tim Early was killed. "The kid has no history of violence. Although you could maybe stretch it to assume he'd kill his grandmother because she wanted to cut him off financially, what's the motive for killing Tim? The captain is theorizing Trevor committed suicide by cop because of his guilt over committing the murders."

"And you don't buy it."

She shook her head. "Do you?"

"Not my case, but if it were, I'd need the same amount of evidence required to convict someone before I'd pin a murder on a dead man."

Charlie understood the paradox between trusting your instincts—your gut feelings—while still demanding evidence before drawing conclusions, but it was nice to hear an experienced investigator like Sean validate what she'd been thinking.

Sean took a sip of his beer and wiped his mouth with the back of his hand. "How are you doing with the shooting?"

"Fine," she answered quickly.

He smiled faintly and looked at her with his big brown eyes. "How are you *really* doing?"

A man of Sean's size could be naturally intimidating, but he had a way of seeming to shrink in size and draw people in with his eyes until he was the least threatening person in the world. She had no doubt he could disarm murder suspects, conveying such deep empathy that they'd *want* to confess their sins to him.

He didn't press. He just sat there, as if he was willing to sit quietly with her all night.

She began telling him about the incident, all the details she had told the SLED shooting team. Then about feeling Trevor wasn't a threat. About seeing the BB gun lying next to him. About holding him as the life drained from him. Her eyes welled, and tears began to form and roll down her cheeks.

He reached in his back pocket and handed her a handkerchief.

Jeez, what kind of man still carries a handkerchief?

She wiped her eyes. "I feel so embarrassed."

"It's okay to feel," he said.

She didn't know why she felt a wave of enormous relief being given permission to feel—to show emotions—to be human. Maybe because she'd tried so hard to shut off that part of her when she joined the department.

For some reason, she felt safe being vulnerable around this big, tough ex-cop whom she hardly knew.

For at least that moment, she didn't have to be that tough cop. "Trevor was the same age as Spencer. He was someone's son." She wiped her eyes again "He didn't need to die."

Sean sat there silently for a few minutes. Finally he spoke very softly. "I killed a young man his age, too. My third shooting on the job."

"Three?"

He nodded with a look of sadness, totally unlike the bravado she'd seen in other cops when they talked about their shootings.

"My partner and I went to a house to interview the girlfriend of a murder suspect. Officers had been there previously looking for the suspect, but he was never there. We were sitting in the living room talking to the girl and taking notes when the suspect, an eighteen-year-old kid who was mixed up in the drug scene, burst out from a bedroom with a nine-millimeter in his hand. He had the drop on us. He ordered us to unholster our guns and throw them to the floor. My partner was scared. He gave up his gun."

"But you didn't," she said.

"The suspect glanced at my partner's gun lying on the floor, maybe thinking about picking it up, and I drew my handgun and shot him."

"He died?"

Sean nodded.

"Did you feel bad?"

"I felt bad that he made me kill him. But I was incredibly happy I was alive," Sean said. "I second-guessed myself for weeks after that, wondering what would've happened if I surrendered my gun. Wasn't he just trying to get away? Would he just've fled?"

"But he might've executed you both."

Sean nodded.

"What happened to your partner? In our academy they stressed to never surrender our weapon."

"He didn't ask me to cover for him. He told the shooting team exactly what happened and supported my decision to shoot. He had his time in and put in for retirement the following week."

She mulled her own incident over in her head. "So, you're saying I should stand by Darryl."

"I'm not suggesting anything. You need to make that decision yourself. I've investigated plenty of officer-involved shootings and interviewed a lot of cops who had to shoot in the line of duty. Not all of them handled the situations as I would've—or how I hoped I would've. But I think they all did the best they could."

She looked at her watch. An hour had passed, and Spencer would be looking for her. "I've gotta go." She stood and handed Sean his handkerchief. "Thanks."

Sean stood and put the handkerchief back in his pocket. "Anytime."

She gave him a quick hug, then stepped on her tiptoes and kissed him on the cheek. She then quickly turned and rushed out the pool gate toward the crowd of tennis players and spectators.

56

Sean lay in bed watching the ceiling fan revolving above him. He normally fell asleep within ten minutes of lying down, but tonight, his head was spinning. Annie snored softly on her dog bed by the door. No regrets from yesterday or worries about tomorrow with her. The moonlight shone through the bedroom windows that looked out on the marsh, outlining the row of pillows he had stacked on the other side of the bed. Lauren's side.

Lauren loved pillows. When she made the bed in the mornings, she placed their sleeping pillows down first. On top of them went three big square pillows that matched the bedspread. Then she added two cylindrical pillows, and on top of them went five smaller square ones in three assorted colors. She said it made the bed inviting. To him, it wasn't inviting when it was a chore to remove the pillows and carefully stack them on two chairs—you couldn't just toss them on the floor—before you could even lie down.

For years, they joked about the pillows, and Sean said—only half in jest—that if anything ever happened to her, the next day, he'd drive to Goodwill with a carload of pillows. But when she died, he couldn't do it, and every night he laid the pillows in a neat row on her side of the bed. In the darkness, it almost looked as if she were lying beside him. In the mornings, he made the bed exactly as Lauren had—pillows and all.

Seeing Lauren's tennis friends had brought back memories of Lauren and rekindled his grief. Grief tossed you around like waves in the ocean. You never knew when it would happen or what memory it would take you back to. He wondered if he'd ever be able to live fully in the present.

So much of what he did every day was automatic, like his routine with the pillows. When they retired and moved to the island, Lauren liked to sleep in, so Sean would get up at six, as he always had, make coffee for himself, feed Annie, and read the paper. Then at seven, he'd make a second pot for Lauren. She liked fresh coffee. For a month after her death, he automatically made the second pot. And every time the coffee maker beeped with the second pot, he realized he didn't need to do that anymore. But the next morning, he forgot and did it again.

He heard the thermostat click and the air conditioner kicked on. The ceiling fan pushed the cool, refreshing air from the ceiling vents down on him. He thought of the murders: Tim Early, Nancy Russo, and Theresa Goldberg. The answers were out there. He just needed to ask the right people the right questions and convince them to tell the truth. But his investigation had stalled as a result of the officer-involved shooting taking precedence.

His investigation? What was he thinking? They were Charlie's cases. He was retired.

His mind kept circling back to Charlie. When he first saw her five days ago, he thought she was a decent looking woman, but condescending, pushy, standoffish, judgmental, and demanding. Skinny in her baggy suits with her hair wound so tight in a bun that it pulled her face as taut as a Sea Island retiree with a fresh facelift.

She was nothing like that this evening. A slender, athletic body with narrow waist and the nicest legs he'd seen in ages. She looked prettier with her face coated in sweat than at work wearing makeup. Once she dropped her guard, he saw a soft, human side underneath her hard shell. There was still an undeniable toughness to her, an essential component of every good cop, but he saw a glimpse of a tender, sweet side to her. And he liked what he saw.

He was wondering what Lauren would think of her as he finally drifted off to sleep.

57

SUNDAY

The grass was still wet with morning dew when Sean looked over at Jeff Keller next to him in his golf cart. "You don't think we should go over and help them?" Sean asked.

"That's the third time those two hit into the trees and they still insist on looking forever."

Sean tried to be patient with fellow golfers, but his patience was wearing thin this morning. "When I can't find my ball in a minute, I just drop. It's not like my score matters anyway and I buy the cheapest balls I can find."

"That's why we like playing with you, Sean. You might not hit 'em straight, but you know when to pick up and move on."

"Have you talked to Ken since his grandson was killed?"

"No, all I've been hearing is the new neighborhood gossip."

"About what?" Sean asked.

"The key club."

Sean laughed. "When we moved here, Lauren heard that rumor. But come on, Jeff, do you really believe that stuff happens here?"

"You mean you never went to parties back in California, dropped your keys in a bowl, and went home with the girl who drew them?"

"Afraid not."

"Debbie says it happens in Sea Island," Jeff said. "She thinks the Russos might've been part of it."

"Let me guess, she heard it from someone, who heard it from someone else, who heard it from—"

"It might be total bullshit, but I was working in my home office one night when there was a party going on at the Russos'. A bunch of cars were parked on the street in front of my house. It could've been a bible study for all I know, but some cars only stayed for an hour, left, and came back in a few hours. It seemed a little weird, so...who knows."

Sean saw a golf ball sailing from the far tree line and down the fairway. "I think he finally decided to drop." Sean drove down the edge of the fairway to where his ball sat in the rough and pulled a club from his bag.

58

Charlie leaned back in the antique desk chair in the home library and read for the third time the case file she had constructed on her father's disappearance. Although Cannon's investigative log and notes didn't conclude her father had committed suicide, it was obvious he had been leaning that way. Cannon had the department boat search the area under the bridge and requested the Coast Guard for a wider search of the intracoastal waterway based on where a body may have traveled with the tidal currents. Divers also scoured the area.

Cannon's notes mentioned no one he interviewed knew why her father would leave his wallet and phone in his car if he was just taking a walk. None thought he'd ever hurt himself. Charlie was disappointed Cannon didn't take formal statements from Boyd Moretti and Roger since they were the last people to see him. His summaries of those interviews only said the three of them discussed the financial realities of the Sea Island Plantation development in light of the recession. Then they both left for home while her father said he was taking a walk to think about what they had discussed.

She placed the photocopied pages into the folder and stuck it in the back of her father's roll-top desk. Lexi, her Siamese-Burmese mix, jumped onto her lap and looked up at her with her aqua eyes. Charlie stroked her mink coat. She purred loudly, obviously understanding Charlie's feelings.

She didn't know how to go ahead or if she even should. The department would never allow her to officially re-open the case. Billy made it clear years ago that the captain was opposed to it. Even if they agreed to re-open it, they would never allow her to be part of the investigation. Permitting a detective to investigate a case involving a relative could produce multiple legal landmines should the case ever go to court. She understood. She wouldn't allow one of her detectives to investigate a crime involving a close friend or relative. She didn't know how she could justify reopening it. She certainly couldn't admit she broke into the captain's file cabinet, reviewed his notes, and saw potential leads.

The biggest shock was seeing that Roger had been there that night. Everyone intentionally withheld that from her. There were a thousand times when Roger could've mentioned that to her. Sure, they had just ended a contentious divorce, and she probably would've directly confronted him, demanding to know exactly what happened in the parking lot, exactly what was said. She wondered if her mother knew, and if so, was she protecting him or thinking she was protecting Charlie by hiding this from her?

It took every ounce of self-restraint not to interrogate Roger when he had arrived earlier that morning to pick up Spencer for his move to Duke University. She was already pissed that she didn't get to help her son move into his dorm, although she understood Spencer's insistence that both of his parents could not be there. He knew the likelihood of an embarrassing blowout between his parents was too great. Although it hurt to miss the beginning of such an important chapter in her son's life, she grudgingly accepted Spencer's decision that he wanted his father to be a greater part of his college life than just paying half the tuition bills.

She carried Lexi to a leather club chair, one of her favorite spots, and opened her briefcase on the massive hand-carved mahogany table in the middle of the room. Whenever she sat there, it brought back fond memories of her childhood, evenings sitting at the table with her brothers doing their homework or reading a book from one of the floor-to-ceiling bookcases while her father worked at his roll-top desk. The library had been her father's room, but the door was nearly always open, and she loved spending time among the scents of leather, furniture polish, and old books, especially when her father was there. After her divorce, she and Spencer moved in with her mother, and Charlie made this her room. Her mother hardly ever stepped foot into the library—too masculine and too many memories, but Charlie had only good memories of her times here, and the memories got even better when Spencer began doing his homework at this same table.

She powered up her laptop and went onto the department's internal website. She checked the folders for the murder cases and was disappointed to see no new entries from her detectives. She clicked on an email from SLED's lab. It said the DNA on the vaginal swabs and the semen stain in Nancy Russo's underwear were the same profile but did not match Ken Russo. The lab ran it through CODIS and received no hits, meaning whoever had sex with Nancy had no arrest record.

It wasn't Nancy's husband and not a known criminal. So Nancy had a lover. Did the lover kill her after they had sex? Or was the killer someone else, maybe someone who discovered the dalliance?

Had Ken's alibi not ruled him out, this had all the earmarks of a jealous spouse—the husband comes home to see his wife in bed with another man and rage consumes him. Keeping secrets in a community filled with retirees would be tough. Someone had to know who her lover was. Her first order of business when she returned to work would be to re-interview all of Nancy's friends and neighbors, paying closer attention to the rumors and gossip. The truth was probably somewhere inside the rumors.

She called Billy. "Are you working today?"

"I just got here," Billy said. "Told everyone to take the morning off for church and family stuff. How are you?"

"Ready to come back. I just checked my email and saw one from SLED." She read him the DNA results and told him her thoughts.

"I agree with going back and talking to all the neighbors and friends. I can get Jay and Sherm on that right away."

"I should be part of it. I have the best feel for the entire case."

"This sounds like the most tangible lead. I'm not so sure we should wait for you."

"I thought you said I'd be back tomorrow."

"I said SLED should have a preliminary finding tomorrow, and then the sheriff and captain would decide."

"You know this is bullshit. I did nothing wrong. I wasn't even the shooter."

"Police shootings are sensitive. The community watches carefully to see how we police our own. They need to feel we're thorough and not just protecting our own."

"I get it, but we have two unsolved murders on our hands. I went online and didn't see that anyone's done anything since I followed the lead that led us to Trevor two days ago."

Charlie heard him breathing over the phone for what seemed like an eternity. Finally, Billy said. "Charlie, you know you're one of my favorite people in the whole world, and you and I go way back, but it sure sounds as if you're questioning my professional ability and dedication."

Charlie immediately felt awful. Billy had not only been her mentor and friend, but he'd also protected her countless times. "Sorry."

"I know how hard this must be for you. You've been through a lot with the two homicides and then the shooting. Enjoy the day off and let me worry about all of these cases until you return."

She had just set her phone on the table when it rang again. "What!" she snapped before looking at the caller ID.

"Did I call at a bad time?" Sean asked.

She was glad to hear his voice. "I just got off the phone with Billy. They haven't done shit on the murder cases and there's no guarantee I'll even be allowed back to work tomorrow."

"Frustrating, huh?"

"Damn straight it is." She felt a tinge of guilt for venting her emotions on Sean two days in a row.

Sean chuckled. "You know you're *a real* cop, one with blue blood flowing in your veins, when you're given free days off and are mad they won't let you work."

"I guess that makes me pretty sick."

"If so, I had that same illness for thirty years. Let me tell you why I called." He summarized his conversation about the key club and the Russos' rumored involvement.

"Swinger parties? Isn't that something that went out in the seventies?"

"Actually, they still go on. My final year in Oakland, the department was trying to find a way to shut down a regular swinger party that was taking place in an upscale residential area. Neighbors complained about the parking and what their kids might think."

"Yeah, but California has always been full of degenerates."

"Can't argue with that, but the truth is those who attended were normal people—just with different attitudes about sex and marriage."

"But you're talking about couples old enough for social security doing this. Sorry, but I don't buy it."

"Not sure if I do either, but I thought I'd pass it on. Secondly, I don't know if you remember the third couple that vacationed down here when Theresa Goldberg was killed."

"Steve and Sandra Nowak," she said. "You told me a few days ago that they now live in Sea Island Plantation."

"Right," he said. "I wanted to talk to them about the cold case, and now after Tim Early's murder, it seems even more relevant that someone interview them."

"Billy reminded me I'm supposed to lay low until I'm cleared."

"I understand."

"I should probably tell Billy about this so he can go out and interview them with Sherm or Jay."

"I guess."

She didn't want to pass on the lead and figured Sean didn't either. She had a better chance of getting the full story out of them than other detectives not as intimately familiar with the cases, and, although she didn't want to admit it, she wanted to be the one to break the case. She waited for Sean to say something else. When he didn't, she told him about the DNA results.

"That's interesting," he said. "Someone other than Ken had sex with her that morning, and that someone has no criminal record."

"At least it throws out the media-spun serial rapist theory."

"Did you see the *Island Gazette* this morning?"

"I wanna puke whenever I read that rag."

"I understand, but they haven't let go of that theory. They're now suggesting there's a serial killer randomly murdering senior citizens. I'm sure your bosses are feeling the heat."

That was above her pay grade, and she didn't want to worry about what the media was printing and blabbering about to increase their readership. "Well, if that's it..."

"Can't think of anything else," Sean said.

She liked talking to him. She wanted to tell him about Spencer going off to college and the void it created in her life. She guessed he had kids—probably grown now—and wondered what it was like for him when they left home. "If you think of anything else, give me a call," she said.

"I will."

She looked at her phone, waiting for him to hang up. Maybe he was waiting for her to say something more or to hang up first. He finally ended the call.

She made a note about Sean's information so she could add it to her log when she returned to work. She went back to her inbox and deleted about twenty emails about trivial pieces of meaningless information people passed on to cover their asses and administrative crap she didn't care about. She stopped at an email from Ken Russo that he'd sent shortly after she met with him two days ago. The email listed eight different companies that had been to their house over the past six months, ranging from a pest control company to a plumber. Following that was a list of social events at their house, including a wine-tasting party they held at their house two months ago. The people in attendance included Steve and Sandra Nowak.

Charlie switched back to the computer file on Nancy Russo's murder and brought up the summary of her interrogation of Ken at the station the day of the murder. She ran a search for Nowak. There it was. Ken said that on Saturday night—a week before Nancy's murder—they went to a wine-tasting party at the Nowaks' house.

59

She stood at the doorstep of the Nowaks' house dressed in tan pants and a light blazer—not quite her normal work attire, but a look people would accept for a detective working on a Sunday. Before she left her house, she had done a quick background on them. Both sixty-six, they moved here a year and a half ago from New Jersey. Neither had any criminal history. Their house was a two-thousand-square-foot, two-bedroom, two-and-a-half bath, single-story stucco model on a lagoon a few streets from the activities center.

Steve Nowak opened the door. He was a stoop-shouldered man about her height, with a neatly trimmed beard that was lighter than the tufts of gray hair that stuck out from the sides of his bald head. He looked significantly older than his driver's license photo. She swept the corner of her coat back to show the badge clipped to her belt. "Mr. Nowak, I'm Sergeant Nash with the sheriff's office. I'd like to talk to you about the murder of your friend, Nancy Russo."

She followed him into the living room, where he muted the sound of a preseason football game on the TV. "My wife's off visiting a neighbor in a nursing home," Steve said. "She knew Nancy better than I did."

"That's okay." Charlie sat on a floral sofa facing a recliner surrounded by a TV remote, magazines, and a can of beer on a small end table. "I can always talk to her later."

Once Steve settled into his chair, Charlie asked, "How long have you known Nancy?"

"We knew them from back in New Jersey."

"And Tim Early?"

"We knew him back then too. Until we read about his death in the paper, we had no idea he had a house down here."

"So you haven't kept in touch with him?"

"It's been over thirty years since we saw him."

"But you kept in touch with Nancy and Ken?"

"They've been friends for a long time, and we see them occasionally down here."

"Like at regular wine-tasting parties?"

Steve shifted in his seat. Charlie had intended to make him uncomfortable by showing him that she'd done her homework and knew a lot about him and his relationship with the two murder victims. When a person realized they couldn't bullshit you, it often speeded up the process of getting to the truth.

"Yeah, a group of us get together once a month or so."

"How's that work?" she asked. "The wine-tasting parties."

He looked baffled. Or it could've been an act. "Whoever hosts the party buys an assortment of different wines, often related to a particular theme. The last one we hosted, we bought German wines. We pour a taste of each wine, and everyone talks about it."

She smiled as if he had enlightened her. Even if wine-tasting party was code for swinger party, she wasn't surprised he didn't mention it. "Let me get right to the crux of why I'm here. Who would want to hurt Nancy and Tim?"

"I have no idea. Like I said, I haven't seen Tim in ages, but everyone loved Nancy."

"Sometimes a person puts themselves at risk through certain activities that could lead to their death," she said. "Not that that means the victim deserved it. But someone who uses drugs could be murdered over a bad drug deal, or a woman who works as a prostitute could encounter a violent john. What was Nancy into?"

Steve looked at his beer can, picked it up, and took a swig. She knew she'd hit a nerve. "Nothing I can think of. Nancy didn't do drugs or anything like that."

"I heard she and Ken had been having some problems. We've ruled him out, by the way. But I was wondering—with those difficulties at home—was Nancy having an affair?"

He sat up straight. "No! Absolutely not."

"How can you be so sure?"

"She wasn't that type."

She decided not to push him at this time but would revisit that subject later. "We're also looking at a cold case, the murder of Theresa Goldberg."

Steve looked down at his lap and sighed.

"You came down here with them on vacation that year, didn't you?" Charlie asked.

He took a deep breath. "I knew all of them back in New Jersey. All three of them. Sandra and I have been wondering if this was just a weird coincidence or something else. But you can't think.... You don't think either of us had something to do with their deaths—that we murdered them?"

Until that moment, the thought had never entered Charlie's mind. But the way he said it made her realize how naïve she'd been to come here alone. To question someone this close to the murders when she wasn't even supposed to be working. To be here without telling anyone where she was.

She tried to hide her nervousness with a confident smile. "If I thought you were a murderer, do you think I'd come here alone?"

"I guess not, but I'm feeling very uncomfortable with this questioning."

"Talking about the murders of three of your friends *should* be uncomfortable. I'm sorry about that."

"Don't you need a warrant to come in my house and question me? Or shouldn't I have a lawyer present?"

"Mr. Nowak, you invited me in. And no, the only people who need a lawyer are those who are under arrest and being questioned as a criminal subject."

"I think I want to talk to my wife before we continue this."

"Why is that?"

"They were her friends, too, and I don't want to say anything that might tarnish their reputations."

"Sir, they're dead. They were murdered. If I know what they were involved in, it might tell me who their killer was."

Steve stood and walked halfway to the door. "Leave me your card, Sergeant, and once my wife and I have time to discuss this, I'll call you."

"More chicken, honey?" Abigail asked.

Charlie's mother made Sunday dinner even when no one was around to enjoy it. That's what Southern women did. It was always one of her traditional Southern dishes, this time chicken and gravy, rice, and okra. She also insisted on eating in the dining room, even though ten of the chairs at the huge table were unoccupied.

"No, thanks, but it was very good," Charlie said.

"The house feels strange with Spencer gone."

"It does," Charlie agreed. "It's going to give you a lot more freedom not having to be around for him." When Charlie and Spencer moved in with her mother after her divorce and her father's disappearance, they filled a void for each other. Taking care of Spencer while Charlie worked gave Abigail a purpose in life. It also gave Charlie and Spencer a safe, comfortable home where all their needs were provided for and allowed Charlie to pursue her career with its erratic schedule.

"What about you?" Abigail asked. "You no longer need to stay in this old house for its built-in babysitter."

Charlie had thought about this day for a while. Of getting her own place, maybe a small house with its own boat dock on the river, or a nice beachfront condo on the island. Places where she could see the water from her house. Places where she could step outside right onto the beach or into her boat. An extra bedroom for when Spencer came home for holidays and the summer. A place that would be her own, where she wouldn't have to abide by her mother's rules. A place where, if she so desired, she could bring a man home to.

"I love this house and how you made it a home for me and Spencer these past ten years."

"Truth is, Spencer hasn't needed me much for the past couple years."

"Oh, Mom, that's not true. He just needed you in a different way. I don't know what I would've done after the divorce without you."

"Maybe you might've been motivated to find yourself a new husband."

"Women today don't need a husband to take care of them or to feel complete." She immediately regretted saying that. Her mother could've remarried once her father was declared legally dead three years ago, but other than attending a few social events with gentlemen friends, as she called them, she seemed to have no desire to date, much less remarry.

"You're still young and very eligible."

"We've been through this before, and you know how hard it is to find a man capable of a real relationship with a female cop."

"What about that fella, Sean?" Abigail asked. "He seems like a nice man and very handsome."

"He's ten years older than me."

"So what? Your father was ten years older than me. That seemed like a lot when I was only twenty and he began courting me, but later, it didn't seem like much."

"And he just lost his wife a year ago."

"I'm sorry. I didn't know that."

"Cancer, it was rather sudden. And I don't want to be in a relationship with a man who's always comparing me to his deceased wife." She recalled how her mother used to complain about things her father did when he was alive, sometimes nagging him half to death, but once he was gone, he became a saint in her eyes.

"Oh, honey, a good man would never do that."

"How about you and your *gentlemen friends*? Tell me you don't compare them to Dad?"

"Your father was a very good man. The best. But he's gone, and I don't dwell on it."

Her mother was an expert at *look-good*, stuffing her feelings to maintain an outward appearance that everything's fine, but Charlie knew her mother had not gotten over the loss of her husband. Charlie figured this was as good a time as any to get some answers to questions that had been nagging her for a decade.

"Did you ever talk with Boyd Moretti about what he and Dad discussed that night?"

"What's bringing this up now?"

"Maybe it's all the murders that have occurred. What did they discuss?"

Abigail pushed her plate back and took a sip of her sweet tea. "If you remember back then, the country was going through a recession. Folks up north weren't moving down here like they were a few years earlier, so new home sales dipped. He and Boyd had a lot of money invested in Sea Island Plantation, but only about a hundred lots were sold, and the other two hundred they had all plotted out and ready for building weren't selling. People didn't have the kind of money to buy those nice lots and build big houses. Boyd presented him with a plan to avoid going bankrupt."

"Was that really a concern? Dad had a lot of other ventures."

"We were going to be fine with all of his other holdings, but Sea Island was a separate entity, and if they had to sit on it with no revenue for years, they could've lost it. And Boyd had investors who were concerned."

"What happened to change Dad's vision about Sea Island?"

"A while after your father disappeared, Boyd asked to meet. He and his lawyer came over and showed me a new plan. Instead of the two hundred large houses on big lots in the section west of the creek, they could build eight hundred smaller homes on normal size lots. Those houses would be affordable for folks who wanted to leave the snow and high taxes up north even during the recession."

"Dad would've never gone for that," Charlie said. "We created the vision for that property together. We wanted to showcase the natural environment and fit the homes, amenities, and a golf course around the land."

"I know how much that had meant to you, but your father was also a realist. Besides, he wasn't around, and I had to make the decision."

"Who was Boyd's lawyer?" Charlie asked, already knowing the answer. "Did he sway you?"

Abigail stared at Charlie for a moment and then said softly, "Roger was his attorney. And no, he didn't try to sway me. He helped me see the reality of the situation."

Charlie wondered if Roger had really changed so drastically from when they first met at Clemson, or if he'd been a slimy narcissist his entire life and she had missed it. Everything had seemed perfect for the first five years of their marriage, both of them working for the regional planning commission and trying to protect the fragile Lowcountry for future generations. Then he needed to make more money than the planning commission paid their attorneys and opened a law practice representing developers. There he used everything he had learned working for the planning commission to circumvent the county and state laws and quash the commission's guidance and rulings in favor of developers.

"Why'd you never tell me Roger was also there with Dad the night he disappeared?"

"I knew you'd blame him," Abigail said. "You despised him so very much. And nothing he said was going to bring your father back."

60

"I need to hit the head," Jeff said. "Anyone want another beer?"

Sean passed, but George Laughlin and Mark and Dave, the other two men at the table, raised their hands. The four men's wives were in Charleston on a shopping and dinner excursion, so Jeff hosted the husbands for poker and invited Sean to join them. Mark and Dave were both in their seventies and lived next to each other on Cormorant Court, which ran between a lagoon and the river off Blue Heron Lane.

"Is anyone else getting a bit concerned for our safety after Nancy was killed and then that guy on MacCrain Island?" Mark asked as they waited for Jeff to return.

"I have an alarm company coming on Tuesday to give me a quote," Dave said.

"We already have a home alarm. For the first time since living here, we started setting it at night. I'm also thinking about getting a gun," Mark said.

"You're more likely to shoot yourself than an intruder," Dave said. "Isn't that right, Sean?"

Sean took a sip of the beer he'd been nursing for the past hour. Having seen the horrendous acts people were capable of doing to others, Sean strongly supported the right to self-defense, but didn't think guns in the hands of untrained citizens was the answer. "I've seen a lot more instances of homeowners shooting themselves or someone else by mistake than instances of legitimate self-defense."

"But those people were probably idiots," Mark said.

"Even with all our training on how to shoot and when to shoot, cops make mistakes," Sean said. "Seriously, Mark, if you're considering a gun for self-defense, I'd be glad to talk more with you about it and other alternatives."

"We have a gun," George said, "but I don't even know where it is."

"Then what good is it?" Mark asked.

"Hell, it was Beth's," George said. "Her father gave it to her after college. I think she keeps it in a dresser drawer with her underwear or something."

Jeff returned and passed out the beers. "Five card draw," he said and dealt the cards.

While everyone was examining his cards, Sean asked George, "Did you know Tim Early, the man killed on MacCrain?"

George looked at his new cards, frowned, and took three. "Not really. He was a member of my country club in Short Hills for a few years, but I was too busy with family and work in those days to socialize much at the club."

Sean took one card, hoping for a one in four chance of matching up his four hearts for a flush. He drew a spade. "But I guess Beth and Nancy knew each other well back then."

George laughed. "Beth was *the* country club socialite in those days. I didn't really get to know her until years later, after she divorced and my own marriage fell apart."

Sean folded when the betting came around to him.

Mark won the hand with two pair, raked the chips his way, and said, "That was your second, but how many for Beth?"

"Four," George said. "She needed more practice to get it right than I did."

It was Sean's turn to deal, and he called seven-card stud. He dealt everyone two cards down and one face up. He had the high card with a king, bet a dime, and dealt everyone another card face up. "The cold case team I volunteer with is looking into Theresa Goldberg's murder from thirty-eight years ago. She was from up there too, wasn't she?"

"I don't know for sure if she and Aaron were members of the country club at that time," George said, "But I ran into Aaron at the club plenty in the years after that."

Dave got a second jack face up, bet a quarter, and said, "Are we here to play poker or chat about the glory days at some highfalutin country club?"

Although Sean had many more questions about the members of George's country club, he'd have to wait for a better place and time.

It was after ten when Sean got home. While Annie peed and sniffed around the backyard, he sat on a bench under a live oak tree overlooking the marsh. The full moon cast eerie shadows through the tree branches swaying gently in the breeze. Annie perked up her ears at the distinctive *who-cooks-for-you* hoot of a barred owl in the distance. The tide was near its low mark, and the river was barely visible in the darkness beyond the sea of Spartina grasses waving back and forth in the wind.

He pulled out his phone. He wanted to share with Charlie his excitement over what he'd learned but thought it might be too late to call. He punched out a text: *Played poker with George Laughlin and others. George said he, Beth, Russos, Goldbergs, Tim Early all members of same country club in NJ.*

Annie sat beside him with her nose twitching as she took in the scents the wind carried from the marsh. His phone jiggled with a return text from Charlie: *Interesting! I interviewed Steve Nowak. No surprise, but he knew all 3 victims. Maybe member of same CC??? Admitted he, wife, and Russos do wine-tasting parties at Sea Island. Got uncomfortable when I asked more.*

Sean: *Does wine-tasting party=swinger party????*

Charlie: *???*

Sean: *George mentioned they own a gun, given to Beth by her father years ago.*

Charlie: *My detectives ran everyone. Don't remember guns registered to them.*

Sean: *Even in NJ, no requirement to register guns years ago.*

Charlie: *Right and lots of people in SC have guns. Doesn't make them killers.*

Sean: *Few days ago, George told me he went to gas station for sausage biscuit early Monday before golf, but didn't tell wife because supposed to be on diet. He may have told your people he was home.*

Charlie: *Thanks. Go to bed. Let's talk in the morning.*

61

MONDAY

Sean opened his eyes and saw the clock on his nightstand read 6:02. Annie was sitting by his bed and looking at him, her nose inches from his face. "Okay, no sleeping in for us," he said and rolled out of bed. Annie followed him into the bathroom then into the closet where he pulled on shorts and a tee shirt. He filled her bowl in the kitchen with dry kibble and started the coffee pot. After she did her business in the backyard, he walked out the front door and sent Annie to gather the morning paper. Ken was walking down his driveway to collect his paper at the same time.

"I'm really sorry about your grandson," Sean said.

"Just about when I'm regaining my senses following Nancy's death, I get a second punch in the gut."

"I can't imagine what it's like."

"I've got coffee on," Ken said. "You wanna come over for a cup?'"

Sean let Annie back into his house then crossed the street to Ken's house and sat at the kitchen table where Ken poured him some coffee.

"Cream and sugar?"

He shook his head. He recalled Beth Laughlin at dinner Monday night saying she and Nancy didn't drink coffee. "Nancy didn't drink coffee, did she?"

"Quit it ten years ago," Ken said. "And never missed it. I pretty much

IVed the stuff when I drank just to clear my head in the mornings. Now I only make it at home if I'm going to be around that morning."

"So you didn't make coffee at the house on Monday because you were going to your AA meeting."

"I got my first cup at McDonald's and another one at the meeting," Ken sipped his coffee quietly for a moment. "The police think Trevor killed Nancy and Tim."

Sean nodded. "I hear they discovered Trevor was on MacCrain Island the day Tim was murdered."

"It doesn't make sense. Trevor would've never hurt anyone."

"I'm sure the truth will come out," Sean said.

Ken looked at his watch. "I need to shower and clean up. I'm meeting my kids at the funeral home in an hour."

Sean stood. "I hate to waste good coffee. You got a to-go cup?"

Ken got a Styrofoam cup out of the pantry and handed it to him. Sean was about to say something but reconsidered. "Good luck today," he said as he walked out the door.

62

Charlie came through the back door into the kitchen after her morning run. Abigail was making breakfast. "You're dripping all over the floor," she said.

Charlie grabbed a dish towel from a drawer and wiped the sweat from her face. Abigail frowned but didn't scold her as she normally did for using a kitchen towel for bathroom purposes. Charlie filled a large glass with water and chugged half of it.

"Are you hungry?" Abigail turned bacon with a fork in a cast iron skillet.

Charlie didn't need to peek under the lid of the small pot to know it held enough grits to feed the neighborhood. "Not that hungry." Although she had never worried about her weight, she still took Southern cooking in small doses.

"I'm making shrimp and grits for some ladies from church who'll be visiting in a little bit," Abigail said. "I can make you some eggs."

"I'm good," she said and popped two slices of bread into the toaster and filled a bowl with berries and sliced peaches from a container in the refrigerator. She sat at the kitchen table and called Sean. "Halfway through my morning run, I became thoroughly convinced the murder of Nancy Russo and Tim Early stems from what happened to Theresa Goldberg thirty-eight years ago."

"And what facts convinced you of that?" he asked.

"No facts, just a gut feeling."

"Gut feelings normally stem from facts," he said. "Try to articulate them."

She loved Sean's manner of brainstorming a case by forcing her to tie together the pieces of known information before jumping to a conclusion or formulating a theory. "The same people are reappearing in all three cases. Six people came down here on vacation from New Jersey: Steve and Sandra Nowak, Tim and Lizzy Early, and Aaron and Theresa Goldberg. Tim and Theresa are dead. Maybe Tim killed Theresa and now someone killed him for revenge."

"That's a theory," he said. "What facts lead you to it?"

She thought for a moment. "I don't have any. I tried to talk to Steve, but he blew me off when I pressed him. I'd like to try Sandra, but I need to wait until I'm returned to full duty so I can bring her to the station. What do we know about Lizzy Early and Aaron Goldberg?"

"I located a current phone number for Aaron back in New Jersey and called him last week. He hung up on me when I questioned him about the night Theresa was killed. Said it was in the past and he wanted to forget it."

"According to the coroner, Tim Early's next of kin is his wife, Susan Early. I don't know what happened to Lizzy or how long she and Tim remained married. The only mention of her is her name in the cold case report."

"I don't have access to anything other than public records on the internet," Sean said. "And I wasn't able to find anything on her either. Maybe she went back to her maiden name or remarried before the internet started capturing people's every move."

"There could've been other murders in New Jersey connected to these people," Charlie said. "I can try criminal and DMV records and maybe call the state of New Jersey vital records and local police when I get back to work."

"I've been playing around with all the names we have and drew up a link diagram containing the people and their connections to each other, the three murders, the country club, and Spartina Island."

"You drew a link analysis by hand?"

Sean chuckled. "I know you probably have a crime analyst who enters all that into a computer that spits out fancy charts and diagrams, but when I started investigating crimes back in the dark ages, we didn't have that. When you see everything on paper with the connecting lines, the relationships are clearer. There's still a lot we don't know, so I have a bunch of dotted lines—"

"Dotted lines represent possible connections?"

"Yeah. As we interview these people and get the truth out of them, I think many of the dotted lines will become solid."

"I'd like to see that," Charlie said.

"Anytime."

"Are you home?"

"I am."

"I'll be over as soon as I shower and change."

On her way to Sean's house she called Billy for an update about her status. He said it probably wouldn't be until later in the day before SLED spoke to the sheriff and gave them a preliminary report. He'd let her know as soon as he heard something, but she shouldn't plan to come back to work until tomorrow at the earliest.

Charlie parked her unmarked Dodge Charger in Sean's driveway. Even though she wasn't officially back at work, she was working, so it made sense to use the department's gas. But she wasn't exactly working, so she dressed in a pair of white capris and a lavender crop top and tied her hair back in a ponytail.

She always liked the Riverside neighborhood of the Sea Island Plantation with its sizable lots. The custom-built houses all looked different from their neighbors, unlike the tract houses on the other side of the development, where buyers choose from a half-dozen different models. She had driven through here with her father when the houses were being built, and she loved how the landscaping had matured and the houses blended into the natural setting. Her father would be proud of what he had built.

She threw her bag over her shoulder and strode to the door as Annie barked to announce her arrival. Sean opened the door barefooted. Wearing shorts and a golf shirt, he didn't appear to have spent a fraction of the time deciding what to wear as she did. His beautiful yellow lab sat by the door obediently. She patted Annie on the head and stepped inside. The house's layout was open and airy with high ceilings, a modern floor plan, and nicely decorated. A large sectional sofa faced a gas fireplace and a flat screen TV on the wall above it. She imagined it as a perfect place to watch a movie at night or to stretch out with an enjoyable book on a rainy afternoon. A stylish leather recliner completed the grouping. Unlike the living room and family room—parlors as her mother called them—in her house, everything here felt casual and relaxed.

"I have sodas and iced tea if you…"

Sean sounded nervous. She wondered if she was the first woman in his house since his wife's death. "Water would be fine."

"A bottle or tap?"

She smiled. "Tap is perfect. I try not to add more plastic to the landfills."

Three hardback novels were neatly stacked next to two TV remotes arranged in a perfect row on the end table between the recliner and sofa. The kitchen was spotless, not even a dirty glass in the sink. She wondered if he was a neat freak or had rushed through the house picking things up before she came over.

He filled a large glass with cold water from the refrigerator door dispenser and handed it to her. "I have my notes and stuff in here," he said, motioning to a round glass-top table in a breakfast alcove off the kitchen.

She set her shoulder bag on the table and looked out the back window to a lush, shaded yard. Beyond that she saw Spartina grass waving in the breeze and sunlight sparkling off the river. "I came out here a few times with my dad when he was plotting out each lot. He made sure each riverfront lot was special."

"He was sure a hands-on developer," Sean said.

She laughed. "He drove the survey crews crazy, tromping forest so thick it looked like a jungle. I still can see him dressed in his boots and work clothes and swinging a machete to clear paths."

"He did an excellent job. We…I mean I…love the home site."

"What ever happened to the original owners—the couple who built the house?"

"They were near seventy when they retired here, and he ended up with some major health issues, so they moved closer to their kids. Good for us, because the house was perfect for us and came on the market at the ideal time."

Charlie sat down at the table, and Sean placed a diagram drawn on two taped-together sheets of paper in front of her. Standing beside her, he spent the next five minutes pointing out the relationships between twenty different people, each represented by a name inside a circle. When he finished, he sat across from her and pulled a file from a stuffed accordion folder. "This is what I have on Aaron Goldberg," he said.

The accordion folder contained files labeled with the names of everyone on the link diagram. She scanned the contents of the folder on Aaron. "Jeez, Sean, you've set up a full case file based on a flimsy murder book we threw together."

He looked at her, surprised, as if to say, *what did you expect? I'm a homicide detective after all.* "I don't mean to take over the investigation, I understand I'm just a civilian volunteer, but I needed to organize it to see the big picture. I also kept a log where I documented my actions, observations, and statements people made to me. Some of that I typed into the cold case team report, which someone should've forwarded to your office."

She laughed. "This is great. Really, really great!"

Her phone beeped. She pulled it from her pocket. "Hello, this is Charlie Nash."

"Sergeant, this is Susan Early. We've been playing phone tag."

Charlie had called the Earlys' Manhattan home the day after Tim's murder, and Susan called her office phone the following day. They finally traded cell numbers over voicemail. "I'm going to put you on speaker so my partner, Sean Tanner, can hear."

Sean winked at her when she called him her partner.

"Your last message said you were thinking about coming down here," Charlie said. "We'd love to talk with you in person about your husband's death."

"I'm here now."

"You're here?"

"Flew into Savannah with my attorney last night. We arranged for a boat to take us to Marta Point this morning."

"Hang on a second," Charlie said and muted the phone. "Are you available if she'll meet with us?"

"Sure, but won't you get in trouble?" Sean said.

"Probably."

Sean's eyes widened, probably wondering if she fully understood the consequences. He then said, "If it was my case, I'd do the same."

Charlie smiled and unmuted the phone. "We can be at your house at Marta Point in just over an hour, if that will work."

"Sure, but maybe we can find another place to talk. My attorney's handling it all, but there's a cleaning crew at the house right now, and contractors are coming over soon to fix the wall and refinish half the floor. I'd just as soon get away from this for a while."

"We can talk on my boat," Charlie said. "I'll call when we're ready to dock at the Marta Point marina."

63

Sean sat in a raised captain's chair alongside Charlie's matching seat as she motored the thirty-six-foot Hinckley Picnic Boat out of the Cusseta Marina, the polished teak-trimmed hull gleaming in the midday sun. Although on the small size for a yacht, the boat was every bit as luxurious as those twice its size. He looked around the cherry-paneled cockpit at the array of gauges and controls surrounding Charlie's perch and through the open doorway between their seats to a compact galley and stateroom below.

He'd felt like they'd been sprinting ever since Charlie's phone call with Susan Early. He had quickly changed clothes and jumped into her car. Charlie then sped through the plantation, onto the public roads, and to her house. He'd ridden with plenty of cops who drove crazy fast over the years, but most slowed down by the time they made detective. Charlie still drove like a rookie street cop. At every stop, she floored the accelerator, and the Charger roared down the street, oblivious to the speed limit.

He had waited in her car as she ran into her house and changed in three minutes. She yanked the shifter into drive and sped to the Cusseta Marina, where the harbormaster was aboard the Hinckley with its diesel engine warmed up and ready to go.

"This was my father's baby." Charlie steered the boat away from the dock. "They're hand built with amazing attention to detail. It's considered a day boat, but it works as an overnighter for one or two people, and he'd taken it all the way up to the Chesapeake and as far south as the Florida Keys."

"It's beautiful." Sean turned toward her, marveling at how comfortable she seemed piloting the boat. Although the attire she had changed into at her house was more appropriate for a witness interview, he missed seeing the bronzed strip of skin that peeked between the crop top and capris she wore at his house. "Do you take it out much?"

"Not as much as I'd like. A few weeks ago, I took it to Savannah with my brothers and their families for an early dinner." She smiled and looked at him. "You'll have to come with us next time."

Sean felt his throat constrict as he formulated a response. If she were one of the guys from the department who threw out an open invitation like that, he would've thought nothing of it—one cop inviting a fellow cop to some off-duty fun. Coming from a sexy, single woman, it felt different. "I'd like that," he finally said.

They sailed slowly past Dufftown the same as they had a few days ago in the much smaller skiff, and then they picked up speed as they approached the wider part of the river. She glanced at her watch and said, "We've got time. I'd like to show you something."

She cranked the wheel to the left and opened the throttle. The bow of the large boat rose, and they sped out of the mouth of the river toward Spartina Island. A few minutes later, she pulled back on the throttle, and they chugged toward what looked like a chunk of rock in the middle of the sound where the Atlantic Ocean met the Cusseta River and Intracoastal Waterway. The big diesel engine idled, and they coasted to within two hundred yards of the piece of land in the middle of the water.

"Boaters and birders call this Chick Island." Charlie handed him a pair of binoculars. "About forty years ago, they started dumping dredging material—dirt, sand, rock, and even chunks of concrete—from the local harbors. The birds figured it out and turned it into a rookery."

Sean scanned the tiny island through the binoculars. Thousands of birds covered the rocks and sand. Brown pelicans flocked on the north end and a mass of smaller white birds congregated on the other side of the tiny island. He saw hundreds of nests among the rocks. Signs warning boats to come no closer ringed the island.

"The pelican chicks hatched a few months ago," she said. "Most have already fledged, but they still hang out with their parents, who'll feed them for another few months. Most of the show is over now, but through last month, I'd come out here every week to watch the chicks hatch and grow up."

"This is amazing," Sean said.

Charlie smiled. Sean couldn't help smiling back. He had mostly seen the mission-focused part of Charlie, where she raced around at a million miles a minute to solve a case. Being out on the water and experiencing nature brought out a different side of her. He felt honored that she wanted to share this with him. She then pushed the throttle forward, swung the boat around, and continued south toward MacCrain Island.

Ten minutes later, she maneuvered the Hinckley into the Marta Point harbor, found an empty slip, and eased into the space. Sean leaned over the side with a rope and tied off the back of the boat, then crept along the edge of the deck with one hand on the railing and did the same with the front.

Charlie shut down the engine, checked the ropes, and retied them. "I once tried to dock here in my little skiff. Within minutes, people were chasing me away. But even though this is a private marina, a boat like the Hinckley is always welcome."

"Sort of like driving up to a valet in a Bentley," Sean said.

"Exactly." She ducked into the galley and returned with two bottles of water, handing one to Sean. They walked onto the open rear deck and sat on one of the white and blue striped cushioned seats.

A woman dressed in loose-fitting white pants with a drawstring waist, sea green top, huge sunglasses, and a broad-brimmed hat waved and walked toward them. Susan Early was a well-preserved woman in her early sixties with platinum-colored hair and a pale complexion that showed she didn't spend much time out of the shaded canyons formed by the Manhattan skyscrapers. Susan kicked her sandals off on the dock and stepped onto the boat.

"Beautiful yacht," she said. "The sheriff's budget must be quite substantial."

"It's my family's boat," Charlie said, as she shook Susan's hand.

Susan scanned Charlie from head to foot. "I figured there couldn't be more than one Charlie Nash. It's really commendable how you decided to devote your life to public service."

"I don't believe we've ever met," Charlie said with a confused look on her face.

"Tim and I came down here twenty-five years ago when we heard someone was developing the island. Henry Nash took us out here on his boat—a different one back then. He told us he was a New York transplant himself, but mostly spoke of his lovely southern wife and his children. You were in college then, I think, and insisting to be called Charlie rather than Charlotte. Tim was always wary of developers offering land deals, but he trusted your father. They had many dinners and cocktails together over the years."

Charlie smiled broadly, obviously pleased that her father had made such an impression on people and was so proud of her he spoke about her to strangers. "Tim sounds like quite a man," she said. "I'm so very sorry for your loss. Why don't we talk inside where it's cool?"

Once everyone stepped inside, Charlie zipped the transparent plastic door at the rear of the cabin closed. She flipped a switch to start the air conditioner and opened a hinged wood table between the two upholstered bench seats located behind the captain chairs. Susan sat on one side and Sean and Charlie sat across from her. She removed her sunglasses to reveal eyes swollen and red from days of crying.

Sean opened his leather folio and prepared to take notes, while Charlie began the interview by gathering background.

Susan said she was a financial analyst when she met Tim thirty years ago. They married and both climbed to management positions in the Wall Street firm where they worked. They finished building the house in Marta Point five years ago and normally spent a long weekend there every month and several weeks in the summer and over the December holidays. After Tim received a call from someone advising him of Nancy Russo's murder last Monday, he told her he was flying down to talk with some people he knew from his days in New Jersey.

"Any idea who?" Charlie asked.

"It might've been her husband, but I don't really know. He was adamant about that part of his life being the past, so I was surprised he wanted to reopen it."

"I have to ask the standard questions: do you know who might want to hurt him, did he have any enemies, and was he troubled by anything recently?"

"Not at all. He was the nicest man in the world. He didn't even have enemies at work."

"We know Tim was down here on vacation thirty-eight years ago with two other couples when Theresa Goldberg was murdered," Charlie said. "Did he ever talk about that?"

Susan leaned forward and rested her hands on the table. "Tim got a job as an investment banker with one of the regional banks in New Jersey right after college. The bank gave him a membership in a country club in Short Hills, a rather exclusive area, so he could rub elbows with all the right people. He married Lizzy Jones, who came from old money in the area."

Sean circled Jones in his notes and drew a line at the margin of the page to remind him to research her further now that he had her maiden name.

"And they vacationed on Spartina Island with the Goldbergs and Nowaks?" Charlie asked.

"Tim told me about his first marriage and behavior he wasn't very proud of as he got older and more mature." Susan took a deep breath and continued. "Back in New Jersey, eight couples met monthly for swinging parties. The Goldbergs and Nowaks were two of them. Times were different back then."

Sean glanced up from his notes to see Charlie's reaction. She maintained her poker face.

"We're not here to judge Tim or anyone else," Charlie said. "We just want to figure out who killed your husband."

"On that vacation, they did a swap one night. Theresa drew Tim. She wanted to get together with him again afterward without the others knowing, but Tim was against it. I know it sounds strange, and I still can't wrap my head around that lifestyle, but Tim explained to me that swinging is not about emotional entanglements with a partner. I don't understand it, but Tim said it was supposed to strengthen marriages, not pull them apart."

"Did he get together with her later?" Charlie asked.

"According to Tim, no. But she insisted they meet so she could share her feelings. Tim agreed, but they didn't know what the rest of the group had planned that evening. He told her that if the ladies weren't doing anything together, she should leave a note in the paperback book he had been reading on the beach with a place and time they could meet. She never did. He spent the evening watching baseball with everyone in the Nowak's rental unit."

"We know everyone didn't stay there all night," Charlie said.

"According to Tim, Sandra went into her bedroom to read, and Theresa went out for cigarettes. It would've been too obvious if Tim got up and followed her, and since she never left a note, he figured she had gotten over her need to talk. A little bit later, Lizzy said she could watch baseball back home, so she was going to a bar."

"But Tim stayed there in the condo?" Charlie asked.

"According to Tim, he didn't go back to his unit until the game was over. Lizzy came home drunk around midnight and passed out on the sofa. A while after that, Aaron knocked at his door and asked if he or Lizzy had seen Theresa. No one had, so Aaron called the police. By that time, the police had found her body at the boat launch."

"Anything else?" Charlie asked.

"That's all he told me about that night, other than the police eventually thinking it was two African American men who'd been robbing tourists."

"What ever happened to Tim and Lizzy?"

"Tim realized his marriage to Lizzy and the wife swapping stuff was all wrong. He had gotten sucked into a lifestyle that wasn't who he was by a woman who was too wild for him. A year or two later, he got a job offer at the investment firm on Wall Street, divorced Lizzy, and moved to Manhattan."

"And Lizzy?"

"Her maiden name was Elizabeth Jones," Susan said. "Tim heard at some point during her third marriage she reinvented herself as Beth. She later married a dentist—her fourth marriage—and moved to an active adult community on Spartina Island."

64

Sean saw the excitement in Charlie's face. "Could her last name be Laughlin?" she asked. "Married to a George Laughlin?"

Susan shrugged her shoulders. "All I know is what Tim told me. Is there a Beth Laughlin on the island?"

Charlie looked at Sean, apparently unsure what, if anything, she should share with Susan.

Sean could tell she was deferring to him. It was as if they'd been homicide partners for years and knew when to hand off the lead to the other. "We know a Beth Laughlin who lives in the Riverside neighborhood of Sea Island Plantation," Sean said. "She's probably the same person Tim knew as Lizzy. She's from New Jersey, and her current husband is a retired dentist."

"It won't be hard for us to verify they're one and the same now that we have her maiden name," Charlie said, and then nodded to Sean to continue, knowing he had a better understanding about this cast of characters than she did.

"What other connection can you think of between Tim, Theresa Goldberg, and Nancy Russo?" Sean asked.

"Nothing other than they all lived in New Jersey together years ago and were members of the same club." Susan's voice lowered and her eyes hardened as she spoke.

It was subtle, but Sean sensed she was holding back. He said softly, "Is there something you aren't telling us?"

Susan dropped her hands to her lap and stared at them. It looked like Charlie was getting ready to press her, but Sean held up a finger. Charlie sat back in her seat, and no one said a word for a long minute.

Finally, Susan looked up at them. "Tim told me Nancy called him out of the blue years ago and said he was the father of one of her sons, that when they were doing their swapping, she wasn't on the pill. She knew her husband wasn't the father the moment the baby was born."

"Was that just a feeling she had, or did she have proof?" Sean asked.

"She emailed Tim a copy of the birth certificate. The timing was right. She also attached a photo of her son. He looked so much like Tim there was little doubt in Tim's mind."

"Did she want anything?" Sean asked. "Money or something?"

"That would've been a red flag since we were doing quite well by then, but she asked for nothing. Nancy asked Tim what he thought they should do."

"And what did Tim say?" Sean asked.

"That it was her decision. If she wanted to tell her son, they should first do a DNA test to be positive and make sure Nancy's husband was on board with her decision. And if it was Tim's son, Tim said he wanted to meet him."

"Did they do the DNA test?"

"Tim was ready to, but Nancy dropped the whole thing. I knew Tim was disappointed in a way. We never had children, but I think he always wished he had a son."

"Did you hear about the Russo's grandson, Trevor, being killed a few days ago?" Sean asked.

Susan nodded. "Tim phoned me Thursday morning and said a young man named Trevor called and wanted to meet. Trevor told him on the phone that a few days before his grandmother died, she blurted out that Ken wasn't his real grandfather. Tim was his biological grandfather."

Sean's first thought was this latest information put Trevor on top of the list of Tim's most likely killers. That Trevor could've been so angry over Tim withholding this from him his entire life that he killed him.

"Did you talk with Tim after he and Trevor met?" Sean asked.

Susan shook her head. "I was expecting to talk with him that evening and hear all about it. Do you think it was Trevor?"

"We haven't reached any conclusions," Charlie said and quickly changed the subject. "We collected Tim's cell phone as evidence, but it's password protected. Would you be willing to contact your service provider and get his call history for the last month?"

"It's a work phone, but I'll call the firm's IT manager and ask them to release it to you."

"Do you know who the other person was that he planned to meet that day?" Charlie asked.

She shook her head.

"Did you ever meet Aaron Goldberg, Lizzy, or Beth as she later called herself, George Laughlin, or Nancy or Ken Russo or their children?"

"No, all I know about them is what Tim told me."

Charlie made eye contact with Sean. He shrugged his shoulders to signify he had no further questions.

"You've been very helpful, Susan," Charlie said. "Is there anything that we didn't ask? Anything you can think of that might be important?"

She shook her head.

On the boat ride back to the mainland, Sean tried to reconcile everything Susan told them with what they already knew, but too many pieces were still missing to see the full picture. "What do you think?"

"I had thought all that talk about the key club was bullshit. It's apparently true, but the question is, does it have anything to do with the murders?"

"Or is it just the common denominator that ties all these people together?"

"If couples willingly swap partners," Charlie said, "does that mean they don't experience the same emotion of jealousy and desire for revenge that normally occurs when one spouse cheats on another?"

"Hard for me to say. I was married to the same woman for thirty years and never considered sleeping with another woman."

"Come on! Every man thinks about it."

A fishing boat with a flying bridge twenty feet above the water came toward them then veered to their right. Two men on board waved as they passed.

"Sure, I've seen an attractive woman and might've thought *what if.* But then I'd immediately consider everything I'd be throwing away and how it would hurt the woman I loved and the wonderful life we'd built together."

Charlie looked his way and smiled. He wasn't sure if his mention of his previous marriage would make her uncomfortable, but it didn't seem to. "According to Susan, Theresa had developed feelings for Tim after their hookup. Is that just a female reaction or do men feel the same way?"

Sean chuckled. "You're asking me to speak for the entire male gender?"

Charlie glanced at him but didn't answer. She wasn't about to let him off the hook.

"I think it's normal for everyone to develop feelings for someone you're intimate with." Sean wasn't sure if Charlie's question was about how Tim and the other men in the key club would feel or if she was investigating his feelings about casual sex and intimacy. "But in a healthy relationship, you develop those feelings *before* you sleep with someone, not the other way around. And this group sex stuff is way beyond my comprehension."

"I just know that if I were in a relationship with a man I loved, it would not be okay for him to screw someone else."

Sean nodded. So this was about his thoughts on the subject and Charlie making it clear what hers were. He needed to move the conversation back to the murders. "I think that leaves the motive of jealousy as a possibility. This began with Theresa's murder. Her husband at the time, Aaron, could be a likely suspect. But if we believe the same person also killed Nancy and Tim, that means Aaron had to have been down here at the time of Nancy and Tim's murders."

Once the boat was out of MacCrain Creek, Charlie opened the throttle and turned left into the wide mouth of the Cusseta River. She spoke louder to be heard over the wind and engine noise. "I can have a friend from the New Jersey State Police look into Aaron for us. See if he's at his home now and whether he's done any travel recently."

"Good idea. We can obviously rule out Tim since he's dead."

"Unless he killed Theresa and Nancy, and someone else killed him as payback," added Charlie.

"Possibility. I guess Ken could've killed Tim if he thought Tim had killed Theresa and Nancy. Susan said Tim flew down here after he learned of Nancy's murder, but do we know independently when Tim arrived?"

"I can check airlines."

"We've only ruled out Ken for Nancy's murder."

"But not for Theresa," Charlie said. "We have no information showing he was on that vacation thirty-eight years ago, but I guess he could've been."

"I think it would've come out, but I agree we need to remain open to the possibility. If Ken did travel to MacCrain Island and shoot Tim, he'd have to be a damn cool killer to make that trip right after his wife's death and with all the attention your office gave him."

"And although Trevor is a possibility for Tim's murder, it doesn't feel right. If he killed Nancy, that still doesn't explain who had sex with her just before."

"Are you thinking the lover was her killer?" Sean asked.

"Jeez, I don't know. Too many possible suspects and too much we still don't know."

"My thought exactly. So what do we do to learn more?"

"I'd still like to talk to the Nowaks, but Steve will need some convincing to cooperate."

"I'll bet he and Sandra might prefer talking with us instead of the world hearing about their kinky lifestyle," Sean said.

"You mean threatening to leak information about their sex club if they don't cooperate? A threat like that only works if we're willing to make good on it. I doubt the sheriff will approve of those tactics."

"When I was working in Oakland, I seldom asked for permission. I never felt bad about coercing a reluctant witness to tell the truth about a murder. If things went sideways and the brass got pissed off, I'd beg for forgiveness afterward."

Charlie was quiet, obviously thinking about it. Sean didn't want to get her in trouble at the department or push her into something she'd later regret.

"I'd need access to the department's interview rooms to isolate and control them if we have any chance of getting the truth out of them," she said. "I'd need to be back on full duty to orchestrate it. What about talking to George and Beth? She was on that vacation during the first murder, lives right down the street from Nancy, and was part of this key club. What else do we know about George?"

"A typical quiet older neighbor," Sean said. "We were fishing the morning of Nancy's murder, and he initially lied to your detectives about his whereabouts before that."

"So, maybe we talk to him first."

"Could he be the killer?" Sean asked.

They entered the no-wake zone as they approached the Dufftown pier, and Charlie slowed to five knots. "We don't know enough to rule him out."

"In my investigations, I always tried to save the suspect interviews for last. I wanted to build a case and know the answers to the questions I planned to ask suspects so I could catch them in their lies."

"You're right. It's best to work around the fringes before going after the likely suspects." Charlie steered wide of two kayakers paddling up the river. "There's something you're not telling me."

"Something less than a hunch at this point," Sean said. "What about talking to Ken again? I'd be interested in hearing what he has to say about the key club and the son who might not actually be his son."

"Are you sure he's not responsible for Tim's death?"

"He might have a motive, but he's been surrounded by his AA friends and neighbors ever since he got out of jail, so sneaking off to MacCrain Island in the middle of the day would be tough."

"Okay, we'll talk to Ken again." She turned toward him and smiled. "That is as long as you're willing to still work with this detective sergeant who's not even supposed to be working."

"There's nothing I'd rather do."

65

The yacht club dockhand grabbed the line she tossed him when she pulled up to her berth. "How ya doing for fuel, Miss Charlotte?" he asked.

"It was just a short trip, so we're still at full."

He tied off the lines. "You and your gentleman friend can hop off. I'll clean her up and get her all closed up for the night."

She thanked him and slipped him a few bills then walked down the dock alongside Sean. She was feeling wonderful. She loved being out on her boat and was excited about the leads they developed during the interview with Susan Early. And being with Sean felt...it felt interesting. And comfortable. He was easy to be around and easy to work with. Nothing like she had first imagined.

"I can't help but think about my father whenever I go out on the Hinckley."

"When we were at Marta Point on Thursday, you mentioned his disappearance was a story for another time," Sean said. "How's this for the time?"

Charlie had told the story often, but it was usually the just-the-facts version. He went to meet his business partner one night and didn't return, his car was found by the bridge to Spartina Island the next morning, and police and boats searched for his body, but never found him. But as they walked to her car, she began telling him the entire story, the story of the loss of her father, and how it changed her life.

By the time they drove out of the Cusseta Country Club gate and turned onto Spartina Island Road, she was telling him about the sheriff's office refusing to allow her to see the investigation file and how she found the captain's office unlocked on Saturday, made a copy of the case file, and discovered Captain Cannon was the original detective and her ex-husband was present the night her father disappeared.

They were halfway across the bridge when Sean spoke for the first time. "It sounds like you believe he didn't take his own life or accidentally fall off the bridge."

"I'm not so naïve to believe I'm unbiased, but there are too many unanswered questions."

"And Captain Cannon is the only one who can re-open the investigation?"

"And since he was the original investigator, he could look bad if it showed he dropped the ball."

"I wonder if his keeping the case file with other sensitive investigations is because of your father's prominence or to protect himself from scrutiny?"

"You investigated cold cases back in Oakland, right? Did re-examining old cases ruffle the feathers of the original investigators?"

"I was assigned cold cases for a while when I was on light duty after an on-duty injury. A few of the investigators didn't like me reviewing and potentially judging their work, but most were thrilled over the possibility of achieving justice for the victim."

"I approached Billy several times about re-opening the case. He said he asked the captain, but he refused."

"I've known Billy a long time, and he's a stand-up guy," Sean said. "But when the boss says no, what's he supposed to do?"

"If I were the lieutenant, I'd take it to the sheriff."

Sean smiled. "I don't know how it is in your department, but going over a boss's head would be career suicide in Oakland. It would have to be pretty damn important to take that risk."

Sean was right. Their new sheriff was a good guy, but he left the day-to-day operations of the department to his subordinate command officers. If she were to bypass Billy and Captain Cannon to ask the sheriff to re-open the case after they already refused, she could find herself back in uniform working permanent night shift. "Someone should look into it."

"But it can't be you," Sean said. "You know that, right?"

She sighed. "Yeah."

They had made it across the bridge and were approaching the turn off that would take them to Sea Island Plantation. Sean pointed down the road. "How about stopping at the gas station mini mart? I need a coffee for a little caffeine jolt."

66

"We need to talk," Charlie said as soon as Ken opened the door. "We can do it here or downtown."

Sean stood behind her and let her do the talking. She had warned him she would be displaying her bad-ass, pissed-off cop attitude, and he should play along.

Ken opened the door and stepped aside as Charlie and Sean entered. "Can I get you some water or iced tea?"

"This isn't a social call," she said. "Let's sit in the kitchen."

Ken sat at the table and placed his shaking hands in front of him. *Good*, Sean thought, Charlie's feigned anger put Ken on the defensive.

She sat across from him. Sean took the chair to her right and set his gas station paper coffee cup in front of him. "I'm pissed at myself for being so nice to you the last time we spoke," she said. "But you'd just lost your wife, so I felt sorry for you. And you later apologized for lying the first time we talked and said you were now telling me the whole truth when we spoke again."

Ken looked at Sean.

"Don't look at your neighbor," she snapped. "He can't help you. I know about your key club. What I want to know is why you failed to tell me about it when you assured me you were telling me everything."

Ken looked down and said softly, "I'm sorry."

"You're sorry! Damn it, Ken. I'm trying to solve a bunch of fucking murders here." She slapped her hand on the table. "One of them being your wife's. And you're still holding out on me."

Ken sat quietly for a few counts. "It started about forty years ago when we all lived in New Jersey."

"Tell me about it."

Ken told them about he and Nancy, the Nowaks and Earlys having dinner and drinks at their country club one night and first broaching the topic of swinging. They had their first party with the Goldbergs and two other couples. Eventually they had over a dozen couples who attended the monthly parties over the next few years. Sean wrote down the names of everyone Ken mentioned.

"After a while, the club dissolved," Ken said. "We grew up, I guess. We had kids and got busy with their lives, our work, and everyday living."

"Were you and Nancy on Spartina Island when Theresa was murdered?"

"No, we didn't come down that year. Nancy was pregnant with our first son at that time, and we decided to get out of the drinking and partying scene after that."

"Did you both stop at that time?"

"Yeah, totally," he said. "Until a few years ago, when they started it up down here."

"How'd that happen?"

"We were having dinner with the Laughlins, and Beth and Nancy started talking about our lives down here needing some excitement."

Charlie glanced at Sean. He kept a blank expression and continued taking notes in his legal pad. "What happened next?" Charlie asked.

"Beth and Nancy talked to Sandra. She was interested, and they recruited a few other couples who live on Sea Island."

Charlie asked him for the names of the other couples and Sean jotted them down.

"Walk me through it. Tell me how these parties work."

"We rotate houses and have a party once or twice a month. If neighbors ask, we say they're wine tasting parties. Everyone shows up, has some drinks, and we get a deck of cards. Each man is dealt two cards of the same number. He keeps one and puts the other one in a pile. One of the women shuffles them and deals them out. If someone draws her husband's number, the card is reshuffled back into the deck."

"No keys?" she asked.

"That doesn't work these days. People have giant car remotes or golf cart keys, and half the people don't even carry a house key."

"Then you go off in separate rooms?"

"The party hostess takes her partner into her bedroom, her husband gets the guest room, and the other women take their partner to their house. Everyone comes back in an hour or two."

Sean tried to visualize these older people screwing their friends' spouses. The image was revolting. He glanced at Charlie and could tell she was fighting to keep a poker face.

"Who was at the last party?" Charlie asked.

"It was at the Nowaks' house a few weeks ago. Only four couples could make it. Us, the Nowaks, Laughlins, and John and Mary Dupree. I was paired with Mary and went to her house, and Nancy drew George and went to our house. Beth picked Steve, and John was with Sandra. They stayed in their house."

"Did anything out of the ordinary happen?"

"It's not like the couples are required to have sex," Ken said. "They could decide not to for whatever reason, and what everyone does is not to be shared, not even with our spouses. I told Mary I couldn't do this anymore."

"You mean that night?"

"That night and for good." Ken leaned forward in his chair. "Once I got sober, I started examining my life. And this key club stuff doesn't fit with who I am. The only way I got through it before was by getting pretty buzzed."

"Did you ever share these concerns with your wife?"

"I tried talking to Nancy about it a few months ago, but she laughed it off. Nancy and her friends were more into it than the men. They say that men, by our very nature, aren't meant to be monogamous. We're wired to screw around, so if they provide us with the opportunity through the key club, we won't have to go out on our own, have affairs, and ruin our marriages."

67

Charlie tried to keep the same neutral expression she saw on Sean's face, so Ken didn't think she was judging him. Maybe these women were right, she thought—men aren't meant to be monogamous. Her ex certainly proved that. But setting up swinging parties was not much better than bringing your husband a hooker, thinking that would ensure he remained faithful. "What do *you* think about that?" she asked Ken.

"I certainly don't buy it today. I'm not sure I ever did. Sure, when we were younger, I guess being with different partners might've spiced up our own sex lives. But now...now, it just feels gross."

"Did you and Mary actually do anything?"

"We just talked. And we assured each other that we would say nothing about it to anyone in the club."

"Do others talk about what went on?"

"We're not supposed to. The men never talked among ourselves."

"Did Nancy say anything about what happened with her and George that night?"

"No, but she never talked about the man she was with. It would be pretty crushing if your wife compared you to another man."

Charlie nodded. "I'm having trouble believing it's the wives who pushed this. I would've thought men would be the instigators of this kind of stuff."

"We all read about swinging in men's magazines, *Playboy* and such, when we started this," Ken said. "It's not as deviant as people want to believe. But you're right. The articles said men usually suggested it and their spouses reluctantly went along. But I'm telling you what happened with us."

"Was Nancy having an affair with any of the men in the club?"

"No," he said quickly.

Charlie made eye contact with him, showing she didn't fully believe him.

"I can't be sure," he finally said. "One of the things the club stressed was absolutely no relations outside the club parties. But after what happened to Nancy, I can't say for sure."

"If she was having an affair, who do you think it would be with?"

"I have no idea. John Dupree, one of the new members, is younger than the rest of us. Maybe women find him more attractive. But I can't imagine John wanting to have an affair with Nancy."

"Do you think any of the men in the group would've killed Nancy? Or killed Theresa?"

He shrugged. "I know all these guys. I can't imagine it."

"We just found out Beth Laughlin used to be married to Tim. Why didn't you tell us?"

"It didn't come up. Everyone knew her back then as Lizzy. She was a party girl. All the men wanted to be with her. As she got older, as we all did, she settled down somewhat and decided the name Lizzy wasn't fitting for a mature woman."

Although it repulsed her, Charlie was fascinated by the history and workings of the key club and could've talked about it longer, but she needed to drop the final bombshell. "We heard Trevor went to see Tim Early because Nancy told him that Tim was his actual grandfather—that Tim Early is the biological father of your son."

She watched Ken's face, expecting a look of shock. But nothing. When he spoke, it was as if he'd rehearsed his response for decades. "Nancy and I were trying to get pregnant back then, so she stopped taking the pill. She didn't want to leave the key club, but assured me she'd take precautions. When Ken Junior was born, I could see his resemblance to Nancy, but not to me. Friends were generous, saying things like, 'he's got your nose,' but they were lying. As he got older, he looked increasingly like Tim. By the time he was in high school, there was no doubt. He was the spitting image of Tim—looks, mannerisms, speech, everything."

"But you still raised him as your son?" Charlie asked.

"Absolutely."

"Did you ever tell him who his biological father was?"

"We never talked about it."

"You and Ken Junior never talked about it?"

"Nancy and I never talked about the fact that he wasn't my son."

Sean stared at Ken with a look as perplexed as she felt. "Wait a minute," she said. "You knew damn well Tim was his father. It was so obvious Nancy had to know too. But you never once broached the topic."

He shook his head. "I kept waiting for her to say something, but she never did. After a while, I figured it was one of those family secrets that was best never discussed. As long as we never acknowledged it, we could pretend it wasn't so."

"And your son never questioned it?"

"He never met Tim, so he never would've seen the resemblance. By the time Ken Junior was two years old, Tim had left the area. A lot of kids don't necessarily look like both of their parents."

Charlie wondered what effect carrying that secret for all those years had on their marriage. The shame and guilt they both held inside and never shared. The proverbial elephant in the room they walked around and pretended didn't exist. "Did you know Nancy told Trevor?"

He shook his head. "I guess it makes sense now. She was angry. No matter what, Ken Junior is still my son and Trevor is…was…my grandson. I wanted to help Trevor into recovery, give him the gift of sobriety I had. I told Nancy that alcoholism and addiction had a genetic component, that children of alcoholic parents are more likely to become alcoholics themselves. I was hoping that might've prompted her to acknowledge my disease could not have been passed to Ken Junior and then to Trevor because I wasn't his grandfather. She only became more entrenched in her belief that Trevor could quit if he wanted to, and we must stop enabling him."

Charlie felt sorry for Ken. He had been living a lie for most of his life.

Staying in a marriage built on secrets and lies. She wondered what other lies and secrets Nancy took to her grave. "Sean, do you have any questions?"

Sean cleared his throat. "Who would you say were Nancy's best friends?"

"Probably Beth and Sandra. They all moved down here to be together. They always did things together."

"What about male friends?"

"Beth and Sandra's husbands, probably. More George than Steve. He was sort of like a brother to Nancy. They could talk about anything."

"We know she had sex with someone the morning she was killed," Sean said. "I suspect it was someone she knew from the key club. Who do you think it would be?"

He shrugged.

"Give me your best guess."

"The women had a pact. The rules of the club included no emotional entanglements. It's just about the physical pleasure. So yes, I understand that she had sex with someone that morning, but I can't imagine she'd break the rules. It would destroy the club the women cared so much about and ruin their friendships with the other women."

Sean jotted some notes on his pad. "That's all the questions I have."

68

Sean opened his front door to Billy's huge mass filling the doorway. He had three deli sandwiches tucked under his arm. Sean set them on the kitchen table, where Charlie was carefully reviewing her notes and jotting things onto a separate page. He poured Billy a tall glass of iced tea and sat down. Billy opened his Philly cheesesteak, stuffed a napkin into his shirt, and slid the other sandwiches toward Sean and Charlie.

"Your pick," Sean said to Charlie.

She grabbed the roast beef, which was fine with Sean because he figured the turkey was healthier. When Annie sat between Charlie and Billy and looked up at them, Sean snapped his fingers and pointed to her dog bed in the living room.

"She's okay with me," Charlie said.

Some people felt Sean was too hard because he didn't feed Annie people food, made her lie down when people were eating, walk at heel instead of pulling on the leash, and lie on the floor—or one of the three dog beds Annie had in the house—instead of the furniture. But Annie was one of the happiest and most confident dogs in the neighborhood. "It's how she was trained," was all he said.

Billy bit into his sandwich and the melted cheese oozed out onto the wax paper wrapper in front of him. "I'm all ears, Charlie. You said this couldn't wait until you got back to work."

Over the next few minutes, Charlie briefed Billy on everything she and Sean had done in the past few days, leaving out her break-in of the captain's file cabinet and subsequent work on her father's disappearance.

When she finished, Billy said, "I guess you didn't understand what was meant by taking some days off."

"It was my fault," Sean said. "I kept feeding her details I picked up around the neighborhood and stuff I dug up on the cold case."

"Nice try, Sean," Billy said, "She should've passed it on to me and gone to the beach."

"You're right," Charlie said. "I should've known better than to drag a civilian into the investigation."

Sean fought back a smile seeing Charlie embrace his style of begging for forgiveness rather than asking for permission.

Billy shook his head. "Hell, I would've thought that if you two actually found a way to work together, Sean would've become a voice of reason, not a co-conspirator."

"The only rules we ignored were the ones keeping us from finding the truth," Sean said.

Billy laughed. "I imagine you were as much a pain in the ass to your bosses back in Oakland as Charlie is to us here."

Sean recognized the hidden compliment. Cops who obey every rule and regulation seldom got the job done. He spent his entire career trying to figure out the right balance, and still, he occasionally stepped over the line until his last day at Oakland PD.

"I don't think we did anything that jeopardized the cases," Sean said. "My participation might require some explanation later on in court, but we didn't break any laws or violate anyone's rights."

"I'm in a fix right now," Billy said. "The sheriff and captain are meeting in an hour or two to discuss the results of SLED's shooting team. I'm sure Charlie will be cleared and brought back to work at that time. If I say nothing to the captain about your recent activities, I'm complicit, and if I tell the captain what you two have been up to, he'll go ape-shit and probably formally suspend Charlie and recommend discipline."

Sean hated placing Billy in that dilemma. He'd done the same with too many bosses he liked and respected in Oakland. The closer to the top they climbed in the department, the less they were willing to risk their careers by covering for their subordinates, even when they were right.

"The captain wants to go public and announce Trevor is responsible for the murders of Nancy and Tim," Billy said. "Indirectly, that will help justify Darryl's shooting."

"We're fairly certain he's not responsible," Charlie said. "The captain has no clue as to what we've uncovered."

"Neither did I until a few minutes ago," Billy said. "You're both convinced George is the man who had sex with Nancy just before her death and could even be her killer?"

"Yes and maybe," Charlie said.

"He told Sean he owns a gun, right?" Billy said.

Sean nodded.

"Just this morning, SLED's ballistics report on Tim Early's murder came back," Billy said.

"We already know the casing at the scene was a three-eighty," Charlie said.

Billy ate the last bite of his sandwich and wiped his mouth with a napkin. "They typed the slug in the wall and sent it to NIBIN, but there were no matches in the national database."

"That figures," Charlie said.

"Frank McDonnel sent me a preliminary report on the cold case team's review of Theresa Goldberg's murder," Billy said. "Among other things, he and your so-called Mudflats Murder Club suggested a reexamination of the slug the medical examiner removed during the autopsy. SLED still says it's too deformed for a comparison, but in addition to measuring it at nominal thirty-eight caliber, they weighed it as eighty-six grains and said it was largely intact."

"That makes it a three-eighty," Charlie said.

Sean was impressed she knew enough about ballistics to come to that conclusion.

"The firearms examiner said it's inconclusive," Billy said. "We all know that three-eighty, nine-millimeter, thirty-eight, and three-fifty-seven bullets are the same diameter. But the actual bullet configurations, especially back forty years ago, varied."

"Exactly," Charlie said. "Most factory ammo for three-eighty metal jacketed cartridges is ninety-five grains and hollow points eighty-eight grains. The lightest nine millimeters or thirty-eight specials were a hundred-ten grains."

"Which tells us the bullet that killed Theresa was most likely a three-eighty hollow point," Sean said. "I think we can rule out the suspects from that old robbery since their gun was a nine-millimeter." Sean said. "It would be very interesting if the Laughlin's gun is a three-eighty."

"Our conservative approach would be to first get a search warrant for the Laughlin's house and collect DNA from George," Billy said. "If we get a DNA match, we have something to confront him with during the interview. If we find a three-eighty pistol and match it to Tim's murder, we've got him."

"How long will it take your state lab to do that work?" Sean asked.

"A week or two if we can get them to rush it," Charlie said.

"More likely a month," Billy said, "unless the solicitor or sheriff calls in a favor."

"And in the meantime, the media is hammering away at your sheriff for answers and the killer is running free," Sean said. "You can't tell the press the crime lab report will *maybe* show something, so someone will leak Trevor is possibly the killer because he's not around to deny it."

"What about Ken and his family?" Charlie said. "Haven't they been through enough? Now they have to bury Trevor as the killer of his grandmother."

"I'm all for a cautious, methodical investigation," Sean said. "But at some point you have to stop collecting and analyzing physical evidence with the hope technology will finger the culprit. In my experience, murders are solved by sitting down with the right people and getting them to tell you the truth."

"If we drag the Laughlins down to the station, it would be construed as a detention or an arrest," Billy said. "We have to Mirandize them and risk them lawyering up. And if the captain wanders into the squad room and sees Charlie and a non-detective volunteer working these cases, I'll have a lot of explaining to do."

"We can talk to them at their house," Charlie said. "We separate George and Beth and interview them one at a time."

"They're also more likely to talk, too, if we use a low-key approach at their house," Sean said. "They're not under arrest, so there's no need to read them their rights. If George did do it and confesses, you can always ease into Miranda and take him downtown for a formal statement."

"We'll still need to get a search warrant," Billy said.

"Unless they both give consent to search," Charlie added.

"I know you've been assisting Charlie on interviews," Billy said to Sean. "But since they're potentially key witnesses or possibly suspects, Charlie and I need to take the lead on these interviews."

"Understandable." As much as Sean wanted to conduct the interview himself, he needed to accept his new role as a civilian. "Since they know me pretty well, I could introduce you and then step aside. They might talk more freely seeing what they think is a friendly face with you."

"This might work," Billy said.

Sean ate the last of his sandwich and crumpled up the wrapper. "I have a theory on how this went down and a way we can maybe get George to flip if he digs in his heels."

Charlie and Billy listened carefully as Sean explained his plan.

69

The single-story stucco house was situated on a large lot that backed up to the tee boxes of the fifteenth hole. When Charlie's father began developing the lots in Sea Island Plantation, he laid out a pricing system based on the desirability of the lot. Lots on the salt marsh were the most expensive, followed by those that were set on one of the many lagoons—or man-made ponds. Next were those on a golf course, and after that were those with a wooded view, although they were surprisingly popular among buyers looking for privacy. The most inexpensive houses were those that backed up to another house, but lots like that were rare in the Riverside neighborhood. The many lagoons and golf fairways running through the neighborhood, as well as the river and salt marsh running along the eastern boundary of the development, supplied magnificent views for most houses.

Like many of the houses in the Riverside neighborhood, the Laughlins' home had a two-car garage with golf cart addition facing perpendicular to the street. From the street, the house didn't look like a large garage with a house attached as did many houses in modern developments. It didn't have a bonus room over the garage, as many of the houses in the neighborhood did, so Charlie figured it was not much larger than the 2500-square-foot minimum requirement for houses in Riverside. Although it was a beautiful house and certainly more than adequate for a retired couple, its size and location made it one of the least expensive houses in Riverside.

It took nearly a minute for the door to open after they rang the bell. George was wearing athletic shorts that hung to his knees and a baggy tee shirt. He looked as if he'd just woken from a nap. "Sean," he said, followed by, "What's going on?" when he saw Charlie and Billy standing behind him.

"Hey, George, this is Sergeant Nash and Lieutenant Green," Sean said. "I'm sorry for the intrusion, but I had to tell them what you shared with me."

"I...I...I meant to call and change my statement," George said.

"Ah, honey, it's no big deal," Charlie said, laying on her slow, sweet Southern drawl. "We can do it now. Is it okay if we come in and talk for a spell?"

Without waiting for a response, Charlie stepped inside. "Is the missus home?"

"Ah, no, she left about an hour ago to visit her sister in Jacksonville."

"Florida?" Charlie asked.

"Yeah, she's spending the night and coming home tomorrow."

She made a mental note to get the address so she could have Jacksonville PD pick her up there if necessary. "Is there a table we can all sit at?"

George showed them to a rectangular cherry table in the dining room that was open to the great room and kitchen. George sat at one of the six high-back upholstered chairs. It wasn't the perfect set up for an interview, Charlie thought, but it would do. She and Billy sat across from George, and Sean sat at the far end of the table.

Charlie gave George her best disarming smile. "We haven't had the chance to meet, but one of my detectives told me he took your statement the afternoon after Mrs. Russo was found dead."

"I should've called and corrected my statement," George said. "Sean told me to, but, I guess, it slipped my mind."

"It's okay. Why don't you tell me what really happened?"

George told her the same story he had told Sean. He woke at six that morning, got dressed, closed the bedroom door so as not to disturb Beth, and drove to the gas station mini mart where he bought two sausage egg biscuits and coffee. He ate them in the gas station parking lot while listening to the morning news on the radio and arrived back to his house a few minutes before Sean picked him up to go fishing.

When he finished, Charlie turned to Billy.

"Are you sure you didn't eat your breakfast in the lot by the River Lodge?" Billy asked. "Sean said he was on his walk with Annie around seven and saw an SUV parked in the front corner of the lot. He could've sworn it was your Acura MDX."

Charlie studied George's face, carefully searching for micro expressions indicating deception to see if Billy's bluff worked. In a few seconds, she knew she didn't need to see tiny signs. Drops of sweat formed on George's upper lip and his hands began trembling.

"Oh, yeah. You're right. The gas station lot can get so busy in the mornings. I came back here and sat in the parking lot by the lodge where it's more peaceful."

"Why didn't you just go home?" Charlie asked.

"This is embarrassing, but Beth would be really pissed if she found out. My cardiologist has me on a low-fat and low-cholesterol diet."

"How long did you sit there?" she asked.

"Not long. I ate, drank my coffee, listened to the morning news. Sean was due to pick me up at seven-thirty. I drove back to my house, parked in the garage, grabbed my fishing gear, and Sean arrived."

"Okay, that makes sense." Charlie didn't believe for a moment that he sat there for a half hour, but now wasn't the time to push him. She was pleased at how readily George flipped once they confronted him with one of his lies. For now, he could think they believed he had merely been mistaken about where he ate his breakfast. The time would come when she'd accuse him of outright lying.

"What we need to talk about now might be a bit uncomfortable for you," Charlie said. "I want to first tell you that my lieutenant and I don't judge people. In our line of work, we've seen all sorts of lifestyles. Since we've discovered an important connection between the murder of Mrs. Russo and that of Theresa Goldberg thirty-eight years ago, we'd be amiss if we didn't talk about it."

George squirmed in his chair. Charlie knew she had touched a nerve. "We understand that what y'all were engaged in is a private affair. It's not against the law since it's between consenting adults, but we need to talk about your key club."

George began to speak, but Charlie held up her hand to stop him. She then methodically laid out pieces of what they knew. George began shaking his head in denial, but Charlie ignored him. She assured him that Ken had told them the entire story and that they knew about Beth's past life as Lizzy. George began listening but showed no reaction. She rattled off the names of the other members of the key club, leaving George to assume they had already interviewed them. Finally, he was nodding in agreement, obviously resigned to the fact that they knew everything. At that point, she said, "Why don't you tell us everything, starting from the beginning?"

For the next half hour, George talked about the key club, how Beth and Nancy had restarted it after they moved to Spartina Island, and how it grew as the women recruited new members. He talked about each monthly meeting as far back as he could recall, who was there, and who was matched with whom. She had to nudge him a few times to continue, but mostly she listened while Billy quietly took notes.

After George finished with a description of their last party where he was paired with Nancy, Billy asked, "Did you and Nancy meet again, after the party, for—how do I say this—additional sexual encounters?"

"Absolutely not! I told you that's against the rules of the club."

"We know someone other than Ken had sex with Nancy that morning," Billy said. "Why don't you tell us about it."

"Not me. No way."

"Are you willing to provide us with a DNA sample?" Billy asked "It's a simple process where we just swab your cheek—"

"I don't want my DNA in some database. I was a medical professional for years and know how that can be compromised."

Charlie was tempted to mention the ease with which she could get a court order forcing him to submit, but worried that might shut him down. All he had to do was mention he wanted a lawyer to end the conversation. She glanced at Billy, who nodded. "If you don't mind, George, Sean told us about when he met you for your fishing trip that morning."

"Remember when I picked you up that morning in my golf cart?" Sean asked.

George nodded.

"You were drinking a cup of coffee."

"Yeah. So?"

"Where'd you get it from?"

"I already told the detectives, from the gas station."

"Your coffee was in a Styrofoam cup," Sean said. "When I dropped you off at your house, you removed the Styrofoam cup from my golf cart's cup holder."

"Yeah, so what?"

"The gas station uses paper cups."

Charlie now realized why Sean wanted to stop for coffee on their way back from MacCrain Island. It certainly wasn't because he liked the gas station's crappy coffee. She watched George stare at Sean, unable to respond. He glanced her way, but she met his gaze with no expression. He was looking for someone to rescue him. Someone to save him from having to face the truth. When she gave him no sign that person was her, George looked back at Sean.

"The sheriff's office asked me to walk through Nancy's house with them that morning," Sean said. "The coffee maker was still on in the kitchen, but Ken didn't make coffee because he left early for an AA meeting. And we know Nancy doesn't drink coffee. I had coffee with Ken this morning at his house. When I left, he gave me coffee to go. In a Styrofoam cup."

Sean paused to let George absorb everything he said. "Exactly like the one you had when I picked you up that morning."

70

Sean knew they had him. George sat in his chair staring straight ahead. They'd caught him in two big lies. Lies he thought he'd get away with. Things he figured the detectives didn't know. Charlie let him walk right into his lies as skillfully as any investigator Sean had ever worked with. She set him up perfectly for Sean to lay out the facts that showed George had sex with Nancy Monday morning and left with a cup of coffee in a Styrofoam cup. The real test would be how she handled the rest of the interview.

George looked deflated. His brain had to be operating at warp speed trying to come up with a new story that they'd buy. He'd be trying to guess how much they knew and how he could weave a tale that matched their known facts while keeping his involvement to a minimum. When suspects repeatedly had their fabricated stories punched full of holes, they typically did one of three things. Some dug in their heels and stuck with their story even though they knew damn well it was a lie. Some surrendered and told the truth. Others totally gave up and asked for a lawyer.

After several moments of silence, Charlie softly said, "Why don't you tell us what really happened that morning?"

George nodded, and Sean could tell he'd selected option two. "Nancy and I talked on the phone Sunday night. She was really upset over a fight she had with Ken. We'd gotten together a few times after that last party. We knew it was wrong—that Beth and Ken would probably never forgive us if they found out. She said on the phone that she really wanted to see me, that she really needed me. Do you know how long it's been since a woman said she needed me?"

Charlie reached across the table, gently patted his arm and parroted, "She said she really needed you."

"It was late, and Beth was in the other room, so I couldn't just leave the house. Nancy told me that Ken leaves by seven every morning for an AA meeting and is gone for a couple of hours. I had until seven-thirty, when I was meeting Sean to go fishing. I thought about cancelling, but Nancy laughed, saying a half hour was plenty of time. What I told you about the sausage biscuits and coffee and eating in the lodge parking lot was true. I waited there until she texted and said Ken left the house."

"What time was that?" Charlie asked.

"Around seven." George pulled out his phone and scrolled through his messages. "She texted me at seven-oh-one and said he was gone. I walked past the greenside bunker, along the back of the houses, and through Nancy's back door. We'd both been anticipating this, so it didn't take long. When we were finished, she made some coffee, and we talked for a few minutes. Then I walked back to my car the same way and drove around to my house to wait for Sean."

Charlie sat quietly, looking at George. Sean hoped she didn't press immediately for the confession. George had taken a huge leap by admitting as much as he had. Now was the time to fill in the empty pieces of the picture, look for inconsistencies, and address them individually.

"What were you wearing?" Charlie asked.

"Shorts and a long-sleeve sun shirt."

"You didn't change your clothes before you and Sean left?"

"No, I told you I didn't even go into my house. Just the garage."

"What was Nancy wearing?"

"At what point?"

Sean fought back a laugh.

"When you first got there?" Charlie asked.

"A thin black robe. More of a negligee."

"And after? When she made you coffee in the kitchen?"

"When we finished, I got dressed and she pulled on her underwear and a robe."

"Where did you do it?"

"In her bed," George said.

"Did she say anything about anyone else coming over?"

He shook his head. "She had an exercise class that day, but joked about already having had a great workout."

"Where was she when you left?"

"She kissed me in the kitchen at the back door. I went out, and that's the last I ever saw her." Tears formed in George's eyes for the first time.

"Tell me about the knife," Charlie said.

George looked puzzled. Then he said, "No! I did not kill her. I would never hurt her."

"You were the last one to see her alive," Charlie said. "You can see why we might think this."

"I'd have to be a real psychopath to stab a woman to death after we had sex, and then a few minutes later paddle off in a kayak."

He had a point, Sean thought. Thinking back, George seemed to be in an especially cheerful mood when he picked him up. He didn't seem at all agitated or in emotional distress. Although he'd encountered more than his share of stone-cold killers in Oakland who could go about their activities as if nothing happened after killing, they were rare.

"Where were you on Thursday?" Charlie asked.

"The MGA tournament."

"MGA?" Charlie asked.

"Men's Golf Association at Sea Island. We have a tournament every Thursday. Shotgun start at nine, so it finishes around one-thirty, followed by lunch and drinks. Probably got home around four."

"I'll need a list of witnesses."

"The golf pro at the club can give you the tee sheet with everyone's name on it. Forty men played. They all saw me."

"What kind of gun do you own?"

"Me? It's Beth's gun. The last time I saw it was when we moved here. After the gun topic came up at poker the other night, I looked in Beth's dresser when I got home. That's where I thought she kept it. But it wasn't there. I'm not much into guns, but she calls it her double-oh-seven pistol. When her father gave it to her years ago, he said it was the gun James Bond carried."

Charlie and Billy exchanged looks. They both shook their heads, signaling neither had any additional questions. Neither did Sean.

"We need you to come down to the station with us and give a formal statement," Charlie said. "If you want to change clothes before we go, Lieutenant Green will accompany you to your room."

71

Once Charlie, Sean, and Billy got to the station with George, Charlie sat him in an interview room and walked into the squad room. Sherm and Jay were at their desks and jumped up when they saw her. "Are you back?" Jay asked.

She held her finger to her lips. "The lieutenant should let me know in a few minutes," she whispered. She summarized her interviews with Susan Early, Ken Russo, and George Laughlin, handed them her interview notes, and asked them to start a search warrant affidavit that would convince a judge they had probable cause to search the Laughlins' house.

Billy strode into their workspace a few minutes later. "The sheriff and captain met an hour ago. SLED found no criminal wrongdoing in the shooting, so you're back on duty. We'll hold a departmental review in a few weeks to look at training issues."

Charlie wanted to hug him but settled for a fist bump.

"I told the captain what we're working," Billy said. "I allowed him to assume Jay, Sherm, and I were the ones who did all the work. Let's let him think this for a while longer. You're back in charge of the cases. What can I do to help?"

She was thrilled that Billy trusted her again after what she'd done, and even more thrilled that her boss was willing to jump in and assist. "I've got

Sherm and Jay working on the warrant for the house. We need to get George's statement on video and then go at him for the murder. You were my partner for the preliminary interview, do you mind continuing?"

"I'd be offended if you didn't ask."

Sean stood by the vacant desk in the squad room without saying a word.

"I'm sorry, Sean," Charlie said, "but it would be inappropriate to have you in the interview room with us."

"I understand," he said, but she knew he had to be disappointed. He'd done so much to get them to where they were.

"You want me to make coffee or go out for pizza?"

She laughed. "I'll bring up the video camera on my computer so you can watch the interview. You can text me with any observations you have or any questions we should ask."

"I can do that," Sean said. "I take it you're going to accuse him of killing Nancy."

"I think we need to," Charlie said.

"Do you think he did it?"

Charlie had been running so frantically for the last few hours, she hadn't paused to think beyond the task at hand. Sure, George was the likely killer. By his own admission, he was the last known person with her. Although they'd have to verify his golf tournament alibi for the period when Tim was murdered, she doubted he'd lie about that since it was so easy to check. In addition, there was no indication George was on Spartina Island thirty-eight years ago. He was married to another woman at that time, and as far as they knew, he didn't get involved in the key club until recently. Because of the sexual component of Nancy Russo's crime scene, Charlie had assumed the killer had to have been a man. But what if it wasn't?

"What if George and Nancy's affair had been discovered?" she asked. "What if thirty-eight years ago, Theresa's plan to meet with Tim had been found out? It's been right in front of us the whole time."

"Beth Laughlin?" Billy asked.

Sean crossed his arms across his chest and nodded.

Charlie wanted to smack him. "You've been thinking it was her for a while, haven't you?"

"It all fits together," Sean said. "Two husbands screwed around on her. Jealousy is a powerful motive."

"And anger at her friends for violating the spirit of the key club," Charlie added. "Something that was very important to her."

"I think you still need to press George," Sean said.

"Agreed," Charlie said. "But I don't think he did it. Whoever stabbed Nancy would've been covered in blood, and George didn't have time to clean up and change before you saw him at seven-thirty. And I don't see a motive. He cared about her. We should rule him out, see what we find in the house, and go from there."

As much as Charlie wanted to immediately drive to Jacksonville and slap the cuffs on Beth, she knew they couldn't jump to conclusions. They needed to follow the trail in front of them. Although everything seemed to fit when they plugged Beth into the puzzle, they needed evidence to present to a jury.

"Should we notify the Jacksonville police?" Charlie asked.

"I'll get a judge ready to sign the warrant on the house and make sure he's available for a subsequent arrest warrant," Billy said. "If we find a three-eighty pistol, ammo, or other evidence, we'll get the arrest warrant and then notify Jacksonville to pick her up."

"Once we get the warrant for their house signed, Sherm and I can head out to MacCrain Island with Beth's photo," Jay said. "If she was the other person Tim was expecting a visit from, someone out there had to have seen her."

"Good idea," Charlie said.

"Beth is one of the nicest neighbors in Riverside," Sean said. "She picks up mail and newspapers and waters plants for half the neighborhood when we're out of town. She's even fed Annie and taken her for walks when I'm away."

"Are you now saying she couldn't have done it?" Charlie asked.

"Oh, no," Sean said. "Everyone's capable of murder. Last week, I saw Beth in the Farmers' house watering the houseplants because they're away for the summer. That's right next door to the Laughlins. I'll bet she had a magnificent view of the Laughlins' back door from the Farmers' house."

"Where she could've seen her husband coming and going from the house," Charlie said.

It took Charlie and Billy an hour to walk George through everything he'd told them at his house. Nothing new came up, but his statement was now preserved on video should he try to recant later to protect his wife. Although her heart wasn't in it, Charlie pushed him to admit he killed Nancy.

She suggested it might've been an accident—he brought the knife into the bathroom and waved it around to warn Nancy not to tell Beth, and in the process, she was cut. Then she suggested that Nancy retrieved the knife, and in the process of taking it from her, he accidentally stabbed her. Billy suggested that George got angry over something after they made love, he had an emotional blackout, and when he came out of it, he was standing over her body with a bloody knife in his hand.

George never wavered. He was adamant he didn't hurt her, didn't touch a knife, would never hurt her, and she was alive and well when he left the house.

Charlie switched her focus. "Tell us again how you and Beth met."

"She'd been a patient at my dental practice for as long as I remember. We were also members of the same country club. By the time my kids were in college, I had brought in three other dentists to my practice and could take more time off. I played golf three days a week at the club. Beth was often there. She was recently divorced. We started talking in the bar and one thing led to another. My wife found out and filed for divorce."

"How long were you married?" Charlie asked.

"Thirty-three years. But the marriage had been dead for a while, so I didn't fight to save it. We settled and split everything down the middle. I hadn't been too excited about practicing dentistry the last few years anyway, so I decided to retire. Beth and I got married and moved down here to enjoy life."

"And you told us that when the Russos retired and moved here two years ago, they started up the key club again."

"That's right."

"Did Beth ever tell you about Theresa Goldberg's murder?"

"I joined the country club a few years after it happened, but people still talked about it. I knew Beth was there, but she never brought it up with me."

"I'm sure you'll see where I'm going with this, but I need to ask. How would Beth react if she found out you were having an affair?"

"Beth's not a killer. She can have a temper, but I've never seen her get physical. But to answer your questions, she'd be disappointed mostly."

"Disappointed with you?"

George chuckled. "Probably to a degree, but she didn't have much faith in the willpower of the male gender. After we got married, she joked about women being the most powerful of the sexes, and that she knew I'd marry her the first time we had a drink together in the club. She said I was powerless against her wily, womanly ways."

"She sounds like a very confident woman," Charlie said.

"Although she joked about it, there was some truth to it. She believed men were weak when it came to women like her, so we weren't really at fault for succumbing to our natural desires."

"If men have no control over their desires," Charlie asked, "then how did she expect any marriage to survive?"

"I'm not saying I agreed with her philosophy. Sure, I cheated on my first wife, but I did it knowingly because there wasn't much left to our marriage by that point. But Beth considered it the responsibility of women not to seduce married men."

An interesting take on the sexes and marital fidelity, thought Charlie. Although she knew some married men seemed to think with their small head rather than the big head when it came to sex outside their marriage, she'd never accept it wasn't equally the responsibility of both husband and wife not to screw around. "That brings us back to how angry Beth would've been with Nancy if she found out she was having an affair with you."

"Nancy was her friend. She would've seen it as a betrayal. I was so stupid for getting involved with her. This is all my fault."

"What's all your fault?" Charlie asked.

George sighed. He seemed resigned to the real possibility that Beth killed Nancy and that he should've seen it coming.

"Knowing Beth as well as you do, could you have really anticipated she would resort to murder?" Charlie asked.

"I'm not saying Beth killed her. I still can't fathom her doing that. But maybe...maybe if we'd restricted our activities to the key club, Nancy would still be alive."

72

Sean watched on the computer screen as Charlie and Billy left the interview room. He rose from Charlie's desk and handed her a sheet of paper. "Jay and Sherm left me with the signed warrant and took off for MacCrain Island ten minutes ago."

She smiled. "I didn't get any texts from you while I was in the interview room."

"That's because you covered all the bases and introduced a nice circumstantial case on Beth," Sean said. "He would never come right out and say it, but I think George was beginning to suspect Beth as well."

Billy removed his phone from his ear. "Voicemail from the captain. There's a press conference in a half hour. I better be there to prevent a premature announcement of our new suspect."

"No problem," Charlie said. "We can handle the search of the house. That is, if Sean doesn't mind continuing to help."

Sean looked at his watch. "As long as we can make a quick stop at my house so I can feed Annie and let her out."

Charlie slid her handgun into her holster. He noted it was a Sig Sauer P320 Compact, a larger pistol than the P365 she carried on their first trip to MacCrain Island when she was dressed in casual boating attire. The more time he spent around her, the more her professionalism impressed him.

She grabbed her shoulder bag from her desk and led the way to her car. On the way across the bridge to Spartina Island, she requested a crime scene technician meet them at the Laughlins' house. Dark clouds were forming to the south and the Spartina grass in the salt marsh swayed in the wind. Sean was deep in thought, weaving the most recent facts into the theory Beth killed all three victims to make sure everything fit.

"You don't seem as excited over knowing who the killer is as the rest of us," Charlie said.

"I am happy. I love it when a case comes together, but it's been quite a while since I've done a victory dance when I solved a murder."

"I hope I never lose that feeling."

"I hope you never do either." He missed that feeling that he got during his first few years in homicide. Back then, he and his partner would walk the suspect down to the jail after getting a confession. Once the jail door slammed, they'd slap hands in a high-five, and head over to the cop bar to celebrate. Maybe being around someone like Charlie would bring back some of that excitement.

He looked out the window for a few counts. "I'm sure it's her, but we still need some physical evidence or a confession to prove it."

"I intend to get a dump on her phone. That should show where she was at the time of Nancy and Tim's murders."

"That'll help, and I'm sure SLED got a load of latents from both houses. Once you print her and collect her DNA, you might get some matches that'll help." Sean didn't want to burst her bubble, but if they didn't get much in the way of physical evidence, he could see her walk if they didn't get her to confess.

Charlie was requesting a records check on Beth when she stopped in his driveway so he could run inside to feed Annie and take her out. When he got back to the car, she said, "They found no criminal history and no firearms registered to her or George. DMV showed a ticket for a stop sign violation a year ago, but other than that, she was squeaky clean." Her radio crackled. The dispatcher advised that the crime scene technician she'd requested was clearing a car larceny scene and would be there in fifteen minutes.

Fat drops of rain began splattering the windshield by the time Charlie made the short trek down Blue Heron Lane and pulled her car in front of the Laughlins' house. Thunder sounded in the distance. She rang the doorbell, knocked and announced, "Sheriff's Office. Search warrant. Open the door." The law required police to "knock and announce" before making entry into a house with a search warrant, and even though it seemed silly when they knew the house was vacant, Sean knew good cops didn't want to give lawyers ammunition to have the search thrown out later in court.

She pulled George's house keys from her shoulder bag and unlocked the door. Thunder cracked nearby and rain pelted the driveway and street. She stepped inside. Sean followed and shut the door.

"Should we start in the master bedroom where the gun's most likely to be?" Charlie asked.

"You wanna do a quick walk-through first?"

"Definitely," she replied. Sean followed her through the great room, into the breakfast alcove, and between the kitchen counters and center island. She peeked into the laundry room and powder room. She entered the short hallway that led to two guest rooms. Queen bed, dresser, two nightstands, and a chair in the corner. The room looked like it hadn't been used in a year. She opened the closet and gave it a cursory look. She bent down and peered under the bed then stepped into the bathroom. It was a Jack-and-Jill set up, so she continued through the bathroom into the other guest room and searched it the same as she had the first one.

They crossed through the living room again and stepped into the master bedroom suite. Sitting on one of the two matching wingback chairs next to the window was Beth. She held a small pistol in her hand.

73

Charlie's hand snaked under her jacket and came out with her Sig. Sean stepped to her side and drew his own gun.

Her heart leaped in her chest. She fought the urge to scream, *Police, drop the gun*, which could startle Beth into doing something reckless. Instead, Charlie assumed a shooting stance with her gun pointed at the center of Beth's chest and said calmly, "Beth, we're with the sheriff's office. I need you to put down the gun."

Beth slowly raised the barrel of the gun and pressed it under her chin. Charlie tightened her grip on her pistol and indexed her finger along the trigger guard. She kept her eyes on Beth, but was confident Sean was locked onto her with his gun as well.

Out of the corner of her eye, Charlie saw Sean slowly sidestepping away from her to triangulate Beth, which would make it harder to shoot them both if she decided to point the gun in their direction.

Beth's eyes bounced between Charlie and Sean.

"Sean, you're designated shooter," Charlie said. "I'll negotiate."

Charlie had been trained as a crisis negotiator and had assumed that role on the department's small SWAT team for the last five years. In a tactical situation with a suicidal suspect, one officer is typically assigned as the designated shooter to avoid a dozen officers all shooting—sympathetic gunfire—in response to the suspect shooting or one nervous officer touching his trigger. Ideally, the designated shooter was an experienced sharpshooter who could stay calm when facing an agitated, armed suspect, yet fire with deadly accuracy if the need arose. She was confident Sean fit all those criteria.

It was equally important that only one officer gave commands to the suspect and attempted negotiation. She'd been in situations where multiple deputies shouted orders to a suspect, one ordering him to freeze, while another ordered him to lie on the ground. No matter what the suspect did, one officer could view it as non-compliance, which could result in unnecessary force.

"Roger that." Sean's voice was strong and confident. "I've got you."

She glanced to her right and saw Sean holding his handgun in a two-handed stance, pointed at Beth. He looked relaxed, yet ready.

If she had any chance of talking the gun out of Beth's hand, she needed to keep her composure and develop rapport with her. It was difficult for a suicidal woman to feel a connection with someone who was pointing a gun at her, but Charlie was reluctant to lower her weapon, knowing Beth could swing her pistol at her in a second.

She glanced at Sean again. He was the picture of calm confidence.

She lowered her gun, trusting Sean with her life.

"Beth, please put the gun down and let's talk," Charlie said.

"There's nothing to talk about." She pressed the barrel of the gun into the soft flesh under her chin. Her finger remained on the trigger. If she pulled the trigger, the bullet would travel upward into the center of her brain.

"There's always something to talk about when you're thinking of ending your life," Charlie said.

"I didn't mean to do it."

"Do what?" Charlie wanted to keep her talking, distract her from pulling the trigger.

"Hurting my best friend."

"You mean Nancy?"

"I just wanted to scare her. Make a point that we women can't violate the trust of the club."

"But she wouldn't listen?" Charlie asked.

"She blamed me." Beth's voice rose. "She said it was my fault my husband strayed."

"That's not fair," Charlie said. "We know how men are."

"Damn straight! It's our responsibility not to wield our power over men in that way. Men are weak and easily influenced by strong women." Beth turned toward Sean.

"Don't worry about him," Charlie said. "Look at me."

Beth returned her eyes to Charlie and continued. "We all know how easily we can manipulate men."

"That we do."

"You're so pretty you surely know the power you have over men." Beth smiled slightly. "I could tell George was up to something. Then I saw him sneaking out Nancy's back door one day when I was next door watering Dorothy's plants. I was tempted to confront him, but I knew it wasn't his fault."

"Of course not," Charlie said. "He's a man."

"When he got up early last Monday and tiptoed around the bedroom so as not to wake me, I knew he was up to no good. I got dressed and went to Dorothy's house and watched. And in no time at all, there he was, creeping out the kitchen door again."

"That must've made you angry."

"I got the knife just to make a point. I didn't mean to stab her."

"I believe you," Charlie said. "But we sometimes lose control."

"I guess." Beth lowered the gun for a moment, but quickly placed it against her neck again. "I'm so sorry I killed my friend."

"I know you are. Why don't you put the gun down?"

"I've been carrying this guilt for too long."

"What guilt, Beth?"

"Theresa." Her eyes teared up. She wiped them with her left hand.

"What happened to Theresa?"

"She knew how much I loved Tim. Why would a woman sleep with her friend's husband? What kind of friend would do that?"

"Not a very good friend."

"They were arranging another tryst. I took the note she slipped into

Tim's book. It asked him to meet her at the boat launch that night. I went there in his place. Just to make her understand that no emotional entanglements were permitted in our club. I was only trying to scare her with the gun. It went off. I really didn't mean to shoot her."

"Accidents happen," Charlie said. "People can understand that. How about you put the gun on the little table beside you so we can talk more?"

"It's too late for that."

"You're a beautiful woman, Beth. You don't want to do it this way. Even the best mortician won't be able to fix your face if a bullet explodes inside your head. You don't want to be remembered that way."

Beth scrunched up her nose, obviously envisioning what she'd look like in her casket.

She slowly lowered the muzzle of the gun from her throat.

Charlie saw Sean's body tighten as he watched the barrel turn slightly toward them as she lowered it. Beth's finger left the trigger and she set the gun on the pedestal table between the two chairs.

"Stand up slowly and walk toward me," Charlie commanded softly.

As soon as Beth stood, Sean stepped behind her, grabbed the gun, and tucked it deeply into his waistband. Charlie holstered her Sig and ratcheted one cuff on Beth's right wrist. Sean grasped Beth's other hand and gently turned her around so Charlie could handcuff her other wrist.

74

TUESDAY

At 7:45 a.m. Sean was sitting at three pushed-together tables in the back of the Crown Café, a British themed breakfast and lunch restaurant two blocks from the sheriff's office. Last night he had received a group text from Frank, saying the sheriff wanted to meet with all the members of the cold case team and buy breakfast. Sean was tempted by the breakfast special—eggs and bangers with grilled tomatoes and an English muffin—but opted for scrambled eggs and multigrain toast.

The word had gotten out last night about the arrest of Beth Laughlin for the three murders, and members of the cold case team began drifting into the sheriff's office to find out what happened. After retelling the story too many times, Sean went home, leaving the group of retired cops and a gaggle of reporters waiting for the sheriff to appear for the announced press conference.

Sean's breakfast had just arrived when Frank and Irish came in. "You done good, kid," Frank said.

Sean figured that was high praise coming from Frank.

"The sheriff gave our little Mudflats Murder Club lots of praise last night at the press conference," Irish said.

In all his time working homicide, Sean had never cared for the spotlight. The only thanks he appreciated was from the family and friends of his victims. It was for them and the deceased victims that he worked his cases.

Stretch and Feebee arrived, exchanged high-fives with Sean and ordered the English breakfast special. Doc and Beagle came in together, congratulated Sean and ordered coffee and scones. A few minutes later, Sheriff Robert Donohue, followed by Captain Clinton Cannon, walked in the door. Donohue had the posture and bearing of a career military officer. He was in his mid-fifties, around six feet tall, and wore his iron gray hair in a crew cut.

"I really appreciate you all making it," Donohue said. He turned to Sean. "We've never formally met, but I'm Bob Donohue."

"Sean Tanner." Sean stood and shook his hand. "Nice to meet you, sheriff."

Donohue ordered coffee and an omelet and then said, "I must be honest with y'all. I cringed when I first heard of your active involvement in this investigation. Especially about Sean traveling to MacCrain Island with Sergeant Nash to find another murder victim and him joining our detectives as they followed the trail to the perpetrator. But then I realized we could not have solved these killings without y'all. So, I thank you. The sheriff's office thanks you. And the citizens of Campbell County thank you."

"We appreciate your support, sheriff," Frank said.

Feebee elbowed Stretch in the ribs, and they both pinned their Mudflats Murder Club buttons on their shirts. Feebee then stood and handed one to Donohue. "We'd like to offer you an honorary membership in the Mudflats Murder Club."

Donohue looked at the button and laughed. He slipped it into his pocket. "I heard some rumors about our cold case team's nickname. How about we keep this among ourselves? I'm not sure all of our citizens would understand law enforcement officers' sense of humor."

While everyone ate and talked, Sean leaned toward Feebee and whispered, "Did Frank know about presenting the sheriff with the button?"

"No way." She grinned. "Me and Stretch took it upon ourselves to do it."

"Have you given one to Cannon?" Sean asked, considering the captain was the official head of the cold case team.

"That dickhead?" she whispered. "Hell no, but we're considering giving one to Charlie."

Sheriff Donohue cleared his throat, and everyone quieted. He looked at Cannon. "What's the next unsolved cold case you got in mind for the team?"

"We all've been so busy, I haven't even thought about it," Cannon said.

"I have an idea," Sean said.

"I'm all ears," Donohue said.

"About ten years ago, a major real estate developer and well-known community member disappeared. He never turned up and his body was never found."

"Yes, Henry Nash," Donohue said. "I was with the state police back then, but it was regional news for quite a while. I recall lots of speculation, but nothing ever came of it. He was Sergeant Nash's father, wasn't he, Clinton?"

"Yes, sir," Cannon said. "I was actually the detective assigned that missing person investigation back then. We exhausted all leads but turned up nothing."

The sheriff swallowed a bite of his food, took a sip of coffee, then said, "That disappearance was a real mystery back then. Seems like a fresh set of eyes wouldn't hurt one bit, don't you think, Clinton?"

Sean saw Clinton's eyes shoot daggers at him. Clinton then smiled at the sheriff. "No, sir, a fresh set of eyes wouldn't hurt one bit."

Later that morning, Sean met Rachel at her school to help her set up her classroom for the start of school the following week. When he stepped into the room, she said, "Dad, I have something to tell you."

He stood there, waiting.

"You know the doctor's appointment I mentioned?"

Worst-case scenarios rushed through his mind—she was sick—cancer like Lauren. He braced himself.

Rachel smiled. "Daddy, I'm pregnant. I'm going to have a baby."

He pulled her into his arms. Tears rolled down his cheeks. Tears of joy.

Although Rachel insisted at seven weeks she looked no different, Sean noticed a glow emanating from his daughter and a smile on her face bigger than he'd ever seen before. While she sat at her desk preparing lesson plans, he did the heavy work: moving desks around, carting stacks of books and supplies to the classroom, and, at Rachel's insistence, cleaning everything the custodial staff had already cleaned. Sean vividly remembered a day thirty years ago when he helped Lauren in her classroom during her second year of teaching when she was pregnant with Rachel. Even while cleaning windows that were already clean, Sean felt happier than he'd been in a long time.

"What are you smiling about?" Rachel asked.

Sean laughed. "I guess I'm having fun washing windows."

"I enjoy spending time with you too," she said.

"And I'm going to be a granddad."

Rachel left her desk and gave him a hug. "You should be quite pleased with that cold case you worked."

He had stayed at the sheriff's office last night as Charlie continued interviewing Beth in one of the video-recorded interview rooms. If he hadn't investigated homicides as long as he had, he would've been sickened by Beth's excuses and rationalizations for the murders. As it was, he expected nothing less.

Sean was impressed with how Charlie controlled her emotions during the long interview. She allowed Beth to continue claiming the stabbing of Nancy and shooting of Theresa were accidents, knowing no jury would buy it. She told Beth about the three witnesses her detectives had located who saw her on MacCrain Island that day, and the bullet that killed Tim came from the same gun as the bullet that killed Theresa—the gun she threatened suicide with. When Beth stuck to her claim she had nothing to do with Tim's death, Charlie didn't press her. Sometimes a denial, especially when it's accompanied by overwhelming evidence, often plays better to a jury because it indicates the suspect's refusal to accept responsibility for their actions and their lack of remorse.

"I had a tiny part in it," he said. "It was the sheriff detectives who solved it."

"I saw the press conference last night. The sheriff, Billy, and Sergeant Nash mentioned you by name and heaped on the praise."

"They were being overly generous. I was just glad I could help."

"Sergeant Nash is really pretty."

"I hadn't noticed."

"Come on, Dad, she's gorgeous. Is she married?"

"I don't know."

"Dad?"

"Okay, she's divorced."

"You should ask her out."

"She's ten years younger than me."

"So what? Just don't hook up with someone younger than me and we're okay."

On the drive home, Sean called Dufftown Self-Help. He expected them to schedule a pickup in a week or so, instead they told him a group of volunteers could be at his house that afternoon. At four o'clock, three women arrived. In less than an hour, they had emptied Lauren's closet, dresser drawers, and bathroom vanity, saying they would sell some of her nicer clothes and shoes in their thrift shop, but everything else would go directly to less fortunate women in the county. After they returned to the bedroom from their final trip to their cars, the volunteers asked if there was anything else. Sean thought about giving them a half dozen pillows off the bed but decided he wasn't ready to give up that part of Lauren yet.

That evening, Sean arrived at the Sandy Feet Bar with Annie at his side. Billy was sitting at an outside table. The sun was low in the sky and its rays danced across the small ripples on the surface of the ocean. A soft breeze blew from the water. A few people still waded in the warm water and sat on the beach watching the hypnotic rhythm of the waves.

Billy drained a beer as Sean approached. "Am I late?"

Dressed in a tee shirt, shorts, and flip-flops, Billy looked like any other bar patron. "Since I'm the boss and we did such a fantastic job on the murder spree in the county, I sent the team—and me—home early."

Sean grabbed a chair where he had a clear view of the beach. "Where's Charlie?"

"She didn't agree that beer-drinking is the only way to celebrate a closed case, so she went for a swim and a walk on the beach," Billy said. "Here she comes now."

Sean watched a tall, slender woman wearing a bikini top and gym shorts trudge through the fluffy sand above the water line. The wind whipped her long blonde beach hair around her face. She climbed the three wooden steps to the deck and strolled toward them.

"Hey, Sean," Charlie removed an oversized tee shirt from a beach bag. She caught Sean's eyes lingering on her and smiled. She pulled the tee shirt over her head, rubbed Annie behind the ears, and sat down.

A server descended on their table, looked at Billy, and asked, "Another Yuengling?"

"Sure."

She glanced at Charlie. "And for you?"

"I'll have the same."

Sean made it three.

"Do you want to order now or wait a bit?" The server asked.

"I'll have the cheeseburger, medium rare, with sweet potato fries," Charlie said.

Sean wasn't surprised when Billy ordered the same but couldn't figure out how Charlie could eat that way and still look the way she did. Although he normally ordered their grilled fish sandwich, he decided to splurge and get the half-pound burger as well.

When the server returned with their beers and a bowl of water for Annie, they clinked their glasses. "To an amazing team of detectives," Billy said.

"The circuit solicitor charged Beth with three counts of murder," Charlie said. "SLED expedited the ballistics tests and matched the slugs from Tim Early's murder to Beth's Walther PPK. I'm sure they'll get some hits with DNA and prints in the next few weeks."

"Sounds like a slam dunk for a prosecutor," Sean said.

"I can't imagine her demanding a trial," Billy said. "Even with a generous plea bargain, I'm sure she'll spend the remainder of her life in prison."

"She took three lives, contributed to the death of a young man, and shattered a lot of families," Sean said. "She won't get any sympathy from me."

"What's ironic is how in today's era, she could give men a pass for their sexual indiscretions and blame women," Billy said. "You can be damn sure if I cheated on my wife, she wouldn't be looking to kill the woman I bedded."

"It takes two to have an affair," Charlie said, "And both are equally responsible."

"And I don't care whether it's a clandestine affair in some seedy motel or wife swapping, it's still cheating," Billy said.

"Agreed," Sean said.

Charlie stared at her beer for a moment then looked at Sean. "I hope you didn't think I really believed all those things I said to Beth when I was trying to convince her to drop the gun."

"You mean like how we men are weak and can't be expected to control our impulses, so it's up to women to keep us in line?"

"Well, there is some truth to that." She grinned.

"Yeah, right." Sean laughed. "But no problem. I'd agree with whatever nonsense a crazy person is spouting if that's what it takes to keep them from pulling a trigger."

"What's going to happen with Darryl?" Charlie asked Billy.

"After their praise of the fantastic job you two did, the sheriff and Captain Cannon discussed that at our meeting today. Although the captain defended Darryl, the sheriff recognized his major screw up. He'll be on limited duty and restricted to the office until he can be scheduled for tactics and shoot-don't-shoot refresher training at the academy."

"I never blamed him for the outcome," Charlie said.

"Of course not," Billy said. "The sheriff expects deputies to have each other's backs, but it was obvious Darryl's poor tactics were at least a contributing factor to the shooting."

"That might cause him to think about retirement," Charlie said. "What about me? Am I looking at discipline for pursuing the investigation when I was supposed to be home?"

"The sheriff never mentioned it. I think he wants to pretend you were on duty the entire time. He was also thoroughly impressed with Sean's contribution and wants to keep him around. Under state law, he can appoint retired law enforcement officers as reserve deputies, an unpaid position with full police powers." Billy looked at Sean. "The sheriff wants to order a special badge for you, one you can pin on if we ever need an old, retired homicide dick to assist on a future case."

Sean thought about it for a moment. "I hung up the uniform and gun belt for a reason. Besides, I don't think I have the patience to deal with a department's rules and regulations and pain-in-the-ass bosses anymore."

"You started off as quite a pain in the ass to work with yourself," Charlie said. "But you have to admit, we ended up making a pretty good team."

"That we did." Sean smiled. "If you need my help again, just call, but I don't need another badge and all that goes with it."

"I hear you suggested to the sheriff the next cold case your team should look into," Billy said.

"Yeah, the mysterious disappearance of one of Spartina Island's largest developers."

Charlie's eyes opened wide, and a huge smile crossed her face. "You're kidding?"

"He's not kidding," Billy said. "Captain Cannon wasn't too happy about it, but there's not much he can do when the sheriff supports it."

Charlie kept smiling for the longest time. "I hope we can still use Sean as a consultant of sorts on active cases."

"No reason why not," Billy said.

For the first time since Lauren's death, Sean felt like his life had a purpose. He knew Charlie liked working with him, although he wasn't sure if she had feelings on another level. But he enjoyed working with her too, and he didn't want to do anything to mess that up. "Any time you can use my help as a consultant or whatever, you know how to reach me."

"Oh, I'll be calling. You can be sure of it." Charlie winked at him, and Sean felt a warm sandy foot sliding along his leg under the table.

A Killer in the Cordgrass
Mudflats Murder Club Mysteries Book 2

The golden years are tainted red with murder on Spartina Island.

When Courtney Evanson's body is found in the dunes of Spartina Island, the peaceful facade of the retirement haven is shattered. Retired detective Sean Tanner teams up with Detective Sergeant Charlie Nash, diving into a case that's far more twisted than they imagined.

A stolen credit card initially offers a promising lead, but when their main suspect turns up dead, all their theories unravel. The investigation grinds to a halt—until The Mudflats Murder Club uncovers a crucial piece of evidence: a ruby pendant hidden in the pocket of the clothes Courtney was wearing when she died. This pendant is more than a simple find—it's the unmistakable link to a 27-year-old cold case involving another young woman's violent death.

The deeper they probe into the case, the more Sean's team unearths, including secrets about Charlie's father, who mysteriously disappeared a decade ago. As the lines between past and present blur, Sean must navigate these buried truths without losing Charlie's trust.

As the body count climbs and three seemingly separate cases collide, the stakes on Spartina Island have never been higher. The Cordgrass Killer is still out there—watching, waiting—and Sean and Charlie's relentless digging has put them squarely in the crosshairs. Can Sean and Charlie outpace a killer who's always a step ahead...or will the sands of Spartina Island claim them next?

Get your copy today at
severnriverbooks.com

ACKNOWLEDGMENTS

My most heartfelt appreciation to Paula Munier, Gina Panettieri, and the rest of the team at Talcott Notch Literary Agency for believing in me, guiding me, and never giving up on me.

Thank you to the entire team at Severn River Publishing: Andrew Watts, Amber Hudock, Julia Hastings, Mo Melten, Megan Copenhaver, and Amie Swope. Your support and encouragement has kept writing fun for me.

I wish to thank Laura Hayden, the author of *Staying Alive*, Ron Fitch, the author of *My Heart*, and several other people who wanted to remain anonymous for helping me understand what it's like to lose a spouse.

Thanks to my friend and neighbor, Robert Drabik, a volunteer at the Bluffton Historical Society, for sharing a wealth of information that helped me create the fictional Spartina Island and Dufftown.

Loads of thanks to the men and women of the Beaufort County Sheriff's Office, especially Major (Ret.) Robert Bromage for inviting me to join the Sheriff's Cold Case Team and teaching me about Southern law enforcement. I couldn't have come up with the premise for this story without you.

Thanks to former Bluffton Police Chief Chris Chapmond for letting me work with your fantastic staff, Sgt. Ryan Fazekas, Det. Zatch Pouchprom, and Det. Adam Thompson, and observe your phenomenal department firsthand. Charlie Nash's character was inspired by the professional officers I worked with and observed.

A million thanks to my beta readers: Rachael Van Sloten, David Griffith, James Mallory, Karen Veazey, and Karen Murray. Your insightful comments and thoughtful suggestions made this story immeasurably better.

And, of course, my deepest appreciation to my most trusted reader, my lovely wife, Cathy, who has shown enormous support when I sit in my office for long hours playing with my make-believe characters.

And thank you to those who generously donated to worthy Lowcountry charities. Jacque Mitro, I hope you and your husband Ray enjoy his character, who will become even more prominent throughout the series. And Doug May, you can now reveal the surprise to your wife Jane. I hope she likes her badass cop persona.

ABOUT THE AUTHOR

Brian Thiem is the author of The Mudflats Murder Club, the first book in the Mudflats Murder Club series, as well as Red Line, Thrill Kill, and Shallow Grave. In his previous life, he spent 25 years with the Oakland Police Department, much of it working Homicide, and retired as a lieutenant. He's also an Iraq War veteran, retiring from the Army as a lieutenant colonel after 28 years of active and reserve service. He holds an MFA in creative writing and is a member of the Mystery Writers of America, Sisters in Crime, International Thriller Writers, and the Island Writers Network. He lives with his wife, yellow Lab, and Tonkinese cat in Hilton Head Island, South Carolina, where he's also a member of the sheriff department's Cold Case Team, consisting of retired law enforcement professionals from around the nation who examine unsolved murders.

Sign up for Brian Thiem's reader list at
severnriverbooks.com

Printed in the United States
by Baker & Taylor Publisher Services